W9-CFH-257

Praise for

THE LAST JUROR

"[GRISHAM] IMBUES HIS WRITING WITH A NEW STRENGTH, GIVING EXUBERANT LIFE TO THIS COMPASSIONATE, COMPULSIVELY READABLE STORY OF A YOUNG MAN'S GROWTH FROM CALLOWNESS TO SOMETHING APPROACHING WISDOM.... HEARTFELT, WISE, SUSPENSEFUL AND FUNNY, ONE OF THE BEST GRISHAMS EVER."
—*Publishers Weekly,* starred review

"IT RANKS AMONG HIS BEST-WRITTEN AND MOST ATMOSPHERIC NOVELS."
—*USA Today*

"A MOST ENTERTAINING NOVEL."
—*Washington Post*

"[GRISHAM WRITES WITH] CRISPNESS, STREAMLINED ENERGY AND SELF-DEPRECATING CHARM.... *THE LAST JUROR* DOES NOT NEED TO COAST ON THE AUTHOR'S MEGAPOPULARITY. IT'S A REMINDER OF HOW THE GRISHAM JUGGERNAUT BEGAN."
—*New York Times*

ALSO BY JOHN GRISHAM

JOHN GRISHAM

THE
LAST
JUROR

A DELL BOOK

THE LAST JUROR
A Dell Book

PUBLISHING HISTORY
Doubleday hardcover edition published March 2004
Dell export mass market edition / October 2004

Published by
Bantam Dell
A Division of Random House, Inc.
New York, New York

This is a work of fiction. Names, characters, businesses, organizations,
places, events, and incidents either are the product of the author's
imagination or are used fictitiously. Any resemblance to actual persons,
living or dead, events, or locales is entirely coincidental.

Library of Congress Catalog Card Number: 2004043818

ISBN 0-440-29631-5

Manufactured in the United States of America

OPM 10 9 8 7 6 5 4 3 2 1

THE
LAST
JUROR

PART
ONE

CHAPTER 1

After decades of patient mismanagement and loving neglect, *The Ford County Times* went bankrupt in 1970. The owner and publisher, Miss Emma Caudle, was ninety-three years old and strapped to a bed in a nursing home in Tupelo. The editor, her son Wilson Caudle, was in his seventies and had a plate in his head from the First War. A perfect circle of dark grafted skin covered the plate at the top of his long, sloping forehead, and throughout his adult life he had endured the nickname of Spot. Spot did this. Spot did that. Here, Spot. There, Spot.

In his younger years, he covered town meetings, football games, elections, trials, church socials, all sorts of activities in Ford County. He was a good reporter, thorough and intuitive. Evidently, the head wound did not affect his ability to write. But sometime after the Second War the plate apparently shifted, and Mr.

Caudle stopped writing everything but the obituaries. He loved obituaries. He spent hours on them. He filled paragraphs of eloquent prose detailing the lives of even the humblest of Ford Countians. And the death of a wealthy or prominent citizen was front page news, with Mr. Caudle seizing the moment. He never missed a wake or a funeral, never wrote anything bad about anyone. All received glory in the end. Ford County was a wonderful place to die. And Spot was a very popular man, even though he was crazy.

The only real crisis of his journalistic career happened in 1967, about the time the civil rights movement finally made it to Ford County. The paper had never shown the slightest hint of racial tolerance. No black faces appeared in its pages, except those belonging to known or suspected criminals. No black wedding announcements. No black honor students or baseball teams. But in 1967, Mr. Caudle made a startling discovery. He awoke one morning to the realization that black people were dying in Ford County, and their deaths were not being properly reported. There was a whole, new, fertile world of obituaries waiting out there, and Mr. Caudle set sail in dangerous and uncharted waters. On Wednesday, March 8, 1967, the *Times* became the first white-owned weekly in Mississippi to run the obituary of a Negro. For the most part, it went unnoticed.

The following week, he ran three black obituaries, and people were beginning to talk. By the fourth week, a regular boycott was under way, with subscriptions being canceled and advertisers holding their money. Mr.

Caudle knew what was happening, but he was too impressed with his new status as an integrationist to worry about such trivial matters as sales and profits. Six weeks after the historic obituary, he announced, on the front page and in bold print, his new policy. He explained to the public that he would publish whatever he damned well pleased, and if the white folks didn't like it, then he would simply cut back on their obituaries.

Now, dying properly is an important part of living in Mississippi, for whites and blacks, and the thought of being laid to rest without the benefit of one of Spot's glorious send-offs was more than most whites could stand. And they knew he was crazy enough to carry out his threat.

The next edition was filled with all sorts of obituaries, blacks and whites, all neatly alphabetized and desegregated. It sold out, and a brief period of prosperity followed.

The bankruptcy was called involuntary, as if others had eager volunteers. The pack was led by a print supplier from Memphis that was owed $60,000. Several creditors had not been paid in six months. The old Security Bank was calling in a loan.

I was new, but I'd heard the rumors. I was sitting on a desk in the front room of the *Times*'s offices reading a magazine, when a midget in a pair of pointed toes strutted in the front door and asked for Wilson Caudle.

"He's at the funeral home," I said.

He was a cocky midget. I could see a gun on his hip under a wrinkled navy blazer, a gun worn in such a manner so that folks would see it. He probably had a permit, but in Ford County one was not really needed, not in 1970. In fact, permits were frowned upon. "I need to serve these papers on him," he said, waving an envelope.

I was not about to be helpful, but it's difficult being rude to a midget. Even one with a gun. "He's at the funeral home," I repeated.

"Then I'll just leave them with you," he declared.

Although I'd been around for less than two months, and though I'd gone to college up North, I had learned a few things. I knew that good papers were not served on people. They were mailed or shipped or hand-delivered, but never served. The papers were trouble, and I wanted no part of them.

"I'm not taking the papers," I said, looking down.

The laws of nature require midgets to be docile, noncombative people, and this little fella was no exception. The gun was a ruse. He glanced around the front office with a smirk, but he knew the situation was hopeless. With a flair for the dramatic, he stuffed the envelope back into his pocket and demanded, "Where's the funeral home?"

I pointed this way and that, and he left. An hour later, Spot stumbled through the door, waving the papers and bawling hysterically. "It's over! It's over!" he kept wailing as I held the Petition for Involuntary Bankruptcy. Margaret Wright, the secretary, and Hardy, the pressman, came from the back and tried to console him. He sat in a chair, face in hands, elbows on knees, sobbing pitifully. I read the petition aloud for the benefit of the others.

It said Mr. Caudle had to appear in court in a week over in Oxford to meet with the creditors and the Judge, and that a decision would be made as to whether the paper would continue to operate while a trustee sorted things out. I could tell Margaret and Hardy were more concerned about their jobs than about Mr. Caudle and his breakdown, but they gamely stood next to him and patted his shoulders.

When the crying stopped, he suddenly stood, bit his lip, and announced, "I've got to tell Mother."

The three of us looked at each other. Miss Emma Caudle had departed this life years earlier, but her feeble heart continued to work just barely enough to postpone a funeral. She neither knew nor cared what color Jell-O they were feeding her, and she certainly cared nothing about Ford County and its newspaper. She was blind and deaf and weighed less than eighty pounds, and now Spot was about to discuss involuntary bankruptcy with her. At that point, I realized that he, too, was no longer with us.

He started crying again and left. Six months later I would write his obituary.

Because I had attended college, and because I was holding the papers, Hardy and Margaret looked hopefully at me for advice. I was a journalist, not a lawyer, but I said that I would take the papers to the Caudle family lawyer. We would follow his advice. They smiled weakly and returned to work.

At noon, I bought a six-pack at Quincy's One Stop in Lowtown, the black section of Clanton, and went for a long drive in my Spitfire. It was late in February, unseasonably warm, so I put the top down and headed for the lake, wondering, not for the first time, just exactly what I was doing in Ford County, Mississippi.

———

I grew up in Memphis and studied journalism at Syracuse for five years before my grandmother got tired of paying for what was becoming an extended education. My grades were unremarkable, and I was a year away from a degree. Maybe a year and a half. She, BeeBee, had plenty of money, hated to spend it, and after five years she figured my opportunity had been sufficiently funded. When she cut me off I was very disappointed, but I did not complain, to her anyway. I was her only grandchild and her estate would be a delight.

I studied journalism with a hangover. In the early days at Syracuse, I aspired to be an investigative reporter with the *New York Times* or the *Washington Post*. I wanted to save the world by uncovering corruption and environmental abuse and government waste and the injustice suffered by the weak and oppressed. Pulitzers were waiting for me. After a year or so of such lofty dreams, I saw a movie about a foreign correspondent who dashed around the world looking for wars, seducing beautiful women, and somehow finding the time to write award-winning stories. He spoke eight languages, wore a beard, combat boots, starched khakis that never wrinkled. So I decided I would become such a journalist. I grew a beard, bought some boots and khakis, tried to learn German, tried to score with prettier girls. During my junior year, when my grades began their steady decline to the bottom of the class, I became captivated by the idea of working for a small-town newspaper. I cannot explain this attraction, except that it was at about this time that I met and befriended Nick Diener. He was from rural Indiana, and for decades his family had owned a rather prosperous county newspaper. He drove a fancy little Alfa Romeo and always had plenty of cash. We became close friends.

Nick was a bright student who could have handled medicine, law, or engineering. His only goal, however, was to return to Indiana and run the family business. This baffled me until we got drunk one night and he told me how much his father cleared each year off their small weekly—circulation six thousand. It was a gold mine, he said. Just local news, wedding announcements, church socials, honor rolls, sports coverage, pictures of basketball teams, a few recipes, a few obituaries, and pages of advertising. Maybe a little politics, but stay away from controversy. And count your money. His father was a millionaire. It was laid-back, low-pressure journalism with money growing on trees, according to Nick.

This appealed to me. After my fourth year, which should've been my last but wasn't close, I spent the summer interning at a small weekly in the Ozark Mountains of Arkansas. The pay was peanuts but BeeBee was

impressed because I was employed. Each week I mailed
her the paper, at least half of which was written by me.
The owner/editor/publisher was a wonderful old gentleman who was delighted to have a reporter who
wanted to write. He was quite wealthy.

After five years at Syracuse my grades were irreparable, and the well ran dry. I returned to Memphis, visited
BeeBee, thanked her for her efforts, and told her I loved
her. She told me to find a job.

At the time, Wilson Caudle's sister lived in Memphis, and through the course of things this lady met
BeeBee at one of those hot tea drinkers' parties. After a
few phone calls back and forth, I was packed and
headed to Clanton, Mississippi, where Spot was eagerly
waiting. After an hour of orientation, he turned me
loose on Ford County.

In the next edition he ran a sweet little story with
a photo of me announcing my "internship" at the
Times. It made the front page. News was slow in those
days.

The announcement contained two horrendous
errors that would haunt me for years. The first and less
serious was the fact that Syracuse had now joined the
Ivy League, at least according to Spot. He informed
his dwindling readership that I had received my Ivy
League education at Syracuse. It was a month before
anyone mentioned this to me. I was beginning to believe that no one read the paper, or, worse, those who
did were complete idiots.

The second misstatement changed my life. I was

born Joyner William Traynor. Until I was twelve I hammered my parents with inquiries about why two supposedly intelligent people would stick Joyner on a newborn. The story finally leaked that one of my parents, both of whom denied responsibility, had insisted on Joyner as an olive branch to some feuding relative who allegedly had money. I never met the man, my namesake. He died broke as far as I was concerned, but I nonetheless had Joyner for a lifetime. When I enrolled at Syracuse I was J. William, a rather imposing name for an eighteen-year-old. But Vietnam and the riots and all the rebellion and social upheaval convinced me that J. William sounded too corporate, too establishment. I became Will.

Spot at various times called me Will, William, Bill, or even Billy, and since I would answer to all of them I never knew what was next. In the announcement, under my smiling face, was my new name. Willie Traynor. I was horrified. I had never dreamed of anyone calling me Willie. I went to a prep school in Memphis and then to college in New York, and I had never met a person named Willie. I wasn't a good ole boy. I drove a Triumph Spitfire and had long hair.

What would I tell my fraternity brothers at Syracuse? What would I tell BeeBee?

After hiding in my apartment for two days, I mustered the courage to confront Spot and demand he do something. I wasn't sure what, but he'd made the mistake and he could damned well fix it. I marched into the *Times* office and bumped into Davey Bigmouth Bass, the sports editor of the paper. "Hey, cool name," he said. I followed him into his office, seeking advice.

"My name's not Willie," I said.

"It is now."

"My name's Will."

"They'll love you around here. A smart-ass from up North with long hair and a little imported sports car. Hell, folks'll think you're pretty cool with a name like Willie. Think of Joe Willie."

"Who's Joe Willie?"

"Joe Willie Namath."

"Oh him."

"Yeah, he's a Yankee like you, from Pennsylvania or some place, but when he got to Alabama he went from Joseph William to Joe Willie. The girls chased him all over the place."

I began to feel better. In 1970, Joe Namath was probably the most famous athlete in the country. I went for a drive and kept repeating "Willie." Within a couple of weeks the name was beginning to stick. Everybody called me Willie and seemed to feel more comfortable because I had such a down-to-earth name.

I told BeeBee it was just a temporary pseudonym.

———

The *Times* was a very thin paper, and I knew immediately that it was in trouble. Heavy on the obits, light on news and advertising. The employees were disgruntled, but quiet and loyal. Jobs were scarce in Ford County in 1970. After a week it was obvious even to my novice eyes that the paper was operating at a loss. Obits are free—ads are not. Spot spent most of his time in his cluttered office, napping periodically and calling the funeral home. Sometimes they called him. Sometimes the families would stop just hours after Uncle Wilber's last breath and hand over a long, flowery, handwritten narrative that Spot would seize and carry delicately to his desk. Behind a locked door, he would write, edit, research, and rewrite until it was perfect.

He told me the entire county was mine to cover. The paper had one other general reporter, Baggy Suggs, a pickled old goat who spent his hours hanging around the courthouse across the street sniffing for gossip and drinking bourbon with a small club of washed-up lawyers too old and too drunk to practice anymore. As I would soon learn, Baggy was too lazy to check sources and dig for anything interesting, and it was not unusual for his front page story to be some dull account of a boundary dispute or a wife beating.

Margaret, the secretary, was a fine Christian lady who ran the place, though she was smart enough to allow Spot to think he was the boss. She was in her early fifties and had worked there for twenty years. She was the rock, the anchor, and everything at the *Times* revolved around her. Margaret was soft-spoken, almost shy, and from day one was completely intimidated by me because I was from Memphis and had gone to school up North for five years. I was careful not to wear my Ivy Leagueness on my shoulder, but at the same time I wanted these rural Mississippians to know that I had been superbly educated.

She and I became gossiping pals, and after a week she confirmed what I already suspected—that Mr. Caudle was indeed crazy, and that the newspaper was indeed in dire financial straits. But, she said, the Caudles have family money!

It would be years before I understood this mystery.

In Mississippi, family money was not to be confused with wealth. It had nothing to do with cash or other assets. Family money was a status, obtained by someone who was white, somewhat educated beyond high school, born in a large home with a front porch—preferably one surrounded by cotton or soybean fields, although this was not mandatory—and partially reared by a beloved black maid named Bessie or Pearl, partially reared by doting grandparents who once owned the ancestors of Bessie or Pearl, and lectured from birth on the stringent social graces of a privileged people. Acreage and trust funds helped somewhat, but Mississippi was full of insolvent blue bloods who inherited the status of family money. It could not be earned. It had to be handed down at birth.

When I talked to the Caudle family lawyer, he explained, rather succinctly, the real value of their family money. "They're as poor as Job's turkey," he said as I sat deep in a worn leather chair and looked up at him across his wide and ancient mahogany desk. His name was Walter Sullivan, of the prestigious Sullivan & O'Hara firm. Prestigious for Ford County—seven lawyers. He studied the bankruptcy petition and rambled on about the Caudles and the money they used to have and how foolish they'd been in running a once profitable paper into the ground. He'd represented them for thirty years, and back when Miss Emma ran things the *Times* had five thousand subscribers and pages filled with advertisements. She kept a $500,000 certificate of deposit at Security Bank, just for a rainy day.

Then her husband died, and she remarried a local alcoholic twenty years her junior. When sober, he was semiliterate and fancied himself as a tortured poet and essayist. Miss Emma loved him dearly and installed him as coeditor, a position he used to write long editorials blasting everything that moved in Ford County. It was the beginning of the end. Spot hated his new stepfather, the feelings were mutual, and their relationship finally climaxed with one of the more colorful fistfights in the history of downtown Clanton. It took place on the sidewalk in front of the *Times* office, on the downtown square, in front of a large and stunned crowd. The locals believed that Spot's brain, already fragile, took additional damage that day. Shortly thereafter, he began writing nothing but those damned obituaries.

The stepfather ran off with her money, and Miss Emma, heartbroken, became a recluse.

"It was once a fine paper," Mr. Sullivan said. "But look at it now. Less than twelve hundred subscriptions, heavily in debt. Bankrupt."

"What will the court do?" I asked.

"Try and find a buyer."

"A buyer?"

"Yes, someone will buy. The county has to have a newspaper."

I immediately thought of two people—Nick Diener and BeeBee. Nick's family had become rich off their county weekly. BeeBee was already loaded and she had only one beloved grandchild. My heart began pounding as I smelled opportunity.

Mr. Sullivan watched me intently, and it was obvious he knew what I was thinking. "It could be bought for a song," he said.

"How much?" I asked with all the confidence of a twenty-three-year-old cub reporter whose grandmother was as stout as lye soap.

"Probably fifty thousand. Twenty-five for the paper, twenty-five to operate. Most of the debts can be bankrupted, then renegotiated with the creditors you need." He paused and leaned forward, elbows on his desk, thick grayish eyebrows twitching as if his brain was working overtime. "It could be a real gold mine, you know."

BeeBee had never invested in a gold mine, but after three days of priming the pump I left Memphis with a check for $50,000. I gave it to Mr. Sullivan, who put it in a trust account and petitioned the court for the sale of the paper. The Judge, a relic who belonged in the bed next to Miss Emma, nodded benignly and scrawled his name on an order that made me the new owner of *The Ford County Times*.

It takes at least three generations to be accepted in Ford County. Regardless of money or breeding, one cannot simply move there and be trusted. A dark cloud of suspicion hangs over any newcomer, and I was no exception. The people there are exceedingly warm and gracious and polite, almost to the point of being nosy with their friendliness. They nod and speak to everyone on the downtown streets. They ask about your health, the weather, and they invite you to church. They rush to help strangers.

But they don't really trust you unless they trusted your grandfather.

Once word spread that I, a young green alien from Memphis, had bought the paper for fifty, or maybe a hundred, or perhaps even two hundred thousand dollars, a great wave of gossip shook the community. Margaret gave me the updates. Because I was single, there was a chance I was a homosexual. Because I went to Syracuse, wherever that was, then I was probably a Communist. Or worse, a liberal. Because I was from Memphis, I was a subversive intent on embarrassing Ford County.

Just the same, as they all conceded quietly among themselves, I now controlled the obituaries! I was somebody!

The new *Times* debuted on March 18, 1970, only three weeks after the midget arrived with his papers. It was almost an inch thick and loaded with more photos than had ever been published in a county weekly. Cub Scout troops, Brownies, junior high basketball teams, garden clubs, book clubs, tea clubs, Bible study groups, adult softball teams, civic clubs. Dozens of photos. I tried to include every living soul in the county. And the dead ones were exalted like never before. The obits were embarrassingly long. I'm sure Spot was proud, but I never heard from him.

The news was light and breezy. Absolutely no editorials. People love to read about crime, so on the bottom left-hand corner of the front page I launched the Crime Notes Section. Thankfully, two pickups had been stolen the week before, and I covered these heists as if Fort Knox had been looted.

In the center of the front page there was a rather large group shot of the new regime—Margaret, Hardy, Baggy Suggs, me, our photographer, Wiley Meek, Davey Bigmouth Bass, and Melanie Dogan, a high school student and part-time employee. I was proud of my staff. We had worked around the clock for ten days, and our first edition was a great success. We printed five thousand copies and sold them all. I sent a box of them to BeeBee, and she was most impressed.

For the next month, the new *Times* slowly took shape as I struggled to determine what I wanted it to become. Change is painful in rural Mississippi, so I decided to do it gradually. The old paper was bankrupt, but it had changed little in fifty years. I wrote more news, sold more ads, included more and more pictures of groups of endless varieties. And I worked hard on the obituaries.

I had never been attracted to long hours, but since I was the owner I forgot about the clock. I was too young and too busy to be scared. I was twenty-three, and through luck and timing and a rich grandmother, I was suddenly the owner of a weekly newspaper. If I had hesitated and studied the situation, and sought advice from bankers and accountants, I'm sure someone would have talked some sense into me. But when you're twenty-three, you're fearless. You have nothing, so there's nothing to lose.

I figured it would take a year to become profitable. And, at first, revenue increased slowly. Then Rhoda Kassellaw was murdered. I guess it's the nature of the business to sell more papers after a brutal crime when people want details. We sold twenty-four hundred papers the week before her death, and almost four thousand the week after.

It was no ordinary murder.

———

Ford County was a peaceful place, filled with people who were either Christians or claimed to be. Fistfights were common, but they were usually the work of the lower classes who hung around beer joints and such. Once a month a redneck would take a shot at a neighbor or perhaps his own wife, and each weekend had at least one stabbing in the black tonks. Death rarely followed these episodes.

I owned the paper for ten years, from 1970 to 1980, and we reported very few murders in Ford County. None was as brutal as Rhoda Kassellaw's; none was as premeditated. Thirty years later, I still think about it every day.

CHAPTER 2

Rhoda Kassellaw lived in the Beech Hill community, twelve miles north of Clanton, in a modest gray brick house on a narrow, paved country road. The flower beds along the front of the house were weedless and received daily care, and between them and the road the long wide lawn was thick and well cut. The driveway was crushed white rock. Scattered down both sides of it was a collection of scooters and balls and bikes. Her two small children were always outdoors, playing hard, sometimes stopping to watch a passing car.

It was a pleasant little country house, a stone's throw from Mr. and Mrs. Deece next door. The young man who bought it was killed in a trucking accident somewhere in Texas, and, at the age of twenty-eight, Rhoda became a widow. The insurance on his life paid off the house and the car. The balance was invested to provide a modest monthly income that allowed her to remain home and dote on the children. She spent hours outside, tending her vegetable garden, potting flowers, pulling weeds, mulching the beds along the front of the house.

She kept to herself. The old ladies in Beech Hill considered her a model widow, staying home, looking sad, limiting her social appearances to an occasional visit to church. She should attend more regularly, they whispered.

Shortly after the death of her husband, Rhoda planned to return to her family in Missouri. She was not from Ford County, nor was her husband. A job took them there. But the house was paid for, the kids were happy, the neighbors were nice, and her family was much too concerned about how much life insurance she'd collected. So she stayed, always thinking of leaving but never doing so.

Rhoda Kassellaw was a beautiful woman when she wanted to be, which was not very often. Her shapely, thin figure was usually camouflaged under a loose cotton drip-dry dress, or a bulky chambray workshirt, which she preferred when gardening. She wore little makeup and kept her long flaxen-colored hair pulled back and stuck together on top of her head. Most of what she ate came from her organic garden, and her skin had a soft healthy glow to it. Such an attractive young widow would normally have been a hot property in the county, but she kept to herself.

After three years of mourning, however, Rhoda became restless. She was not getting younger; the years were slipping by. She was too young and too pretty to sit at home every Saturday and read bedtime stories. There had to be some action out there, though there was certainly none in Beech Hill.

She hired a young black girl from down the road to baby-sit, and Rhoda drove north for an hour to the Tennessee line, where she'd heard there were some respectable lounges and dance clubs. Maybe no one would know her there. She enjoyed the dancing and the flirting, but she never drank and always came home early. It became a routine, two or three times a month.

Then the jeans got tighter, the dancing faster, the hours longer and longer. She was getting noticed and talked about in the bars and clubs along the state line.

He followed her home twice before he killed her. It was March, and a warm front had brought a premature hope of spring. It was a dark night, with no moon. Bear, the family mutt, sniffed him first as he crept behind a tree in the backyard. Bear was primed to growl and bark when he was forever silenced.

Rhoda's son Michael was five and her daughter Teresa was three. They wore matching Disney cartoon pajamas, neatly pressed, and watched their mother's glowing eyes as she read them the story of Jonah and the whale. She tucked them in and kissed them good night, and when Rhoda turned off the light to their bedroom, he was already in the house.

An hour later she turned off the television, locked the doors, and waited for Bear, who did not appear. That was no surprise because he often chased rabbits and squirrels into the woods and came home late. Bear would sleep on the back porch and wake her howling at dawn. In her bedroom, she slipped out of her light cotton dress and opened the closet door. He was waiting in there, in the dark.

He snatched her from behind, covered her mouth with a thick and sweaty hand, and said, "I have a knife. I'll cut you and your kids." With the other hand he held up a shiny blade and waved it before her eyes.

"Understand?" he hissed into her ear.

She trembled and managed to shake her head. She couldn't see what he looked like. He threw her to the floor of the cluttered closet, facedown, and yanked her hands behind her. He took a brown wool scarf an old aunt had given her and wrapped it roughly around her face. "Not one sound," he kept growling at her. "Or I'll cut your kids." When the blindfold was finished he grabbed her hair, snatched her to her feet, and dragged her to her bed. He poked the tip of the blade into her chin and said, "Don't fight me. The knife's right here." He cut off her panties and the rape began.

He wanted to see her eyes, those beautiful eyes he'd seen in the clubs. And the long hair. He'd bought her drinks and danced with her twice, and when he'd finally made a move she had stiff-armed him. Try these moves, baby, he mumbled just loud enough for her to hear.

He and the Jack Daniel's had been building courage for three hours, and now the whiskey numbed him. He moved slowly above her, not rushing things, enjoying every second of it. He mumbled in the self-satisfying grunts of a real man taking and getting what he wanted.

The smell of the whiskey and his sweat nauseated her, but she was too frightened to throw up. It might anger him, cause him to use the knife. As she started to accept the horror of the moment, she began to think. Keep it quiet. Don't wake up the kids. And what will he do with the knife when he's finished?

His movements were faster, he was mumbling louder. "Quiet, baby," he hissed again and again. "I'll use the knife." The wrought-iron bed was squeaking; didn't get used enough, he told himself. Too much noise, but he didn't care.

The rattling of the bed woke Michael, who then got Teresa up. They eased from their room and crept down the dark hall to see what was happening. Michael opened the door to his mother's bedroom, saw the strange man on top of her, and said, "Mommy!" For a second the man stopped and jerked his head toward the children.

The sound of the boy's voice horrified Rhoda, who bolted upward and thrust both hands at her assailant, grabbing whatever she could. One small fist caught him in the left eye, a solid shot that stunned him. Then she yanked off her blindfold while kicking with both legs. He slapped her and tried to pin her down again. "Danny Padgitt!" she shouted, still clawing. He hit her once more.

"Mommy!" Michael cried.

"Run, kids!" Rhoda tried to scream, but she was struck dumb by her assailant's blows.

"Shut up!" Padgitt yelled.

"Run!" Rhoda shouted again, and the children backed away, then darted down the hallway, into the kitchen, and outside to safety.

In the split second after she shouted his name, Padgitt realized he had no choice but to silence her. He took the knife and hacked twice, then scrambled from the bed and grabbed his clothing.

———

Mr. and Mrs. Aaron Deece were watching late television from Memphis when they heard Michael's voice calling and getting closer. Mr. Deece met the boy at the front door. His pajamas were soaked with sweat and dew and his teeth were chattering so violently he had trouble speaking. "He hurt my mommy!" he kept saying. "He hurt my mommy!"

Through the darkness between the two houses, Mr. Deece saw Teresa running after her brother. She was almost running in place, as if she wanted to get to one place without leaving the other. When Mrs. Deece finally got to her by the Deece garage, she was sucking her thumb and unable to speak.

Mr. Deece raced into his den and grabbed two shotguns, one for him, one for his wife. The children were in the kitchen, shocked to the point of being paralyzed. "He hurt Mommy," Michael kept saying. Mrs. Deece cuddled them, told them everything would be fine. She looked at her shotgun when her husband laid it on the table. "Stay here," he said as he rushed out of the house.

He did not go far. Rhoda almost made it to the Deece home before she collapsed in the wet grass. She was completely naked, and from the neck down covered in blood. He picked her up and carried her to the front porch, then shouted at his wife to move the children toward the back of the house and lock them in a bedroom. He could not allow them to see their mother in her last moments.

As he placed her in the swing, Rhoda whispered, "Danny Padgitt. It was Danny Padgitt."

He covered her with a quilt, then called an ambulance.

———

Danny Padgitt kept his pickup in the center of the road and drove ninety miles an hour. He was half-drunk and scared as hell but unwilling to admit it. He'd be home in ten minutes, secure in the family's little kingdom known as Padgitt Island.

Those little faces had ruined everything. He'd think about it tomorrow. He took a long pull on the fifth of Jack Daniel's and felt better.

It was a rabbit or a small dog or some varmint, and when it darted from the shoulder he caught a glimpse of it and reacted badly. He instinctively hit the brake pedal, just for a split second because he really didn't care what he hit and rather enjoyed the sport of roadkilling, but he'd punched too hard. The rear tires locked and the pickup fishtailed. Before he realized it Danny was in serious trouble. He jerked the wheel one way, the wrong way, and the truck hit the gravel shoulder where it began to spin like a stock car on the backstretch. It slid into the ditch, flipped twice, then crashed into a row of pine trees. If he'd been sober he would've been killed, but drunks walk away.

He crawled out through a shattered window, and for a long while leaned on the truck, counting his cuts and scratches and considering his options. A leg was suddenly stiff, and as he climbed up the bank to the road he realized he could not walk far. Not that he would need to.

The blue lights were on him before he realized it. The deputy was out of the car, surveying the scene with a long black flashlight. More flashing lights appeared down the road.

The deputy saw the blood, smelled the whiskey, and reached for the handcuffs.

CHAPTER 3

The Big Brown River drops nonchalantly south from Tennessee and runs as straight as a hand-dug channel for thirty miles through the center of Tyler County, Mississippi. Two miles above the Ford County line it begins twisting and looping, and by the time it leaves Tyler County it looks like a scared snake, curling desperately and going nowhere. Its water is thick and heavy, muddy and slow, shallow in most places. The Big Brown is not known for its beauty. Sand, silt, and gravel bars line its innumerable bends and curves. A hundred sloughs and creeks feed it with an inexhaustible supply of slow-moving water.

Its journey through Ford County is brief. It dips and forms a wide circle around two thousand acres in the northeasternmost corner of the county, then leaves and heads back toward Tennessee. The circle is almost perfect and an island is almost formed, but at the last moment the Big Brown turns away from itself and leaves a narrow strip of land between its banks.

The circle is known as Padgitt Island, a deep, dense woodland covered in pine, gum, elm, oak, and a myriad of swamps and bayous and sloughs, some connected but most isolated. Little of the rich soil had ever been cleared. Nothing was harvested on the island except timber and lots of corn—for illegal whiskey. And marijuana, but that was a later story.

On the thin strip of land between the banks of the Big Brown a paved road entered and left, came and went, always with someone watching. The road was built long ago by the county, but very few taxpayers ever dared to use it.

The entire island had been in the Padgitt family since Reconstruction, when Rudolph Padgitt, a carpetbagger from the North, arrived a bit late after the War and found all the prime land taken. He searched in vain, found nothing attractive, then somehow stumbled upon the snake-infested island. On the map, it looked promising. He put together a band of newly freed slaves and, with guns and machetes, fought his way onto the island. No one else wanted it.

Rudolph married a local whore and began cutting timber. Since timber was in great demand after the War, he became prosperous. The local proved to be quite fertile and soon there was a horde of little Padgitts on the island. One of his ex-slaves had learned the art of distillery. Rudolph became a corn farmer who neither ate nor sold his crop, but instead used it to produce what was soon known as one of the finest whiskeys in the Deep South.

For thirty years Rudolph made moonshine until he died of cirrhosis in 1902. By then an entire clan of Padgitts inhabited the island, and were quite proficient at milling timber and producing illegal whiskey. Scattered about the island were half a dozen distilleries, all well protected and concealed, all operating with state-of-the-art machinery.

The Padgitts were famous for their whiskey, though fame was not something they sought. They were secretive and clannish, fiercely private and deathly afraid that someone might infiltrate their little kingdom and disrupt their considerable profits. They said they were loggers, and it was well known that they produced timber and were prosperous at it. The Padgitt Lumber Company was very visible on the main highway near the river. They claimed to be legitimate people, taxpayers and such, with their children in the public schools.

During the 1920s and 1930s, when alcohol was illegal and the nation was thirsty, Padgitt whiskey could not be distilled fast enough. It was shipped in oak barrels across the Big Brown and hauled by trucks up North, as far away as Chicago. The patriarch, president, and director of production and marketing was a tight-fisted old warrior named Clovis Padgitt, eldest son of Rudolph and the local. Clovis had been taught at an early age that the best profits were those from which no taxes were extracted. That was lesson number one. Number two preached the marvelous message of dealing strictly in cash. Clovis was a hard-nosed cash and no-taxes man, and the Padgitts were rumored to have more money than the Mississippi state treasury.

In 1938, three revenue agents sneaked across the Big Brown in a rented flatboat in search of the source of Old Padgitt. Their covert invasion of the island was flawed in many ways, the obvious being the original idea itself. But for some reason they chose midnight as their hour to cross the river. They were dismembered and buried in deep graves.

In 1943, a strange event occurred in Ford County— an honest man was elected Sheriff. Or High Sheriff, as he is commonly known. His name was Koonce Lantrip, and he wasn't really that honest but certainly sounded good on the stump. He vowed to end corruption, to clean up county government, to put the bootleggers and moonshiners, even the Padgitts, out of business. It made for a nice speech and Lantrip won by eight votes.

His supporters waited and waited, and, finally, six months after taking office he organized his deputies and crossed the Big Brown on the only bridge, an ancient wooden structure that had been built by the county in 1915 at the insistence of Clovis. The Padgitts sometimes used it in the springtime when the river was high. No one else was allowed to cross it.

Two of the deputies were shot in the head, and Lantrip's body was never found. It was carefully laid to rest on the banks of a swamp by three Padgitt Negroes. Buford, the eldest son of Clovis, supervised the burial.

The massacre was hot news in Mississippi for weeks,

and the Governor threatened to send in the National Guard. But the Second War was raging, and D-Day soon captured the attention of the country. There wasn't much left of the National Guard anyway, and those who were able to fight had little interest in attacking Padgitt Island. The beaches of Normandy would be more inviting.

With the noble experiment of an honest Sheriff behind them, the good people of Ford County elected one from the old school. His name was Mackey Don Coley and his father had been the High Sheriff back in the twenties when Clovis was in charge of Padgitt Island. Clovis and the senior Coley had been rather close, and it was widely known that the Sheriff was a rich man because Old Padgitt was allowed to move so freely out of the county. When Mackey Don announced his candidacy, Buford sent him $50,000 in cash. Mackey Don won in a landslide. His opponent claimed to be honest.

There was a widely held but unprofessed belief in Mississippi that a good Sheriff must be a little crooked to ensure law and order. Whiskey, whoring, and gambling were simply facts of life, and a good Sheriff must be knowledgeable in these affairs to properly regulate them and protect the Christians. Those vices could not be eliminated, so the High Sheriff must be able to coordinate them and synchronize the orderly flow of sin. For his coordinating efforts, he was to be paid a little extra from the purveyors of such wickedness. He expected it. Most of the voters expected it. No honest man could live on such a humble salary. No honest man could move quietly through the shadows of the underworld.

For the better part of a hundred years following the Civil War, the Padgitts owned the Sheriffs of Ford County. They bought them outright with sacks of cash. Mackey Don Coley received a hundred thousand a year (it was rumored), and during election years he got whatever he needed. And they were generous with other politicians. They quietly bought and kept influence. They asked little; they just wanted to be left alone on their island.

After the Second War, the demand for moonshine began a steady decline. Since generations of Padgitts had been schooled to operate outside the law, Buford and the family began to diversify into other forms of illicit commerce. Selling only timber was dull, and subject to too many market factors, and, most important, did not generate the piles of cash the family expected. They ran guns, stole cars, counterfeited, bought and burned buildings to collect insurance. For twenty years they operated a highly successful brothel on the county line, until it mysteriously burned in 1966.

They were creative and energetic people, always scheming and searching for opportunity, always waiting for someone to rob. There were rumors, quite significant at times, that the Padgitts were members of the Dixie Mafia, a loose-knit gang of redneck thieves who ran rampant through the Deep South in the sixties. These rumors were never verified and were in fact discounted by many because the Padgitts were simply too secretive to share their business with anyone. Nonetheless, the rumors persisted for years, and the Padgitts were the source of endless gossip in the cafés and coffee shops around the square in Clanton. They were never considered local heroes, but certainly legends.

In 1967, a younger Padgitt fled to Canada to avoid the draft. He drifted to California where he tried marijuana and realized he had a taste for it. After a few months as a peacenik, he got homesick and sneaked back to Padgitt Island. He brought with him four pounds of pot, which he shared with all his cousins, and they, too, were quite taken with it. He explained that the rest of the country, and primarily California, was toking like crazy. As usual, Mississippi was at least five years behind the trend.

The stuff could be grown cheaply, then hauled to the cities where there was demand. His father, Gill Padgitt, grandson of Clovis, saw the opportunity, and soon many of the old cornfields were converted to cannabis. A two-thousand-foot strip of land was cleared for a runway and the Padgitts bought themselves an airplane. Within a year there were daily flights to the outskirts of Memphis and Atlanta, where the Padgitts had established their network. To their delight and with their help, marijuana finally became popular in the Deep South.

The moonshining slowed considerably. The brothel was gone. The Padgitts had contacts in Miami and Mexico and the cash was coming in by the truckloads. For years, no one in Ford County had a hint that the

Padgitts were trafficking in drugs. And they never got caught. No Padgitt was ever indicted for a drug-related offense.

In fact, not a single Padgitt had ever been arrested. A hundred years of moonshining, stealing, gunrunning, gambling, counterfeiting, whoring, bribing, even killing, and eventually drug manufacturing, and not a single arrest. They were smart people, careful, deliberate, patient with their schemes.

Then Danny Padgitt, Gill's youngest son, was arrested for the rape and murder of Rhoda Kassellaw.

CHAPTER 4

Mr. Deece told me the next day that when he was certain Rhoda was dead he finally left her in the swing on the front porch. He went to his bathroom, where he stripped and showered and saw her blood spin down the drain. He changed into work clothes and waited for the police and the ambulance. He watched her house while holding a loaded shotgun, anxious to blast anything that moved. But there was no movement, no sound. In the distance he could barely hear a siren.

His wife kept the children locked in the back bedroom, where she huddled with them in the bed, under a blanket. Michael kept asking about his mother, and who was that man? But Teresa was too traumatized to speak. She managed only a low groaning sound as she sucked her fingers and shook as if she were freezing.

Before long Benning Road was alive with red and blue flashing lights. Rhoda's body was photographed at length before it was taken away. Her home was cordoned off by a squad of deputies, led by Sheriff Coley himself. Mr. Deece, still holding his shotgun, gave his statement to an investigator, then to the Sheriff.

Shortly after 2 A.M., a deputy arrived with the news that a doctor in town had been notified and had suggested that the children be brought in for a look. They rode in the backseat of a patrol car, Michael clutching Mr. Deece, and Teresa in the lap of his wife. At the hospital, they were given a mild sedative and placed together in a semiprivate room where the nurses brought them cookies and milk until they finally went to sleep. Later in the day an aunt arrived from Missouri and took them away.

———

My phone rang seconds before midnight. It was Wiley Meek, the paper's photographer. He'd picked up the story on the police scanner and was already hanging around the jail waiting to ambush the suspect. Cops were everywhere, he said, his excitement barely under control. Hurry, he urged me. This could be the big one.

At the time I lived above an old garage next to a decaying but still grand Victorian mansion known as the Hocutt House. It was filled with elderly Hocutts, three sisters and a brother, and they took turns being my landlord. Their five-acre estate was a few blocks from the Clanton square and had been built a century earlier with family money. It was covered with trees, overgrown flower beds, thick patches of mature weeds, and enough animals to stock a game preserve. Rabbits, squirrels, skunks, possums, raccoons, a million birds, a frightening assortment of green and black snakes—all non-poisonous I was reassured—and dozens of cats. But no dogs. The Hocutts hated dogs. Each cat had a name, and a major clause in my verbal lease was that I would respect the cats.

Respect them I did. The four-room loft apartment was spacious and clean and cost me the ridiculous sum of $50 a month. If they wanted their cats respected at that price, fine with me.

Their father, Miles Hocutt, had been an eccentric doctor in Clanton for decades. Their mother died during childbirth, and, according to local legend, Dr. Hocutt became very possessive of the children after her death. To protect them from the world, he concocted one of the biggest lies ever told in Ford County. He explained to his children that insanity ran deeply in the family, and thus they should never marry lest they produce some hideous strain of idiot offspring. His children worshiped him, believed him, and were probably already exposed to some measure of unbalance. They never married. The son, Max Hocutt, was eighty-one when he leased me the apartment. The twins, Wilma and Gilma, were seventy-seven, and Melberta, the baby, was seventy-three and completely out of her mind.

It was Gilma, I think, who was peeking from the kitchen window as I descended the wooden stairway at midnight. A cat was asleep on the bottom step, directly in my path, but I respectfully stepped over it. I wanted to kick it into the street.

Two cars were parked in the garage. One was my Spitfire, top up to keep the cats out, and the other was a long, shiny black Mercedes with red-and-white butcher knives painted on the doors. Under the knives were phone numbers in green paint. Someone had once told Mr. Max Hocutt that he could completely write off the cost of a new car, any car, if he used it for business and some sort of logo was painted on the doors. He bought a new Mercedes and became a knife sharpener. He said his tools were in the trunk.

The car was ten years old and had been driven less than eight thousand miles. Their father had also preached to them the sinfulness of women driving, so Mr. Max was the chauffeur.

I eased the Spitfire down the gravel drive and waved at Gilma peeking from behind the curtain. She jerked her head away and disappeared. The jail was six blocks away. I had slept for about thirty minutes.

Danny Padgitt was being fingerprinted when I arrived. The Sheriff's office was in the front section of the jail, and it was packed with deputies and reserves and volunteer firemen and everybody with access to a uniform and a police scanner. Wiley Meek met me on the front sidewalk.

"It's Danny Padgitt!" he said with great excitement.

I stopped for a second and tried to think. "Who?"

"Danny Padgitt, from the island."

I'd been in Ford County less than three months and

had yet to meet a single Padgitt. They, as always, kept to themselves. But I'd heard various installments of their legend, with much more to follow. Telling Padgitt stories was a common form of entertainment in Ford County.

Wiley gushed on, "I got some great shots just as they got him out of the car. Had blood all over him. Great pictures! The girl's dead!"

"What girl?"

"The one he killed. Raped her too, at least that's the rumor."

Danny Padgitt, I mumbled to myself as the sensational story began to sink in. I had my first glimpse of the headline, no doubt the boldest one the *Times* had run in many years. Poor old Spot had shied away from the jolting stories. Poor old Spot had gone bankrupt. I had other plans.

We pushed our way inside and looked around for Sheriff Coley. I'd met him twice during my brief stint with the *Times* and I had been impressed with his polite and warm nature. He called me mister and said sir and ma'am to everyone, always with a smile. He'd been the Sheriff since the massacre in 1943, so he was pushing seventy years of age. He was tall and gaunt without the obligatory thick stomach required of most Southern sheriffs. On the surface he was a gentleman, and both times I'd met him I'd later wondered how such a nice man could be so corrupt. He emerged from a back room with a deputy, and I, practicing my assertiveness, rushed to him.

"Sheriff, just a couple of questions," I said sternly. There were no other reporters present. His boys—the real deputies, the part-timers, the wannabes, the jackleg constables with homemade uniforms—they all got quiet and gave me their sneers. I was still very much the brash new rich boy who'd somehow wrangled control of their newspaper. I was a foreigner, with no right to barge in at a time like this and start asking questions.

Sheriff Coley smiled as usual, as if these encounters happened all the time around midnight. "Yes sir, Mr. Traynor." He had a slow rich drawl that was very soothing. This man couldn't tell a lie, could he?

"What can you tell us about the murder?"

With his arms folded across his chest, he gave a few of the basics in copspeak. "White female, age thirty-one, was attacked in her home on Benning Road. Raped, stabbed, murdered. Can't give you her name until we talk to her kinfolks."

"And you've made an arrest?"

"Yes sir, but no details now. Just give us a couple of hours. We're investigatin'. That's all, Mr. Traynor."

"Rumor has it that you have Danny Padgitt in custody."

"I don't deal in rumors, Mr. Traynor. Not in my profession. Yours neither."

Wiley and I drove to the hospital, sniffed around for an hour, heard nothing we could print, then drove to the scene on Benning Road. The cops had cordoned off the house and a few of the neighbors were huddled quietly behind a strand of yellow police ribbon near the mailbox. We eased next to them, listening intently, hearing almost nothing. They seemed too stunned to talk. After a few minutes of gawking at the house, we crept away.

Wiley had a nephew who was a part-time deputy, and we found him guarding the Deece home where they were still inspecting the front porch and the swing where Rhoda took her last breath. We pulled him off to the side, behind a row of Mr. Deece's crepe myrtles, and he told us everything. All off the record, of course, as if the gory details would somehow be kept quiet in Ford County.

———

There were three small cafés around the square in Clanton, two for the whites, one for the blacks. Wiley suggested we get an early table and just listen.

I do not eat breakfast, and I'm usually not awake during the hours in which it is served. I don't mind working until midnight, but I prefer to sleep until the sun is overhead and in full view. As I quickly realized, one of the advantages of owning a small weekly was that I could work late and sleep late. The stories could be written anytime, as long as the deadlines were met. Spot himself was known to drift in not long before noon, after, of course, dropping by the funeral home. I liked his hours.

The second day I lived in my apartment above the Hocutt garage, Gilma banged on my door at nine-thirty in the morning. And banged and banged. I finally staggered through my small kitchen in my underwear and saw her squinting through the blinds. She announced that she was just about to call the police. The other Hocutts were down below, wandering around the garage, looking at my car, certain that a crime had been committed.

She asked what I was doing. I said that I had been sleeping until I heard somebody banging on the damned door. She asked me why I was still asleep at nine-thirty on a Wednesday morning. I rubbed my eyes and tried to think of an appropriate response. I was suddenly aware that I was almost nude and standing in the presence of a seventy-seven-year-old virgin. She kept looking at my thighs.

They'd been up since five, she explained. Nobody sleeps till nine-thirty in Clanton. Was I drunk? They were just concerned, that's all. As I closed the door I told her I was sober, still sleepy, thanks for being concerned but I would often be in bed past 9 A.M.

I'd been to the Tea Shoppe a couple of times for late morning coffee and once for lunch. As the owner of the paper, I felt it necessary to circulate and be seen, at a reasonable hour. I was keenly aware that I would be writing about Ford County, its people and places and happenings, for years to come.

Wiley said the cafés would be crowded early. "Always after football games and car wrecks," he said.

"What about murders?" I asked.

"It's been a long time," he said.

He was right, the place was packed when we walked in, just after 6 A.M. He offered some hellos, shook some hands, exchanged a couple of insults. He was from Ford County and knew everyone. I nodded and smiled and caught the odd looks. It would take years. The people were friendly, but also wary of outsiders.

We found two seats at the counter and I asked for coffee. Nothing else. The waitress did not approve of this. She warmed to Wiley, though, when he reconsidered and ordered scrambled eggs, country ham, biscuits, grits, and a side of hash browns, enough cholesterol to choke a mule.

The talk was of the rape and murder and nothing else. If the weather could cause arguments, imagine what such a heinous crime could stir up. The Padgitts had had the run of the county for a hundred years; it was time to send 'em all to jail. Surround the island with the National Guard if necessary. Mackey Don had to go; he'd been in their pockets for too long. Let a bunch of crooks run free and they think they're above the law. Now this.

Not much was said about Rhoda because little was known. Someone knew she'd been hanging around the lounges on the state line. Someone said she'd been sleeping with a local lawyer. Didn't know his name. Just a rumor.

The rumors roared around the Tea Shoppe. A couple of the loudmouths took turns holding court, and I was surprised at how reckless they were with their versions of the truth. Too bad I couldn't print all the wonderful gossip we heard.

CHAPTER 5

We did, however, print a lot. The headline proclaimed that Rhoda Kassellaw had been raped and murdered, and that Danny Padgitt had been arrested for it. The headline could've been read from twenty yards down any sidewalk around the courthouse square.

Under it were two photos; one of Rhoda as a senior in high school, and one of Padgitt as he was led into the jail in handcuffs. Wiley had ambushed him all right. It was a perfect shot, with Padgitt sneering at the camera. There was blood on his forehead from the wreck, and blood on his shirt from the attack. He looked nasty, mean, insolent, drunk, and guilty as hell, and I knew the photo would cause a sensation. Wiley thought we'd better avoid it, but I was twenty-three years old and too young to be restrained. I wanted my readers to see and know the ugly truth. I wanted to sell newspapers.

The photo of Rhoda had been obtained from a sister in Missouri. The first time I talked to her, by phone, she had had almost nothing to say and quickly hung up. The second time she thawed just a little, said the children were being seen by a doctor, that the funeral would take place Tuesday afternoon in a small town near Springfield, and, as far as the family was concerned, the entire state of Mississippi could burn in hell.

I told her that I understood completely, that I was from Syracuse, that I was one of the good guys. She finally agreed to send me a photo.

Using a host of unnamed sources, I described in detail what happened the previous Saturday night on Benning Road. When I was sure of a fact, I drove it home. When I wasn't so sure, I nibbled around the edges with enough innuendo to convey what I thought happened. Baggy Suggs sobered up long enough to reread and edit the stories. He probably kept us from getting sued or shot.

On page two there was a map of the crime scene and a large photo of Rhoda's home, one taken the morning after the crime, complete with cop cars and yellow police ribbon everywhere. The photo also included the bikes and toys of Michael and Teresa scattered around the front yard. In many ways, the photo was more ominous than one of the corpse itself, which I didn't have but tried to get. The photo stated plainly that children lived there, and that children were involved in a crime so brutal that most Ford Countians were still trying to believe it really happened.

How much did the children see? That was the burning question.

I didn't answer it in the *Times*, but I got as close as possible. I described the house and its interior layout. Using an unnamed source, I estimated that the children's beds were about thirty feet from their mother's. The children fled the house before Rhoda, they were in shock by the time they got next door, they were seen by a doctor in Clanton and were undergoing therapy of some nature back home in Missouri. They saw a lot.

Would they testify at a trial? Baggy said there was no way; they were simply too young. But I pulled the question out of the air and posed it anyway, to give the readers something else to argue and fret over. After exploring the possibility of parading the children into a courtroom, I concluded that "experts" agreed that such a scenario was unlikely. Baggy enjoyed being considered an expert.

Rhoda's obituary was as long as I could possibly make it, which, given the tradition of the *Times*, was not unusual.

We went to press about 10 P.M. on Tuesday night; the paper was in the racks around the Clanton square by 7 A.M. on Wednesday. The circulation had dropped to fewer than twelve hundred at the time of the bankruptcy, but after a month of my fearless leadership we had close to twenty-five hundred subscribers—five thousand was a realistic goal.

For the Rhoda Kassellaw murder we printed eight thousand copies and put them everywhere—by the

doors of the cafés around the square, in the halls of the
courthouse, on the desks of every county employee, in
the lobbies of the banks. We mailed three thousand free
copies to potential subscribers, as part of a sudden, one-
time special promotion effort.

According to Wiley, it was the first murder in eight
years. It was a Padgitt! It was a wonderfully sensational
story and I saw it as my golden moment. Sure I went for
the shock, for the sensational, for the bloodstains. Sure
it was yellow journalism, but what did I care?

I had no idea the response would be so quick and
unpleasant.

———

At 9 A.M., Thursday morning, the main courtroom on
the second floor of the Ford County Courthouse was
full. It was the domain of the Honorable Reed Loopus,
an aging Circuit Court Judge from Tyler County, who
passed through Clanton eight times a year to dispense
justice. He was a legendary old warrior who ruled with
an iron fist and, according to Baggy—who spent most
of his working life hanging around the courthouse either picking up gossip or creating it—was a thoroughly
honest Judge who had somehow managed to avoid the
tentacles of the Padgitt money. Perhaps because he was
from another county, Judge Loopus believed criminals
should serve long sentences, preferably at hard labor,
though he could no longer order such.

The Monday after the murder, the Padgitt lawyers
had scrambled around trying to get Danny out of jail.

Judge Loopus was preoccupied with a trial in another county—his district covered six of them—and he refused to be pushed into a quick bail hearing. Instead, he set the matter for 9 A.M. Thursday, thus allowing the town several days to ponder and speculate.

Because I was a member of the press, indeed the owner of the local paper, I felt it was my duty to arrive early and get a good seat. Yes, I was a bit smug. The other spectators were there out of curiosity. I, however, had very important work to do. Baggy and I were sitting in the second row when the crowd began to assemble.

Danny Padgitt's principal lawyer was a character named Lucien Wilbanks, a man I would quickly learn to hate. He was what was left of a once prominent clan of lawyers and bankers and such. The Wilbanks family had worked long and hard to build Clanton, then Lucien came along and had pretty much ruined a fine family name. He fancied himself as a radical lawyer, which, for that part of the world in 1970, was quite rare. He wore a beard, swore like a sailor, drank heavily, and preferred clients who were rapists and murderers and child molesters. He was the only white member of the NAACP in Ford County, which alone was enough to get you shot there. He didn't care.

Lucien Wilbanks was abrasive and fearless and downright mean, and he waited until everyone was settled in the courtroom—just before Judge Loopus entered—to walk slowly over to me. He was holding a copy of the latest *Times*, which he began waving as he started swearing. "You little son of a bitch!" he said, quite loudly, and the courtroom became perfectly still. "Who in hell do you think you are?"

I was too mortified to attempt an answer. I felt Baggy inch away. Every single person in the courtroom was staring at me, and I knew I had to say something. "Just telling the truth," I managed to say with as much conviction as I could muster.

"It's yellow journalism!" he roared. "Sensational tabloid garbage!" The paper was just a few inches from my nose.

"Thank you," I said, like a real wise guy. There were at least five deputies in the courtroom, none of whom were showing any interest in breaking this up.

"We'll file suit tomorrow!" he said, his eyes glowing. "A million dollars in damages!"

"I got lawyers," I said, suddenly terrified that I was about to be as bankrupt as the Caudle family. Lucien tossed the paper into my lap, then turned and went back to his table. I was finally able to exhale; my heart was pounding. I could feel my cheeks burning from embarrassment and fear.

But I managed to keep a stupid grin on my face. I couldn't show the locals that I, the editor/publisher of their paper, was afraid of anything. But a million dollars in damages! I immediately thought of my grandmother in Memphis. That would be a difficult conversation.

There was a commotion up behind the bench and a bailiff opened a door. "Everyone rise," he announced. Judge Loopus crept through it and shuffled to his seat, his faded black robe trailing behind him. Once situated, he surveyed the crowd, and said, "Good morning. A rather nice turnout for a bail hearing." Such routine matters generally attracted no one, except for the accused, his lawyer, and perhaps his mother. There were three hundred people watching this one.

It wasn't just a bail hearing. It was round one of a rape/murder trial, and few people in Clanton wanted to miss it. As I was keenly aware, most folks would not be able to attend the proceedings. They would rely on the *Times*, and I was determined to give them the details.

Every time I looked at Lucien Wilbanks, I thought about the lawsuit for a million dollars. Surely he wasn't going to sue my paper, was he? For what? There had been no libel, no defamation.

Judge Loopus nodded at another bailiff and a side door opened. Danny Padgitt was escorted in, his hands cuffed at his waist. He was wearing a neatly pressed white shirt, khaki pants, and loafers. His face was clean shaven and free of any apparent injuries. He was twenty-four, a year older than me, but he looked much younger. He was clean cut, handsome, and I couldn't help but think he ought to be in college somewhere. He managed a slow strut, then the sneer as the bailiff removed the handcuffs. He looked around at the crowd, and for a moment seemed to enjoy the attention. He showed all the confidence of someone whose family had unlimited cash, which it would use to get him out of his little jam.

Seated directly in back of him, behind the bar in the

first row, were his parents and various other Padgitts. His father Gill, grandson of the infamous Clovis Padgitt, had a college degree and was rumored to be the chief money launderer in the gang. His mother was well dressed and somewhat attractive, which I found unusual for someone dimwitted enough to marry into the Padgitt clan and spend the rest of her life secluded on the island.

"I've never seen her before," Baggy whispered to me.

"How often have you seen Gill?" I asked.

"Maybe twice, in the last twenty years."

The State was represented by the county prosecutor, a part-timer named Rocky Childers. Judge Loopus addressed him: "Mr. Childers, I assume the State is opposed to bail."

Childers stood and said, "Yes sir."

"On what grounds?"

"The horrific nature of the crimes, Your Honor. A vicious rape, in the victim's own bed, in front of her small children. A simultaneous murder caused by at least two knife wounds. The attempted flight of the accused, Mr. Padgitt." Childers's words cut through the hushed courtroom. "The great likelihood that if Mr. Padgitt leaves jail we will never see him again."

Lucien Wilbanks couldn't wait to stand up and start bickering. He was on his feet immediately. "We object to that, Your Honor. My client has no criminal record whatsoever, never been arrested before."

Judge Loopus looked calmly over his reading glasses

and said, "Mr. Wilbanks, I do hope that is the first and last time you interrupt anyone in this proceeding. I suggest you sit down, and when the Court is ready to hear from you, then you will be so advised." His words were icy, almost bitter, and I wondered how many times these two had tangled in this very courtroom.

Nothing bothered Lucien Wilbanks; his skin was as thick as rawhide.

Childers then gave us a bit of history. Eleven years earlier, in 1959, a certain Gerald Padgitt had been indicted for stealing cars over in Tupelo. It took a year to find a couple of deputies willing to enter Padgitt Island to serve a warrant, and though they survived, they were unsuccessful. Gerald Padgitt either fled the country or secluded himself somewhere on the island. "Wherever he is," Childers said, "he's never been arrested, never been found."

"You ever hear of Gerald Padgitt?" I whispered to Baggy.

"Nope."

"If this defendant is released on bail, Your Honor, we'll never see him again. It's that simple." Childers sat down.

"Mr. Wilbanks," His Honor said.

Lucien stood slowly and waved a hand at Childers. "As usual, the prosecutor is confused," he began pleasantly. "Gerald Padgitt is not charged with these crimes. I don't represent him and really don't give a damn what happened to him."

"Watch your language," Loopus said.

"He's not on trial here. This is about Danny Padgitt, a young man with no criminal record whatsoever."

"Does your client own real estate in this county?" Loopus asked.

"No, he does not. He's only twenty-four."

"Let's get to the bottom line, Mr. Wilbanks. I know his family owns considerable acreage. The only way I'll grant bail is if it's all pledged to secure his appearance for trial."

"That's outrageous," Lucien growled.

"So are his alleged crimes."

Lucien flung his legal pad onto the table. "Give me a minute to consult with the family."

This caused quite a stir among the Padgitts. They huddled behind the defense table with Wilbanks and there was disagreement from the very start. It was almost funny watching these very wealthy crooks shake their heads and get mad at each other. Family fights are quick and bitter, especially when money is at stake, and every Padgitt present seemed to have a different opinion about which course to take. One could only imagine what it was like when they were dividing their loot.

Lucien sensed that an agreement was unlikely, and to avoid embarrassment he turned and addressed the Court. "That's impossible, Your Honor," he announced. "The Padgitt land is owned by at least forty people, most of them absent from this courtroom. What the Court is requiring is arbitrary and overly burdensome."

"I'll give you a few days to put it together," Loopus said, obviously enjoying the discomfort he was causing.

"No sir. It's just not fair. My client is entitled to a reasonable bail, same as any other defendant."

"Then bail is denied until the preliminary hearing."

"We waive the preliminary."

"As you wish," Loopus said, taking notes.

"And we request that the case be presented to the grand jury as soon as possible."

"In due course, Mr. Wilbanks, same as all other cases."

"Because we will move for a change of venue as soon as possible." Lucien said this boldly, as if an important proclamation was needed.

"It's a bit early for that, don't you think?" Loopus said.

"It will be impossible for my client to get a fair trial in this county." Wilbanks was gazing around the courtroom as he continued, almost ignoring the Judge, who, for the moment, seemed curious.

"An effort is already under way to indict, try, and convict my client before he has the chance to defend himself, and I think the Court should intervene immediately with a gag order."

Lucien Wilbanks was the only one who needed gagging.

"Where are you going with this, Mr. Wilbanks?" Loopus asked.

"Have you seen the local paper, Your Honor?"

"Not lately."

All eyes seemed to settle upon me, and once again my heart stopped dead still.

Wilbanks glared at me as he continued. "Front page stories, bloody photographs, unnamed sources, enough half-truths and innuendos to convict any innocent man!"

Baggy was inching away again, and I was very much alone.

Lucien stomped across the courtroom and tossed a copy up to the bench. "Take a look at this," he growled. Loopus adjusted his reading glasses, pulled the *Times* up high, and sank back into his fine leather chair. He began reading, apparently in no particular hurry.

He was a slow reader. At some point my heart began functioning again, returning with the fury of a jackhammer. And I noticed my collar was wet where it rested on the back of my neck. Loopus finished the front page and slowly opened it up. The courtroom was silent. Would he toss me into jail right there? Nod to a bailiff to slap handcuffs on me and drag me away? I wasn't a lawyer. I'd just been threatened with a million-dollar lawsuit, by a man who'd certainly filed many, and now the Judge was reading my rather lurid accounts while the entire town waited for his verdict.

A lot of hard glances were coming my way, so I found it easier to scribble on my reporter's pad, though I couldn't read anything I was writing. I worked hard at keeping a straight face. What I really wanted to do was bolt from the courtroom and race back to Memphis.

Pages rattled, and His Honor was finally finished.

He leaned slightly forward to the microphone and uttered words that would instantly make my career. He said, "It's very well written. Engaging, perhaps a bit macabre, but certainly nothing out of line."

I kept scribbling, as if I hadn't heard this. In a sudden, unforeseen, and rather harrowing skirmish, I had just prevailed over the Padgitts and Lucien Wilbanks. "Congratulations," Baggy whispered.

Loopus refolded the newspaper and laid it down. He allowed Wilbanks to rant and rave for a few minutes about leaks from the cops, leaks from the prosecutor's office, potential leaks from the grand jury room, all of them somehow coordinated by a conspiracy of unnamed people determined to treat his client unfairly. What he was really doing was performing for the Padgitts. He had lost his attempt to get bail, so he had to impress them with his zealousness.

Loopus bought none of it.

As we would soon learn, Lucien's act had been nothing but a smokescreen. He had no intention of moving the case from Ford County.

CHAPTER 6

When I bought the *Times*, its prehistoric building came with the deal. It had very little value. It was on the south side of the Clanton square, one of four decaying structures built wall to wall by someone in a hurry; long and narrow, three levels, with a basement that all employees feared and shied away from. There were several offices in the front, all with stained and threadbare carpet, peeling walls, the smell of last century's pipe smoke forever fused to the ceilings.

In the rear, as far away as possible, was the printing press. Every Tuesday night, Hardy, our pressman, somehow coaxed the old letterpress to life and managed to produce yet another edition of our paper. His space was rank with the sharp odor of printer's ink.

The room on the first floor was lined with bookshelves sagging under the weight of dusty tomes that had not been opened in decades; collections of history and Shakespeare and Irish poetry and rows of badly outdated British encyclopedias. Spot thought such books would impress anyone who ventured in.

Standing in the front window, and looking through dingy panes of glass, across which someone had long ago painted the word "TIMES," one could see the Ford County Courthouse and the bronze Confederate sentry guarding it. A plaque below his feet listed the names of the sixty-one county boys who died in the Great War, most at Shiloh.

The sentry could also be seen from my office, which was on the second floor. It, too, was lined with bookshelves holding Spot's personal library, an eclectic collection that appeared to have been as neglected as the one downstairs. It would be years before I moved any of his books.

The office was spacious, cluttered, filled with useless artifacts and worthless files and adorned with fake portraits of Confederate generals. I loved the place. When Spot left he took nothing, and after a few months no one seemed to want any of his junk. So it remained where it was, neglected as always, virtually untouched by me, and slowly becoming my property. I boxed up his personal things—letters, bank statements, notes, postcards—and stored them in one of the many unused rooms down the hall where they continued to gather dust and slowly rot.

My office had two sets of French doors that opened to a small porch with a wrought-iron railing, and there was enough room out there for four people to sit in wicker chairs and watch the square. Not that there was much to see, but it was a pleasant way to pass the time, especially with a drink.

Baggy was always ready for a drink. He brought a bottle of bourbon after dinner, and we assumed our positions in the rockers. The town was still buzzing over the bail hearing. It had been widely assumed that Danny Padgitt would be sprung as soon as Lucien Wilbanks and Mackey Don Coley could get matters arranged. Promises would be made, money would change hands, Sheriff Coley would somehow personally guarantee the boy's appearance at trial. But Judge Loopus had other plans.

Baggy's wife was a nurse. She worked the night shift in the emergency room at the hospital. He worked days, if his rather languid observations of the town could be considered labor. They rarely saw each other, which was evidently a good thing because they fought constantly. Their adult children had fled, leaving the two of them to wage their own little war. After a couple of drinks, Baggy always began the cutting remarks about his wife. He was fifty-two, looked at least seventy, and I suspected that the booze was the principal reason he was aging badly and fighting at home.

"We kicked their butts," he said proudly. "Never before has a newspaper story been so clearly exonerated. Right there in open court."

"What's a gag order?" I asked. I was an ill-informed rookie, and everybody knew it. No sense in pretending I knew something when I didn't.

"I've never seen one. I've heard of them, and I think they're used by judges to shut up the lawyers and the litigants."

"So they don't apply to newspapers?"

"Never. Wilbanks was grandstanding, that's all. The guy is a member of the ACLU, only one in Ford County. He understands the First Amendment. There's no way a court can tell a newspaper not to print something. He was having a bad day, it was apparent his client was staying in jail, so he had to showboat. Typical maneuver by lawyers. They teach it in law school."

"So you don't think we'll get sued?"

"Hell no. Look, first of all, there's no lawsuit. We didn't libel or defame anyone. Sure we got kinda loose with some of the facts, but it was all small stuff, and it was probably true anyway. Second, if Wilbanks had a lawsuit he would have to file it here, in Ford County. Same courthouse, same courtroom, same Judge. The Honorable Reed Loopus, who, this morning, read our stories and declared them to be just fine. The lawsuit was shot down before Wilbanks typed the first word. Brilliant."

I certainly didn't feel brilliant. I'd been worrying about the million dollars in damages and wondering where I might find such a sum. The bourbon was finally settling in and I relaxed. It was Thursday night in Clanton and few people were out. Every shop and store and office around the square was locked tight.

Baggy, as usual, had been relaxed for a long time. Margaret had whispered to me that he often had bourbon for breakfast. He and a one-legged lawyer called Major liked to have a nip with their coffee. They would meet on the balcony outside Major's office across the square and smoke and drink and argue law and politics while the courthouse came to life. Major lost a leg at Guadalcanal, according to his version of the Second War. His law practice was specialized to the point that he did nothing but type wills for the elderly. He typed them himself—had no need for a secretary. He worked about as hard as Baggy, and the two were often seen in the courtroom, half-soused, watching yet another trial.

"I guess Mackey Don's got the boy in the suite," Baggy said, his words starting to slur.

"The suite?" I asked.

"Yeah—have you seen the jail?"

"No."

"It's not fit for animals. No heat, no air, plumbing works about half the time. Filthy conditions. Rotten food. And that's for the whites. The blacks are at the other end, all in one long cell. Their only toilet is a hole in the floor."

"I think I'll pass."

"It's an embarrassment to the county, but, sadly, it's the same in most places around here. Anyway, there's one little cell with air conditioning and carpet on the floor, one clean bed, color television, good food. It's called the suite and Mackey Don puts his favorites there."

I was mentally taking notes. To Baggy, it was business as usual. To me, a recent college attendee and sometime journalism student, a real muckraking story was in the works. "You think Padgitt's in the suite?"

"Probably. He came to court in his own clothes."

"As opposed to?"

"Those orange jail coveralls everybody else wears. You haven't seen them?"

Yes, I had seen them. I had been in court one time, a month or so earlier, and I suddenly recalled seeing two or three defendants sitting in the courtroom, waiting for a judge, all wearing different shades of faded orange coveralls. "Ford County Jail" was printed across the front and back of the shirts.

Baggy took a sip and expounded. "You see, for the preliminary hearings and such, the defendants, if they're still in jail, always come to court dressed like prisoners. In the old days, Mackey Don would make them wear the coveralls even during their trials. Lucien Wilbanks got a guilty verdict reversed on the grounds that the jury was predisposed to convict since his client certainly looked guilty as hell in his orange jail suit. And he was right. Kinda hard to convince a jury you're not guilty when you're dressed like an inmate and wearing rubber shower shoes."

I marveled once again at the backwardness of Mississippi. I could see a criminal defendant, especially a black one, facing a jury and expecting a fair trial, wearing jail garb designed to be spotted from half a mile away. "Still fightin' the War," was a slogan I'd heard several times in Ford County. There was a frustrating

resistance to change, especially where crime and punishment were concerned.

———

Around noon the following day I walked to the jail looking for Sheriff Coley. Under the pretext of asking him
questions about the Kassellaw investigation, I planned to
see as many of the inmates as possible. His secretary informed me, rather rudely, that he was in a meeting, and
that was fine with me.

Two prisoners were cleaning the front offices. Outside, two more were pulling weeds from a flower bed. I
walked around the block and behind the jail I saw a
small open area with a basketball goal. Six prisoners
were loitering under the shade of a small oak tree. On
the east side of the jail I saw three prisoners standing in
a window, behind bars, gazing down at me.

Thirteen inmates in all. Thirteen orange suits.

Wiley's nephew was consulted about things around
the jail. At first he was reluctant to talk, but he had a deep
hatred of Sheriff Coley, and he thought he could trust
me. He confirmed what Baggy had suspected—Danny
Padgitt was living the good life in an air-conditioned cell
and eating whatever he wanted. He dressed as he wished,
played checkers with the Sheriff himself, and made
phone calls all day long.

———

The next edition of the *Times* did much to solidify my
reputation as a hard-charging, fearless, twenty-three-

year-old fool. On the front page was a huge photo of Danny Padgitt being led into the courthouse for his bail hearing. He was handcuffed and wore street clothes. He was also giving the camera one of his patented go-to-hell looks. Just above it was the massive headline: BAIL DENIED FOR DANNY PADGITT. The story was lengthy and detailed.

Alongside was another story, almost as long and much more scandalous. Quoting unnamed sources, I described at length the conditions of Mr. Padgitt's incarceration. I mentioned every possible perk he was getting, including personal time with Sheriff Coley over the checkerboard. I talked about his food and diet, color television, unlimited phone use. Everything I could possibly verify. Then I compared this with how the other twenty-one inmates were living.

On page two, I ran an old black-and-white file photo of four defendants being led into the courthouse. Each, of course, was wearing the coveralls. Each had handcuffs and unruly hair. I blacked out their faces so, whoever they were, they would not suffer any more embarrassment. Their cases had long since been closed.

I'd placed another picture of Danny Padgitt as he was led into the courthouse next to the file photo. Except for the handcuffs, he could've been on his way to a party. The contrast was startling. The boy was being pampered by Sheriff Coley, who, so far, had refused to discuss the matter with me. Big mistake.

In the story, I detailed my efforts to chat with the Sheriff. My phone calls had not been returned. I'd gone to the jail twice and he wouldn't meet with me. I'd left a list of questions for him, which he chose to ignore. I painted the picture of an aggressive young reporter desperately searching for the truth and being stiff-armed by an elected official.

Since Lucien Wilbanks was one of the least popular men in Clanton, I included him in the fray. Using the phone, which I was quickly learning was a great equalizer, I called his office four times before he called me back. At first he had no comment about his client or the charges, but when I persisted with questions about his treatment at the jail he erupted. "I don't run the damned jail, son!" he growled, and I could almost see his red eyes glowing at me. I quoted him on that.

"Have you interviewed your client at the jail?" I asked.

"Of course."

"What was he wearing?"

"Don't you have better things to report?"

"No sir. What was he wearing?"

"Well, he wasn't naked."

That was too good a quote to pass up, so I put it in bold print in a sidebar.

With a rapist/murderer, a corrupt Sheriff, and a radical lawyer on one side, and me standing alone on the other, I knew I couldn't lose the fight. The response to the story was astounding. Baggy and Wiley reported that the cafés were buzzing with admiration for the fearless young editor of the paper. The Padgitts and Lucien had been despised for a long time. Now it was time to get rid of Coley.

Margaret said we were swamped with phone calls from readers incensed with the soft treatment Danny was receiving. Wiley's nephew reported that the jail was in chaos and Mackey Don was at war with his deputies. He was coddling a murderer—1971 was an election year. Folks were angry out there and they might all lose their jobs.

———

Those two weeks at the *Times* were crucial to its survival. The readers were hungry for details, and, through timing, dumb luck, and some guts, I gave them just what they wanted. The paper was suddenly alive; it was a force. It was trusted. The people wanted it to report with detail and without fear.

Baggy and Margaret told me that Spot would have never used the bloody pictures and challenged the Sheriff. But they were still quite timid. I can't say that my brashness had in any way emboldened my staff. The *Times* was, and would be, a one-man show with a rather weak supporting staff.

Little did I care. I was telling the truth and damning the consequences. I was a local hero. Subscriptions jumped to almost three thousand. Ad revenue doubled. Not only was I shining a new light into the county, I was making money at the same time.

CHAPTER 7

The bomb was a rather basic incendiary device that, if detonated, would have quickly engulfed our printing room. There the fire would have been energized by various chemicals and no less than 110 gallons of printer's ink, and would have raced quickly through the front offices. After a few minutes, with no sprinkler system and no alarms, who knows how much of the upper two floors could have been saved. Probably not much. It was very likely that the fire, if properly detonated in the early hours of Thursday morning, would've burned most of the four buildings in our row.

It was discovered sitting ominously, still intact, next to a pile of old papers in the printing room, by the village idiot. Or, I should say, one of the village idiots. Clanton had more than its share.

His name was Piston, and he, like the building and the ancient press and the untouched libraries upstairs and down, came with the deal. Piston was not an official employee of the *Times*, but he nonetheless showed up every Friday to collect his $50 in cash. No checks. For this fee he sometimes swept the floors and occasionally rearranged the dirt on the front windows, and he hauled out the trash when someone complained. He kept no hours, came and went as he pleased, didn't believe in knocking on doors when meetings were in progress, liked to use our phones and drink our coffee, and though he at first looked rather sinister—eyes wide apart and covered with thick glasses, oversized trucker's cap pulled down low, scraggly beard, hideous buck teeth—he was harmless. He provided his janitorial services for several businesses around the square, and somehow survived. No one knew where he lived, or with whom, or how he got about town. The less we knew about Piston, the better.

Piston was in early Thursday morning—he'd had a key for decades—and said that he first heard something ticking. Upon closer examination he noticed three five-gallon plastic cans laced together with a wooden box sitting on the floor next to them. The ticking sound came from the box. Piston had been around the printing room for many years and occasionally helped Hardy on Tuesday nights when he ran the paper.

For most folks, panic would quickly follow curiosity, but for Piston it took a while. After poking around the cans to make sure that they were in fact filled with gasoline, and after determining that a series of dangerous-looking wires tied everything together, he walked to

Margaret's office and called Hardy. He said the ticking was getting louder.

Hardy called the police, and around 9 A.M. I was awakened with the news.

Most of downtown was evacuated by the time I arrived. Piston was sitting on the hood of a car, by then thoroughly distraught at having survived such a close call. He was being attended by some acquaintances and an ambulance driver, and he seemed to be enjoying the attention.

Wiley Meek had photographed the bomb before the police removed the gasoline cans and placed them safely in the alley behind our building. "Woulda blown up half of downtown," was Wiley's uneducated evaluation of the bomb. He nervously darted around the scene, recording the excitement for future use.

The chief of police explained to me that the area was off limits because the wooden box had not been opened and whatever was in there was still ticking. "It might explode," he said gravely, as if he was the first one smart enough to realize the danger. I doubted if he had much experience with bombs, but I went along. An official from the state crime lab was being rushed in. It was decided that the four buildings in our row would remain unoccupied until this expert finished his business.

A bomb in downtown Clanton! The news spread faster than the fire would have, and all work stopped. The county offices emptied, as well as the banks and stores and cafés, and before long large groups of spectators were crowded across the street, under the huge oaks on the south side of the courthouse, a safe distance away. They gawked at our little building, obviously concerned and frightened but also waiting for some excitement. They'd never seen a bomb blast before.

The Clanton city police had been joined by the Sheriff's deputies, and every uniform in the county was soon present, milling about on the sidewalks, doing absolutely nothing. Sheriff Coley and the police chief huddled and conferred and watched the throng across the street, then barked some orders here and there, but if any of their orders were followed it wasn't noticeable. It was obvious to all that the city and county had no bomb drills.

Baggy needed a drink. It was too early for me. I followed him into the rear of the courthouse, up a narrow flight of stairs I'd not seen before, through a cramped hallway, then up another twenty steps to a small dirty room with a low ceiling. "Used to be the old jury room," he said. "Then it was the law library."

"What is it now?" I asked, almost afraid of the answer.

"The Bar Room. Get it? Bar? Lawyers? Booze?"

"Got it." There was a card table with folding legs and a beaten look that indicated years of use. Around it were half a dozen mismatched chairs, all county hand-me-downs that had been passed from one county office to another and finally ditched in this dingy little room.

In one corner there was a small refrigerator with a padlock. Baggy, of course, had a key, and inside he found a bottle of bourbon. He poured a generous shot into a paper cup and said, "Grab a chair." We pulled two of them up to the window, and below was the scene we had just left. "Not a bad view, huh?" he said proudly.

"How often you come here?"

"Twice a week, maybe, sometimes more. We play poker every Tuesday and Thursday at noon."

"Who's in the club?"

"It's a secret society." He took a sip and smacked his lips as if he'd been in the desert for a month. A spider made its way down a thick web along the window. Dust was half an inch thick on the sills.

"I guess they're losin' their touch," he said, gazing down at the excitement.

"They?" I was almost afraid to ask.

"The Padgitts." He said this with a certain smugness, then allowed it to hang in the air for my benefit.

"You're sure it's the Padgitts?" I asked.

Baggy thought he knew everything, and he was right about half the time. He smirked and grunted, took another sip, then said, "They've been burnin' buildings forever. It's one of their scams—insurance fraud. They've made a bloody fortune off insurance companies." A quick sip. "Odd, though, that they would use gasoline. Your more talented arsonists stay away from gasoline because it's easily detected. You know that?"

"No."

"True. A good fire marshal can smell gasoline within minutes after the blaze is out. Gasoline means arson. Arson means no insurance payoffs." A sip. "Of course, in this case, they probably wanted you to know it's arson. Makes sense, doesn't it?"

Nothing made sense at that moment. I was too confused to say much.

Baggy was content to do the talking. "Come to think of it, that's probably the reason it wasn't detonated. They wanted you to see it. If it went off, then the county wouldn't have the *Times*, which might upset some folks. Might make some other folks happy."

"Thanks."

"Anyway, that explains it better. It was a subtle act of intimidation."

"Subtle?"

"Yes, compared to what could've been. Believe me, those guys know how to burn buildings. You were lucky."

I noticed how he had quickly disassociated himself from the paper. It was "I" who was lucky, not "we."

The bourbon had found its way to the brain and was loosening the tongue. "About three years ago, maybe four, there was a large fire at one of their lumber mills, the one on Highway 401, just off the island. They never burn anything on the island because they don't want the authorities snoopin' around. Anyway, the insurance company smelled a rat, refused to pay, so Lucien Wilbanks filed this big lawsuit. It came to trial, in front of the Honorable Reed Loopus. I heard ever' word of it." A long, satisfying drink.

"Who won?"

He ignored me completely because the story was not

yet properly laid out. "It was a big fire. The boys from Clanton took off with all their trucks. The volunteers from Karaway took off, ever' yokel with a siren went screamin' off toward Padgitt Island. Nothin' like a good fire around here to get the boys worked up. That and a bomb, I guess, but I can't remember the last bomb."

"And so . . ."

"Highway 401 runs through some lowland near Padgitt Island, real swampy. There's a bridge over Massey's Creek, and when the fire trucks came flyin' up to the bridge they found a pickup layin' on its side, like it had rolled over. The road was completely blocked; couldn't go around because there was nothin' but swamps and ditches." He smacked his lips and poured more from the bottle. It was time for me to say something, but whatever I said would be completely ignored anyway. This was the way Baggy preferred to be prompted.

"Whose pickup was it?" I asked, the words barely out of my mouth before he was shaking his head as if the question was completely off the mark.

"The fire was ragin' like hell. Fire trucks backed up all along 401 because some clown had flipped his pickup. Never found him. No sign of a driver. No sign of an owner because there was no registration. No tags. The vehicle ID had been sanded off. The truck was never claimed. Wasn't damaged much either. All this came out at trial. Ever'body knew the Padgitts set the fire, flipped one of their stolen trucks to block the road, but the insurance company couldn't prove it."

Down below Sheriff Coley had found his bullhorn. He was asking the people to please stay off the street in front of our office. His shrieking voice added urgency to the situation.

"So the insurance company won?" I said, anxious to get to the end.

"Helluva trial. Went on for three days. Wilbanks can usually cut a deal with one or two people on the jury. Been doin' it for years and never gets caught. Plus he knows ever'body in the county. The insurance boys were up from Jackson, and they didn't have a clue. The jury stayed out for two hours, came back with a verdict for the claim, a hundred grand, and for good measure, tacked on a million in punitive damages."

"One point one million!" I said.

"You got it. The first million-dollar verdict in Ford County. Lasted about a year until the Supreme Court took an ax to it and cut out the punitive."

The notion of Lucien Wilbanks having such sway over jurors was not comforting. Baggy neglected his bourbon for a moment and gazed at something below. "This is a bad sign, son," he finally said. "Really bad."

I was his boss and didn't like to be referred to as "son," but I let it slide. I had more pressing matters at hand. "The intimidation?" I said.

"Yep. The Padgitts rarely leave the island. The fact that they've brought their little show on the road means they're ready for war. If they can intimidate the newspaper, then they'll try it with the jury. They already own the Sheriff."

"But Wilbanks said he wants a change of venue."

He snorted and rediscovered his drink. "Don't bet on it, son."

"Please call me Willie." Odd how I was now clinging to that name.

"Don't bet on it, Willie. The boy's guilty; his only chance is to have a jury that can be bought or scared. Ten to one odds the trial takes place right here, in this building."

After two hours of waiting in vain for the ground to shake, the town was ready for lunch. The crowd broke up and drifted away. The expert from the state crime lab finally arrived and went to work in the printing room. I wasn't allowed in the building, which was fine with me.

Margaret, Wiley, and I had a sandwich in the gazebo on the courthouse lawn. We ate quietly, chatted briefly, the three of us keeping an eye on our office across the street. Occasionally someone would see us and stop for an awkward word or two. What do you say to bombing victims when the bomb doesn't go off? Fortunately, the townsfolk had had little practice in that area. We collected some sympathy and a few offers of help.

Sheriff Coley ambled over and gave a preliminary report on our bomb. The clock was of the wind-up alarm variety, available in stores everywhere. At first glance the expert thought there was a problem with the wiring. Very amateurish, he said.

"How will you investigate this?" I asked with an edge.

"We'll check for prints, see if we can find any witnesses. The usual."

"Will you talk to the Padgitts?" I asked, even edgier. I was, after all, in the presence of my employees. And though I was scared to death, I wanted to impress them with how utterly fearless I was.

"You know somethin' I don't?" he shot back.

"They're suspects, aren't they?"

"Are you the Sheriff now?"

"They're the most experienced arsonists in the county, been burning buildings for years with impunity. Their lawyer threatened me in court last week. We've had Danny Padgitt on the front page twice. If they're not suspects, then who is?"

"Just go ahead and write the story, son. Call 'em by name. You seem determined to get sued anyway."

"I'll take care of the paper," I said. "You catch the criminals."

He tipped his hat to Margaret and walked away.

"Next year's reelection year," Wiley said as we watched Coley stop and chat with two ladies near a drinking fountain. "I hope he has an opponent."

———

The intimidation continued, at Wiley's expense. He lived a mile from town on a five-acre hobby farm, where his wife raised ducks and watermelons. That night as he parked in his drive and was getting out of his car, two goons jumped from the shrubs and assaulted him. The larger man knocked him down and kicked him in the face, while the other one rummaged through his backseat and pulled out two cameras. Wiley was fifty-eight years old and an ex-Marine, and at some point in the melee he managed to land a kick that sent the larger assailant to the ground. There they exchanged blows and as Wiley was gaining the upper hand the other thug banged him over the head with one of his cameras. Wiley said he didn't remember much after that.

His wife eventually heard the ruckus. She found Wiley on the ground, semiconscious, with both cameras shattered. In the house, she put ice packs on his face and determined that there were no broken bones. The ex-Marine did not want to go to the hospital.

A deputy arrived and made a report. Wiley had caught only a glimpse of his attackers and he'd certainly never seen them before. "They're back on the island by now," he said. "You won't find them."

His wife prevailed, and an hour later they called me from the hospital. I saw him between X rays. His face was a mess, but he managed to smile. He grabbed my hand and pulled me close. "Next week, front page," he said through cut lips and swollen jaws.

A few hours later I left the hospital and went for a long drive through the countryside. I kept glancing at my mirror, half-expecting another load of Padgitts to come roaring up, guns blazing.

It was not a lawless county, where organized criminals

ran roughshod over the law-abiding people. It was just the opposite—crime was rare. Corruption was generally frowned upon. I was right and they were wrong, and I decided I'd be damned before I knuckled under. I'd buy myself a gun; hell, everybody else in the county carried two or three. And if necessary I'd hire a guard of some sort. My paper would grow even bolder as the murder trial approached.

CHAPTER 8

Prior to the bankruptcy, and my unlikely rise in prominence in Ford County, I had heard a fascinating story about a local family. Spot never pursued it because it would've required some light research and a trip across the railroad tracks.

Now that the paper was mine, I decided it was too good to pass up.

Over in Lowtown, the colored section, there lived an extraordinary couple—Calia and Esau Ruffin. They had been married for over forty years and had raised eight children, seven of whom had earned PhD's and were now college professors. Details on the remaining one were sketchy, though, according to Margaret, his name was Sam and he was hiding from the law.

I called the house and Mrs. Ruffin answered the phone. I explained who I was and what I wanted, and she seemed to know everything about me. She said she'd been reading the *Times* for fifty years, front to back, everything including the obits and the want ads, and after a moment or two offered the opinion that the paper was in much better hands now. Longer stories. Fewer mistakes. More news. She spoke slowly, clearly, with precise diction I had not heard since I left Syracuse.

When I finally had an opening, I thanked her and said I'd like to meet and talk about her remarkable family. She was flattered and insisted that I come over for lunch.

Thus began an unusual friendship that opened my eyes to many things, not the least of which was Southern cuisine.

———

My mother died when I was thirteen. She was anorexic; there were only four pallbearers. She weighed less than a hundred pounds and looked like a ghost. Anorexia was only one of her many problems.

Because she did not eat, she did not cook. I cannot remember a single hot meal she prepared for me. Breakfast was a bowl of Cheerios, lunch a cold sandwich, dinner some frozen mess I usually ate in front of the television, alone. I was an only child and my father was never at home, which was a relief because his presence caused friction between them. He preferred to eat, she did not. They feuded over everything.

I never went hungry; the pantry was always full of peanut butter and cereal and such. I occasionally ate with a friend and I always marveled at how real families cooked and spent so much time at the table. Food was simply not important around our house.

As a teenager I existed on frozen dinners. At Syracuse it was beer and pizza. For the first twenty-three years of my life, I ate only when I was hungry. This was wrong, I soon learned in Clanton. In the South, eating has little to do with hunger.

———————

The Ruffin home was in a nicer section of Lowtown, in a row of neatly preserved and painted shotgun houses. The street addresses were on the mailboxes, and when I rolled to a stop I was smiling at the white picket fence and flowers—peonies and irises—that lined the sidewalk. It was early April, I had the top down on my Spitfire, and as I turned off the ignition I smelled something delicious. Pork chops!

Calia Ruffin met me at the low swing-gate that opened into her immaculate front lawn. She was a stout woman, thick in the shoulders and trunk, with a handshake that was firm and felt like a man's. She had gray hair and was showing the effects of raising so many children, but when she smiled, which was constantly, she lit up the world with two rows of brilliant, perfect teeth. I had never seen such teeth.

"I'm so glad you came," she said, halfway up the brick walkway. I was so glad too. It was about noon. Typically, I had yet to eat a bite, and the aromas wafting from the porch were making me dizzy.

"A lovely house," I said, gazing at the front of it. It was clapboard, painted a sparkling white, and gave the impression that someone was usually hanging around with a brush and bucket. A green tin-roofed porch ran across the entire front.

"Why, thank you. We've owned it for thirty years."

I knew that most of the dwellings in Lowtown were owned by white slumlords across the tracks. To own a home was an unusual accomplishment for blacks in 1970.

"Who's your gardener?" I asked as I stopped to smell a yellow rose. There were flowers everywhere—edging the walkway, along the porch, down both sides of their property line. "That would be me," she said with a laugh, teeth gleaming in the sunlight.

Up three steps and onto the porch, and there it was—the spread! A small table next to the railing was prepared for two people—white cotton cloth, white napkins, flowers in a small vase, a large pitcher of iced tea, and at least four covered dishes.

"Who's coming?" I asked.

"Oh, just the two of us. Esau might drop by later."

"There's enough food for an army." I inhaled as deeply as possible and my stomach ached in anticipation.

"Let's eat now," she said, "before it gets cold."

I restrained myself, walked casually to the table, and pulled back a chair for her. She was delighted that I was such a gentleman. I sat across from her and was ready to yank off the lids and dive headfirst into whatever I found when she took both my hands and lowered her head. She began to pray.

It would be a lengthy prayer. She thanked the Lord for everything good, including me, "her new friend." She prayed for those who were sick and those who might become so. She prayed for rain and sun and health and humility and patience, and though I began to worry about the food getting cold I was mesmerized by her voice. Her cadence was slow, with thought given to each word. Her diction was perfect, every consonant treated equally, every comma and period honored. I had to peek to make sure I wasn't dreaming. I had never heard such speech from a Southern black, or a Southern white for that matter.

I peeked again. She was talking to her Lord, and her face was perfectly content. For a few seconds, I actually forgot about the food. She squeezed my hands as she petitioned the Almighty with eloquence that came only from years of practice. She quoted Scripture, the King James Version for sure, and it was a bit odd to hear her use words like "thou" and "thine" and "whither" and "goest." But she knew precisely what she was doing. In the clutches of this very holy woman, I had never felt closer to God.

I couldn't imagine such a lengthy devotional over a table crowded with eight children. Something told me, though, that when Calia Ruffin prayed everybody got still.

Finally, she ended with a flourish, a long burst in which she managed to appeal for the forgiveness of her sins, which I presumed were few and far between, and for my own, which, well, if she only knew.

She released me and began removing lids from bowls. The first contained a pile of pork chops smothered in a sauce that included, among many ingredients, onions and peppers. More steam hit my face and I wanted to eat with my fingers. In the second there was a mound of yellow corn, sprinkled with green peppers, still hot from the stove. There was boiled okra, which, she explained as she prepared to serve, she preferred over the fried variety because she worried about too much grease in her diet. She was taught to batter and fry everything, from tomatoes to pickles, and she had come to realize that this was not altogether healthy. There were butter beans, likewise unbattered and unfried, but rather cooked with ham hocks and bacon. There was a platter of small red tomatoes covered with pepper and olive oil. She was one of the very few cooks in town who used olive oil, she said as she continued her narrative. I was hanging on every word as my large plate was being tended to.

A son in Milwaukee shipped her good olive oil because such was unheard of in Clanton.

She apologized because the tomatoes were store bought; hers were still on the vine and wouldn't be ready until summertime. The corn, okra, and butter beans had been canned from her garden last August. In fact, the only real "fresh" vegetables were the collard greens, or "spring greens" as she called them.

A large black skillet was hidden in the center of the

table, and when she pulled the napkin off it there were at least four pounds of hot corn bread. She removed a huge wedge, placed it in the center of my plate, and said, "There. That will get you started." I had never had so much food placed in front of me. The feast began.

I tried to eat slowly, but it was impossible. I had arrived with an empty stomach, and somewhere in the midst of the competing aromas and the beauty of the table and the rather long-winded blessing and the careful description of each dish, I had become thoroughly famished. I packed it in, and she seemed content to do the talking.

Her garden had produced most of the meal. She and Esau grew four types of tomatoes, butter beans, string beans, black-eyed peas, crowder peas, cucumbers, eggplant, squash, collards, mustard greens, turnips, vidalia onions, yellow onions, green onions, cabbage, okra, new red potatoes, russet potatoes, carrots, beets, corn, green peppers, cantaloupes, two varieties of watermelon, and a few other things she couldn't recall at the moment. The pork chops were provided by her brother, who still lived on the old family place out in the country. He killed two hogs for them every winter and they stuffed their freezer. In return, they kept him in fresh vegetables.

"We don't use chemicals," she said, watching me gorge myself. "Everything is natural."

It certainly tasted like it.

"But it's all put-up, you know, from the winter. It'll taste better in the summertime when we pick and eat it just a few hours later. Will you come back then, Mr. Traynor?"

I grunted and nodded and somehow managed to convey the message that I would return any time she wanted.

"Would you like to see my garden?" she asked.

I nodded again, both jaws filled to capacity.

"Good. It's out back. I'll pick you some lettuce and greens. They're coming in nicely."

"Wonderful," I managed to utter.

"I figure a single man like you needs all the help he can get."

"How'd you know I was single?" I took a gulp of tea. It could have served as dessert—there was so much sugar in it.

"Folks are talking about you. Word gets around. There are not too many secrets in Clanton, on both sides of the tracks."

"What else have you heard?"

"Let's see. You rent from the Hocutts. You come from up North."

"Memphis."

"That far?"

"It's an hour away."

"Just joking. One of my daughters went to college there."

I had many questions about her children, but I was not ready to take notes. Both hands were busy eating. At some point I called her Miss Calia, instead of Miss Ruffin.

"It's Callie," she said. "Miss Callie will do just fine."
One of the first habits I picked up in Clanton was refer-
ring to the ladies, regardless of age, by sticking the word
"Miss" in front of their names. Miss Brown, Miss Webster, for new acquaintances who had a few years on
them. Miss Martha, Miss Sara, for the younger ones. It
was a sign of chivalry and good breeding, and since I
had neither it was important to seize as many local cus-
toms as possible.

"Where did Calia come from?" I asked.

"It's Italian," she said, as if that would explain
everything. She ate some butter beans. I carved up a
pork chop. Then I said, "Italian?"

"Yes, that was my first language. It's a long story, one
of many. Did they really try to burn down the paper?"

"Yes, they did," I said, wondering if I'd heard this
black lady in rural Mississippi just say that her first language was Italian.

"And they assaulted Mr. Meek?"

"They did."

"Who is they?"

"We don't know yet. Sheriff Coley is investigating." I
was anxious to get her impression of our Sheriff. While
I waited, I went after another wedge of corn bread.
Soon there was butter dripping from my chin.

"He's been the Sheriff for a long time, hasn't he?"
she said.

I'm sure she knew the exact year in which Mackey
Don Coley had first bought himself into office. "What
do you think of him?" I asked.

She drank some tea and contemplated. Miss Callie did not rush her answers, especially when talking about others. "On this side of the tracks, a good Sheriff is one who keeps the gamblers and the bootleggers and the whoremongers away from the rest of us. In that regard, Mr. Coley has done a proper job."

"Can I ask you something?"

"Certainly. You're a reporter."

"Your speech is unusually articulate and precise. How much education did you receive?" It was a sensitive question in a society where, for many decades, education had not been stressed. It was 1970, and Mississippi still had no public kindergartens and no mandatory school attendance laws.

She laughed, giving me the full benefit of those teeth. "I finished the ninth grade, Mr. Traynor."

"The ninth grade?"

"Yes, but my situation was unusual. I had a wonderful tutor. It's another long story."

I began to realize that these wonderful stories Miss Callie was promising would take months, maybe years to develop. Perhaps they would evolve on the porch, over a weekly banquet.

"Let's save it for later," she said. "How is Mr. Caudle?"

"Not well. He will not come out of his house."

"A fine man. He will always be close to the heart of the black community. He had such courage."

I thought Spot's "courage" had more to do with widening the range of his obituaries than with a commitment to the fair treatment of all. But I had learned how important dying was to black folks—the ritual of the wake, often lasting a week; the marathon memorial services, with open caskets and much wailing; the mile-long funeral processions; and, lastly, the final graveside farewells fraught with emotion. When Spot had so radically opened his obituary page to blacks he had become a hero in Lowtown.

"A fine man," I said, reaching for my third pork chop. I was beginning to ache a bit, but there was so much food left on the table!

"You're doing him proud with your obituaries," she said with a warm smile.

"Thank you. I'm still learning."

"You have courage too, Mr. Traynor."

"Could you call me Willie? I'm only twenty-three."

"I prefer Mr. Traynor." And that issue was settled. It would take four years before she could break down and use my first name. "You have no fear of the Padgitt family," she announced.

That was news to me. "It's just part of my job," I said.

"Do you expect the intimidation to continue?"

"Probably so. They are accustomed to getting whatever they want. They are violent, ruthless people, but a free press must endure." Who was I kidding? One more bomb or assault and I'd be back in Memphis before sunrise.

She stopped eating and her eyes turned toward the

street, where she looked at nothing in particular. She was deep in thought. I, of course, kept stuffing my face.

Finally, she said, "Those poor little children. Seeing their mother like that."

That image finally caused my fork to stop. I wiped my mouth, took a long breath, and let the food settle for a moment. The horror of the crime was left to everyone's imagination, and for days Clanton had whispered about little else. As always happens, the whispers and rumors got amplified, different versions were spun off and repeated, and enlarged yet again. I was curious as to how the stories were playing in Lowtown.

"You told me on the phone you've been reading the *Times* for fifty years," I said, almost belching.

"Indeed I have."

"Can you remember a more brutal crime?"

She paused for a second as she reviewed five decades, then slowly shook her head. "No, I cannot."

"Have you ever met a Padgitt?"

"No. They stay on the island, and always have. Even their Negroes stay out there, making whiskey, doing their voodoo, all sorts of foolishness."

"Voodoo?"

"Yes, it's common knowledge on this side of the tracks. Nobody here messes with the Padgitt Negroes, never have."

"Do people on this side of the tracks believe Danny Padgitt raped and killed her?"

"The ones who read your newspaper certainly do."

That stung more than she would ever know. "We just

report the facts," I said smugly. "The boy was arrested. He's been charged. He's in jail awaiting trial."

"Isn't there a presumption of innocence?"

Another squirm on my side of the table. "Of course."

"Do you think it was fair to use a photograph of him handcuffed, with blood on his shirt?" I was struck by her sense of fairness. Why would she, or any other black in Ford County, care if Danny Padgitt was treated fairly? Few people had ever worried about black defendants getting decent treatment by the police or the press.

"He had blood on his shirt when he arrived at the jail. We didn't put it there." Neither one of us was enjoying this little debate. I took a sip of tea and found it difficult to swallow. I was stuffed all the way down.

She looked at me with one of those smiles and had the nerve to say, "What about some dessert? I baked a banana pudding."

I could not say no. Nor could I hold another bite. A compromise was called for. "Let's wait a while, give things a chance to settle."

"Then have some more tea," she said, already re-filling my glass. Breathing was difficult, so I reclined as much as possible in my chair and decided to act like a journalist. Miss Callie, who'd eaten far less than I, was finishing a serving of okra.

According to Baggy, Sam Ruffin had been the first black student to enroll in the white schools in Clanton. It happened in 1964 when Sam was a seventh grader, age twelve, and the experience had been difficult for everyone. Especially Sam. Baggy warned me that Miss Callie might not talk about her youngest child. There was a warrant for his arrest and he had fled the area.

She was reluctant at first. In 1963, the courts ruled that a white school district could not deny admission to a black student. Forced integration was still years in the future. Sam was her youngest, and when she and Esau made the decision to take him to the white school they hoped they would be joined by other black families. They were not, and for two years Sam was the only black student at Clanton Junior High School. He was tormented and beaten, but he quickly learned to handle his fists and with time was left alone. He begged his parents to take him back to the Negro school, but they held their ground, even after he moved to the senior high. Relief was coming, they kept telling themselves. The desegregation fight was raging across the South and blacks were continually promised that the mandate of *Brown versus Board of Education* would be carried out.

"It is hard to believe that it is now 1970, and the schools here are still segregated," she said. Federal lawsuits and appellate decisions were pummeling white resistance throughout the South, but, typically, Mississippi was fighting to the bitter end. Most white folks I knew in Clanton were convinced that their schools would never be integrated. I, a Northerner from Memphis, could see the obvious.

"Do you regret sending Sam to the white school?"

"Yes and no. Someone had to be courageous. It was painful knowing he was very unhappy, but we had taken a stand. We were not going to retreat."

"How is he today?"

"Sam is another story, Mr. Traynor, one I might talk about later, or not. Would you like to see my garden?"

It was more of a command than an invitation. I followed her through the house, down a narrow hallway lined with dozens of framed photographs of children and grandchildren. The inside was as meticulous as the outside. The kitchen opened to the back porch and from there the Garden of Eden stretched to the rear fence. Not a single square foot was wasted.

It was a postcard of beautiful colors, neat rows of plants and vines, narrow dirt footpaths so that Callie and Esau could tend to their spectacular bounty.

"What do you do with all this food?" I asked in amazement.

"We eat some, sell a little, give most away. No one goes hungry around here." At that moment my stomach was aching like never before. Hunger was a notion I couldn't comprehend. I followed her into the garden, moving slowly along the footpaths as she pointed out the herb patch and melons and all the other delicious fruits and vegetables she and Esau tended to with great care. She commented on every plant, including an occasional weed, which she snatched almost with anger and flung back into some vines. It was impossible for her to walk through the garden and ignore the details.

She looked for insects, killed a nasty green worm on a tomato vine, searched for weeds, made mental notes about future chores for Esau. The leisurely stroll was doing wonders for my digestive system.

So this is where food comes from, I thought to my ignorant self. What did I expect? I was a city kid. I'd never been in a vegetable garden before. I had many questions, all banal, so I held my tongue.

She examined a stalk of corn and was not pleased with whatever she saw. She tore off a snap bean, broke it in two, analyzed it like a scientist, and offered the guarded opinion that they needed much more sun. She saw a patch of weeds and informed me Esau would be sent to pull them as soon as he got home. I did not envy Esau.

After three hours, I left the Ruffin home stuffed yet again with banana pudding. I also left with a sack of "spring greens," which I had no idea what to do with, and precious few notes on which to write a story. I also had an invitation to return the following Thursday for another lunch. Lastly, I had Miss Callie's handwritten list of all the errors she'd found in that week's edition of the *Times*. Almost all were typographical errors and misspelled words—twelve in all. Under Spot, the average had been about twenty. Now it was down to around ten. It was a lifelong habit of hers. "Some folks like crossword puzzles," she said. "I like to look for mistakes."

It was hard not to take this personally. She certainly didn't intend to criticize anyone. I vowed to proofread the copy with much more enthusiasm.

I also left with the feeling that I had entered a new and rewarding friendship.

CHAPTER 9

We ran another large photo on the front page. It was Wiley's shot of the bomb before the police dismantled it. The headline above it screamed: BOMB PLANTED IN *TIMES* OFFICE.

My story began with Piston and his unlikely discovery. It included every detail I could substantiate, and a few I could not. No comment from the chief of police, a few meaningless sentences from Sheriff Coley. It ended with a summary of the findings by the state crime lab, and a prediction that, if detonated, the bomb would have caused "massive" damage to the buildings on the south side of the square.

Wiley would not allow me to use a photo of his badly bruised face, though I pleaded desperately with him to do so. On the bottom half of the front page I ran the headline *TIMES* PHOTOGRAPHER ASSAULTED AT

HOME. Again, my story spared no detail, though Wiley insisted he be allowed to edit it.

In both stories, and with no effort at being subtle, I linked the crimes and implied rather strongly that little was being done by the authorities, especially Sheriff Coley, to prevent further intimidation. I never named the Padgitts. I didn't have to. Everyone in the county knew they were bullying me and my newspaper.

Spot had been too lazy for editorials. He'd written only one during my stint as an employee. A congressman from Oregon had filed some nutty bill that would somehow affect the cutting of redwood trees—more cutting or maybe less, it really wasn't clear. This had upset Spot. For two weeks he labored over an editorial and finally ran a two-thousand-word tirade. It was obvious to anyone with a high school education that he wrote with a pen in one hand and a dictionary in the other. The first paragraph was filled with more six-syllable words than anyone had ever seen and was virtually unreadable. Spot was shocked when there was no response from the community. He expected a flood of sympathetic letters. Few of his readers could have survived the flood from Webster's.

Finally, three weeks later, a hand-scrawled note was slid under the front door of the office. It read:

Dear Editor: I'm sorry you're so worked up over the redwoods, which we don't have in Mississippi. If Congress starts messing with pulpwood, would you please let us know?

It was unsigned, but Spot ran it anyway. He was relieved that someone out there was paying attention. Baggy told me later that the note was written by one of his drinking buddies in the courthouse.

My editorial began, "A free and uninhibited press is crucial to sound democratic government." Without being windy or preachy, I went on for four paragraphs extolling the importance of an energetic and inquisitive newspaper, not only for the country but for every small community as well. I vowed that the *Times* would not be frightened away from reporting local crimes, whether they were rapes and murders or corrupt acts by public officials.

It was bold, gutsy, and downright brilliant. The townsfolk were on my side. It was, after all, the *Times* versus the Padgitts and their Sheriff. We were taking a mighty stand against bad people, and though they were dangerous they were evidently not intimidating me. I kept telling myself to act brave, and I really had no choice. What was my paper supposed to do—ignore the Kassellaw murder? Take it easy on Danny Padgitt?

My staff was elated with the editorial. Margaret said it made her proud to work for the *Times*. Wiley, still nursing his wounds, was now carrying a gun and looking for a fight. "Give 'em hell, rookie," he said.

Only Baggy was skeptical. "You're gonna get yourself hurt," he said.

And Miss Callie once again described me as courageous. Lunch the following Thursday lasted for only two hours and included Esau. I actually began taking notes about her family. More important, she'd found only three errors in that week's edition.

I was alone in my office early Friday afternoon when someone made a noisy entrance downstairs, then came clamoring up. He shoved my door open without so much as a "Hello" and stuck both hands in his pants pockets. He looked vaguely familiar; we'd met somewhere around the square.

"You got one of these, boy?" he growled, yanking his right hand out and momentarily freezing my heart and lungs. He slid a shiny pistol across my desk as if it were a set of keys. It spun wildly for a few seconds before resting directly before me, the barrel mercifully pointing toward the windows.

He lunged across the desk, thrust out a massive hand, and said, "Harry Rex Vonner, a pleasure." I was too stunned to speak or move, but eventually honored him with an embarrassingly weak handshake. I was still watching the gun.

"It's a Smith and Wesson thirty-eight, six-shooter, damned fine firearm. You carry one?"

I shook my head no. The name alone sent chills to my feet.

Harry Rex kept a nasty black cigar tucked into the left side of his mouth. It gave the impression of having spent most of the day there, slowly disintegrating like a plug of chewing tobacco. No smoke because it wasn't lit. He dropped his massive body into a leather chair as if he might stay for a couple of hours.

"You a crazy sumbitch, you know that?" He didn't speak as much as he growled. Then I caught the name. He was a local lawyer, once described by Baggy as the meanest divorce attorney in the county. He had a large fleshy face with short hair that shot in all directions like windblown straw. His ancient khaki suit was wrinkled and stained and said to the world that Harry Rex didn't give a damn about anything.

"What am I supposed to do with this?" I asked, pointing at the gun.

"First you load it, I'll give you some bullets, then you stick it in your pocket and carry it with you everywhere you go, and when one of them Padgitt thugs jumps out from behind the bushes you blast him right between the eyes." To help convey his message, he moved his index finger through the air like a bullet and poked himself between the eyes.

"It's not loaded?"

"Hell no. Don't you know anything about guns?"

"Afraid not."

"Well, you'd better learn, boy, at the rate you're goin'."

"That bad, huh?"

"I did a divorce one time, ten years ago I guess, for a man whose young wife liked to sneak over to the brothel and make a few bucks. The guy worked offshore, stayed gone all the time, had no idea what she was up to. He finally found out. The Padgitts owned the whorehouse and one of them had taken a shine to the young lady." Somehow the cigar stayed in place, bobbing up and down with the narrative. "My client was heartbroken and he wanted blood. He got it. They caught him out one night and beat him senseless."

"They?"

"The Padgitts I'm sure, or some of their operatives."

"Operatives?"

"Yeah, they got all sorts of thugs who work for them. Leg breakers, bomb throwers, car stealers, hit men."

He allowed the "hit men" to hang in the air while he watched me flinch. He gave the impression of one who could tell stories forever without being unduly burdened by veracity. Harry Rex had a nasty grin and a twinkle in his eyes, and I strongly suspected some embellishment was under way.

"And of course they were never caught," I said.

"Padgitts never get caught."

"What happened to your client?"

"He spent a few months in the hospital. The brain damage was pretty severe. In and out of institutions, really sad. Broke his family. He drifted to the Gulf Coast where they elected him to the state senate."

I smiled and nodded at what I hoped was a lie, but I didn't pursue it. Without touching the cigar with his hands, he flicked his tongue somehow and cocked his head, and it slid to the right side of his mouth.

"You ever eat goat?" he asked.

"Say what?"

"Goat?"

"No. I didn't know it was edible."

"We're roastin' one this afternoon. The first Friday of each month I throw a goat party at my cabin in the woods. Some music, cold beer, fun and games, about fifty folks, all carefully selected by me, the cream of society. No doctors, no bankers, no country club assholes. A classy bunch. Why don't you stop by? I got a firin' range out behind the pond. I'll take the pistol and we'll figure out how to use the damned thing."

Harry Rex's ten-minute drive into the country took almost half an hour, and that was on the paved county road. When I crossed the "third creek past Heck's old Union 76 station," I left the asphalt and turned onto gravel. For a while it was a nice gravel road with mailboxes indicating some hope of civilization, but after three miles the mail route stopped and so did the gravel. When I saw a "rusted-out Massey Ferguson tractor with no tires," I turned left onto a dirt road. His crude map referred to it as a pig trail, though I had never seen one of those. After the pig trail disappeared into a dense forest, I gave serious thought to turning back. My Spitfire wasn't designed for the terrain. By the time I saw the roof of his cabin, I'd been driving for forty-five minutes.

There was a barbed-wire fence with an open metal gate, and I stopped there because the young man with the shotgun wanted me to. He kept it on his shoulder as he looked scornfully at my car. "What kind is it?" he grunted.

"Triumph Spitfire. It's British." I was smiling, trying not to offend him. Why did a goat party need armed security? He had the rustic look of someone who'd never seen a car made in another country.

"What's your name?" he asked.

"Willie Traynor."

I think the "Willie" made him feel better, so he nodded at the gate. "Nice car," he said as I drove through.

The pickup trucks outnumbered the cars. Parking was haphazard in a field in front of the cabin. Merle Haggard was wailing from two speakers placed in the windows. One group of guests huddled over a pit where smoke was rising and the goat was roasting. Another group was tossing horseshoes beside the cabin. Three well-dressed ladies were on the porch, sipping something that was certainly not beer. Harry Rex appeared and greetly me warmly.

"Who's the boy with the shotgun?" I asked.

"Oh him. That's Duffy, my first wife's nephew."

"Why is he out there?" If the goat party included something illegal, I at least wanted some notice.

"Don't worry. Duffy ain't all there, and the gun ain't loaded. He's been guardin' nothin' for years."

I smiled as if this made perfect sense. He guided me to the pit where I saw my first goat, dead or alive. With the exception of head and hide, it appeared to be intact. I was introduced to the many chefs. With each name I got an occupation—a lawyer, a bail bondsman, a car dealer, a farmer. As I watched the goat spin slowly on a spit, I soon learned that there were many competing theories on how to properly barbecue one. Harry Rex handed me a beer and we moved on to the cabin, speaking to anyone we bumped into. A secretary, a "crooked real estate agent," the current wife of Harry Rex. Each seemed pleased to meet the new owner of the *Times*.

The cabin sat on the edge of a muddy pond, the kind snakes find attractive. A deck protruded over the water, and there we worked the crowd. Harry Rex took great delight in introducing me to his friends. "He's a good boy, not your typical Ivy League asshole," he said more than once. I didn't like to be referred to as a "boy," but then I was getting used to it.

I settled into a small group that included two ladies who looked as though they'd spent years in the local honky-tonks. Heavy eye makeup, teased hair, tight clothing, and they immediately took an interest in me. The conversation began with the bomb and the assault on Wiley Meek and the prevailing cloud of fear the Padgitts had spread over the county. I acted as if it was just another routine episode in my long and colorful career in journalism. They drilled me with questions and I did more talking than I wanted to.

Harry Rex rejoined us and handed me a suspicious-looking jar of clear liquid. "Sip it slowly," he said, much like a father.

"What is it?" I asked. I noticed that others were watching.

"Peach brandy."

"Why is it in a fruit jar?" I asked.

"That's the way they make it," he said.

"It's moonshine," one of the painted ladies said. The voice of experience.

Not often would these rural folks see an "Ivy Leaguer" take his first drink of moonshine, so the crowd drew closer. I was certain I had consumed more alcohol in the prior five years at Syracuse than anyone else present, so I threw caution to the wind. I lifted the jar, said, "Cheers," and took a very small sip. I smacked my lips, said, "Not bad." And tried to smile like a freshman at a fraternity party.

The burning began at the lips, the point of initial contact, and spread rapidly across the tongue and gums and by the time it hit the back of my throat I thought I was on fire. Everyone was watching. Harry Rex took a sip from his jar.

"Where does it come from?" I asked, as nonchalantly as possible, flames escaping through my teeth.

"Not far from here," someone said.

Scorched and numb, I took another sip, quite anxious for the crowd to ignore me for a while. Oddly enough, the third sip revealed a hint of peach flavoring, as if the taste buds had to be shocked before they could work. When it was apparent that I was not going to breathe fire, vomit, or scream, the conversation resumed. Harry Rex, ever anxious to speed along my education, thrust forward a plate of fried something. "Have one of these," he said.

"What is it?" I asked, suspicious.

Both of my painted ladies curled up their noses and

turned away, as if the smell might make them ill. "Chitlins," one of them said.

"What's that?"

Harry Rex popped one in his mouth to prove they weren't poison, then shoved the plate closer to me. "Go ahead," he said, chomping away at this delicacy.

Folks were watching again, so I picked out the smallest piece and put it in my mouth. The texture was rubbery, the taste was acrid and foul. The smell had a barnyard essence. I chewed as hard as possible, choked it down, then followed with a gulp of moonshine. And for a few seconds I thought I might faint.

"Hog guts, boy," Harry Rex said, slapping me on the back. He threw another one in his large mouth and offered me the plate. "Where's the goat?" I managed to ask. Anything would be an improvement.

Whatever happened to beer and pizza? Why would these people eat and drink such disagreeable things?

Harry Rex walked away, the putrid smell of the chitlins following him like smoke. I placed the fruit jar on the railing, hoping it would tumble and disappear. I watched others pass around their moonshine, one jar usually good for an entire group. There was absolutely no concern over germs and such. No bacteria could've survived within three feet of the vile brew.

I excused myself from the deck, said I needed to find a restroom. Harry Rex emerged from the back door of the cabin holding two pistols and a box of ammo. "We'd better take a few shots before it gets dark," he said. "Follow me."

We stopped at the goat spit where a cowboy named Rafe joined us. "Rafe's my runner," Harry Rex said as the three of us headed for the woods.

"What's a runner?" I asked.

"Runs cases."

"I'm the ambulance chaser," Rafe said helpfully. "Although usually the ambulance is behind me."

I had so much to learn, though I was making some real progress. Chitlins and moonshine in one day were no small feat. We walked a hundred yards or so down an old field road, through some woods, then came to a clearing. Between two magnificent oaks Harry Rex had constructed a semicircle wall of hay bales twenty feet high. In the center was a white bedsheet, and in the middle of it was the crude outline of a man. An attacker. The enemy. The target.

Not surprisingly, Rafe whipped out his own handgun. Harry Rex was handling mine. "Here's the deal," he said, beginning the lesson. "This is a double action revolver with six cartridges. Press here and the cylinder pops out." Rafe reached over and deftly loaded six bullets, something he had obviously done many, many times. "Snap it back like this, and you're ready to fire."

We were about fifty feet from the target. I could still hear the music from the cabin. What would the other guests think when they heard gunfire? Nothing. It happened all the time.

Rafe took my handgun and faced the target. "For starters, spread your legs to shoulders' width, bend the knees slightly, use both hands like this, and squeeze the trigger with your right index finger." He demonstrated as he spoke, and, of course, everything looked easy. I was standing less than five feet away when the gun fired, and the sharp crack jolted my nerves. Why did it have to be so loud?

I had never heard live gunfire.

The second shot hit the target square in the chest, and the next four landed around the midsection. He turned to me, opened the cylinder, spun out the empty cartridges, and said, "Now you do it."

My hands were shaking as I took the gun. It was warm and the smell of gunpowder hung heavy around us. I managed to shove in the six cartridges and snap the cylinder shut without hurting anyone. I faced the target, lifted the gun with both hands, crouched like someone in a bad movie, closed my eyes, and pulled the trigger. It felt and sounded like a small bomb of some sort.

"You gotta keep your eyes open, dammit," Harry Rex growled.

"What did I hit?"

"That hill beyond the oak trees."

"Try it again," Rafe said.

I tried to look down the gunsight but it was shaking too badly to be of any use. I squeezed the trigger again, this time with my eyes open, waiting to see where my bullet hit. I noticed no entry wound anywhere near the target.

"He missed the sheet," Rafe mumbled behind me.

"Fire again," Harry Rex said.

I did, and again couldn't see where the bullet landed. Rafe gently took my left arm and eased me forward another ten feet. "You're doin' fine," he said. "We got plenty of ammo."

I missed the hay on the fourth shot, and Harry Rex said, "I guess the Padgitts are safe after all."

"It's the moonshine," I said.

"It just takes practice," Rafe said, moving me forward yet again. My hands were sweating, my heart was galloping away, my ears were ringing.

On number five I hit the sheet, barely, in the top right-hand corner, at least six feet from the target. On number six I missed everything again and heard the bullet hit a branch up in one of the oaks.

"Nice shot," Harry Rex said. "You almost hit a squirrel."

"Shut up," I said.

"Relax," Rafe said. "You're too tense." He helped me reload, and this time he squeezed my hands around the gun. "Breathe deeply," he said over my shoulder. "Exhale right before you pull the trigger." He steadied the gun as I looked down the sight, and when it fired the target took a hit in the groin.

"Now we're in business," Harry Rex said.

Rafe released me, and, like a gunslinger at high noon, I unloaded the next five shots. All hit the sheet, one would've taken off the target's ear. Rafe approved and we loaded up again.

Harry Rex had a 9-millimeter Glock automatic from his vast collection, and as the sun slowly disappeared we took turns blasting away. He was good and had no trouble drilling ten straight shots into the upper torso from fifty feet. After four rounds, I began to relax and enjoy the sport of it. Rafe was an excellent teacher, and as I progressed he passed on tips here and there. "It just takes practice," he kept saying.

When we finished, Harry Rex said, "The gun's a gift. You can come out here anytime for target practice."

"Thanks," I said. I stuck the gun in my pocket like a real redneck. I was delighted that the ritual was over, that I had accomplished something that every other male in the county had experienced by his twelfth birthday. I didn't feel any safer. Any Padgitt who jumped from the bushes would have the advantage of surprise, and the benefit of years of target practice. I could almost envision myself grappling with my own gun in the darkness and finally unloading a bullet that would more likely hit me than any assailant.

As we were walking back through the woods, Harry Rex said from behind me, "That bleached blonde you met, Carleen."

"Yeah," I said, suddenly nervous.

"She likes you."

Carleen had lived at least forty very hard years. I could think of nothing to say.

"She's always good for a hop in the sack."

I doubted if Carleen had missed too many sacks in Ford County. "No thanks," I said. "I got a girl in Memphis."

"So?"

"Good call," Rafe said under his breath.

"A girl here, a girl there. What's the big difference?"

"I gotta deal for you, Harry Rex," I said. "If I need your help picking up women, I'll let you know."

"Just a roll in the hay," he mumbled.

I did not have a girl in Memphis, but I knew several. I'd rather make the drive than stoop to the likes of Carleen.

————

The goat had a distinctive taste; not good, but, after the chitlins, not nearly as bad as I had feared. It was tough and smothered in sticky barbeque sauce, which, I suspected, was applied in generous layers to counter the taste of the meat. I toyed with a slice of it and washed it down with beer. We were on the deck again with Loretta Lynn in the background. The moonshine had made the rounds for a while and some of the guests were dancing above the pond. Carleen had disappeared earlier with someone else, so I felt safe. Harry Rex sat nearby, telling everyone how effective I'd been shooting squirrels and rabbits. His talent for storytelling was remarkable.

I was an oddity but every effort was made to include me. Driving the dark roads home, I asked myself the same question I posed every day. What was I doing in Ford County, Mississippi?

CHAPTER 10

The gun was too big for my pocket. For a few hours I tried walking around with it, but I was terrified the thing would discharge down there very near my privates. So I decided to carry it in a ragged leather briefcase my father had given me. For three days the briefcase went everywhere, even to lunch, then I grew weary of that too. After a week I left the pistol under the seat of my car, and after three weeks I had pretty much forgotten about it. I did not go to the cabin for more target practice, though I did attend a few other goat parties in which I avoided chitlins, moonshine, and an increasingly aggressive Carleen.

The county was quiet, a lull before the frenzy of the trial. The *Times* said nothing about the case because nothing was happening. The Padgitts were still refusing to pledge their land for Danny's bail, so he remained a guest in Sheriff Coley's special cell, watching television, playing cards or checkers, getting plenty of rest, and eating better food than the common inmates.

The first week in May, Judge Loopus was back in town, and my thoughts returned to my trusty Smith & Wesson.

Lucien Wilbanks had filed a motion requesting a change of venue, and the Judge set it for a hearing at 9 A.M. on a Monday morning. Half the county was there, it seemed. Certainly most of the regulars from around the square. Baggy and I got to the courtroom early and secured good seats.

The defendant's presence was not required, but evidently Sheriff Coley wanted to show him off. They brought him in, handcuffed and wearing new orange coveralls. Everyone looked at me. The power of the press had brought about change.

"It's a setup," Baggy whispered.

"What?"

"They're baitin' us into runnin' a picture of Danny in his cute little jail outfit. Then Wilbanks can run back to the Judge and claim the jury pool has been poisoned yet again. Don't fall for it."

My naïveté shocked me again. Wiley had been positioned outside the jail in another effort to ambush Padgitt when they loaded him up for court. I could see a large front page photo of him in his orange coveralls.

Lucien Wilbanks entered the courtroom from behind the bench. As usual, he seemed angry and perturbed, as if he'd just lost an argument with the Judge. He walked to the defense table, tossed down his legal pad, and scanned the crowd. His eyes locked onto me. They narrowed and his jaws clenched, and I thought he might hop over the bar and attack. His client turned around and began looking too. Someone pointed, and Mr. Danny Padgitt himself commenced glaring at me as if I might be his next victim. I was having trouble breathing, but I tried to keep calm. Baggy inched away.

In the front row behind the defense crowd were several Padgitts, all older than Danny. They, too, joined the staring, and I had never felt so vulnerable. These were violent men who knew nothing but crime, intimidation, leg breaking, killing, and there I was in the same room with them while they dreamed of ways to cut my throat.

A bailiff called us to order and everybody stood to acknowledge the entrance of His Honor. "Please be seated," he said.

Loopus scanned the papers while we waited, then he adjusted his reading glasses and said, "This is a motion to change venue, filed by the defense. Mr. Wilbanks, how many witnesses do you have?"

"Half a dozen, give or take. We'll see how things go."

"And the State?"

A short round man with no hair and a black suit bounced to his feet and said, "About the same." His name was Ernie Gaddis, the longtime, part-time District Attorney from up in Tyler County.

"I don't want to be here all day," Loopus mumbled, as if he had an afternoon golf game. "Call your first witness, Mr. Wilbanks."

"Mr. Walter Pickard."

The name was unknown to me, which was expected, but Baggy had never heard of him either. During the preliminary questions it was established that he had lived in Karaway for over twenty years, went to church every Sunday and the Rotary Club every Thursday. For a living he owned a small furniture factory.

"Must buy lumber from the Padgitts," Baggy whispered.

His wife was a schoolteacher. He had coached Little League baseball and worked with the Boy Scouts. Lucien pressed on and did a masterful job of laying the groundwork that Mr. Pickard knew his community well.

Karaway was a smaller town eighteen miles west of Clanton. Spot had always neglected the place and we sold very few papers there. And even fewer ads. In my youthful eagerness, I was already contemplating the expansion of my empire. A small weekly in Karaway would sell a thousand copies, I thought.

"When did you first hear that Miss Kassellaw had been murdered?" Wilbanks asked.

"Couple of days after it happened," Mr. Pickard said. "News is sometimes slow getting to Karaway."

"Who told you?"

"One of my employees came in with the story. She has a brother who lives around Beech Hill, where it happened."

"Did you hear that someone had been arrested for the murder?" Lucien asked. He prowled around the courtroom like a bored cat. Just going through the motions, yet missing nothing.

"Yes, the rumor was that one of the young Padgitts had been arrested."

"Did you later confirm this?"

"Yes."

"How?"

"I saw the story in *The Ford County Times*. There was a large photo of Danny Padgitt on the front page, right next to a large photo of Rhoda Kassellaw."

"Did you read the reports in the *Times?*"

"I did."

"And did you form an opinion about Mr. Padgitt's guilt or innocence?"

"He looked guilty to me. In the photo he had blood all over his shirt. His face was placed right next to that of the victim's, you know, side by side. The headline was huge and said something like, DANNY PADGITT ARRESTED FOR MURDER. "

"So you assumed he was guilty?"

"It was impossible not to."

"What's been the reaction to the murder in Karaway?"

"Shock and outrage. This is a peaceful county. Serious crimes are rare."

"In your opinion, do folks over there generally believe Danny Padgitt raped and murdered Rhoda Kassellaw?"

"Yes, especially after the way the newspaper has treated the story."

I could feel stares from all directions, but I kept telling myself that we had done nothing wrong. People suspected Danny Padgitt because the rotten sonofabitch had committed the crimes.

"In your opinion, can Mr. Padgitt receive a fair trial in Ford County?"

"No."

"Upon what do you base this opinion?"

"He's already been tried and convicted by the newspaper."

"Do you think your opinion is shared by most of your friends and neighbors over in Karaway?"

"I do."

"Thank you."

Mr. Ernie Gaddis was on his feet, holding a legal pad as if it were a weapon. "Say you're in the furniture business, Mr. Pickard?"

"Yes, that's correct."

"You buy lumber locally?"

"We do."

"From whom?"

Pickard readjusted his weight and pondered the question. "Gates Brothers, Henderson, Tiffee, Voyles and Sons, maybe one or two others."

Baggy whispered, "Padgitt owns Voyles."

"You buy any lumber from the Padgitts?" Gaddis asked.

"No sir."

"Now or at any time in the past?"

"No sir."

"Any of these lumberyards owned by the Padgitts?"

"Not to my knowledge."

The truth was that no one really knew what the Padgitts owned. For decades they'd had their tentacles in so many businesses, legitimate or otherwise. Mr. Pickard may not have been well known in Clanton, but, at that moment, he was suspected of having some relationship with the Padgitts. Why would he voluntarily testify on Danny's behalf?

Gaddis shifted gears. "Now, you said that the bloody photograph had much to do with your assumption that the boy is guilty, that right?"

"It made him look very suspicious."

"Did you read the entire story?"

"I believe so."

"Did you read where it says that Mr. Danny Padgitt was involved in an auto accident, that he was injured, and that he was also charged with drunk driving?"

"I believe I read that, yes."

"Would you like for me to show it to you?"

"No, I remember it."

"Good, then why were you so quick to assume the blood came from the victim and not from Mr. Padgitt himself?"

Pickard shifted again and looked frustrated. "I simply said that the photos and the stories, when taken together, make him look guilty."

"You ever serve on a jury, Mr. Pickard?"

"No sir."

"Do you understand what's meant by the presumption of innocence?"

"Yes."

"Do you understand that the State of Mississippi must prove Mr. Padgitt guilty beyond a reasonable doubt?"

"Yes."

"Do you believe everyone accused of a crime is entitled to a fair trial?"

"Yes, of course."

"Good. Let's say you got a summons for jury service in this case. You've read the newspaper reports, listened to all the gossip, all the rumors, all that mess, and you arrive in this very courtroom for the trial. You've already testified that you believe Mr. Padgitt to be guilty. Let's say you're selected for the jury. Let's say that Mr. Wilbanks, a very skilled and experienced lawyer, attacks the State's case and raises serious doubts about our proof. Let's say there's doubt in your mind, Mr. Pickard. Could you at that point vote not guilty?"

He nodded as he followed along, then said, "Yes, under those circumstances."

"So, regardless of how you now feel about guilt or innocence, you would be willing to listen to the evidence and weigh it fairly before you decide the case?"

The answer was so obvious that Mr. Pickard had no choice but to say "Yes."

"Of course," Gaddis agreed. "And what about your wife? You mentioned her. She's a schoolteacher, right? She would be as openminded as you, wouldn't she?"

"I think so. Yes."

"And what about those Rotarians over there in Karaway. Are they as fair as you?"

"I suppose so."

"And your employees, Mr. Pickard. Surely you hire honest, fair-minded people. They'd be able to ignore what they've read and heard and try this boy justly, wouldn't they?"

"I suppose."

"No further questions, Your Honor."

Mr. Pickard hustled off the witness stand and hurried from the courtroom. Lucien Wilbanks stood and said, rather loudly, "Your Honor, the defense calls Mr. Willie Traynor."

A brick to the nose could not have hit Mr. Willie Traynor with more force. I gasped for air and heard Baggy say, too loudly, "Oh shit."

Harry Rex was sitting in the jury box with some other lawyers, taking in the festivities. As I wobbled to my feet, I looked at him desperately for help. He was rising too.

"Your Honor," he said. "I represent Mr. Traynor, and this young man has not been notified that he would be a witness." Go Harry Rex! Do something!

The Judge shrugged and said, "So? He's here. What's the difference?" There was not a trace of concern in his voice, and I knew I was nailed.

"Preparation for one thing. A witness has a right to be prepped."

"I believe he's the newspaper editor, is he not?"

"He is."

Lucien Wilbanks was walking toward the jury box as if he might take a swing at Harry Rex. He said, "Your Honor, he's not a litigant, and he will not be a witness at trial. He wrote the stories. Let's hear from him."

"It's an ambush, Judge," Harry Rex said.

"Sit down, Mr. Vonner," His Honor said, and I took a seat in the witness chair. I fired a look at Harry Rex as if to say, "Nice work, lawyer."

A bailiff stood in front of me and said, "Are you armed?"

"What?" I was beyond nervous and nothing made sense.

"A gun. Do you have a gun?"

"Yes."

"Can I have it, please?"

"Uh, it's in the car." Most of the spectators thought this was funny. Evidently, in Mississippi, one cannot properly testify if one is armed. Another silly rule. Moments later the rule made perfect sense. If I'd had a gun, I would've begun firing in the direction of Lucien Wilbanks.

The bailiff then swore me to tell the truth, and I watched as Wilbanks began pacing. The crowd behind him looked even larger. He began pleasantly enough with some preliminary inquiries about me and my purchase of the paper. I managed the correct answers, though I was extremely suspicious of every question. He was going somewhere; I had no idea where.

The crowd seemed to enjoy this. My sudden

takeover of the *Times* was still the source of interest and speculation, and, suddenly, there I was, in plain view of everyone, chatting about it under oath and on the record.

After a few minutes of niceties, Mr. Gaddis, who I assumed was on my side since Lucien certainly was not, stood and said, "Your Honor, this is all very informative. Where, exactly, is it going?"

"Good question. Mr. Wilbanks?"

"Hang on, Judge."

Lucien then produced copies of the *Times* and passed them to me, Gaddis, and Loopus. He looked at me and said, "Just for the record, Mr. Traynor, how many subscribers does the *Times* have now?"

"About forty-two hundred," I answered with a little pride. When the bankruptcy hit, Spot had squandered all but twelve hundred or so.

"And how many copies are sold at the newsstand?"

"Roughly a thousand."

Roughly twelve months earlier I had been living on the third floor of a fraternity house in Syracuse, New York, attending class occasionally, working hard to be a good soldier in the sexual revolution, drinking prodigious amounts of alcohol, smoking pot, sleeping until noon anytime I felt like it, and for exercise I'd hustle over to the next antiwar rally and scream at the police. I thought I had problems. How I'd gone from there to a witness chair in the Ford County courtroom was suddenly very unclear to me.

However, at that crucial moment in my new career, I

had several hundred of my fellow citizens, and subscribers, staring at me. It was not the time to appear vulnerable.

"What percentage of your newspapers are sold in
Ford County, Mr. Traynor?" he asked, as casually as if
we were talking business over coffee.

"Virtually all. I don't have the exact numbers."

"Well, do you have any newsstands outside of Ford
County?"

"No."

Mr. Gaddis attempted another lame rescue. He
stood and said, "Your Honor, please, where is this
going?"

Wilbanks suddenly raised his voice and lifted a finger toward the ceiling. "I will argue, Your Honor, that
potential jurors in this county have been poisoned by
the sensational coverage thrust upon us by *The Ford
County Times*. Mercifully, and justifiably, this newspaper
has not been seen or read in other parts of the state. A
change of venue is not only fair, but mandatory."

The word "poisoned" changed the tone of the proceedings dramatically. It stung me and frightened me,
and once again I asked myself if I had done something
wrong. I looked at Baggy for consolation, but he was
ducking behind the lady in front of him.

"I'll decide what's fair and mandatory, Mr.
Wilbanks. Proceed," Judge Loopus said sharply.

Mr. Wilbanks held up the paper and pointed to the
front page. "I refer to the photograph of my client," he
said. "Who took this photograph?"

"Mr. Wiley Meek, our photographer."

"And who made the decision to put it on the front page?"

"I did."

"And the size? Who determined that?"

"I did."

"Did it occur to you that this might be considered sensational?"

Damned right. Sensational was what I was after. "No," I replied coolly. "It happened to be the only photo we had of Danny Padgitt at the moment. He happened to be the only person arrested for the crime. We ran it. I'd run it again."

My haughtiness surprised me. I glanced at Harry Rex and saw one of his nasty grins. He was nodding. Go get 'em, boy.

"So in your opinion it was fair to run this photo?"

"I don't think it was unfair."

"Answer my question. In your opinion, was it fair?"

"Yes, it was fair, and it was accurate."

Wilbanks seemed to record this, then filed it away for future use. "Your report has a rather detailed description of the interior of the home of Rhoda Kassellaw. When did you inspect the home?"

"I have not."

"When did you enter the home?"

"I have not."

"You've never seen the interior of the house?"

"That's correct."

He flipped open the newspaper, scanned it for a moment, then said, "You report that the bedroom of Miss Kassellaw's two small children was down a short hallway, approximately fifteen feet from her bedroom door, and you estimate that their beds were about thirty feet from hers. How do you know this?"

"I have a source."

"A source. Has your source been in the house?"

"Yes."

"Is your source a police officer or a deputy?"

"He will remain confidential."

"How many confidential sources did you use for these stories?"

"Several."

From my journalism studies I vaguely remembered the case of a reporter who, in a similar situation, relied on sources and then refused to reveal their identity. This had somehow upset the Judge, who ordered the reporter to divulge his sources. When he refused again, the Judge held him in contempt and the cops hauled him away to jail where he spent many weeks hiding the identity of his informants. I couldn't remember the ending, but the reporter was eventually let go and the free press endured.

In a flash, I saw myself being handcuffed by Sheriff Coley and dragged away, screaming for Harry Rex, then thrown into the jail where I'd be stripped and handed a pair of those orange coveralls.

It would certainly be a bonanza for the *Times*. Boy, the stories I could write from in there.

Wilbanks continued, "You report that the children were in shock. How do you know this?"

"I spoke with Mr. Deece, the next-door neighbor."

"Did he use the word 'shock'?"

"He did."

"You report that the children were examined by a doctor here in Clanton on the night of the crime. How did you know this?"

"I had a source, and later I confirmed this with the doctor."

"And you report that the children are now undergoing some type of therapy back home in Missouri. Who told you that?"

"I talked to their aunt."

He tossed the newspaper on the table and took a few steps in my direction. His bloodshot eyes narrowed and glared at me. Here, the pistol would've been useful.

"The truth is, Mr. Traynor, you tried to paint the unmistakable picture that these two little innocent children saw their mother get raped and murdered in her own bed, isn't that right?"

I took a deep breath and weighed my response. The courtroom was silent, waiting. "I have reported the facts as accurately as possible," I said, staring straight at Baggy, who, though he was peeking around the lady in front of him, at least was nodding at me.

"In an effort to sell newspapers, you relied on unnamed sources and half-truths and gossip and wild speculation, all in an effort to sensationalize this story."

"I have reported the facts as accurately as possible," I said again, trying to remain calm.

He snorted and said, "Is that so?" He grabbed the

newspaper again and said, "I quote: 'Will the children testify at trial?' Did you write that, Mr. Traynor?"

I couldn't deny it. I kicked myself for writing it. It was the last section of the reports that Baggy and I had haggled over. We'd both been a little squeamish, and, with hindsight, we should have followed our instincts.

Denial was not possible. "Yes," I said.

"Upon what accurate facts did you base that question?"

"It was a question I heard asked many times after the crime," I said.

He flung the newspaper back on his table as if it were pure filth. He shook his head in mock bewilderment. "There are two children, right, Mr. Traynor?"

"Yes. A boy and a girl."

"How old is the little boy?"

"Five."

"And how old is the little girl?"

"Three."

"And how old are you, Mr. Traynor?"

"Twenty-three."

"And in your twenty-three years, how many trials have you covered as a reporter?"

"None."

"How many trials have you seen, period?"

"None."

"Since you are so ignorant about trials, what type of legal research did you do in order to accurately prepare yourself for these stories?"

At this point I would have probably turned the gun on myself.

"Legal research?" I repeated, as if he were speaking another language.

"Yes, Mr. Traynor. How many cases did you find where children age five or younger were allowed to testify in a criminal trial?"

I glanced in the direction of Baggy, who, evidently was now under the wooden bench. "None," I said.

"Perfect answer, Mr. Traynor. None. In the history of this state, no child under the age of eleven has ever testified in a criminal trial. Please write that down somewhere, and remember it the next time you attempt to inflame your readers with yellow journalism."

"Enough, Mr. Wilbanks," Judge Loopus said, a little too gently for my liking. I think he and the other lawyers, probably including Harry Rex, were enjoying this quick butchering of someone who'd meddled in legal affairs and gotten it all wrong. Even Mr. Gaddis seemed content to let me bleed.

Lucien was wise enough to stop when the blood was flowing. He growled something like, "I'm through with him." Mr. Gaddis had no questions. The bailiff motioned for me to step down, off the witness chair, and I tried desperately to walk upright back to the bench where Baggy was still hunkering down, like a stray dog in a hailstorm.

I scribbled notes through the rest of the hearing, but it was a failing effort to look busy and important. I could feel the stares. I was humiliated and wanted to lock myself in my office for a few days.

Wilbanks ended things with an impassioned plea to move the case somewhere far away, maybe even the Gulf Coast, where perhaps a few folks had heard of the crime but no one had been "poisoned" by the *Times*'s coverage of it. He railed against me and my newspaper, and he went overboard. Mr. Gaddis, in his closing remarks, reminded the Judge of the old saying, "Strong and bitter words indicate a weak cause."

I wrote that down. Then I hustled out of the courtroom as if I had an important deadline.

CHAPTER 11

Baggy rushed into my office late the following morning with the hot news that Lucien Wilbanks had just withdrawn his motion to change venue. As usual, he was full of analysis.

His first windy opinion was that the Padgitts didn't want the trial moved to another county. They knew Danny was dead guilty and that he would almost certainly be convicted by a properly selected jury anywhere. Their sole chance was to get a jury they could either buy or intimidate. Since all guilty verdicts must be unanimous, they needed only a single vote in Danny's favor. Just one vote and the jury would hang itself; the Judge would be required by law to declare a mistrial. It would certainly be retried, but with the same result. After three or four attempts, the State would give up.

I was sure Baggy had been at the courthouse all morning, replaying with his little club the venue hearing and borrowing the conclusions of the lawyers. He explained gravely that the hearing the day before had been staged by Lucien Wilbanks, for two reasons. First, Lucien was baiting the *Times* into running another large photo of Danny, this one in jailhouse garb. Second, Wilbanks wanted to get me on the witness stand to peel off some skin. "He damned sure did that," Baggy said.

"Thanks, Baggy," I said.

Wilbanks was setting the stage for the trial, one that he knew all along would take place in Clanton, and he wanted the *Times* to tone down its coverage.

The third, or fourth, reason was that Lucien Wilbanks never missed an opportunity to grandstand in front of a crowd. Baggy had seen it many times and he shared a few stories.

I'm not sure I followed all of his expansive thinking, but at that moment nothing else made sense. It seemed such a waste of time and effort to put on a two-hour hearing, knowing full well it was all a show. I figured worse things have happened in courtrooms.

———

The third feast was a pot roast, and we ate on the porch as it rained steadily.

As usual, I confessed that I'd never had a pot roast, so Miss Callie described the recipe and the preparation in detail. She lifted the lid off a large iron pot in the center of the table and closed her eyes as the thick aroma wafted upward. I had only been awake for an hour, and at that moment I could've eaten the tablecloth.

It was her simplest dish, she said. Take a beef rump roast, leave the fat on it, place it in the bottom of the pot, then cover it with new potatoes, onions, turnips, carrots, and beets; add some salt, pepper, and water, put it in the oven on slow bake, and wait five hours. She filled my plate with beef and vegetables, then covered it all with a thick sauce. "The beets give it all a purple tint," she explained.

She asked me if I wanted to say the blessing, and I declined. Praying was not something I had done in a long time. She was far more gifted. She took my hands and we closed our eyes. As she spoke to heaven the rain tapped the tin roof above our heads.

"Where's Esau?" I asked after my first three large bites.

"At work. Sometimes he can get free for lunch, often he cannot." She was preoccupied with something and finally said, "Can I ask you a question that's somewhat personal?"

"Sure, I guess."

"Are you a Christian child?"

"I'm sure I am. My mother used to take me to church on Easter."

That was not satisfactory. Whatever she was looking for, that wasn't it. "What kind of church?"

"Episcopalian. St. Luke's in Memphis."

"I'm not sure we have one of those in Clanton."

"I haven't seen one." Not that I'd been searching diligently for a house of worship. "What kind of church do you attend?" I asked.

"Church of God in Christ," she answered quickly and her entire face had a serene glow. "My pastor is the Reverend Thurston Small, a fine man of God. A powerful preacher too. You should come hear him."

I'd heard stories about how blacks worship, how the entire Sabbath was spent at church, how services ran late into the night and broke up only when the spirit was finally exhausted. I had vivid memories of suffering through Episcopal Easter services that, by law, could run no longer than sixty minutes.

"Do white people worship with you?" I asked.

"Only during the election years. Some of the politicians come sniffing around like dogs. They make a bunch of promises."

"Do they stay for the entire service?"

"Oh no. They're always too busy for that."

"So it's possible to come and go?"

"For you, Mr. Traynor, yes. We'll make an exception." She launched into a long story about her church, which was within walking distance of her home, and a fire that destroyed it not too many years earlier. The fire department, which of course was on the white side of town, was never in a hurry when responding to calls in Lowtown. They lost their church, but it was a blessing! Reverend Small rallied the congregation. For nearly three years they met in a warehouse loaned to them by Mr. Virgil Mabry, a fine Christian man. The building was one block off Main Street and many white folks didn't like the idea of Negroes worshiping on their side of town. But Mr. Mabry held firm. Reverend Small raised the money, and three years after the fire they cut the ribbon on a new sanctuary, one twice as big as the old. Now it was full every Sunday.

I loved it when she talked. It allowed me to eat non-stop, which was a priority. But I was still captivated by her precise diction, her cadence, and her vocabulary, which had to be college level.

When she finished with the new sanctuary, she asked, "Do you read the Bible often?"

"No," I said, shaking my head and chewing on a hot turnip.

"Never?"

Lying never crossed my mind. "Never."

That disappointed her again. "How often do you pray?"

I paused for a second and said, "Once a week, right here."

She slowly placed her knife and fork beside her plate and frowned at me as if something profound was about to be said. "Mr. Traynor, if you don't go to church, don't read your Bible, and don't pray, I'm not so sure you're really a Christian child."

I wasn't so sure either. I kept chewing so I wouldn't have to speak and defend myself. She continued, "Jesus said, 'Judge not, that ye be not judged.' It's not my place to pass judgment on anyone's soul, but I must confess that I'm worried about yours."

I was worried too, but not to the point of disrupting lunch.

"Do you know what happens to those who live outside the will of God?" she asked.

Nothing good, I knew that much. But I was too hungry and too frightened to answer. She was preaching now, not eating, and I was not enjoying myself.

"Paul wrote in Romans, 'The wages of sin is death, but the gift of God is eternal life through Jesus Christ our Lord.' Do you know what that means, Mr. Traynor?"

I had a hunch. I nodded and took a mouthful of beef. Had she memorized the entire Bible? Was I about to hear it all?

"Death is always physical, but a spiritual death means eternity away from our Lord Jesus. Death means an eternity in hell, Mr. Traynor. Do you understand this?"

She was making things very clear. "Can we change the subject?" I said.

Miss Callie suddenly smiled and said, "Of course. You're my guest and it's my job to make sure you feel welcome." She took up her fork again and for a long time we ate and listened to the rain.

"It's been a very wet spring," she said. "Good for beans but my tomatoes and melons need some sunshine."

I was comforted to know she was planning future meals. My story about Miss Callie and Esau and their remarkable children was almost complete. I was dragging out the research in hopes of spending a few more Thursday lunches on her porch. At first I had felt guilty for having so much food prepared just for me; we ate only a fraction of it. But she assured me that nothing was thrown out. She and Esau and perhaps some friends would make sure the leftovers were properly put away. "Nowadays, I only cook three times a week," she admitted with a hint of shame.

Dessert was peach cobbler and vanilla ice cream. We agreed to wait an hour so we could pace ourselves. She brought two cups of strong black coffee and we moved to the rocking chairs where we did our work. I pulled out my reporter's pad and pen and began making up questions. Miss Callie loved it when I wrote down things she said.

Her first seven children had Italian names—Alberto (Al), Leonardo (Leon), Massimo (Max), Roberto (Bobby), Gloria, Carlota, and Mario. Only Sam, the youngest and the one rumored to be on the lam, had an American name. During my second visit she had explained that she had been raised in an Italian home, right there in Ford County, but it was a very long story and she was saving it for later.

The first seven had all been valedictorians of their classes at Burley Street High, the colored school. Each had earned a PhD and now taught in college. The biographical details filled pages, and Miss Callie, rightly so, could talk about her children for hours.

And so she talked. I scribbled notes, rocked gently in my chair, listened to the rain, and finally fell asleep.

CHAPTER 12

Baggy had some reservations about the Ruffin story. "It's really not news," he said as he read it. I'm sure Hardy had alerted him that I was considering a large, front page story about a family of Negroes. "This stuff is usually on page five," he said.

Absent a murder, Baggy's notion of front page news was a hot property line dispute being waged in the courtroom with no jurors, a handful of half-asleep lawyers, and a ninety-year-old Judge brought back from the grave to referee such matters.

In 1967, Mr. Caudle had shown guts in running black obituaries, but in the three years since then the *Times* had taken little interest in anything on the other side of the railroad tracks. Wiley Meek was reluctant to go over with me and photograph Callie and Esau in front of their home. I managed to schedule the picture taking on a Thursday, at midday. Fried catfish, hush puppies, and coleslaw. Wiley ate until he had trouble breathing.

Margaret was also skittish about the story, but, as always, she deferred to the boss. In fact, the entire office was cool to the idea. I didn't care. I was doing what I thought was right; plus there was a big trial around the corner.

And so, on Wednesday, May 20, 1970, during a week in which there was absolutely nothing to print about the Kassellaw murder, the *Times* devoted more than half of its front page to the Ruffin family. It began with a large headline—RUFFIN FAMILY BOASTS SEVEN COLLEGE PROFESSORS. Under it was a large photo of Callie and Esau sitting on their front steps, smiling proudly at the camera. Below them were the senior portraits of all eight children—Al through Sam. My story began:

When Calia Harris was forced to drop out of school in the tenth grade, she promised herself her children would be able to finish not only high school but college as well. The year was 1926, and Calia, or Callie as she prefers to be called, was, at the age of fifteen, the oldest of four children. Education became a luxury when her father died of tuberculosis. Callie worked for the DeJarnette family until 1929, when she married Esau Ruffin, a carpenter and part-time preacher. They rented a small duplex in Lowtown for $15 a month and began saving every penny. They would need all they could save.

In 1931, Alberto was born.

In 1970, Dr. Alberto Ruffin was a professor of sociology at the University of Iowa. Dr. Leonardo Ruffin was a professor of biology at Purdue. Dr. Massimo Ruffin was a professor of economics at the University of Toledo. Dr. Roberto Ruffin was a professor of history at Marquette. Dr. Gloria Ruffin Sanderford taught Italian at Duke. Dr. Carlota Ruffin was a professor of urban studies at UCLA. Dr. Mario Ruffin had just completed his PhD in medieval literature and was a professor teaching at Grinnell College in Iowa. I mentioned Sam but didn't dwell on him.

By phone I had talked to all seven of the professors, and I quoted liberally from them in my story. The themes were common—love, sacrifice, discipline, hard work, encouragement, faith in God, faith in family, ambition, perseverance; no tolerance for laziness or failure. Each of the seven had a success story that could have filled an entire edition of the *Times*. Each had worked at least one full-time job while struggling through college and grad school. Most had worked two jobs. The older ones helped the younger ones. Mario told me he received five or six small checks each month from his siblings and parents.

The five older ones had been so tenacious in their studies that they had postponed marriage until in their late twenties and early thirties. Carlota and Mario were still single. Likewise, the next generation was being carefully planned. Leon had the oldest grandchild, age five. There were a total of five. Max and his wife were expecting their second.

There was so much material on the Ruffins that I ran only Part One that week. When I went to Lowtown for lunch the next day, Miss Callie met me with tears in her eyes. Esau met me too, with a firm handshake and a stiff, awkward, manly hug. We devoured a lamb stew and compared notes on how the story was being received. Needless to say, it was the talk of Lowtown, with neighbors stopping by all Wednesday afternoon and Thursday morning with extra copies. I had mailed a half dozen or so to each of the professors.

Over coffee and fried apple pies, their preacher, Reverend Thurston Small, parked in the street and made his way to the porch. I was introduced, and he seemed pleased to meet me. He quickly accepted a dessert and began a lengthy summary of how important the Ruffin story was to the black community of Clanton. Obituaries were fine, and in most Southern towns dead black folks were still ignored. Thanks to Mr. Caudle, progress was being made on one front. But to run such a grand and dignified profile of an outstanding black family on the front page was a giant step for racial tolerance in the town. I didn't see it that way. It was just a good human interest story about Miss Callie Ruffin and her extraordinary family.

The reverend enjoyed food and he also had a knack for embellishment. On his second pie, he became monotonous in his praise for the story. He gave no indication of leaving anytime that afternoon, so I finally excused myself.

Other than being the unofficial and somewhat un-reliable janitor for several businesses around the square, Piston had another job. He had an unlicensed courier service. Every hour or so he would appear inside the front doors of his clients—primarily law offices, but also the three banks, some Realtors, insurance agents, and the *Times*—and he would stand there for a few moments waiting for something to deliver. A simple shake of the head by a secretary would send him on his way to his next stop. If a letter or small package needed to be delivered, the secretaries would wait for Piston to pop in. He would grab whatever it was and jog it over to its destination. If it weighed over ten pounds, forget it. Since he was on foot, his service was limited to the square and maybe one or two blocks around it. At al-most any hour of the working day Piston could be seen downtown—walking, if he had no package, and jog-ging if he did.

The bulk of his traffic was letters between law of-fices. Piston was much faster than the mail, and much cheaper. He charged nothing. He said it was his service to his community, though at Christmas he fully ex-pected a ham or a cake.

He darted in late Friday morning with a hand-addressed letter from Lucien Wilbanks. I was almost afraid to open it. Could it be the million- dollar lawsuit he'd promised? It read:

Dear Mr. Traynor:

I enjoyed your profile on the Ruffin family, a most remarkable clan. I had heard of their achievements, but your story provided great insight. I admire your courage.

I hope you continue in this more positive vein.

Sincerely,
Lucien Wilbanks

I detested the man, but who wouldn't have appreciated the note? He enjoyed his reputation as a wild-eyed radical liberal who embraced unpopular causes. As such, his support at that moment gave limited comfort. And I knew it was only temporary.

There were no other letters. No anonymous phone calls. No threats. School was out and the weather was hot. The ominous and much-dreaded winds of desegregation were gathering strength. The good folks of Ford County had more important matters to worry about.

After a decade of strife and tension over civil rights, many white Mississippians were fearful that the end was near. If the federal courts could integrate the schools, could churches and housing be next?

The following day, Baggy went to a public meeting in the basement of a church. The organizers were trying to measure the support for a private, all-white school in Clanton. The crowd was large, frightened, angry, and determined to protect the children. A lawyer summarized the status of various federal appeals and delivered the distressing opinion that the final mandate would come that summer. He predicted that black kids in grades ten through twelve would be sent to Clanton High School and that white kids in grades seven through nine would be sent to Burley Street in Lowtown. This caused men to shake their heads and women to cry. The thought of white kids being shipped across the tracks was simply unacceptable.

A new school was organized. We were asked not to report the story, at least not then. The organizers wanted to gain some financial commitments before going public. We complied with their requests. I was anxious to avoid controversy.

A federal judge in Memphis ordered a massive busing plan that ripped the city apart. Inner-city black kids would be hauled to the white suburbs, and along the way they would pass the white kids going in the other direction. Tension was even greater there, and I found myself trying to avoid the city for a while.

It would be a long, hot summer. It seemed as if we were waiting for things to explode.

———

I skipped a week, then ran the second part of Miss Callie's story. On the bottom of the front page I lined up current photos of the seven Ruffin professors. My story dealt with where they were now and what they were doing. Without exception they professed great love for Clanton and Mississippi, though none planned to ever return permanently. They refused to judge a place that had kept them in inferior schools, kept them on one side of the tracks, kept them from voting and eating in most restaurants and drinking water from the fountain on the courthouse lawn. They refused to dwell on anything negative. Instead, they thanked God for his goodness, for health, for family, for their parents, and for their opportunities.

I marveled at their humility and kindness. Each of the seven promised to meet me during the Christmas vacation when we would sit on Miss Callie's porch and eat pecan pie and tell stories.

I finished my lengthy profile with an intriguing detail about the family. From the day each Ruffin child left home, he or she was instructed by Esau to write at least one letter a week to their mother. This they did, and the letters never stopped. At some point, Esau decided that Callie should receive a letter a day. Seven professors. Seven days in a week. So Alberto wrote his letter on Sunday, and mailed it. Leonardo wrote his on Monday, and mailed it. And so on. Some days Callie received two or three letters, some days none. But the short walk to the mailbox was always exciting.

And she kept every letter. In a closet in the front bedroom, she showed me a stack of cardboard boxes, all filled with hundreds of letters from her children.

"I'll let you read them sometime," she said, but for some reason I didn't believe her. Nor did I want to read them. They would be far too personal.

CHAPTER 13

Ernie Gaddis, the District Attorney, filed a motion to enlarge the jury pool. According to Baggy, who was becoming more of an expert each day, in the typical criminal trial the Circuit Court clerk summoned about forty people for jury duty. About thirty-five would show up and at least five of those would be too old or too sick to be qualified. Gaddis argued in his motion that the increased notoriety of the Kassellaw murder would make it more difficult to find impartial jurors. He asked the Court to summon at least a hundred prospective jurors.

What he didn't say in writing, but what everybody knew, was that the Padgitts would have a harder time intimidating one hundred than forty. Lucien Wilbanks objected strenuously and demanded a hearing. Judge Loopus said one was not necessary and ordered a larger jury pool. He also took the unusual step of sealing the list of prospective jurors. Baggy and his drinking buddies, and everyone else around the courthouse, were shocked by this. It had never been done. The lawyers and litigants always got a complete list of the jury pool two weeks before trial.

The order was generally viewed as a major setback to the Padgitts. If they didn't know who was in the pool, then how could they bribe or frighten them?

Gaddis then asked the Court to have the jury summons mailed, not personally served by the Sheriff's office. Loopus liked this idea too. Evidently he was well aware of the cozy relationship between the Padgitts and our Sheriff. Not surprisingly, Lucien Wilbanks screamed over this plan. In his rather frantic responses he made the point that Judge Loopus was treating his client differently and unfairly. Reading his filings, I was amazed at how he could rant so clearly for so many pages.

It was becoming obvious that Judge Loopus was determined to preside over a secure and unbiased trial. He had been the District Attorney back in the 1950s before ascending to the bench, and he was known for his pro-prosecution leanings. He certainly appeared to have little concern for the Padgitts and their legacy of corruption. Plus, on paper (and certainly in my paper), the case against Danny Padgitt appeared to be airtight.

On Monday, June 15, amid great secrecy, the Circuit Court clerk mailed a hundred summonses for jury duty to registered voters all over Ford County. One arrived in the rather busy mailbox of Miss Callie Ruffin, and when I arrived for lunch on Thursday she showed it to me.

———

In 1970, Ford County was 26 percent black, 74 percent white, with no fractions for Others or those who weren't certain. Six years after the tumultuous summer of 1964 and its massive push to register blacks, and five years after the Voting Rights Act of 1965, few bothered to sign up in Ford County. In the statewide elections of 1967, almost 70 percent of the eligible whites in the county had voted, while only 12 percent of the blacks did so. Registration drives in Lowtown were met with general indifference. One reason was that the county was so white that no black could ever be elected to a local office. So why bother?

Another reason was the historical abuse at the point of enrolling. For a hundred years whites had used a variety of tricks to deny blacks proper registration. Poll taxes, literacy exams, the list was long and miserable.

Yet another reason was the hesitancy by most blacks to be registered in any manner by white authorities. Registration could mean more taxes, more supervision, more surveillance, more intrusions. Registration could mean serving on juries.

According to Harry Rex, who was a slightly more reliable courthouse source than Baggy, there had never been a black juror in Ford County. Since potential jurors were selected from the voter registration rolls and nowhere else, few showed up in a jury pool. Those who survived the early rounds of questioning were routinely excused before the final twelve were empaneled. In criminal cases, the prosecution routinely challenged blacks under the belief that they would be too sympathetic to the accused. In civil cases, the defense challenged them because they were feared as too liberal with the money of others.

However, these theories had never been tested in Ford County.

———

Callie and Esau Ruffin registered to vote in 1951. Together, they marched into the office of the Circuit Court clerk and asked to be added to the voter rolls. The deputy clerk, as she was trained to do, handed them a laminated card with the words "Declaration of Independence" across the top. The text was written in German.

The clerk, assuming that Mr. and Mrs. Ruffin were as illiterate as most blacks in Ford County, said, "Can you read this?"

"This is not English," Callie said. "It's German."

"Can you read it?" the clerk asked, realizing that she might have her hands full with this couple.

"I can read as much of it as you can," Callie said politely.

The clerk withdrew the card and handed over another. "Can you read this?" she asked.

"I can," Callie said. "It's the Bill of Rights."

"What does number eight say?"

Callie read it slowly, then said, "The Eighth Amendment prohibits excessive fines and cruel punishments."

At about this time, depending on whose version was being described, Esau leaned in and said, "We are property owners." He placed the deed to their home on the counter and the deputy clerk examined it. Property ownership was not a prerequisite to voting, but it was a huge asset if you were black. Not knowing what else to do, she said, "Fair enough. The poll tax will be two dollars each." Esau handed over the money, and with that they joined the voter rolls with thirty-one other blacks, none of whom were women.

They never missed an election. Miss Callie had always worried because so few of her friends bothered to register and vote, but she was too busy raising eight children to do much about it. Ford County was spared the racial unrest that was common throughout most of the state, so there was never an organized drive to register blacks.

———

At first I couldn't tell if she was anxious or excited. I'm not sure she knew either. The first black female voter might now become the first black juror. She had never backed away from a challenge, but she had grave moral concerns about judging another person. "'Judge not, that ye be not judged,'" she said more than once, quoting Jesus.

"But if everyone followed that verse of Scripture, our entire judicial system would fail, wouldn't it?" I asked.

"I don't know," she said, gazing away. I had never seen Miss Callie so preoccupied.

We were eating fried chicken with mashed potatos and gravy. Esau had not made it home for lunch.

"How can I judge a man I know to be guilty?" she asked.

"First, you listen to the evidence," I said. "You have an open mind. It won't be difficult."

"But you know he killed her. You all but said so in your paper." Her brutal honesty hit hard every time.

"We just reported the facts, Miss Callie. If the facts make him look guilty, then so be it."

The gaps of silence were long and many that day. She was deep in thought and ate little.

"What about the death penalty?" she asked. "Will they want to put that boy in the gas chamber?"

"Yes ma'am. It's a capital murder case."

"Who decides whether he is put to death?"

"The jury."

"Oh my."

She was unable to eat after that. She said her blood pressure had been up since she received the jury summons. She had already been to the doctor. I helped her to the sofa in the den and took her a glass of ice water. She insisted that I finish my lunch, which I happily did in silence. Later, she rallied a bit and we sat on the porch in the rockers, talking about anything but Danny Padgitt and his trial.

I finally hit paydirt when I asked her about the Italian influence in her life. Over our first lunch she had told me that she learned Italian before she learned English. Seven of her eight children had Italian names.

She needed to tell me a long story. I had absolutely nothing else to do.

In the 1890s, the price of cotton rose dramatically as demand increased around the world. The fertile regions of the South were under pressure to produce more. The large plantation owners in the Mississippi Delta desperately needed to increase their crops, but they faced a severe labor shortage. Many of the blacks who were physically able had fled the land their ancestors toiled as slaves for better jobs and certainly better lives up North. Those left behind were, understandably, less than enthusiastic about chopping and picking cotton for brutally low wages.

The landowners hit upon a scheme to import industrious and hardworking European immigrants to raise cotton. Through contacts with Italian labor agents in New York and New Orleans, connections were made, promises swapped, lies told, contracts forged, and in 1895 the first boatload of families arrived in the Delta. They were from northern Italy, from the region of Emilia-Romagna, near Verona. For the most part they were poorly educated and spoke little English, though in any language they quickly realized they were on the bad end of a huge scam. They were given miserable living accommodations, in a subtropical climate, and while battling malaria and mosquitoes and snakes and rotten drinking water they were told to raise cotton for wages no one could live on. They were forced to borrow money at scandalous rates from the landowners. Their food and supplies came from the company store, at steep prices.

Because the Italians worked hard the landowners wanted more of them. They dressed up their operations, made more promises to more Italian labor agents, and the immigrants kept coming. A system of peonage was fine-tuned, and the Italians were treated worse than most black farmworkers.

Over time some efforts were made to divide profits and transfer ownership of land, but the cotton markets fluctuated so wildly that the arrangements could never be stabilized. After twenty years of abuse, the Italians finally scattered and the experiment became history.

Those who remained in the Delta were considered second-class citizens for decades. They were excluded from schools, and because they were Catholic they were not welcome in churches. The country clubs were off limits. They were "dagos" and shoved to the bottom of the social ladder. But because they worked hard and saved their money, they slowly accumulated land.

The Rossetti family landed near Leland, Mississippi, in 1902. They were from a village near Bologna, and had the misfortune of listening to the wrong labor agent in that city. Mr. and Mrs. Rossetti brought with them four daughters, the oldest of which was Nicola, age twelve. Though they often went hungry the first year, they managed to avoid outright starvation. Penniless when they arrived, after three years of peonage the family had racked up $6,000 in debts to the plantation with no possible way of paying them off. They fled the Delta in the middle of the night and rode a boxcar to Memphis, where a distant relative took them in.

At the age of fifteen, Nicola was stunningly beautiful. Long dark hair, brown eyes—a classic Italian beauty. She looked older than her years and managed to get a job in a clothing store by telling the owner she was eighteen. After three days, the owner offered her a marriage proposal. He was willing to divorce his wife of twenty years and say good-bye to his children if Nicola would run away with him. She said no. He offered Mr. Rossetti $5,000 as an incentive. Mr. Rossetti said no.

In those days, the wealthy farming families in northern Mississippi did their shopping and socializing in Memphis, usually within walking distance of the Peabody Hotel. It was there that Mr. Zachary DeJarnette of Clanton had the blind luck of bumping into Nicola Rossetti. Two weeks later they were married.

He was thirty-one, a widower with no children and in the midst of a serious search for a wife. He was also the largest landowner in Ford County, where the soil was not as rich as in the Delta, but still quite profitable if you owned enough of it. Mr. DeJarnette had inherited over four thousand acres from his family. His grandfather had once owned the grandfather of Calia Harris Ruffin.

The marriage was a package deal. Nicola was wise

beyond her years, and she was also desperate to protect her family. They had suffered so much. She saw an opportunity and took full advantage of it. Before she agreed to marriage, Mr. DeJarnette promised to not only employ her father as a farm supervisor but to provide his family with very comfortable housing. He agreed to educate her three younger sisters. He agreed to pay off the peonage debts from the Delta. So smitten was Mr. DeJarnette that he would've agreed to anything.

The first Italians in Ford County arrived not in a broken ox cart, but rather by first-class passage on the Illinois Central Rail Line. A welcoming party unloaded their brand-new luggage and helped them into two 1904 Ford Model T's. The Rossettis were treated like royalty as they followed Mr. DeJarnette from party to party in Clanton. The town was instantly abuzz with descriptions of how beautiful the bride was. There was talk of a formal wedding ceremony, to sort of buttress the quickie service in Memphis, but since there was no Catholic church in Clanton the idea was scrapped. The bride and groom had yet to address the sticky issue of religious preference. At that time, if Nicola had asked Mr. DeJarnette to convert to Hinduism he would have quickly done so.

They finally made it to the main house at the edge of town. When the Rossettis turned into the long front drive and glimpsed the stately antebellum mansion built by the first Mr. DeJarnette, they all broke into tears.

It was decided that they would live there until an overseer's house could be renovated and made suitable. Nicola assumed her duties as the lady of the manor and tried her best to get pregnant. Her younger sisters were provided with private tutors, and within weeks were speaking good English. Mr. Rossetti spent each day with his son-in-law, who was only three years his junior, and learned how to run the plantation.

And Mrs. Rossetti went to the kitchen where she met Callie's mother, India.

"My grandmother cooked for the DeJarnettes, so did my mother," Miss Callie was saying. "I thought I would too, but it didn't work out that way."

"Did Zack and Nicola have children?" I asked. I was on my third or fourth glass of tea. It was hot and the ice had melted. Miss Callie had been talking for two hours, and she had forgotten about the jury summons and the murder trial.

"No. It was very sad because they wanted children so badly. When I was born in 1911, Nicola practically took me away from my mother. She insisted I have an Italian name. She kept me in the big house with her. My mother didn't mind—she had plenty of other children, plus she was in the house all day long."

"What did your father do?" I asked.

"Worked on the farm. It was a good place to work, and to live. We were very lucky because the DeJarnettes took care of us. They were good, fair people. Always. It wasn't that way for a lot of Negro folk. Back then your life was controlled by the white man who owned your house. If he was mean and abusive, then your life was miserable. The DeJarnettes were wonderful people. My father, grandfather, and great-grandfather worked their land, and they were never mistreated."

"And Nicola?"

She smiled for the first time in an hour. "God blessed me. I had two mothers. She dressed me in clothes she bought in Memphis. When I was a toddler she taught me to speak Italian while I was learning English. She taught me to read when I was three years old."

"You still speak Italian?"

"No. It was a long time ago. She loved to tell me stories of being a little girl in Italy, and she promised me that one day she would take me there, to see the canals in Venice and the Vatican in Rome and the tower in Pisa. She loved to sing and she taught me about the opera."

"Was she educated?"

"Her mother had some education, Mr. Rossetti did not, and she had made sure Nicola and her sisters could read and write. She promised me I would go to college somewhere up North, or maybe even in Europe where folks were more tolerant. The notion of a black woman going to college in the 1920s was downright crazy."

The story was running in many directions. I wanted to record some of it but I had not brought a notepad. The image of a young black girl living in an antebellum home speaking Italian and listening to the opera in Mississippi fifty years earlier had to be unique.

"Did you work in the house?" I asked.

"Oh yes, when I got older. I was a housekeeper, but I never had to work as hard as the others. Nicola wanted me close by. At least an hour every day we would sit in her parlor and practice speaking. She was determined to lose her Italian accent, and she was just as determined that I would have perfect diction. There was a retired schoolteacher from town, a Miss Tucker, an old maid, I'll never forget her, and Nicola would send a car for her every morning. Over hot tea we would read a lesson and Miss Tucker would correct even the slightest mispronunciation. We studied grammar. We memorized vocabulary. Nicola drilled herself until she spoke perfect English."

"What happened to college?"

She was suddenly exhausted and story time was over. "Ah, Mr. Traynor, it was very sad. Mr. DeJarnette lost everything back in the 1920s. He'd invested heavily in railroads and ships and stocks and such stuff, and went broke almost overnight. He shot himself, but that's another story."

"What happened to Nicola?"

"She managed to hold on to the big house until the Second War, then she moved back to Memphis with Mr. and Mrs. Rossetti. We swapped letters every week for years. I still have them. She died four years ago, at the age of seventy-six. I cried for a month. I still cry when I think of her. How I loved that woman." Her words trailed off and I knew from experience that she was ready for a nap.

Late that night I buried myself in the *Times* archives.

On September 12, 1930, there was a front page story about the suicide of Zachary DeJarnette. Despondent over the collapse of his businesses, he had left a new will and a farewell note for his wife, Nicola, then, to make things easier for everyone, he had driven to the funeral home in Clanton. He walked in the rear door with a double-barreled shotgun, found the embalming room, took a seat, took off a shoe, put the gun in his mouth, and pulled the trigger with a big toe.

CHAPTER 14

On Monday, June 22, all but eight of the hundred jurors arrived for the trial of Danny Padgitt. As we soon found out, four were dead and four had simply vanished. For the most part, the rest looked very anxious. Baggy said that usually jurors have no idea what kind of case they might be selected to decide when they arrive. Not so with the Padgitt trial. Every breathing soul in Ford County knew that the big day had finally come.

Few things draw a crowd in a small town like a good murder trial, and the courtroom was full long before 9 A.M. The prospective jurors filled one side, spectators the other. The old balcony practically sagged above us. The walls were lined with people. As a show of strength, Sheriff Coley had every available uniformed body milling around, looking important, doing nothing productive. What a perfect time to pull a bank heist, I thought.

Baggy and I were in the front row. He had convinced the Circuit Court clerk that we were entitled to press credentials, thus special seating. Next to me was a reporter from the newspaper in Tupelo, a pleasant gentleman who reeked of cheap pipe tobacco. I filled him in on the details of the murder, off the record. He seemed impressed with my knowledge.

The Padgitts were there in full force. They sat in chairs pulled close to the defense table and huddled around Danny and Lucien Wilbanks like the den of thieves they really were. They were arrogant and sinister and I couldn't help but hate every one of them. I didn't know them by name; few people did. But as I watched them I wondered which one had been the incompetent arsonist who'd sneaked into our printing room with gallons of gasoline. I had my pistol in my briefcase. I'm sure they had theirs close by. A false move here or there and an old-fashioned gunfight would erupt. Throw in Sheriff Coley and his poorly trained but trigger-happy boys, and half the town would get wiped out.

I caught a few stares from the Padgitts, but they were much more worried about the jurors than me. They watched them closely as they filed into the courtroom and took their instructions from the clerk. The Padgitts and their lawyers looked at lists that they had found somewhere. They compared notes.

Danny was nicely but casually dressed in a white long-sleeved shirt and a pair of starched khakis. As instructed by Wilbanks, he was smiling a lot, as if he were really a nice kid whose innocence was about to be revealed.

Across the aisle, Ernie Gaddis and his smaller crew were likewise observing the prospective jurors. Gaddis had two assistants, one a paralegal and one a part-time prosecutor named Hank Hooten. The paralegal carried the files and briefcases. Hooten seemed to do little but just be there so Ernie would have someone to confer with.

Baggy leaned over as if it was time to whisper. "That guy there, brown suit," he said, nodding at Hooten. "He was screwin' Rhoda Kassellaw."

I was shocked and my face showed it. I jerked to the right and looked at Baggy. He nodded smugly and said what he always said when he had the scoop on something really nasty. "That's what I'm tellin' you," he whispered. This meant that he had no doubts. Baggy was often wrong but never in doubt.

Hooten appeared to be about forty with prematurely gray hair, nicely dressed, somewhat handsome. "Where's he from?" I whispered. The courtroom was noisy as we waited for Judge Loopus.

"Here. He does some real estate law, low-pressure stuff. A real jerk. Been divorced a couple of times, always on the prowl."

"Does Gaddis know his assistant was seeing the victim?"

"Hell no. Ernie would pull him from the case."

"You think Wilbanks knows?"

"Nobody knows," Baggy said with even greater

smugness. It was as if he had personally caught them in bed, then kept it to himself until that very moment in the courtroom. I wasn't sure I believed him.

Miss Callie arrived a few minutes before nine. Esau escorted her into the courtroom, then had to leave when he couldn't find a seat. She checked in with the clerk and was placed in the third row; she was given a questionnaire to fill out. She looked around for me but there were too many people between us. I counted four other blacks in the pool.

A bailiff bellowed for us to rise, and it sounded like a stampede. Judge Loopus told us to sit, and the floor shook. He went straight to work and appeared to be in good spirits. He had a courtroom full of voters and he was up for reelection in two years, though he had never had an opponent. Six jurors were excused because they were over the age of sixty-five. Five were excused for medical reasons. The morning began to drag. I couldn't take my eyes off Hank Hooten. He certainly had the look of a ladies' man.

When the preliminary questions were over, the panel was down to seventy-nine duly qualified jurors. Miss Callie was now in the second row, not a good sign if she wanted to avoid jury service. Judge Loopus yielded the floor to Ernie Gaddis, who introduced himself to the panel again and explained in great length that he was there on behalf of the State of Mississippi, the taxpayers, the citizens who had elected him to prosecute those who commit crimes. He was the people's lawyer.

He was there to prosecute Mr. Danny Padgitt, who had been indicted by a grand jury, made up of their fellow citizens, for the rape and murder of Rhoda Kassellaw. He asked if it was possible that anyone had not heard something about the murder. Not a single hand went up.

Ernie had been talking to juries for thirty years. He was friendly and smooth and gave the impression that you could discuss almost anything with him, even in open court. He moved slowly into the area of intimidation. Has anyone outside your family contacted you about this case? A stranger? Has a friend tried to influence your opinion? Your summons was mailed to you; the jury list is locked under seal. No one is supposed to know that you're a potential juror. Has anyone mentioned it to you? Anyone threatened you? Anyone offered you anything? The courtroom was very quiet as Ernie led them through these questions.

No one raised a hand; none was expected. But Ernie was successful in conveying the message that these people, the Padgitts, had been moving through the shadows of Ford County. He hung an even darker cloud above them, and he left the impression that he, as the District Attorney and the people's lawyer, knew the truth.

He began his finish with a question that cut through the air like a rifle shot. "Do all of you folks understand that jury tampering is a crime?"

They seemed to understand.

"And that I, as the prosecutor, will pursue, indict,

bring to trial, and do my utmost to convict any person involved with jury tampering. Do you understand this?"

When Ernie finished we all felt as though we'd been tampered with. Anyone who'd talked about the case, which of course was every person in the county, seemed in danger of being indicted by Ernie and hounded to the grave.

"He's effective," whispered the reporter from Tupelo.

Lucien Wilbanks began with a lengthy and quite dull lecture about the presumption of innocence and how it is the foundation of American jurisprudence. Regardless of what they'd read in the local newspaper, and here he managed a scornful glance in my general direction, his client, sitting right there at the moment, was an innocent man. And if anyone felt otherwise, then he or she was duty bound to raise a hand and say so.

No hands. "Good. Then by your silence you're telling the Court that you, all of you, can look at Danny Padgitt right now and say he is innocent. Can you do that?" He hammered them on this for far too long, then shifted to the burden of proof with another lecture on the State's monumental challenge to prove his client guilty beyond a reasonable doubt.

These two sacred protections—the presumption of innocence and proof beyond a reasonable doubt— were granted to all of us, including the jurors, by the very wise men who wrote our Constitution and Bill of Rights.

We were approaching noon and everybody was anxious for a break. Wilbanks seemed to miss this and he kept rattling on. When he sat down at twelve-fifteen, Judge Loopus announced that he was starving. We would recess until two o'clock.

Baggy and I had a sandwich upstairs in the Bar Room with several of his cronies, three aging washed-up lawyers who hadn't missed a trial in years. Baggy really wanted a glass of whiskey, but for some odd reason felt the call of duty. His pals did not. The clerk had given us a list of jurors as they were currently seated. Miss Callie was number twenty-two, the first black and the third female.

It was the general feeling that the defense would not challenge her because she was black, and blacks, according to the prevailing theory, were sympathetic to those accused of crimes. I wasn't sure how a black person could be sympathetic to a white thug like Danny Padgitt, but the lawyers were unshakable in their belief that Lucien Wilbanks would gladly take her.

Under the same theory, the prosecution would exercise one of its arbitrary, peremptory challenges and strike her from the panel. Not so, said Chick Elliot, the oldest and drunkest of the gang. "I'd take her if I were prosecuting," he argued, then knocked back a potent shot of bourbon.

"Why?" Baggy asked.

"Because we know her so well now, thanks to the *Times*. She came across as a sensible, God-fearing, Bible-quoting

patriot, who raised all those kids with a heavy hand and a
swift kick in the ass if they screwed up."

"I agree," said Tackett, the youngest of the three.
Tackett, though, had a tendency to agree with whatever
the prevailing theory happened to be. "She'd make an
ideal juror for the prosecution. Plus, she's a woman. It's
a rape case. I'd take all the women I could get."

They argued for an hour. It was my first session with
them, and I suddenly understood how Baggy collected
so many differing opinions about so many issues.
Though I tried not to show it, I was deeply concerned
that my long and generous stories about Miss Callie
would somehow come back to haunt her.

After lunch, Judge Loopus moved into the most serious
phase of questioning—the death penalty. He explained
the nature of a capital offense and the procedures
that would be followed, then he yielded again to Ernie
Gaddis.

Juror number eleven was a member of some obscure
church and he made it very clear that he could never
vote to send a person to the gas chamber. Juror number
thirty-four was a veteran of two wars and he felt rather
strongly that the death penalty wasn't used often
enough. This, of course, delighted Ernie, who singled
out individual jurors and politely asked them questions
about judging others and imposing the death sentence. He eventually made it to Miss Callie. "Now, Mrs.

Ruffin, I've read about you, and you seem to be a very religious woman. Is this correct?"

"I do love the Lord, yes sir," she answered, as clear as always.

"Are you hesitant to sit in judgment of another human?"

"I am, yes sir."

"Do you want to be excused?"

"No sir. It's my duty as a citizen to be here, same as all these other folks."

"And if you're on the jury, and the jury finds Mr. Padgitt guilty of these crimes, can you vote to put him to death?"

"I certainly wouldn't want to."

"My question was, 'Can you?' "

"I can follow the law, same as these other folks. If the law says that we should consider the death penalty, then I can follow the law."

———

Four hours later, Calia H. Ruffin became the last juror chosen—the first black to serve on a trial jury in Ford County. The drunks up in the Bar Room had been right. The defense wanted her because she was black. The State wanted her because they knew her so well. Plus, Ernie Gaddis had to save his jury strikes for less-appealing characters.

Late that night I sat alone in my office working on a story about the opening day and jury selection. I heard a familiar noise downstairs. Harry Rex had a way of shoving open the front door and stomping on the wooden floors so that everybody at the *Times*, regardless of the time of day, knew he had arrived. "Willie boy!" he yelled from below.

"Up here," I yelled back.

He rumbled up the stairs and fell into his favorite chair. "Whatta you think of the jury?" he said. He appeared to be completely sober.

"I only know one of them," I said. "How many do you know?"

"Seven."

"You think they picked Miss Callie because of my stories?"

"Yep," he said, brutally honest as always. "Everybody's been talkin' about her. Both sides felt like they knew her. It's 1970 and we've never had a black juror. She looked as good as any. Does that worry you?"

"I guess it does."

"Why? What's wrong with servin' on a jury? It's about time we had blacks doin' it. She and her husband have always been anxious to break down barriers. Ain't like it's dangerous. Well, normally it ain't dangerous."

I hadn't talked to Miss Callie and I would not be able to do so until after the trial. Judge Loopus had ordered the jurors sequestered for the week. By then they were hiding in a motel in another town.

"Any suspicious characters on the jury?" I asked.

"Maybe. Everybody's worried about that crippled boy from out near Dumas. Fargarson. Hurt his back in a sawmill owned by his uncle. The uncle sold timber to

the Padgitts many years ago. The boy has some atti-
tude. Gaddis wanted to bump him but he ran out of
challenges."

The crippled boy walked with a cane and was at
least twenty-five years old. Harry Rex referred to anyone younger than himself, and especially me, as "boy."

"But with the Padgitts you never know," he continued. "Hell, they could own half the jury by now."

"You don't really believe that, do you?"

"Naw, but a hung jury wouldn't surprise me either. It
might take two or three shots at this boy before Ernie
gets him."

"But he will go to prison, won't he?" The thought of
Danny Padgitt escaping punishment frightened me. I
had invested myself in the town of Clanton, and if its
justice was so corruptible then I didn't want to stay.

"They'll hang his ass."

"Good. The death penalty?"

"I'd bet on it, eventually. This is the buckle of the
Bible Belt, Willie. An eye for an eye, all that crap. Loopus'll do everything he can to help Ernie get a death
verdict."

I then made the mistake of asking him why he was
working so late. A divorce client had left town on business, then sneaked back to catch his wife with her
boyfriend. The client and Harry Rex had spent the last
two hours in a borrowed pickup behind a hot-sheets
motel north of town. As it turned out, the wife had two
boyfriends. The story took half an hour to tell.

CHAPTER 15

Tuesday morning, almost two hours were wasted as the lawyers wrangled over some hotly contested motions back in the Judge's chambers. "Probably the photographs," Baggy kept saying. "They always fight over the photographs." Since we were not privy to their little war, we waited impatiently in the courtroom, holding our seats. I wrote pages of useless notes in a chicken-scratch handwriting that any veteran reporter would admire. The scribbling kept me busy and it kept my eyes away from the ever-present stares of the Padgitts. With the jury out of the room they turned their attention to the spectators, especially me.

The jurors were locked away in the deliberation room, with deputies at the door as if someone might gain something by attacking them. The room was on the second floor, with large windows that looked upon the east side of the courthouse lawn. At the bottom of one window was a noisy air-conditioning unit that could be heard from any point on the square when it was at full throttle. I thought of Miss Callie and her blood pressure. I knew she was reading the Bible and maybe this was calming her. I had called Esau early that morning. He was very upset that she had been sequestered and hauled away.

Esau was in the back row, waiting with the rest of us.

When Judge Loopus and the lawyers finally appeared they looked as though they had all been fistfighting. The Judge nodded at the bailiff and the jurors were led in. He welcomed them, thanked them, asked about their accommodations, apologized for the inconvenience, apologized for the delay that morning, then promised that things would move forward.

Ernie Gaddis assumed a position behind the podium and began his opening statement to the jury. He had a yellow legal pad, but he didn't look at it. With great efficiency, he rattled off the necessary elements the State would prove against Danny Padgitt. When all the exhibits were in, and all the witnesses were finished, and the lawyers were quiet, and the Judge had spoken, it would be left to the jury to serve justice. There was no doubt in his mind that they would find Danny Padgitt guilty of rape and murder. He didn't waste a word, and every word found its mark. He was mercifully brief. His confident tone and concise remarks conveyed the clear message that he had the facts, the case, and he would get his verdict. He did not need long, emotional arguments to convince the jury.

Baggy loved to say, "When lawyers have a weak case they do a lot more talking."

Oddly, Lucien Wilbanks deferred his opening remarks until the defense put on its case, an option rarely exercised. "He's up to something," Baggy mumbled as if he and Lucien were thinking together. "No surprise there."

The first witness for the State was Sheriff Coley himself. Part of his job was testifying in criminal cases, but it was doubtful he'd ever dreamed of doing so against a Padgitt. In a few months he would be up for re-election. It was important for him to look good before the voters.

With Ernie's meticulous planning and prodding, they walked through the crime. There were large diagrams of the Kassellaw home, the Deece home, the roads around Beech Hill, the exact spot where Danny Padgitt was arrested. There were photographs of the area. Then, there were photographs of Rhoda's corpse, a series of eight by ten's that were handed to the jurors and passed around. Their reactions were amazing. Every face was shocked. Some winced. A few mouths flew open. Miss Callie closed her eyes and appeared to pray. Another lady on the jury, Mrs. Barbara Baldwin, gasped at first sight and turned away. Then she looked at Danny Padgitt as if she could shoot him at point-blank range. "Oh my God," one of the men mumbled. Another covered his mouth as if he might throw up.

The jurors sat in padded swivel chairs that rocked slightly. As the gruesome photos were passed around,

not a single chair was still. The pictures were inflamma-
tory, highly prejudicial, yet always admissible, and as
they caused a commotion in the jury box I thought
Danny Padgitt was as good as dead. Judge Loopus allowed only six as exhibits. One would have sufficed.

It was just after 1 P.M., and everyone needed a break.
I doubted that the jurors had much of an appetite.

———————

The State's second witness was one of Rhoda's sisters
from Missouri. Her name was Ginger McClure, and I
had talked to her several times after the murder. When
she realized I had gone to school at Syracuse and was
not a native of Ford County, she had thawed somewhat.
She had reluctantly sent me a photo for the obituary.
Later, she had called and asked if I could send her
copies of the *Times* when it mentioned Rhoda's case.
She expressed frustration in getting details from the
District Attorney's office.

Ginger was a slim redhead, very attractive and well
dressed, and when she settled into the witness chair she
had everyone's attention.

According to Baggy, someone from the victim's family always testified. Death became real when the loved
ones took the stand and looked at the jurors.

Ernie wanted Ginger to be viewed by the jury and
arouse their sympathy. He also wanted to remind the jury
that the mother of two small children had been taken
from them in a premeditated murder. Her testimony
was brief. Wisely, Lucien Wilbanks had no questions on

cross-examination. When she was excused, she walked to a reserved chair behind the bar, near the seat of Ernie Gaddis, and assumed the position as representative of the family. Her every move was watched until the next witness was called.

Then it was back to the gore. A forensic pathologist from the state crime lab was called to discuss the autopsy. Though he had plenty of photos, none were used. None were needed. In layman's terms, her cause of death was obvious—a loss of blood. There was a four-inch gash beginning just below her left ear and running almost straight down. It was almost two inches deep, and, in his opinion, and he'd seen many knife wounds, it was caused by a rapid and powerful thrust from a blade that was approximately six inches long and an inch wide. The person using the knife was, more than likely, right-handed. The gash cut completely through the left jugular vein, and at that point the victim had only a few minutes to live. A second gash was six-and-a-half inches long, one inch deep, and ran from the tip of the chin to the right ear, which it almost sliced in two. This wound by itself probably would not have resulted in death.

The pathologist described these wounds as if he were talking about a tick bite. No big deal. Nothing unusual. In his business he saw this carnage every day and talked about it with juries. But for everyone else in the courtroom, the details were unsettling. At some point during his testimony, every single juror looked at Danny Padgitt and silently voted "Guilty."

Lucien Wilbanks began his cross pleasantly enough. The two had hooked up before in trials. He made the pathologist admit that some of his opinions might possibly be wrong, such as the size of the murder weapon and whether the assailant was right-handed. "I stated that these were probabilities," the doctor said patiently. I got the impression that he'd been grilled so many times nothing rattled him. Wilbanks poked and probed a bit, but he was careful not to revisit the damning evidence. The jury had heard enough of the cuts and gashes; it would be foolish to cover this ground again.

A second pathologist followed. Concurrent with the autopsy, he had made a thorough examination of the body and found several clues as to the identity of the killer. In the vaginal area, he found semen that matched perfectly with Danny Padgitt's blood. Under the nail of Rhoda's right index finger he had found a tiny piece of human skin. It too matched the defendant's blood type.

On cross-examination, Lucien Wilbanks asked him if he had personally examined Mr. Padgitt. No, he had not. Where on his body was Mr. Padgitt scraped or scratched or clawed in such a way?

"I did not examine him," the pathologist said.

"Did you examine photographs of him?"

"I did not."

"So if he lost some skin, you can't tell the jury where it came from, can you?"

"I'm afraid not."

After four hours of graphic testimony, everybody in the courtroom was exhausted. Judge Loopus sent the jury away with stern warnings about avoiding outside contact. It seemed overkill in light of the fact that they were being hidden in another town and guarded by police.

Baggy and I raced back to the office and typed frantically until almost ten. It was Tuesday, and Hardy liked to have the presses running no later than 11 P.M. On those rare weeks when there were no mechanical problems, he could run five thousand copies in less than three hours.

Hardy set the type as quickly as possible. There was no time for editing and proofreading, but I wasn't too concerned about that edition because Miss Callie was on the jury and wouldn't be able to catch our mistakes. Baggy was hitting the sauce as we finished up and couldn't wait to leave. I was about to head for my apartment when Ginger McClure strolled in the front door and said hello as if we were old friends. She was wearing tight jeans and a red blouse. She asked if I had anything to drink. Not at the office, but that wouldn't stop us.

We left the square in my Spitfire and drove to Quincy's, where I bought a six-pack of Schlitz. She wanted to see Rhoda's house one last time, from the road, not too close. As we headed that way I cautiously inquired about the two children. The report was mixed. Both were living with another sister—Ginger was quick to tell me she was recently divorced—and both were undergoing intense counseling. The little boy appeared to be almost normal, though he sometimes drifted off into prolonged periods of silence. The little girl was much worse. She had constant nightmares about her mother and had lost the ability to control her bladder. She was often found curled in a fetal position, sucking her fingers and groaning pitifully. The doctors were experimenting with various drugs.

Neither child would tell the family or the doctors how much they saw that night. "They saw their mother get raped and stabbed," she said, killing off the first beer. Mine was still half full.

The Deece home looked as if Mr. and Mrs. Deece had been asleep for days. We turned into the gravel driveway of what was once the happy little Kassellaw home. It was empty, dark, and had an abandoned look to it. There was a FOR SALE sign in the yard. The house was the only significant asset in Rhoda's small estate. The proceeds would all go to the children.

At Ginger's request, I cut the lights and turned off the engine. It was not a good idea because the neighbors were understandably jumpy. Plus, my Triumph Spitfire was the only one of its kind in Ford County and as such was naturally a suspicious vehicle.

She gently placed her hand on mine and said, "How did he get in the house?"

"They found some footprints at the patio door. It was probably unlocked." And during a long silence both of us replayed the attack, the rape, the knife, the children fleeing through the darkness, yelling for Mr. Deece to come save their mother.

"Were you close to her?" I asked, then I heard the distant approach of a vehicle.

"When we were kids, but not recently. She left home ten years ago."

"How often did you visit here?"

"Twice. I moved away too, to California. We sort of lost touch. After her husband died, we begged her to come back to Springfield, but she said she liked it here. Truth was, she and my mother never got along."

A pickup truck slowed on the road just behind us. I tried to act unconcerned, but I knew how dangerous things could be in such a dark part of the county. Ginger was staring at the house, lost in some horrible image, and seemed not to hear. Thankfully, the truck did not stop.

"Let's go," she said, squeezing my hand. "I'm scared."

When we drove away, I saw Mr. Deece crouching in the shadows of his garage, holding a shotgun. He was scheduled to be the last witness called by the State.

Ginger was staying at a local motel, but she did not want to go there. It was after midnight, our options were thin, so we drove to the Hocutt place, where I led her up the stairs, over the cats, and into my apartment.

"Don't get any ideas," she said as she kicked off her shoes and sat on the sofa. "I'm not in the mood."

"Neither am I," I lied.

Her tone was almost flippant, as though her mood

might change real soon and when it did then we could have a go at it. I was perfectly happy to wait.

I found colder beer in the kitchen and we settled into our places as if we might talk until sunrise. "Tell me about your family," she said.

It was not my best subject, but, for this lady, I could talk. "I'm an only child. My mother died when I was thirteen. My father lives in Memphis, in an old family house that he never leaves because both he and the house have a few loose boards. He has an office in the attic, and he stays there all day and night trading stocks and bonds. I don't know how well he trades, but I have a hunch he loses more than he gains. We speak by phone once a month."

"Are you wealthy?"

"No, my grandmother is wealthy. My mother's mother, BeeBee. She loaned me the money to buy the paper."

She thought about this as she sipped her beer. "There were three of us girls, two now. We were pretty wild growing up. My father went out for milk and eggs one night and never came home. My mother has tried twice more since then, can't seem to get it right. I'm divorced. My older sister is divorced. Rhoda is dead." She reached across with the bottle and tapped mine. "Here's to a couple of screwed-up families."

We drank to that.

Divorced, childless, wild, and very cute. I could spend time with Ginger.

She wanted to know about Ford County and its

characters—Lucien Wilbanks, the Padgitts, Sheriff Coley, and so on. I talked and talked and kept waiting for her mood to change.

It did not. Sometime after 2 A.M. she stretched out on the sofa, and I went to bed alone.

CHAPTER 16

Three of the Hocutts—Max, Wilma, and Gilma—were loitering around the garage under my apartment when Ginger and I made our exit a few hours later. I guess they wanted to meet her. They looked at her scornfully as I made cheerful introductions. I half-expected Max to say something ridiculous like, "We did not contemplate illicit sex when we leased this place to you." But nothing offensive was said, and we quickly drove to the office. She jumped in her car and disappeared.

The latest edition was stacked floor to ceiling in the front room. I grabbed a copy for a quick perusal. The headline was fairly restrained—DANNY PADGITT TRIAL BEGINS: JURY SEQUESTERED. There were no photos of the defendant. We had used enough of those already, and I wanted to save a big one for the following week when, hopefully, we could nail the little thug leaving the courthouse after receiving his death sentence. Baggy and I had filled the columns with the things we'd seen and heard during the first two days, and I was quite proud of our reporting. It was straightforward, factual, detailed, well written, and not the least bit lurid. The trial itself was big enough to carry the moment. And, truthfully, I had already learned my lesson about trying to sensationalize things. By 8 A.M. the courthouse and the square were blanketed with complimentary copies of the *Times.*

There were no preliminary skirmishes on Wednesday morning. At precisely 9 A.M. the jurors were led in and Ernie Gaddis called his next witness. His name was Chub Brooner, the longtime investigator for the Sheriff's department. According to both Baggy and Harry Rex, Brooner was famous for his incompetence.

To wake up the jury and captivate the rest of us, Gaddis produced the bloody white shirt Danny Padgitt was wearing the night he was arrested. It had not been washed; the splotches of blood were dark brown. Ernie gently waved it around the courtroom for all to see as he chatted with Brooner. It had been removed from the body of Danny Padgitt by a deputy named Grice, in the presence of Brooner and Sheriff Coley. Tests had revealed two types of blood—O Positive and B Positive. Further tests by the state crime lab matched the B Positive with the blood of Rhoda Kassellaw.

I watched Ginger as she looked at the shirt. After a

few minutes she looked away and began writing something. Not surprisingly, she looked even better her second day in the courtroom. I was very concerned about her moods.

The shirt was ripped across the front. Danny had cut himself when he crawled out of his wrecked truck and had received twelve stitches. Brooner did a passable job of explaining this to the jury. Ernie then pulled out an easel and placed on it two enlarged photographs of the footprints found on the patio of Rhoda's home. On the exhibit table he picked up the shoes Padgitt was wearing when he arrived at the jail. Brooner stumbled through testimony that should have been much easier, but the point was made that everything matched.

Brooner was terrified of Lucien Wilbanks and began stuttering at the first question. Lucien wisely ignored the fact that Rhoda's blood was found on Danny's shirt, and chose instead to hammer Brooner on the art and science of matching up footprints. The investigator's training had not been comprehensive, he finally admitted. Lucien zeroed in on a series of ridges on the heel of the right shoe, and Brooner couldn't locate them in the print. Because of weight and motion, a heel usually leaves a better print than the rest of the sole, according to Brooner's testimony on direct. Lucien harangued him to the point of confusing everyone, and I had to admit that I was skeptical of the footprints. Not that it mattered. There was plenty of other evidence.

"Was Mr. Padgitt wearing gloves when he was arrested?" Lucien asked.

"I don't know. I didn't arrest him."

"Well, you boys took his shirt and his shoes. Did you take any gloves?"

"Not to my knowledge."

"You've reviewed the entire evidence file, right, Mr. Brooner?"

"I have."

"In fact, as chief investigator, you're very familiar with every aspect of this case, aren't you?"

"Yes sir."

"Have you seen any reference to any gloves worn by or taken from Mr. Padgitt?"

"No."

"Good. Did you dust the crime scene for finger-prints?"

"Yes."

"Routine, isn't it?"

"Yes, always."

"And of course you fingerprinted Mr. Padgitt when he was arrested, right?"

"Yes."

"Good. How many of Mr. Padgitt's fingerprints did you find at the crime scene?"

"None."

"Not a single one, did you?"

"None."

With that, Lucien picked a good moment to sit down. It was difficult to believe that the murderer could enter the house, hide there for a while, rape and murder his victim, then escape without leaving behind fingerprints. But Chub Brooner did not inspire a lot of confidence. With him in charge of the investigation, there seemed an excellent chance that dozens of fingerprints could have been missed.

Judge Loopus called for the morning recess, and as the jurors stood to leave I made eye contact with Miss Callie. Her face exploded into one huge grin. She nodded, as if to say, "Don't worry about me."

We stretched our legs and whispered about what we had just heard. I was delighted to see so many people in the courtroom reading the *Times*. I walked to the bar and leaned down to speak to Ginger. "You doin' okay?" I asked.

"I just want to go home," she said softly.

"How about lunch?"

"You got it."

The State's last witness was Mr. Aaron Deece. He walked to the stand shortly before 11 A.M., and we braced for his recollection of that night. Ernie Gaddis led him through a series of questions designed to personalize Rhoda and her two children. They had lived next door for seven years, perfect neighbors, wonderful people. He missed them greatly, couldn't believe they were gone. At one point Mr. Deece wiped a tear from his eye.

This was completely irrelevant to the issues at hand, and Lucien gamely allowed it for a few minutes. Then he stood and politely said, "Your Honor, this is very touching, but it's really not admissible."

"Move along, Mr. Gaddis," Judge Loopus said.

Mr. Deece described the night, the time, the temperature, the weather. He heard the panicked voice of little Michael, age five, calling his name, crying for help. He found the children outside, in their pajamas, wet with dew, in shock from fear. He took them inside where his wife put blankets on them. He got his shoes and his guns and was flying out of the house when he saw Rhoda, stumbling toward him. She was naked and, except for her face, she was completely covered in blood. He picked her up, carried her to the porch, placed her on a swing.

Lucien was on his feet, waiting.

"Did she say anything?" Ernie asked.

"Your Honor, I object to this witness testifying to anything the victim said. It's clearly heresay."

"Your motion is on file, Mr. Wilbanks. We've had our debate in chambers, and it is on the record. You may answer the question, Mr. Deece."

Mr. Deece swallowed hard, inhaled and exhaled, and looked at the jurors. "Two or three times, she said, 'It was Danny Padgitt. It was Danny Padgitt.'"

For dramatic effect, Ernie let those bullets crack through the air, then ricochet around the courtroom while he pretended to look at some notes. "You ever met Danny Padgitt, Mr. Deece?"

"No sir."

"Had you ever heard his name before that night?"

"No sir."

"Did she say anything else?"

"The last thing she said was, 'Take care of my babies.'"

Ginger was touching her eyes with a tissue. Miss Callie was praying. Several of the jurors were looking at their feet.

He finished his story—he called the Sheriff's department; his wife had the children in a bedroom behind a locked door; he took a shower because he was covered with blood; the deputies showed up, did their investigating; the ambulance came and took away the body; he and his wife stayed with the children until around two in the morning, then rode with them to the hospital in Clanton. They stayed with them there until a relative arrived from Missouri.

There was nothing in his testimony that could be challenged or impeached, so Lucien Wilbanks declined a cross-examination. The State rested, and we broke for lunch. I drove Ginger to Karaway, to the only Mexican place I knew, and we ate enchiladas under an oak tree and talked about everything but the trial. She was subdued and wanted to leave Ford County forever.

I really wanted her to stay.

———

Lucien Wilbanks began his defense with a little pep talk about what a nice young man Danny Padgitt really was. He had finished high school with good grades, he worked long hours in the family's timber business, he dreamed of one day running his own company. He had no police record whatsoever. His only brush with the law had been one, just one, speeding ticket when he was sixteen years old.

Lucien's persuasive skills were reasonably well honed, but he was collapsing under the weight of the effort. It was impossible to make a Padgitt appear warm and cuddly. There was quite a bit of squirming in the courtroom, some smirks here and there. But we weren't the ones deciding the case. Lucien was talking to the jurors, looking them in the eyes, and no one knew if he and his client had already locked up a vote or two.

However, Danny was not a saint. Like most handsome young men he had discovered he enjoyed the company of ladies. He had met the wrong one, though, a woman who happened to be married to someone else. Danny was with her the night Rhoda Kassellaw was murdered.

"Listen to me!" he bellowed at the jurors. "My client did not kill Miss Kassellaw! At the time of this horrible murder, he was with another woman, in her home not far from the Kassellaw place. He has an airtight alibi."

This announcement sucked the air out of the courtroom, and for a long minute we waited for the next surprise. Lucien played the drama perfectly. "This woman, his lover, will be our first witness," he said.

They brought her in moments after Lucien finished his opening remarks. Her name was Lydia Vince. I whispered to Baggy and he said he'd never heard of her; didn't know any Vinces from out in Beech Hill.

There were a lot of whispers in the courtroom as folks tried to place her, and gauging from the frowns and puzzled looks and head shakes it appeared as though the woman was a complete unknown. Lucien's preliminary questions revealed that she was living in a rented house on Hurt Road back in March but was now living in Tupelo, that she and her husband were going through a divorce, that she had one child, that she grew up in Tyler County, and that she was currently unemployed. She was about thirty years old, somewhat attractive in a cheap way—short skirt, tight blouse over a big chest, bottle-blond hair—and she was utterly terrified of the proceedings.

She and Danny had been having an adulterous affair for about a year. I glanced at Miss Callie and was not surprised to see this was not sitting well.

On the night Rhoda was murdered, Danny was at her house. Malcolm Vince, her husband, was supposedly in Memphis, doing something with the boys, she really didn't know what. He was gone a lot in those days. She and Danny had sex twice and sometime around midnight he was preparing to leave when her husband's truck turned into the driveway. Danny sneaked out the rear door and disappeared.

The shock of a married woman admitting in open court that she had committed adultery was designed to convince the jury that she had to be telling the truth. No one, respectable or otherwise, would admit this. It would damage her reputation, if she cared about such things. It would certainly impact her divorce, perhaps jeopardize custody of her child. It might even allow her husband to sue Danny Padgitt for alienation of affection, though it was doubtful the jurors were thinking that far ahead.

Her answers to Lucien's questions were brief and very well rehearsed. She refused to look at the jurors or at her alleged former lover. Instead, she kept her eyes down and appeared to be looking at Lucien's shoes. Both the lawyer and the witness were careful not to venture outside the script. "She's lyin'," Baggy whispered loudly, and I agreed.

When the direct examination was over, Ernie Gaddis stood and walked deliberately to the podium, staring with great suspicion at this self-confessed adulteress. He kept his reading glasses on the tip of his nose, and looked above them with wrinkled brow and narrow eyes. Very much the professor who'd just caught a bad student cheating.

"Miss Vince, this house on Hurt Road. Who owned it?"

"Jack Hagel."

"How long did you live there?"

"About a year."

"Did you sign a lease?"

She hesitated for a split second too long, then said, "Maybe my husband did. I really don't remember."

"How much was the rent each month?"

"Three hundred dollars."

Ernie wrote down each answer with great effort, as though each detail was about to be diligently investigated and lies would be revealed.

"When did you leave this house?"

"I don't know, about two months ago."

"So how long did you live in Ford County?"

"I don't know, a couple of years."

"Did you ever register to vote in Ford County?"

"No."

"Did your husband?"

"No."

"What's his name again?"

"Malcolm Vince."

"Where does he live now?"

"I'm not sure. He moves around a lot. Last I heard he was somewhere around Tupelo."

"And y'all are getting a divorce now, right?"

"Yes."

"When did you file for divorce?"

Her eyes lifted quickly and she glanced at Lucien, who was listening hard but refusing to watch her. "We haven't actually filed papers yet," she said.

"I'm sorry, I thought you said you were going through a divorce."

"We've split, and we've both hired lawyers."

"And who is your attorney?"

"Mr. Wilbanks."

Lucien flinched, as if this was news to him. Ernie let it settle in, then continued, "Who is your husband's lawyer?"

"I can't remember his name."

"Is he suing you for divorce, or is it the other way around?"

"It's a mutual thing."

"How many other men were you sleeping with?"

"Just Danny."

"I see. And you live in Tupelo, right?"

"Right."

"You say you're unemployed, right?"

"For now."

"And you've separated from your husband?"

"I just said we've split."

"Where do you live over in Tupelo?"

"An apartment."

"How much is the rent?"

"Two hundred a month."

"And you live there with your child?"

"Yes."

"Does the child work?"

"The child is five years old."

"So how do you pay the rent and utilities?"

"I get by." No one could have possibly believed her answer.

"What kind of car do you drive?"

She hesitated again. It was the kind of question that required an answer that could be verified with a few phone calls. "A '68 Mustang."

"That's a nice car. When did you get it?"

Again, there was a paper trail here, and even Lydia, who wasn't bright, could see the trap. "Coupla months ago," she said, defiantly.

"Is the car titled in your name?"

"It is."

"Is the apartment lease in your name?"

"It is."

Paperwork, paperwork. She couldn't lie about it, and she certainly couldn't afford it. Ernie took some notes from Hank Hooten and studied them suspiciously.

"How long did you sleep with Danny Padgitt?"

"Fifteen minutes, usually."

In a tense courtroom, the answer provided scattered laughter. Ernie removed his glasses, rubbed them with the end of his tie, gave her a nasty grin, and rephrased the question. "Your affair with Danny Padgitt, how long did it last?"

"Almost a year."

"Where did you first meet him?"

"At the clubs, up at the state line."

"Did someone introduce the two of you?"

"I really don't remember. He was there, I was there, we had a dance. One thing led to another."

There was no doubt that Lydia Vince had spent many nights in many honky-tonks, and she'd never run from a new dance partner. Ernie needed just a few more lies that he could nail down.

He asked a series of questions about her background and her husband's—birth, education, marriage, employment, family. Names and dates and events that could be verified as true or false. She was for sale. The Padgitts had found a witness they could buy.

As we left the courtroom late that afternoon, I was confused and uneasy. I had been convinced for many months that Danny Padgitt killed Rhoda Kassellaw, and I still had no doubts. But the jury suddenly had something to hang itself with. A sworn witness had committed a dreadful act of perjury, but it was possible that a juror could have a reasonable doubt.

Ginger was more depressed than me, so we decided to get drunk. We bought burgers and fries and a case of beer and went to her small motel room where we ate and then drowned our fears and hatred of a corrupt judicial system. She said more than once that her family, fractured as it was, could not hold up if Danny Padgitt were let go. Her mother was not stable anyway, and a not-guilty verdict would push her over the cliff. What would they tell Rhoda's children one day?

We tried watching television, but nothing held our interest. We grew weary of worrying about the trial. As I was about to fall asleep, Ginger walked out of the bathroom naked, and the night took a turn for the better. We made love off and on until the alcohol prevailed and we fell asleep.

CHAPTER 17

Unknown to me—and there was no reason it should have been known to me because I was such a newcomer to the community and certainly not involved in judicial affairs, and besides I literally had my hands full of Ginger and for a few wonderful hours we lost interest in the trial—a secret meeting took place shortly after adjournment on Wednesday. Ernie Gaddis went to Harry Rex's office for a post-trial drink and both admitted they were sick over Lydia's testimony. They began making phone calls, and within an hour they had rounded up a group of lawyers they could trust, and a couple of politicians as well.

The opinion was unanimous that the Padgitts were in the process of wiggling out of what appeared to be a solid case against them. They had managed to find a witness they could bribe. Lydia had obviously been paid to concoct her story, and she was either too broke or too stupid to understand the risks of perjury. Regardless, she had given the jury a reason, albeit a weak one, to second-guess the prosecution.

An acquittal in such an open-and-shut case would infuriate the town and mock the court system. A hung jury would send a similar message—justice could be bought in Ford County. Ernie, Harry Rex, and the other lawyers worked hard every day manipulating the system on behalf of their clients, but the rules were applied fairly. The system worked because the judges and jurors were impartial and unbiased. To allow Lucien Wilbanks and the Padgitts to corrupt the process would cause irreparable damage.

There was a consensus that a hung jury was entirely possible. As a believable witness, Lydia Vince left much to be desired, but the jurors were not as savvy about fabricated testimony and crooked clients. The lawyers agreed that Fargarson, "the crippled boy," appeared hostile to the prosecution. After two full days and almost fifteen hours of watching the jurors, the lawyers felt they could read them.

Mr. John Deere also had them worried. His real name was Mo Teale and he'd been a mechanic down at the tractor place for over twenty years. He was a simple man with a limited wardrobe. Late Monday afternoon when the jury was finally selected and Judge Loopus sent them home to hurriedly pack for the bus, Mo had simply loaded up his week's supply of work uniforms. Each morning he marched into the jury box wearing a bright yellow shirt with green trim and green pants with

yellow trim, as if he was ready for another vigorous day
of pulling wrenches.

Mo sat with his arms crossed and frowned whenever
Ernie Gaddis was on his feet. His body language terrified the prosecution.

Harry Rex thought it was important to find Lydia's
estranged husband. If they were in fact going through a
divorce, it was more than likely not an amicable one. It
was difficult to believe she was having an affair with
Danny Padgitt, but at the same time it seemed likely
that the woman was no stranger to extramarital activity.
The husband might have testimony that could severely
discredit Lydia's.

Ernie wanted to dig into her private life. He wanted
to create doubt about her finances so he could yell at
the jury, "How can she live so comfortably when she's
unemployed and going through a divorce?"

"Because she got twenty-five thousand dollars from
the Padgitts," one of the lawyers said. Speculation
about the amount of the bribe became a running debate as the night wore on.

The search for Malcolm Vince began with Harry
Rex and two others calling every lawyer within five
counties. Around 10 P.M. they found a lawyer in
Corinth, two hours away, who said he had met with a
Malcolm Vince once about a divorce, but had not been
retained. Mr. Vince was living in a trailer somewhere
out in the boondocks near the Tishomingo County line.
He could not remember where he worked, but he was
sure he had written it down in his file at the office. The

District Attorney himself got on the phone and coaxed the lawyer back to the office.

At eight o'clock the next morning, about the time I was leaving Ginger at the motel, Judge Loopus readily agreed to order a subpoena for Malcolm Vince. Twenty minutes later, a Corinth city policeman stopped a fork-lift in a warehouse and informed its operator that a sub-poena had just been issued for his appearance in a murder trial over in Ford County.

"What the hell for?" Mr. Vince demanded.

"I'm just following orders," the policeman said.

"What am I supposed to do?"

"You got two choices, pal," explained the cop. "Stay here with me till they come get you, or we can leave now and get it over with." Malcolm's boss told him to leave and hurry back.

After a ninety-minute delay, the jury was brought in. Mr. John Deere was as spiffy as ever, but the rest were beginning to look tired. It seemed like the trial had been going on for a month.

Miss Callie searched me out and gave me a restrained grin, not one of her spectacular day-brighteners. She was still clutching a small New Testament.

Ernie rose and informed the court that he had no further questions for Lydia Vince. Lucien said he was through with her too. Ernie said he had a rebuttal wit-ness he would like to call out of order. Lucien Wilbanks objected and they haggled over it at the bench. When Lucien learned who the witness was, he became visibly upset. A good sign.

Evidently Judge Loopus was concerned about a bad verdict as well. He ruled against the defense, and a thoroughly bewildered Malcolm Vince was called into the packed courtroom to testify. Ernie had spent less than ten minutes with him in a back room, so he was as unprepared as he was confused.

Ernie started slow, with the basics—name, address, employment, recent family history. Malcolm somewhat reluctantly admitted being married to Lydia and shared her desire to escape from the union. He said he had seen neither his wife nor his child in about a month. His recent employment history was spotty at best, but he tried to send her $50 a week to support the child.

He knew she was unemployed but living in a nice apartment. "You're not paying for her apartment?" Ernie asked with great suspicion, glancing warily at the jury.

"No sir, I am not."

"Is her family paying for her apartment?"

"Her family couldn't pay for one night in a motel," Malcolm said with no small amount of satisfaction.

Once excused, Lydia had left the courtroom and was probably in the process of fleeing the country. Her act was complete, her performance over, her fee collected. She would never again set foot in Ford County. It's doubtful her presence would have inhibited Malcolm's testimony, but her absence gave him free rein to take all the cheap shots he wanted.

"You're not close to her family?" Ernie asked, a throwaway question.

"Most of them are in jail."

"I see. She testified yesterday that a couple of months ago she bought a 1968 Ford Mustang. Did you help her with this purchase?"

"I did not."

"Any idea how this unemployed woman could make this purchase?" Ernie asked, glancing at Danny Padgitt.

"No."

"Do you know if she's made any other unusual purchases lately?"

Malcolm looked at the jury, saw some friendly faces, and said, "Yeah, she bought a new color television for herself and a new motorcycle for her brother."

It appeared as if everyone at the defense table had stopped breathing. The strategy over there had been to sneak Lydia in quietly, let her tell her lies, verify the alibi, get her off the stand, then push the case to a verdict before she could be discredited. She had known very few people in the county and now lived an hour away.

The strategy was unraveling with disastrous results, and the entire courtroom could see and feel the tension between Lucien and his client.

"Do you know a man by the name of Danny Padgitt?" Ernie asked.

"Never heard of him," Malcolm said.

"Your wife testified yesterday that she had been having an affair with him for almost a year."

It's rare to see an unsuspecting husband confronted with such news in such a public manner, but Malcolm seemed to handle it well. "That so?" he said.

"Yes sir. She testified the affair ended about two months ago."

"Well, sir, I'll tell you—that's kinda hard to believe."

"And why is that?"

Malcolm was squirming, suddenly interested in his feet. "Well, it's really kinda personal, you know," he said.

"Yes, Mr. Vince, I'm sure it is. But sometimes personal matters have to be discussed in open court. A man is on trial here, charged with murder. This is serious business, and we need to know the truth."

Malcolm swung his left leg over his right knee and scratched his chin for a few seconds. "Well, sir, it's like this. We stopped havin' sex about two years ago. That's why we're gettin' a divorce, you know."

"Any particular reason you stopped having sex?" Ernie asked as he held his breath.

"Yes sir. She told me she hated sex with me, said it made her sick to her stomach. Said she preferred sex with, you know, other ladies."

Though he knew what answer was coming, Ernie managed to appear sufficiently shocked. Along with everyone else. He backed away from the podium and huddled with Hank Hooten, just a brief break to allow the jurors to fully absorb the blow. Finally, he said, "No further questions, Your Honor."

———

Lucien approached Malcolm Vince as if he were staring at a loaded gun. He picked around the edges for a few minutes. According to Baggy, a good trial lawyer never asks a question unless he knows the answer, especially with a witness as dangerous as Malcolm Vince. Lucien was a good lawyer, and he had no idea what Malcolm might blurt out.

He admitted he had no affection for Lydia, that he couldn't wait to get through with the divorce, that the last few years with her had not been pleasant, and so on. Typical divorce chatter. He remembered hearing of the Kassellaw murder the next morning. He'd been out the night before and returned home very late. Lucien scored a very weak point by proving that Lydia was indeed alone that night, as she had testified.

But it mattered little. The jurors and the rest of us were still struggling with the enormity of Lydia's sins.

After a long recess, Lucien rose slowly and addressed the Court. "Your Honor, the defense has no other witnesses. However, my client wishes to testify. I want it stated clearly in the record that he will testify against my advice."

"Duly noted," Loopus said.

"A very stupid mistake. Unbelievable," Baggy whispered loud enough for half the courtroom to hear.

Danny Padgitt jumped up and strutted to the witness stand. His attempt at smiling came across as nothing but a smirk. His attempt at confidence came across as cockiness. He was sworn to tell the truth, but no one expected to hear it.

"Why do you insist on testifying?" was Lucien's first

question, and the courtroom was still and silent.

"Because I want these good people to hear what really happened," he answered, looking at the jurors.

"Then tell them," Lucien said, waving his hand at the jury.

His version of events was wonderfully creative because there was no one to rebut him. Lydia was gone, Rhoda was dead. He began by saying that he had spent a few hours with his girlfriend, Lydia Vince, who lived less than half a mile from Rhoda Kassellaw. He knew exactly where Rhoda lived because he had visited her on several occasions. She wanted a serious romance but he'd been too occupied with Lydia. Yes, he and Rhoda had had intimate relations on two occasions. They'd met at the clubs at the state line and spent many hours drinking and dancing. She was hot and loose and known to sleep around.

As insult was added to injury, Ginger lowered her head and covered her ears. It was not missed by the jury.

He didn't believe Lydia's husband's garbage about her homosexual tendencies; the woman enjoyed the intimacy of men. Malcolm was lying so he could win custody of their child.

Padgitt was not a bad witness, but then he was testifying for his life. Every answer was quick, there were too many fake smiles toward the jury box, his narrative was clean and neat and fit too nicely together. I listened to him and watched the jurors and I didn't see much sympathy. Fargarson, the crippled boy, appeared just as skeptical as he had with every other witness. Mr. John Deere still sat with his arms wrapped across his chest, frowning. Miss Callie had no use for Padgitt, but then she would probably send him to prison for the adultery as quickly as for the murder.

Lucien kept it brief. His client had plenty of rope with which to hang himself, no sense making it easier for the State. When Lucien sat down he glared at the elder Padgitts as if he truly hated them. Then he braced himself for what was about to come.

Cross-examining such a guilty criminal is a prosecutor's dream. Ernie deliberately walked to the exhibit table and lifted Danny's bloody shirt. "Exhibit number eight," he said to the court reporter, holding it up for the jury to see again.

"Where'd you buy this shirt, Mr. Padgitt?"

Danny froze, uncertain as to whether he should deny it was his, or admit ownership, or try and recall where he bought the damned thing.

"You didn't steal it, did you?" Ernie roared at him.

"I did not."

"Then answer my question, and please try to remember you're under oath. Where did you buy this shirt?" As Ernie talked he held the shirt in front of him with his fingertips, as if the blood was still wet and might spot his suit.

"Over in Tupelo, I think. I really don't remember. It's just a shirt."

"How long have you owned it?"

Another pause. How many men can remember when they bought a particular shirt?

"A year or so, maybe. I don't keep notes on clothes."

"Neither do I," Ernie said. "When you were in bed with Lydia that night, had you removed this shirt?"

A very cautious, "Yes."

"Where was it while the two of you were, uh, having relations?"

"On the floor, I guess."

Now that it was firmly established that the shirt was his, Ernie was free to slaughter the witness. He pulled out the report from the state crime lab, read it to Danny, and asked him how his own blood came to be stained on the shirt. This led to a discussion about his driving abilities, his tendency to speed, the type of vehicle, and the fact that he was legally drunk when he flipped his truck. With Ernie pounding away, I doubt if a case of driving under the influence had ever sounded so deadly. Not surprisingly, Danny had a thin skin and began to bristle at Ernie's pointed and sardonic questioning.

On to Rhoda's bloodstains. If he was in bed with Lydia, with the shirt on the floor, how in the world did Rhoda's blood find its way from her bedroom to Lydia's, a half mile away?

It was a conspiracy, Danny said, advancing a new theory and digging a hole he would never get out of. Too much time alone in a jail cell can be dangerous for a guilty criminal. Well, he tried to explain, someone either stained his shirt with Rhoda's blood, a theory that lightened up the crowd considerably, or, it was more likely that some mysterious person who examined the shirt was simply lying, all in an effort to convict him. Ernie had a field day with both scenarios, but he landed his heaviest blows with a series of brutal questions about why Danny, who certainly had the money to hire the best lawyers around, didn't hire his own expert to come to court and explain the tainted blood exams to the jury.

Perhaps no expert was found because no expert could reach the ridiculous conclusions Padgitt wanted.

Same for the semen. If Danny had been producing it over at Lydia's, how could it arrive at Rhoda's? No problem—it was part of a broad conspiracy to nail him for the crime. The lab reports were fabricated; the police work was faulty. Ernie hammered him until we were all exhausted.

At twelve-thirty, Lucien stood and suggested a break for lunch. "I'm not done!" Ernie yelled across the courtroom. He wanted to finish the annihilation before Lucien could get his hands on his client and try to rehabilitate him, a task that seemed impossible. Padgitt was on the ropes, battered and gasping for air, and Ernie was not going to a neutral corner.

"Continue," Judge Loopus said, and Ernie suddenly shouted at Padgitt, "What did you do with the knife?"

The question startled everyone, especially the witness, who jerked backward and quickly said, "I, uh—" then went silent.

"You what! Come on, Mr. Padgitt, tell us what you did with the knife, the murder weapon."

Danny shook his head fiercely and looked too scared to speak. "What knife?" he managed to say. He could not have looked guiltier if the knife had dropped out of his pocket onto the floor.

"The knife you used on Rhoda Kassellaw."

"It wasn't me."

Like a slow and cruel executioner, Ernie took a long pause and huddled with Hank Hooten again. He then picked up the autopsy report and asked Danny if he remembered the testimony of the first pathologist. Was his report also a part of this conspiracy? Danny wasn't sure how to answer. All of the evidence was being used against him, so, yes, he figured it must be bogus as well.

And the piece of his skin found under her fingernail, that was part of the conspiracy? And his own semen? And on and on; Ernie hammered away. Occasionally, Lucien would glance over his shoulder at Danny's father with a look that said, "I told you so."

Danny's presence on the stand allowed Ernie to once more trot out all the evidence, and the impact was devastating. His weak protests that everything was tainted by a conspiracy sounded ridiculous, even laughable. Watching him get thoroughly decimated before the jury was quite gratifying. The good guys were winning. The jury seemed primed to pull out rifles and form a firing squad.

Ernie tossed his legal pad on his table and appeared ready for lunch, finally. He jammed both hands into his front pockets, glared at the witness, and said, "Under oath, you're telling this jury you didn't rape and murder Rhoda Kassellaw?"

"I didn't do it."

"You didn't follow her home from the state line that Saturday night?"

"No."

"You didn't sneak in her patio door?"

"No."

"And hide in her closet until she put her children to bed?"

"No."

"And you didn't attack her when she came in to put on her night clothes?"

"No."

Lucien stood and said angrily, "Objection, Your Honor, Mr. Gaddis is testifying here."

"Overruled!" Loopus snapped at the defense table. The Judge wanted a fair trial. To counteract all the lying done by the defense, the prosecution was being allowed considerable freedom in describing the murder scene.

"You didn't blindfold her with a scarf?"

Padgitt was continually shaking his head as the narrative approached its climax.

"And cut off her panties with your knife?"

"No."

"And you didn't rape her in her own bed, with her two little children asleep not far away?"

"I did not."

"And you didn't wake them with your noise?"

"No."

Ernie walked as close to the witness chair as the Judge would allow, and he looked sadly at his jury. Then he turned to Danny and said, "Michael and Teresa ran to check on their mother, didn't they, Mr. Padgitt?"

"I don't know."

"And they found you on top of her, didn't they?"

"I wasn't there."

"Rhoda heard their voices, didn't she? Did they yell at you, beg you to get off?"

"I wasn't there."

"And Rhoda did what any mother would do—she yelled for them to run, didn't she, Mr. Padgitt?"

"I wasn't there."

"You weren't there!" Ernie bellowed, and the walls seemed to shake. "Your shirt was there, your footprints were there, you left your semen there! You think this jury is stupid, Mr. Padgitt?"

The witness kept shaking his head. Ernie walked slowly to his chair and pulled it from under the table. As he was about to sit, he said, "You're a rapist. You're a murderer. And you're a liar, aren't you, Mr. Padgitt?"

Lucien was up and yelling. "Objection, Your Honor. This is enough."

"Sustained. Any further questions, Mr. Gaddis?"

"No, Your Honor, the State is finished with this witness."

"Any redirect, Mr. Wilbanks?"

"No, Your Honor."

"The witness may step down." Danny slowly got to

his feet. Long gone was the smirk, the swagger. His face was red with anger and wet with sweat.

As he was about to step out of the witness box and return to the defense table, he suddenly turned to the jury and said something that stunned the courtroom. His face wrinkled into pure hatred, and he jabbed his right index finger into the air. "You convict me," he said, "and I'll get every damned one of you."

"Bailiff!" Judge Loopus said as he grabbed for his gavel. "That's enough, Mr. Padgitt."

"Every damned one of you!" Danny repeated, louder. Ernie jumped to his feet, but could think of nothing to say. And why should he? The defendant was strangling himself. Lucien was on his feet, equally uncertain about what to do. Two deputies raced forward and shoved Padgitt toward the defense table. As he walked away he glared at the jurors as if he might just throw a grenade right then.

When things settled, I realized my heart was pounding with excitement. Even Baggy was too stunned to speak.

"Let's break for lunch," His Honor said, and we fled the courtroom. I was no longer hungry. I felt like racing to my apartment and taking a shower.

CHAPTER 18

The trial resumed at 3 P.M. All the jurors were present; the Padgitts hadn't knocked one off during lunch. Miss Callie gave me a grin, but her heart was not in it.

Judge Loopus explained to the jury that it was now time for the closing arguments, after which he would read to them his formal instructions, and they should have the case to decide in a couple of hours or so. They listened carefully, but I'm sure they were still reeling from the shock of being so flagrantly intimidated. The entire town was reeling. The jurors were a sampling of us, the rest of the community, and to threaten them was to do the same to everyone.

Ernie went first, and within minutes the bloody shirt was back in play. He was careful, though, not to overdo it. The jurors understood. They knew the evidence well.

The District Attorney was thorough but surprisingly brief. As he made his last appeal for a verdict of guilty, we watched the faces of the jurors. I saw no sympathy for the defendant. Fargarson, the crippled boy, was actually nodding as he followed along with Ernie. Mr. John Deere had uncrossed his arms and was listening to every word.

Lucien was even briefer, but then he had far less to work with. He began by addressing his client's final words to the jury. He apologized for his behavior. He blamed it on the pressure of the moment. Imagine, he asked the jurors, being twenty-four years old and facing either life in prison or, worse, the gas chamber. The stress on his young client—he always referred to him as "Danny" as if he was an innocent little boy—was so enormous that he was concerned about his mental stability.

Since he could not pursue the goofy conspiracy theory advanced by his client, and since he knew better than to dwell on the evidence, he spent half an hour or so praising the heroes who'd written our Constitution and the Bill of Rights. The way Lucien interpreted the presumption of innocence and the requirement that the State prove its case beyond a reasonable doubt made me wonder how any criminal ever got convicted.

The State had the chance for a rebuttal; the defense did not. So Ernie got the last word. He ignored the evidence and did not mention the defendant, but chose instead to talk about Rhoda. Her youth and beauty, her simple life out in Beech Hill, the death of her husband, and the challenge of raising two small children alone.

This was very effective, and the jurors were absorbing every word. "Let's not forget about her," was Ernie's refrain. A polished orator, he saved the best for last.

"And let's not forget about her children," he said as he looked into the eyes of the jurors. "They were there when she died. What they saw was so horrible that they will be forever scarred. They have a voice here in this courtroom, and their voice belongs to you."

Judge Loopus read his instructions to the jury, then sent them back to begin their deliberations. It was after 5 P.M., a time when the shops around the square were closed and the merchants and their customers were long gone. Traffic was normally light, parking was easy.

But not when a jury is out!

Much of the crowd lingered on the courthouse lawn, smoking, gossiping, predicting how long a verdict would take. Others crowded into the cafés for a late coffee or an early dinner. Ginger followed me to my office where we sat on the balcony and watched the activity around the courthouse. She was emotionally wasted and wanted to do nothing but get out of Ford County.

"How well do you know Hank Hooten?" she asked at one point.

"Never met him. Why?"

"He caught me during lunch, said he knew Rhoda well, said he knew for a fact that she was not sleeping around, especially not with Danny Padgitt. I told him I did not believe for an instant that she was seeing that scumbag."

"Did he say he dated her?" I asked.

"He wouldn't say, but I got the impression he did. When we were going through her things, a week or so after the funeral, I found his name and phone number in her address book."

"You've met Baggy," I said.

"Yes."

"Well, Baggy's been around forever, thinks he knows it all. He told me Monday when the trial started that Rhoda and Hank were seeing each other. He said Hank's been through a couple of wives, likes to be known as a ladies' man."

"So he's not married?"

"I don't think so. I'll ask Baggy."

"I guess I should feel better knowing my sister was sleeping with a lawyer."

"Why would that make you feel better?"

"I don't know."

She'd kicked off her heels and her short skirt was even higher up her thighs. I began to rub them, and my thoughts drifted away from the trial.

But only for a moment. There was a commotion around the front door of the courthouse, and I heard someone yell something about a "verdict."

————

After deliberating for less than one hour, the jury was ready. When the lawyers and spectators were in place, Judge Loopus told a bailiff, "Bring 'em in."

"Guilty as hell," Baggy whispered to me as the door

opened and Fargarson came limping out first. "Quick verdicts are always guilty."

For the record, Baggy had predicted a hung jury, but I didn't remind him of that, not then anyway.

The foreman handed a folded sheet of paper to the bailiff, who then gave it to the Judge. Loopus examined it for a long time, then leaned down close to his microphone. "Would the defendant please rise," he said. Both Padgitt and Lucien stood, slowly and awkwardly, as if the firing squad was taking aim.

Judge Loopus read, "As to count one, the charge of rape, we the jury find the defendant, Danny Padgitt, guilty. As to count two, the charge of capital murder, we the jury find the defendant, Danny Padgitt, guilty."

Lucien didn't flinch and Padgitt tried not to. He looked at the jurors with as much venom as he could convey, but he was getting more of it in return.

"You may be seated," His Honor said, then turned to the jury. "Ladies and gentlemen, thank you for your service so far. This completes the guilt-or-innocence phase of the trial. Now we move to the capital phase in which you will be asked to decide whether this defendant gets a death sentence or life in prison. You will now return to your hotel, and we will recess until nine in the morning. Thank you and good night."

It was over so quickly that most of the spectators didn't move for a moment. They led Padgitt out, in handcuffs this time, and his family seemed completely bewildered. Lucien had no time to chat with them.

Baggy and I went to the office where he began

typing with a fury. The deadline was days away, but we wanted to capture the moment. Typically, though, he faded after half an hour when the sour mash called. It was almost dark when Ginger returned, in tight jeans, tight shirt, hair down, a look that said "Take me somewhere."

We stopped at Quincy's again, where I bought another six-pack for the road, and with the top down and the warm muggy air blowing by us, we headed for Memphis, ninety minutes away.

She said little, and I didn't poke around. She had been forced by her family to attend the trial. She hadn't asked for this nightmare. Luckily, she'd found me for a little fun.

I'll never forget that night. Racing the dark empty backroads, drinking a cold beer, holding hands with a beautiful lady who'd come looking for me, one I'd already slept with and was sure to do so again.

Our sweet little romance had but a few hours left. I could almost count them. Baggy thought the penalty phase would take less than a day, so the trial would end tomorrow, Friday. Ginger couldn't wait to leave Clanton and shake the dust off her shoes, and of course there was no way I could leave with her. I'd checked an atlas—Springfield, Missouri, was far away, at least a six-hour drive. Commuting would be difficult, though I'd certainly try if she wanted me to.

But something told me Ginger would vanish from my life as quickly as she had appeared. I was sure she had a boyfriend or two back home, so I wouldn't be wel-

come. And if she saw me in Springfield she would be reminded of Ford County and its horrible memories.

I squeezed her hand and vowed to make the most of
those last few hours.

In Memphis, we headed for the tall buildings by the
river. The most famous restaurant in town was a rib
place called the Rendezvous, a landmark owned by a
family of Greeks. Almost all of the good food in Memphis was cooked by either Greeks or Italians.

Downtown Memphis in 1970 was not a safe place. I
parked in a garage and we hustled across an alley to the
door of the Rendezvous. Smoke from its pits boiled
from vents and hung like thick fog among the buildings.
It was the most delicious smell I had ever encountered,
and I, like most other patrons, was famished by the time
we walked down a flight of stairs and entered the
restaurant.

Thursdays were slow. We waited five minutes, and
when they called my name we followed a waiter as he
zigzagged around tables, through smaller rooms,
deeper into the caverns. He winked at me and gave us a
table for two in a dark corner. We ordered ribs and beer
and groped each other while we waited.

The guilty verdict was a huge relief. Anything else
would've been a civic disaster, and Ginger would've fled
town and never looked back. She would flee tomorrow,
but I had her for the moment. We drank to the verdict.
For Ginger it meant justice had indeed prevailed. For
me, it meant that too, but it also gave us another night
together.

She ate little, which allowed me to finish my slab of ribs and go to work on hers. I told her about Miss Callie and the lunches on her porch, about her remarkable children, and her background. Ginger said she adored Miss Callie, same as she adored the other eleven.

Such admiration would not last long.

As I had expected, my father was holed up in the attic, which is what he had always called his office. It was really the top floor of a Victorian tower at the front corner of our shabby and ill-maintained home in midtown Memphis. Ginger wanted to see it, and in the darkness it looked much more imposing than in daylight. It was in a wonderful, shady old neighborhood filled with declining homes owned by declining families surviving gamely in genteel poverty.

"What does he do up there?" she asked. We were sitting in my car, with the engine off, at the curb. Mrs. Duckworth's ancient schnauzer was barking at us four doors down.

"I told you already. He trades stocks and bonds."

"At night?"

"He's doing market research. He never comes out."

"And he loses money?"

"He certainly doesn't make any."

"Are we going to say hello?"

"No. It'll just piss him off."

"When was the last time you saw him?"

"Three, four months ago." Visiting with my father was the last thing I wanted to do at that moment. I was consumed with lust and anxious to get started. We drove out of the city, into the suburbs, and found a Holiday Inn next to the interstate.

CHAPTER 19

Friday morning, in the hallway outside the courtroom, Esau Ruffin found me and had a pleasant surprise. Three of his sons, Al, Max, and Bobby (Alberto, Massimo, and Roberto), were with him, anxious to say hello to me. I had spoken to all three a month earlier when I was doing the feature on Miss Callie and her children. We shook hands and exchanged pleasantries. They politely thanked me for my friendship with their mother, and for the kind words I'd written about their family. They were as soft-spoken, pleasant, and as articulate as Miss Callie.

They had arrived late the night before to give her moral support. Esau had talked to her once all week—each juror had been given one phone call—and she was holding up well but worried about her blood pressure.

We chatted for a moment as the crowd pushed toward the courtroom and walked in together. They sat directly behind me. A few moments later when Miss Callie took her seat, she looked at me and saw her three sons. The smile was like a bolt of lightning. The fatigue around her eyes vanished immediately.

During the trial, I had seen in her face a certain amount of pride. She was sitting where no black person had ever sat, shoulder to shoulder with fellow citizens, judging a white person for the first time in Ford County. I'd also had hints of the anxiety that comes with venturing into untested waters.

Now that her sons were there to watch, pride filled her face, and there was no evidence of fear. She sat a bit straighter, and though she'd missed nothing in the courtroom so far, her eyes darted everywhere, anxious to capture what was coming and finish her task.

Judge Loopus explained to the jurors that in the penalty phase the State would offer evidence of aggravating circumstances in support of its request for the death penalty. The defense would offer mitigating proof. He did not expect it to take long. It was Friday; the trial had already lasted forever; the jurors and everybody else in Clanton wanted Padgitt shipped off so life could return to normal.

Ernie Gaddis correctly gauged the mood in the courtroom. He thanked the jurors for their proper verdict of guilty and confessed that he felt no further testimony was necessary. The crime was so heinous that nothing more aggravating could be added to it. He asked the jurors to remember the graphic photos of Rhoda in the swing on Mr. Deece's front porch, and the pathologist's testimony about her vicious wounds and how she died. And her children, please don't forget her children.

As if anybody could.

He delivered an impassioned plea for the death penalty. He gave a brief history of why we, as good solid Americans, believed so strongly in it. He explained why it was a deterrent and a punishment. He quoted Scripture.

In almost thirty years of prosecuting crimes in six counties, he had never seen a case that so mightily begged for the death penalty. Watching the faces of the jurors, I was convinced he was about to get what he asked for.

He wrapped it up by reminding the jurors that each had been selected on Monday after promising that they could follow the law. He read them the law enacting the death penalty. "The State of Mississippi has proven its case," he said, closing the thick green law book. "You have found Danny Padgitt guilty of rape and murder. The law now calls for the death penalty. You are duty bound to deliver it."

Ernie's spellbinding performance lasted for fifty-one minutes—I was trying to record everything—and when he finished I knew the jury would hang Padgitt not once but twice.

According to Baggy, in a capital case the defendant, after protesting his innocence throughout the trial and being nailed by the jury, usually took the stand and said he was very sorry for whatever crime he'd been denying all week. "They beg and cry," Baggy had said. "It's quite a show."

But Padgitt's disaster the day before precluded him from getting near the jury. Lucien called to the witness stand his mother, Lettie Padgitt. She was a fiftyish woman with pleasant features and short graying hair, and she wore a black dress as if she was already mourning the death of her son. Led by Lucien, she unsteadily began testimony that seemed scripted down to every pause in her cadence. There was Danny the little boy, fishing every day after school, breaking his leg falling from a tree house, and winning the spelling bee in the fourth grade. He was never any trouble in those days, none at all. In fact, Danny had caused no trouble at all growing up, a real joy. His two older brothers were always into something, but not Danny.

The testimony was so silly and self-serving that it bordered on ridiculous. But there were three mothers on the jury—Miss Callie, Mrs. Barbara Baldwin, and Maxine Root—and Lucien was aiming for one of them. He needed just one.

Not surprisingly, Mrs. Padgitt was soon in tears. She would never believe that her son had committed such a terrible crime, but if the jury felt so, then she would try and accept it. But why take him away? Why kill her little boy? What would the world gain if he were put to death?

Her pain was real. Her emotions were raw and difficult to watch, to sit through. Any human being would feel sympathy for a mother about to lose a child. She finally collapsed and Lucien left her sobbing on the witness stand. What began as a stilted performance ended in a gut-wrenching plea that forced most of the jurors to lower their eyes and study the floor.

Lucien said he had no other witnesses. He and Ernie made brief final summations, and by 11 A.M. the jury once again had the case.

———

Ginger disappeared into the crowd. I went to the office and waited, and when she didn't show I walked across the square to Harry Rex's office. He sent his secretary out for sandwiches and we ate in his cluttered conference room. Like most lawyers in Clanton, he'd spent the entire week in the courtroom watching a case that meant nothing to him financially.

"Is your gal gonna stick?" he asked with a mouth full of turkey and Swiss.

"Miss Callie?" I asked.

"Yeah. She okay with the gas chamber?"

"I have no idea. We haven't discussed it."

"She's got us worried, along with that damned crippled boy."

Harry Rex had quietly involved himself in the case in such a way that one would think he was working for Ernie Gaddis and the State. But he wasn't the only lawyer in town secretly abetting the prosecution.

"It took them less than sixty minutes to find him guilty," I said. "Isn't that a good sign?"

"Maybe, but jurors do strange things when it's time to sign a death warrant."

"So? Then he'll get life. From what I hear about Parchman, life there would be worse than the gas chamber."

"Life ain't life, Willie," he said, wiping his face with a paper towel.

I put my sandwich down while he took another bite.

"What is life?" I asked.

"Ten years, maybe less."

I tried to understand this. "You mean a life sentence in Mississippi is ten years?"

"You got it. After ten years, less with good time, a murderer sent to prison for life is eligible for parole. Insane, don't you think?"

"But why—"

"Don't try and understand it, Willie, it's just the law. Been on the books for fifty years. And what's worse is the jury doesn't know it. Can't tell 'em. Want some coleslaw?"

I shook my head.

"Our distinguished Supreme Court has said that the jury, if it knows how light a life sentence really is, might be more inclined to give the death penalty. Thus, it's unfair to the defendant."

"Life is ten years," I mumbled to myself. In Mississippi, the liquor stores are locked up on Election Day, as if the voters would otherwise get drunk and elect the wrong people. Another unbelievable law.

"You got it," Harry Rex said, then finished his

sandwich with one huge bite. He pulled an envelope off a shelf, opened it, then slid a large black-and-white photo across to me. "Busted, buddy," he said with a laugh.

It was a photo of me, making my quick exit from Ginger's room at the motel on Thursday morning. I looked tired, hungover, guilty of something, but also oddly satisfied.

"Who took this?" I asked.

"One of my boys. He was working on a divorce case, saw your little Communist car pull in that night, decided to have some fun."

"He wasn't the only one."

"She's a hot one. He tried to shoot through the curtains, but couldn't get an angle."

"Shall I autograph it for you?"

"Just keep it."

———

After three hours of deliberation, the jury slipped a note to Judge Loopus. They were deadlocked and making little progress. He called things to order, and we raced across the street.

If the jury could not reach a unanimous verdict for the death penalty, then, by law, the judge imposed a life sentence.

Fear pervaded the crowd as we waited for the jurors. Something was going wrong back there. Had the Padgitts finally found their mark?

Miss Callie was stonefaced, a look I'd never seen.

Mrs. Barbara Baldwin had obviously been crying. Several of the men gave the impression that their fistfight had just been broken up, and that they were anxious to resume the brawl.

The foreman stood and very nervously explained to His Honor that the jury was divided and had made absolutely no progress in the last hour. He was not optimistic about a unanimous verdict, and all were ready to go home.

Judge Loopus then asked each juror if he or she thought a unanimous verdict could be reached. They unanimously said no.

I could feel the anger rise among the crowd. People were fidgeting and whispering, and this certainly didn't help the jurors.

Judge Loopus then delivered what Baggy later described as the "dynamite charge," an off-the-cuff lecture about following the law and keeping promises made during jury selection. It was a stern and lengthy admonishment, loaded with no small measure of desperation.

It didn't work. Two hours later, a stunned courtroom listened as Judge Loopus quizzed the jurors again, with the same result. He grudgingly thanked them and sent them home.

When they were gone, he called Danny Padgitt forward, and on the record, gave him a tongue lashing that made my skin crawl. He called him a rapist, murderer, coward, liar, and worst of all a thief for having taken from two small children the only parent they had. It was a scalding, withering assault. I tried to write it word for word, but it was so compelling I had to stop and listen. A rabid street preacher could not have heaped such abuse upon sin.

If he had the power, he would sentence him to death, and a rapid and painful one at that.

But the law was the law, and he had to follow it. He sentenced him to life and ordered Sheriff Coley to immediately transport him to the state penitentiary at Parchman. Coley slapped handcuffs on him and he was gone.

Loopus banged his gavel and bolted from the courtroom. A fight erupted in the back of the courtroom when one of Danny's uncles bumped into Doc Crull, a local barber and noted hothead. It quickly drew a crowd and several others cursed the Padgitts and told them to get back to their island. "Go back to your swamp!" someone kept yelling. Deputies broke it up, and the Padgitts left the courtroom.

The crowd lingered for a while, as if the trial weren't finished, as if justice had not been completely served. There was anger and cursing, and I got a whiff of how lynch mobs got organized.

————

Ginger didn't show. She said she would stop by the office after she checked out and say good-bye, but she obviously changed her mind. I could see her speeding through the night, crying and cursing and counting the miles until she was out of Mississippi. Who could blame her?

Our three-day fling came to an abrupt end the way both of us expected but neither had admitted. I could not imagine our paths ever crossing again, and if they did it would be another round or two in the sack before we got distracted with life and moved on. She would go through many men before she found one who would last. I sat on the porch outside my office and waited for her to park below, knowing she was probably in Arkansas by then. We'd started the day in bed together, anxious to return to court to watch her sister's murderer get his death sentence.

In the heat of the moment, I began writing an editorial about the verdict. It would be a scathing attack on the criminal laws of the State. It would be honest and heartfelt, and it would also play well with the audience.

Esau called and interrupted me. He was at the hospital with Miss Callie and asked me to hurry down.

She had fainted as she was getting into the car outside the courthouse. Esau and the three sons had rushed her in, and wisely so. Her blood pressure was dangerously high, and the doctor was worried about a stroke. After a couple of hours, though, she had stabilized and her outlook was better. I held her hand briefly, told her I was very proud of her, and so on. What I really wanted was the inside story on what happened back in the jury room.

It was a story I would never get.

I drank coffee with Al, Max, Bobby, and Esau until

midnight in the hospital canteen. She had not said a word about the jury's deliberations.

We talked about them and their brothers and sisters, and their children and careers and life growing up in Clanton. The stories poured forth, and I almost pulled out a pen and notepad.

CHAPTER 20

For the first six months I lived in Clanton, I usually fled the place on weekends. There was so little to do. Other than an occasional goat roasting at Harry Rex's, and one dreadful cocktail party, which I left twenty minutes after I arrived, there had been no socializing. Virtually all the young people my age were married, and their idea of a blowout was an ice cream "supper" on Saturday night at one of the innumerable churches in town. Most of those who went away to college never came back.

Out of boredom, I occasionally spent the weekends in Memphis, usually at the apartment of a friend, almost never at home. I made several trips to New Orleans where an old girlfriend from high school was living and enjoying the party life. But the *Times* was mine for the near future anyway. I was a resident of Clanton. I had to come to grips with life in a small town, dull weekends and all. The office became my refuge.

I went there on Saturday after the verdict, around noon. I had several stories about the trial I wanted to write, plus my editorial was far from finished. There were seven letters lying on the floor, just inside the front door. This had been a tradition at the *Times* for many years. On those rare occasions when Spot wrote something that prompted a reaction from a reader, more often than not the letter to the editor was hand-delivered and slid under the front door.

Four were signed, three were anonymous. Two were typed, the rest handwritten, one I could hardly read. All seven expressed outrage that Danny Padgitt had escaped with his life. I was not surprised by the town's thirst for blood. I was also dismayed that six of the seven made some reference to Miss Callie. The first one was typed and unsigned. It read:

> *Dear Editor: Our community has sunk to a new low when an outlaw like Danny Padgitt can rape and murder and get by with it. The presence of a Negro on the jury should wake us up to the fact that these people do not think the way law-abiding white people think.*

Mrs. Edith Caravelle from Beech Hill, in a beautiful hand, wrote:

> *Dear Editor: I live one mile from where the murder took place. I am the mother of two teenagers. How do I*

explain the verdict to them? The Bible says: "An eye for
an eye." I guess that doesn't apply to Ford County.

Another anonymous author wrote, on perfumed
pink stationery with flowers around the border:

Dear Editor: See what happens when blacks are placed in
positions of responsibility. An all-white jury would have
strung up Padgitt in the courtroom. Now the Supreme
Court is telling us that blacks should teach our children,
police our streets, and run for public office. God help us.

As the editor (and owner and publisher) I had complete control over what was printed in the *Times.* I could
edit the letters, ignore them, pick and choose the ones I
wanted to print. On controversial issues and events,
letters to the editor stoked the fires and got folks upset.
And they sold newspapers, because that's the only place
they could be printed. They were absolutely free and allowed anyone the forum to sound off.

As I read the first wave, I decided that I would print
nothing that would harm Miss Callie. And I became angry that people were assuming she had somehow hung
the jury and prevented a death sentence.

Why was the town so anxious to blame an unpopular
verdict on the only black on the jury? And with no proof
whatsover? I vowed to find out what really happened in
the jury room, and I immediately thought of Harry Rex.
Baggy, of course, would stumble in Monday morning
with his customary hangover and pretend to know exactly

how the jury split. Odds were he'd be wrong. If anyone could get to the truth, it would be Harry Rex.

Wiley Meek stopped by with the town gossip. Folks were hot in the coffee shops. Padgitt was a dirty word. Lucien Wilbanks was despised, but that was nothing new. Sheriff Coley might as well retire; he wouldn't get fifty votes. Two opponents were already making noise and the election was half a year away.

One story had eleven voting for the gas chamber and one holding out. "Probably the nigger," someone had said, echoing the prevailing sentiment at the Tea Shoppe around seven that morning. A deputy guarding the jury room allegedly whispered to someone somebody knew that it was a six-six split, but this was widely discounted around nine o'clock at the coffee shops. There were two primary theories roaring around the square that morning: first, Miss Callie had screwed things up simply because she was black; second, the Padgitts had dropped some cash on two or three of the jurors, same as they had done on that "lyin' bitch," Lydia Vince.

Wiley thought the second had more supporters than the first, though many seemed perfectly willing to believe anything. I was learning that coffee shop gossip was useless.

———

Late Saturday afternoon, I crossed the tracks and drove slowly through Lowtown. The streets were alive with kids on bikes, pickup basketball games, crowded porches, music from the open doors of the honky-tonks, laughter from the men in front of the stores. Everyone was outside, sort of limbering up for the rigors of Saturday night. People waved and stared, more amused at my little car than my pale skin.

There was a crowd on Miss Callie's porch. Al, Max, and Bobby were there along with Reverend Thurston Small and another well-dressed deacon from the church. Esau was in the house tending to his wife. She had been discharged that morning with strict instructions to stay in bed for three days and not lift a finger. Max led me back to her bedroom.

She was sitting in bed, propped up with pillows, reading the Bible. She flashed a smile when she saw me, and said, "Mr. Traynor, so nice of you to come. Please sit. Esau, fetch Mr. Traynor some tea." Esau, as always, jumped when she gave orders.

I sat in a stiff wooden chair close to her bed. She did not appear to be the least bit ill to me. "I'm really concerned about lunch next Thursday," I began, and we laughed.

"I'm cooking," she said.

"No you're not. I have a better idea. I'll bring the food."

"Why does that worry me?"

"I'll buy it somewhere. Something a bit lighter, like a sandwich."

"A sandwich will be fine," she said, patting my knee. "My tomatoes will be ready shortly."

She stopped patting and smiling and looked away

for a moment. "We didn't do a good job, did we, Mr. Traynor?" Her words were filled with both sadness and frustration.

"It's not a popular verdict," I said.

"It's not what I wanted," she said.

And that was as close to the deliberations as she would get for many years. Esau told me later that the other eleven jurors had sworn on a Bible not to talk about their decision. Miss Callie wouldn't swear on the Bible, but she gave them her word that she would guard their secrets.

I left her there to rest and went to the porch, where I spent several hours listening to her sons and their guests talk about life. I sat in a corner, sipping tea, trying to keep myself out of their conversations. At times I would drift away and absorb the sounds of Lowtown on a Saturday night.

The reverend and the deacon left, leaving only Ruffins on the porch. The talk eventually came around to the trial, and the verdict, and how was it playing on the other side of the tracks?

"Did he really threaten the jury?" Max asked me. I told the story, with Esau adding emphasis when needed. They were as shocked as those of us who'd seen it.

"Thank God he's locked up for life," Bobby said, and I didn't have the heart to tell them the truth. They were extremely proud of their mother, as they had been forever.

I was tired of the trial. I left around nine, drove

slowly and aimlessly back through Lowtown, alone and missing Ginger.

————

Clanton seethed over the verdict for days. We received eighteen letters to the editor, six of which I ran in the next edition. Half of it was devoted to the trial, and this of course stirred things up even worse.

As the summer dragged on, I was beginning to think the town would never stop talking about Danny Padgitt and Rhoda Kassellaw.

Then suddenly, the two became history. Instantly, in the blink of an eye, literally in less than twenty-four hours, the trial was forgotten.

Clanton, both sides of the tracks, had something much more important to fret over.

PART
TWO

PART
TWO

CHAPTER 21

In a sweeping ruling that left no room for doubt or delay, the Court ordered the immediate termination of the dual school system. No more stalling, no more lawsuits, no more promises. Instant integration, and Clanton was as shocked as every other town in the South.

Harry Rex brought me the Court's opinion and tried to explain its intricacies. It wasn't that complicated. Every school district had to immediately implement a desegregation plan.

"This'll sell some newspapers," he predicted, unlit cigar crammed in his mouth.

All sorts of meetings were instantly arranged around town, and I covered them all. On a sweltering night in mid-July, a public gathering took place in the gym of the high school. The stands were packed, the floor covered with concerned parents. Mr. Walter Sullivan, the *Times*'s lawyer, also served as the attorney for the school board. He did most of the talking because he wasn't elected in any way. The politicians preferred to hide behind him. He was blunt and said that in six weeks the Ford County school system would open and be fully desegregated.

A smaller meeting was held at the black school on Burley Street. Baggy and I were there, along with Wiley Meek, who took photos. Again Mr. Sullivan explained to the crowd what was about to happen. Twice his remarks were interrupted by applause.

The difference in those two meetings was astounding. The white parents were angry and frightened and I saw several women crying. The fateful day had finally arrived. At the black school there was an air of victory. The parents were concerned, but they were also elated that their children would finally be enrolled in the better schools. Though they had miles to go in housing, employment, and health care, integration into the public schools was an enormous step forward in their battle for civil rights.

Miss Callie and Esau were there. They were treated with great respect by their neighbors. Six years earlier they had walked into the front door of the white school with Sam and fed him to the lions. For three years he was the only black kid in his class, and the family paid a price for it. Now it all seemed worth it, at least to them. Sam wasn't around to interview.

There was also a meeting in the sanctuary of the First Baptist Church. Whites only, and the crowd was slightly upper middle class. Its organizers had been rais-

ing money to build a private academy, and now suddenly the fund-raising was more urgent. Several doctors
and lawyers were there, and most of the country-club
types. Their children were apparently too good to go to
school with black children.

They were quickly putting together a plan to open
classes in an abandoned factory south of town. The
building would be leased for a year or two until their
capital campaign was complete. They were scrambling
to hire teachers and order books but the most pressing
concern, other than running from the blacks, was what
to do about a football team. At times there was an air of
hysteria, as if a 75 percent white school system would
pose grave dangers for their kids.

I wrote long reports and ran bold headlines, and
Harry Rex was right. The newspapers were selling. In
fact, by late July 1970 our circulation topped five thousand, a stunning turnaround. After Rhoda Kassellaw
and desegregation, I was getting a glimpse of what my
friend Nick Diener said back at Syracuse. "A good small
town weekly doesn't print newspapers. It prints money."

I needed news, and in Clanton it was not always
available. In a slow week, I would run an overblown
story on the latest filing in the Padgitt appeal. It was
usually at the bottom of the front page and sounded as
if the boy might walk out of Parchman at any minute.
I'm not sure my readers cared much anymore. In early
August, though, the paper got another boost when
Davey Bigmouth Bass explained to me the rituals of
high school football.

Wilson Caudle had no interest in sports, which was fine except that everyone else in Clanton lived and died with the Cougars on Friday night. He shoved Bigmouth to the back of the paper and rarely ran photos. I smelled money, and the Cougars became front page news.

———————

My football career ended in the ninth grade, at the hands of a sadistic ex-Marine my soft little prep school had for some reason hired to coach us. Memphis in August is the tropics; football practice should be banned then and there. I was running laps around the practice field, in full gear, helmet and all, in ninety-five-degree heat and humidity, and the coach for some reason refused to give us water. The tennis courts were next to the field, and after I finished vomiting I gazed upon them and saw two girls swatting tennis balls with two guys. With the girls in the scene everything was very pleasant, but what really got my attention were the large bottles of cold water they drank whenever they wanted.

I quit football and took up tennis and girls, and never for an instant regretted it. My school played its games on Saturday afternoons, so I was not baptized in the religion of Friday night football.

I happily became a later convert.

———————

When the Cougars assembled for their first practice, Bigmouth and Wiley were there to cover it. We ran a large front page photo of four players, two white and two black, and another of the coaching staff, which included a black assistant. Bigmouth wrote columns about the team and its players and prospects, and this was only the first week of practice.

We covered the opening of school, including interviews with students, teachers, and administrators, and our slant was openly positive. In truth, Clanton had little of the racial unrest that was common throughout the Deep South when schools opened that August.

The *Times* did big stories about the cheerleaders, the band, the junior high teams—everything we could possibly think of. And every story had several photos. I don't know how many kids failed to make the pages of our paper, but there weren't many.

The first football game was an annual family brawl against Karaway, a much smaller town that had a much better coach. I sat with Harry Rex and we screamed until we were hoarse. The game was a sell-out and the crowd was mostly white.

But those white folks who had been so adamantly opposed to accepting black students were suddenly transformed that Friday night. In the first quarter of the first game, a star was born when Ricky Patterson, a pint-size black kid who could fly, ran eighty yards the first time he touched the ball. The second time he went forty-five, and from then on whenever they tossed it to him the entire crowd stood and yelled. Six weeks after the desegregation order hit the town, I saw narrow-minded, intolerant rednecks screaming like maniacs and bouncing up and down whenever Ricky got the ball.

Clanton won 34–30 in a cliffhanger, and our coverage of the game was shameless. The entire front page was nothing but football. We immediately initated a Player-of-the-Week, with a $100 scholarship award that went into some vague fund that took us months to figure out. Ricky was our first honoree, and so that required yet another interview with another photo.

When Clanton won its first four games, the *Times* was there to stir up the frenzy. Our circulation reached fifty-five hundred.

———

One very hot day in early September, I was strolling around the square, going from my office to the bank. I was wearing my usual garb—faded jeans, rumpled cotton button-down shirt with rolled-up sleeves, loafers, no socks. I was then twenty-four years old and because I owned a business I was slowly turning my thoughts away from college and toward a career. Very slowly. I had long hair and still dressed like a student. I generally gave little thought to what I wore or what image I portrayed.

This lack of concern was not shared by all.

Mr. Mitlo grabbed me on the sidewalk and shoved me into his small haberdashery. "I been waiting for you," he said with a thick accent, one of the few in Clanton. He was a Hungarian and had some colorful history of escaping from Europe while leaving behind a child or two. He was on my list of human interest stories to pursue as soon as football season was over.

"Look at you!" he sneered as I stood just inside his door, by a rack of belts. But he was smiling and with foreigners it's easy to dismiss their bluntness due to translation problems.

I sort of looked at myself. What exactly was the problem?

Evidently, there were many. "You are a professional," he informed me. "A very important man in this town, and you are dressed like, uh, well . . ." He scratched his bearded chin as he searched for the proper insult.

I tried to help. "A student."

"No," he said, wagging an index finger back and forth as if no student had ever looked that bad. He gave up on the put-down and continued the lecture.

"You are unique—how many people own a newspaper? You are educated, which is rare around here. And from up North! You are young, but you shouldn't look so, so, immature. We must work on your image."

We went to work, not that I had a choice. He advertised heavily in the *Times*, so I certainly couldn't tell him to take a hike. Plus, he made sense. The student days were gone, the revolution was over. I had escaped Vietnam and the sixties and college, and, though I wasn't ready to settle down to a wife and parenthood, I was beginning to feel my age.

"You must wear suits," he decided as he went through racks of clothes. Mitlo had been known to walk up to the president of a bank and, in a crowd, comment on a faulty shirt and suit combo, or a drab tie. He and Harry Rex didn't get along at all.

I was not about to start wearing gray suits and wing tips. He pulled out a light blue seersucker suit, found a white shirt, then went straight for the tie rack where he picked out the perfect red-and-gold-striped bow tie. "Let's try this," he announced when his selections were finished. "Over there," he said, pointing to a dressing room. Thankfully, the store was empty. I had no choice.

I gave up on the bow tie. Mitlo reached up and in a skillful flourish had it fixed in a second. "Much better," he said, examining the finished product. I looked at myself in the mirror for a long time. I wasn't sure, but then I was intrigued by the transformation. It gave me character and individuality.

Whether I wanted it or not, the outfit was about to become mine. I had to wear it at least once.

To top it off, he found a white Panama hat that fit nicely on my shaggy head. As he adusted it here and there, he tugged at a patch of hair over my ear and said, "Too much hair. You are a professional. Cut it."

He altered the slacks and jacket and pressed the shirt, and the following day I arrived to collect my new outfit. I planned to simply pick it up, take it home, then wait and wait until there was a slow day around town and wear it. I intended to walk straight to Mitlo's so he could see me in his creation.

He, of course, had other plans. He insisted I try it

on, and when I did he then insisted that I walk around
the entire square to collect my compliments.

"I'm really in a hurry," I said. Chancery court was in
session and downtown was busy.

"I insist," he said dramatically, wagging the finger as
if he would not negotiate for a second.

He adjusted the hat, and the final prop was a long
black cigar which he cut, stuffed in my mouth, and lit
with a match. "A powerful image," he said proudly.
"The town's only publisher. Now off."

No one recognized me for the first half block. Two
farmers in front of the feed store gave me a look, but
then I didn't like the way they were dressed either. I felt
like Harry Rex with the cigar. Mine was lit, though, and
very strong. I sprinted by his office. Mrs. Gladys Wilkins
ran her husband's insurance agency. She was about
forty, very pretty and always well dressed. When she
saw me she stopped dead in her tracks, then said, "Why,
Willie Traynor. Don't you look distinguished."

"Thank you."

"Sorta reminds me of Mark Twain."

I walked on, feeling better. Two secretaries did
double-takes. "Love that bow tie," one of them called to
me. Mrs. Clare Ruth Seagraves stopped me and talked
on and on about something I'd written months earlier
and had forgotten. As she talked she examined my suit
and bow tie and hat and didn't even mind the cigar.
"You look quite handsome, Mr. Traynor," she said finally, and seemed embarrassed by her candor. I walked
slower and slower around the square and decided that

Mitlo was right. I was a professional, a publisher, an important person in Clanton even if I didn't feel too important, and a new image was in order.

We'd have to find some weaker cigars, though. By the time I completed my tour of the square, I was dizzy and had to sit down.

Mr. Mitlo ordered another blue seersucker and two light gray ones. He decided my wardrobe would not be dark like lawyers' and bankers', but light and cool and a bit unconventional. He dedicated himself to finding me some unique bow ties and proper fabrics for the fall and winter.

Within a month Clanton was accustomed to having a new character around the square. I was getting noticed, especially by the opposite sex. Harry Rex laughed at me, but then his own outfits were comical.

The ladies loved it.

CHAPTER 22

In late September there were two notable deaths in one week. The first was Mr. Wilson Caudle. He died at home, alone, in the bedroom where he'd secluded himself since the day he walked out of the *Times*. It was odd that I had not spoken to him once in the six months I'd owned the paper, but I'd been too busy to fret over it. I certainly didn't want any advice from Spot. And, sadly, I knew of no one who'd either seen him or talked to him in the past six months.

He died on a Thursday and was buried on a Saturday. On Friday I hustled over to Mr. Mitlo's and we had a wardrobe session regarding the proper funeral attire for someone of my stature. He insisted on a black suit, and he had just the perfect bow tie. It was narrow with black and maroon stripes, very dignified, very respectful, and when it was tied and I was properly turned out, I had to admit that the image was impressive. He pulled out a black felt fedora from his personal collection and proudly loaned it to me for the funeral. He said often that it was a shame American men didn't wear hats anymore.

The final touch was a shiny black wooden cane. When he produced it I just stared. "I don't need a cane," I said. It seemed quite foolish.

"It's a walking stick," he said, thrusting it at me.

"What's the difference?"

He then launched into a baffling history of the crucial role walking sticks had played in the evolution of modern European male fashion. He felt passionately about it, and the more worked up he got, the thicker his accent became, and the less I understood. To shut him up I took the stick.

The following day, when I walked into the Methodist church for Spot's funeral, the ladies stared at me. Some of the men did too, most of them wondering what the hell I was doing with a black hat and a cane. In a whisper just loud enough for me to hear, Stan Atcavage, my banker, said behind me, "I guess he's gonna sing and dance for us."

"Been hangin' around Mitlo's again," someone whispered back.

I accidentally whacked the cane on the pew in front of me, and the noise jolted the mourners. I wasn't sure what one did with a cane while one was seated for a funeral. I squeezed it between my legs and placed the hat in my lap. Portraying the right image took work. I looked around and saw Mitlo. He was beaming at me.

The choir began "Amazing Grace," and we fell into a somber mood. Reverend Clinkscale then recited Mr. Caudle's basics—born in 1896, the only child of our beloved Miss Emma Caudle, a widower with no children of his own, a veteran of the First War, and for over fifty years the editor of our county weekly. There he brought to an art form the obituaries, which would forever be Spot's claim to fame.

The reverend rambled on a bit, then a soloist broke the monotony. It was my fourth funeral since landing in Clanton. Except for my mother's, I had never attended one before. They were social events in the small town, and often I heard such gems as, "Wasn't that a lovely service," and "Take care, I'll see you at the funeral," and, my favorite, "She would have loved it."

"She," of course, was the deceased.

Folks took off work and wore their Sunday best. If you didn't go to funerals, then you were downright peculiar. Since I had enough oddities working against me, I was determined to properly honor the dead.

The second death occurred later that night, and when I heard about it on Monday I went to my apartment and found my pistol.

Malcolm Vince was shot twice in the head as he left a honky-tonk in a very remote part of Tishomingo County. Tishomingo was dry, the tonk was illegal, and that's why it was hidden so deep in the sticks.

There were no witnesses to the killing. Malcolm had

been drinking beer and shooting pool, behaving himself generally and causing no trouble. Two acquaintances told the police that Malcolm left by himself around 11 P.M. after about three hours in the tonk. He was in good spirits and was not drunk. He said good-bye to them, walked outside, and within seconds they heard gunfire. They were almost certain he was not armed.

The joint was at the end of a dirt trail, and a quarter of a mile up the road a sentry guarded a passageway with a shotgun. In theory his job was to alert the owner if the police or other unsavory characters were approaching. Tishomingo was on the state line, and there had historically been feuds with some hoodlums over in Alabama. Tonks were favorite places to settle scores and such. The sentry heard the shots that killed Malcolm, and he was certain no car or truck had fled the scene afterward. Any such vehicle would've had to pass by him.

Whoever killed Malcolm had come from the woods, on foot, and carried out the hit. I talked to the Sheriff of Tishomingo County. He was of the opinion that someone was after Malcolm. It certainly wasn't a garden-variety honky-tonk flare-up.

"Any idea who might be after Mr. Vince?" I asked, desperately hoping that Malcolm had made some enemies two hours away.

"No idea," he said. "The boy hadn't lived here long."

For two days I carried the pistol in my pocket, then, again, grew weary of that. If the Padgitts wanted to get me or one of the jurors, or Judge Loopus or Ernie Gaddis or anyone they deemed guilty of helping send Danny away, then there was little we could do to stop them.

————

The paper that week was devoted to Mr. Wilson Caudle. I pulled out some old photos from the archives and plastered them all over the front page. We ran testimonials, stories, and lots of paid announcements of sympathy from his many friends. I then rehashed everything I'd written about him into the longest obituary in the history of the newspaper.

Spot deserved it.

I wasn't sure what to do with the story about Malcolm Vince. He was not a resident of Ford County, thus not entirely eligible for an obituary. Our rules were quite flexible when it came to that issue. A prominent Ford Countian who'd moved away would still qualify for an obituary, but obviously there had to be something to write about. One who'd just passed through the county and either had no family or contributed little could not qualify. Such was the case of Malcolm Vince.

If I exaggerated the story, the Padgitts would get the satisfaction of further intimidating the county. They would frighten us again. (Of those who'd heard of the killing, no one thought it might be the work of anyone other than the Padgitts.)

If I ignored the story, then I would be running scared and shirking my responsibility as a journalist. Baggy thought it was front page material, but there was no room when I was finished with our farewell to Mr. Caudle. I ran it at the top of page three, with the headline PADGITT WITNESS MURDERED IN TISHOMINGO COUNTY. My first headline had been MALCOLM VINCE MURDERED IN TISHOMINGO COUNTY, but Baggy felt strongly that we should use the Padgitt name with the word "murdered" in the headline. The story was three hundred words.

I drove to Corinth to snoop around. Harry Rex gave me the name of Malcolm's divorce lawyer, a local act who went by the name of Pud Perryman. His office was on Main Street, between a barbershop and a Chinese seamstress, and when I opened the door I immediately knew that Mr. Perryman was the least successful lawyer I would ever meet. The place reeked of lost cases, dissatisfied clients, and unpaid bills. The carpet was stained and threadbare. The furniture was left over from the fifties. A rancid haze of old and new cigarette smoke hung in layers, dangerously close to my head.

Mr. Perryman himself showed no signs of prosperity. He was around forty-five, potbellied, unkempt, unshaven, red-eyed. The last hangover was wearing off slowly. He informed me he was a divorce and property guy, and I was supposed to be impressed by this. Either he didn't charge enough or he attracted clients with little to sell or fight over.

He hadn't seen Malcolm in a month, he said as he looked for a file among the landfill that covered his desk. The divorce had never been filed. His efforts to work out an agreement with Lydia's lawyer had gone nowhere. "She flew the coop," he said.

"Beg your pardon?"

"She's gone. Packed up after the trial over there and hit the road. Took the kid, vanished."

I really didn't care what happened to Lydia. I was much more concerned with who shot Malcolm. Pud offered a couple of vague theories, but they broke down after a few basic questions. He reminded me of Baggy—a local courthouse gossipmonger who'd make up a rumor if he doesn't hear a new one within an hour.

Lydia had no boyfriends or brothers or anyone else who might want to shoot Malcolm in the heat of a bad divorce. And, of course, there was no divorce. The bad blood hadn't even begun!

Mr. Perryman gave the impression of one who preferred to prattle and tell lies all day, as opposed to tending to his files. I was in his office for almost an hour, and when I finally managed to leave I ran outside for fresh air.

I drove thirty minutes to Iuka, the Tishomingo County seat, where I found Sheriff Spinner just in time to buy him lunch. Over barbecued chicken in a crowded café, he brought me up to date on the murder. It was a clean hit by someone who knew the area well. They had found nothing—no footprints, no shell casings, nothing. The weapon had been a .44 Magnum, and the two shots had practically blown off Malcolm's head. For drama, he unholstered his service revolver and passed it over. "This is a forty-four," he said. It was twice as heavy as my meager weapon. I lost what little appetite I had.

They had talked to every acquaintance they could find. Malcolm had lived in the area for about five months. He had no criminal record, no arrests, no reports of fistfights, no dice shooting, disturbances, or drunken brawls. He went to the tonk once a week, where he shot pool and drank beer and never raised his voice. There were no loans or bills past due for more than sixty days. There appeared to be no illicit affairs or jealous husbands.

"I can't find a motive," the Sheriff said. "It doesn't make sense."

I told him about Malcolm's testimony in the Padgitt trial, and about how Danny threatened the jury. He listened intently, and said little afterward. I got the clear impression he preferred to stay in Tishomingo County and wanted no part of the Padgitts.

"That could be your motive," I said when I finished.

"Revenge?"

"Sure. These are nasty people."

"Oh, I've heard of them. Guess we're lucky we weren't on that jury, huh?"

Driving back to Clanton, I could not erase the image of the Sheriff's face when he said that. Gone was the swagger of a well-armed man of the law. Spinner was truly grateful he was two counties away, and had nothing to do with the Padgitts.

His investigation was dead. Case closed.

CHAPTER 23

The only Jew in Clanton was Mr. Harvey Kohn, a dapper little man who'd been selling shoes and handbags to ladies for decades. His store was on the square, next door to the Sullivan law firm, in a row of buildings he'd bought during the Depression. He was a widower and his children had fled Clanton after high school. Once a month Mr. Kohn drove to Tupelo to worship in the nearest synagogue.

Kohn's Shoes aimed at the higher end of the market, which was tricky in a small town like Clanton. The few wealthy ladies in town preferred shopping in Memphis, where they could pay higher prices and talk about it back home. To make his shoes attractive, Mr. Kohn put shockingly high prices on them, then slashed them with deep discounts. The local ladies could then throw out any price they wanted when they showed off their latest purchases.

He ran the store himself, opening early and staying late, usually with the help of a part-time student. Two years before I arrived in Clanton he hired a sixteen-year-old black kid named Sam Ruffin to unpack inventory, move stock, clean the place, answer the phone. Sam proved to be bright and industrious. He was courteous, mannerly, well dressed, and before long he could be trusted to run the store while Mr. Kohn went home every day at precisely eleven forty-five for a quick lunch and a long nap.

A lady by the name of Iris Durant dropped in around noon one day and found Sam all alone. Iris was forty-one years old, the mother of two teenage boys, one in Sam's class at Clanton High. She was mildly attractive, liked to flirt and wear mini-skirts, and usually selected shoes from Mr. Kohn's more exotic inventory. She tried about two dozen varieties, bought nothing, and took her time about it. Sam knew his products and was very careful with her feet.

She was back the next day, same time, shorter skirt, heavier makeup. Barefoot, she seduced Sam on Mr. Kohn's desk in his small office just behind the cash register. Thus began a torrid affair that would change both their lives.

Several times a week, Iris went shoe shopping. Sam found a more comfortable spot upstairs on an old sofa. He would lock the store for fifteen minutes, turn off the lights, and dash up.

Iris's husband was a sergeant in the Mississippi Highway Patrol. Alarmed at the number of new shoes in her closet, he became suspicious. Suspicion had been a way of life with Iris.

He hired Harry Rex to investigate. A Cub Scout could've caught the lovers. Three straight days she walked into Kohn's at the same time; three straight days Sam quickly locked the front door, eyes darting in all directions; three straight days the lights went off, etc. On the fourth day, Harry Rex and Rafe sneaked in the back of the store. They heard noises upstairs. Rafe barged into the love nest and in five seconds gathered enough evidence to send both of them packing.

Mr. Kohn fired Sam an hour later. Harry Rex filed the divorce that afternoon. Iris was later admitted to the hospital with cuts, abrasions, and a broken nose. Her husband beat her with his fists until she was unconscious. After dark, three uniformed state troopers knocked on the door of Sam's home in Lowtown. They explained to his parents that he was wanted by the police in connection with some vague embezzling charge at Kohn's. If convicted he could be sentenced to twenty years in prison. They also told them, off the record of course, that Sam had been caught having sex with a white lady, another man's wife, and there was a contract on his head. Five thousand bucks.

Iris left town disgraced, divorced, without her children, and afraid to return.

I had heard different versions of Sam's story. It was old gossip by the time I arrived in Clanton, but it was still sensational enough to find its way into many conversations. In the South, it was not unusual for white men to keep black mistresses, but Sam's was the first documented case of a white woman crossing the color line in Clanton.

Baggy had been the one to tell me the story. Harry Rex had confirmed much of it.

Miss Callie refused to talk about it. Sam was her youngest, and he couldn't come home. He had fled, dropped out of high school, and spent the past two years living off his brothers and sisters. Now he was calling me.

I went to the courthouse and dug through drawers of old files. I found no record of an indictment against Sam Ruffin. I asked Sheriff Coley if he had an outstanding warrant. He dodged the question and wanted to know why I was poking around in such an old case. I asked him if Sam would be arrested if he came home. Again, no direct answer. "Be careful, Mr. Traynor," he warned, but would not elaborate.

I went to Harry Rex and asked about the now legendary contract on Sam's head. He described his client, Sergeant Durant, as a former Marine, an expert marksman with any number of weapons, a career cop, a hothead who was horribly embarrassed by Iris's indiscretion, and who felt the only honorable way out was to kill her lover. He had thought about killing her, but didn't want to go to prison. He felt safer killing a black kid. A Ford County jury would be more sympathetic.

"And he wants to do it himself," Harry Rex explained. "That way he can save the five grand."

He enjoyed delivering such dire news to me, but he did admit that he hadn't seen his client in a year and a half, and he wasn't sure if Mr. Durant hadn't already remarried.

———

Thursday at noon we settled down at the table on the porch and thanked the Lord for the delicious meal we were about to receive. Esau was at work.

As the garden ripened in late summer, we had enjoyed many vegetarian lunches. Red and yellow tomatoes, cucumbers and onions in vinegar, butter beans, snap beans, peas, okra, squash, boiled potatoes, corn on the cob, and always hot corn bread. Now, as the air was cooler and the leaves were turning, Miss Callie was preparing heartier dishes—duck stew, lamb stew, chili, red beans and rice with pork sausage, and the old standby, pot roast.

The meal that day was chicken and dumplings. I was eating slowly, something she had encouraged me to do. I was half through when I said, "Sam called me, Miss Callie."

She paused and swallowed, then said, "How is he?"

"He's fine. He wants to come home this Christmas, said everybody else was coming back, and he wants to be here."

"Do you know where he is?" she asked.

"Do you?"

"No."

"He's in Memphis. We're supposed to meet tomorrow, up there."

"Why are you meeting with Sam?" She seemed very suspicious of my involvement.

"He wants me to help him. Max and Bobby told him about our friendship. He said he thinks I'm a white person who can be trusted."

"It could be dangerous," she said.

"For who?"

"Both of you."

Her doctor was concerned about her weight. At times she was too, but not always. With particularly heavy dishes, like stews and dumplings, she took small portions and ate slowly. The news of Sam gave her a reason to stop eating altogether. She folded her napkin and began talking.

———————

Sam left Clanton in the middle of the night on a Greyhound bus headed for Memphis. He called Callie and Esau when he arrived there. The next day a friend drove up with some money and clothing. As the story about Iris broke fast around town, Callie and Esau were convinced their youngest son was about to be murdered by the cops. Highway patrol cars eased by their house at all hours of the day and night. There were anonymous phone calls with threats and abusive language.

Mr. Kohn filed some papers in court. A hearing date

came and went without Sam's appearance. Miss Callie never saw an official indictment, but then she wasn't sure what one looked like.

Memphis seemed too close, so Sam drifted to Milwaukee where he hid with Bobby for a few months. For two years now, he had drifted from one sibling to the next, always traveling at night, always afraid that he was about to be caught. The older Ruffin children called home often and wrote once a week, but they were afraid to mention Sam. Someone might be listening.

"He was wrong to get involved with a woman like that," Miss Callie said, sipping tea. I had effectively ruined her lunch, but not mine. "But he was so young. He didn't chase her."

———

The next day I became the unofficial go-between for Sam Ruffin and his parents.

We met in a coffee shop in a shopping mall in south Memphis. From somewhere in the distance, he watched me wait for thirty minutes before he popped in from nowhere and sat across from me. Two years on the run had taught him a few tricks.

His youthful face was showing the strain of life on the lam. Out of habit, he continually looked right and left. He tried mightily to hold eye contact, but he could do it only for a few seconds. Not surprisingly, he was soft-spoken, articulate, very polite. And quite thankful that I had been willing to step forward and explore the possibility of helping him.

He thanked me for the courtesies and friendship I'd shown his mother. Bobby in Milwaukee had shown him the *Times* stories. We talked about his siblings, his movements from UCLA to Duke, then to Toledo, then to Grinnell in Iowa. He couldn't live like that much longer. He was desperate for a resolution to the mess at home so he could get on with a normal life. He finished high school in Milwaukee, and planned eventually to go to law school. But he couldn't do it living like a fugitive.

"There's a fair amount of pressure on me, you know," he said. "Seven brothers and sisters, seven PhD's."

I described my fruitless search for an indictment, my inquiries to Sheriff Coley, and my conversation with Harry Rex about Mr. Durant's current mood. Sam thanked me profusely for this information, and for my willingness to get involved.

"There's no threat of being arrested," I assured him. "There is, however, the threat of catching a bullet."

"I'd rather be arrested," he said.

"Me too."

"He's a very scary man," Sam said of Mr. Durant. A story followed, one in which I did not get all the details. Seems as though Iris was now living in Memphis. Sam kept in touch. She had told him some horrible things about her ex-husband and her two teenaged boys and the threats they'd made against her. She was not welcome anywhere in Ford County. Her life might be in danger too. The boys repeatedly said they hated her and never wanted to see her again.

She was a broken woman who was racked with guilt and suffering a nervous breakdown.

"And it's my fault," Sam said. "I was raised better."

Our meeting lasted an hour, and we promised to get together in a couple of weeks. He handed me two thick letters he'd written to his parents, and we said good-bye. He disappeared in a crowd of shoppers and I couldn't help but ask myself where an eighteen-year-old kid hides? How does he travel, move around? How does he survive day to day? And Sam was not some street kid who'd learned to live by his wits and fists.

———

I told Harry Rex about our meeting in Memphis. My lofty goal was to somehow convince Mr. Durant to leave Sam alone.

Since I was living under the assumption that my name was on a not-so-favored list somewhere on Padgitt Island, I had no desire to have it added to another list. I swore Harry Rex to secrecy, and had no trouble believing he would protect my role as the intermediary.

Sam would agree to leave Ford County, to finish high school up North, then stay there for college and probably for the rest of his life. The kid simply wanted to be able to see his parents, to have short visits in Clanton, and to be able to live without looking over his shoulder.

Harry Rex didn't care, nor did he want to get involved. He promised to relay the message to Mr. Durant, but he wasn't optimistic it would get a sympathetic ear. "He's a nasty sumbitch," he said more than once.

CHAPTER 24

In early December, I returned to Tishomingo County for a follow-up with Sheriff Spinner. I was not surprised to learn that the investigation of the murder of Malcolm Vince had produced nothing new. More than once, Spinner described it as a "clean hit," with nothing left behind but a dead body and two bullets that were virtually untraceable. His men had talked to every possible friend, acquaintance, and coworker, and found no one who knew of any reason why Malcolm would meet such a violent end.

Spinner had also talked to Sheriff Mackey Don Coley, and not surprisingly, our Sheriff had expressed doubt that the murder had anything to do with the Padgitt trial over in Ford County. It appeared as though the two sheriffs had some history, and I was relieved to hear Spinner say, "Ol' Coley couldn't catch a jaywalker on Main Street."

I laughed real loud and added, helpfully, "Yeah, he and the Padgitts go way back."

"I told him you'd been over, snoopin' around. He said, 'That boy's gonna get hurt.' Just thought you'd like to know."

"Thanks," I said. "Me and Coley see things differently."

"Election's a few months away."

"Yes it is. I hear Coley's got two or three opponents."

"Just takes one."

Again, he promised to call if something new developed, but both of us knew that was not going to happen. I left Iuka and drove to Memphis.

———

Trooper Durant had been quite pleased to learn that his threats were still hanging over the head of Sam Ruffin. Harry Rex had eventually delivered the word that the boy was still on the run but desperately wanted to come home and see his momma.

Durant had not remarried. He was very much alone and extremely bitter and embarrassed about his wife's affair. He ranted at Harry Rex about how his life had been destroyed, and worse, how his two sons were subject to ridicule and abuse because of what their mother did. The white kids at school taunted them daily. The black kids, their new classmates at Clanton High, were smug and made wisecracks about it.

Both boys were expert marksmen and avid hunters, and the three Durants had vowed to put a bullet into

Sam Ruffin's head if given the chance. They knew exactly where the Ruffins lived in Lowtown. Durant commented on the annual pilgrimage many blacks from the North made at Christmastime. "If that boy sneaks home, we'll be waitin'," he promised Harry Rex.

He also had some venom for me, and for my heartwarming stories about Miss Callie and her older children. He guessed correctly that I was the family's contact with Sam.

"You'd better get your nose outta this mess," Harry Rex warned me after his meeting with Durant. "This is a nasty character."

I wasn't anxious to have someone else dreaming of my painful death.

I met Sam at a truck stop near the state line, about a mile into Tennessee. Miss Callie had sent cakes and pies and letters and some cash, an entire cardboard box that filled the other seat in my little Spitfire. It was the first time in two years she had been able to touch him in any way. He tried to read one of her letters, but became emotional and put it back in the envelope. "I'm so homesick," he said, wiping huge tears while at the same time trying to hide them from the truckers eating nearby. He was a lost, scared little boy.

With brutal honesty, I recounted the conversation with Harry Rex. Sam had naively thought his offer to stay away from Ford County but visit occasionally would be acceptable to Mr. Durant. He had little grasp of the hatred he had inspired. He did, however, seem to appreciate the danger.

"He'll kill you, Sam," I said gravely.

"And he'll get by with it, won't he?"

"What difference will that make to you? You'll be just as dead. Miss Callie would rather have you alive up North than dead in the Clanton cemetery."

We agreed to meet again in two weeks. He was doing his Christmas shopping, and he would have gifts for his parents and family.

We said good-bye and left the dining area. I was almost to my car when I decided to step back inside and use the men's room. It was in the rear of a tacky gift shop next to the café. I glanced out a window and saw Sam, very suspiciously, jump into a car driven by a white woman. She looked to be older, early forties. Iris, I presumed. Some people never learn.

The Ruffin clan began arriving three days before Christmas. Miss Callie had been cooking for a week. She sent me to the grocery store twice for emergency supplies. I was quickly adopted into the family and given full privileges, the highest of which was to eat whenever and whatever I wanted.

Growing up in that house, the children's lives had been centered around their parents, each other, the Bible, and the kitchen table. And for the holidays there was always a fresh dish of something on the table, and another two or three on the stove or in the oven. The announcement "Pecan pies are ready!" sent shockwaves through the small house, across the porch, and even into the street. The family gathered at the table where Esau rather quickly thanked the Lord yet again for his family and their health and for the food they were about to "partake"; then the pies would be cut into thick wedges, laid on saucers, and carried off in all directions.

The same ritual was followed for pumpkin pies, co-conut pies, strawberry cakes, the list went on and on. And those were just the light little snacks that carried them from one major meal to the next.

Unlike their mother, the Ruffin children were not the slightest bit heavy. And I soon learned why. They complained that they were unable to eat like this any-more. The food where they lived was bland and much of it was frozen and mass-produced. There were a lot of ethnic foods they simply could not digest. And the peo-ple ate in a hurry. The list of complaints grew.

My hunch was that they had been so spoiled by Miss Callie's cooking that nothing would ever measure up.

Carlota, who was single and taught urban studies at UCLA, was especially entertaining when telling stories of the latest wacky food trends sweeping California. Raw foods were the current rage—lunch was a plate of raw carrots and raw celery, all to be choked down with a small cup of hot herbal tea.

Gloria, who taught Italian at Duke, was considered the luckiest of the seven because she was still in the South. She and Miss Callie compared notes on the dif-ferent recipes for things such as corn bread, Brunswick stew, and even collard greens. These discussions often turned serious, with the men offering opinions and observations, and more than one argument erupted.

After a three hour lunch, Leon (Leonardo), who taught biology at Purdue, asked me to go for a ride. He was the second oldest, and carried a slight academic air that the others had managed to avoid. He had a beard, smoked a pipe, wore a tweed blazer with worn arm patches, and used a vocabulary that he must've spent hours practicing.

We roamed the streets of Clanton in his car. He wanted to know about Sam, and I told him everything. In my opinion, whatever that was worth, it was too dangerous for him to enter Ford County.

And he wanted to know about the trial of Danny Padgitt. I had sent copies of the *Times* to all of the Ruffins. One of Baggy's reports had emphasized the threat made by Danny to the jurors. The exact quote had been highlighted, "You convict me, and I'll get every damned one of you."

"Will he ever be released from prison?" Leon asked.

"Yes," I said, reluctantly.

"When?"

"No one knows. He got life for murder, life for rape. Ten years is the minimum for each, but I'm told weird things happen in the Mississippi parole system."

"So it's twenty years minimum?" I'm sure he was thinking about his mother's age. She was fifty-nine.

"No one's sure. There is the possibility of good time, which reduces the minimum."

He seemed as confused by this as I had been. Truth

was, no one connected to either the judicial system or the penal system had been able to answer my questions about Danny's sentence. Parole in Mississippi was a vast dark pit, and I was afraid to get too close.

Leon told me that he had quizzed his mother at length about the verdict. Specifically, did she vote for the life sentence, or did she want death? Her response had been that the jury vowed to keep its deliberations a secret. "What do you know?" he asked me.

Not much. She had strongly implied to me that she had not agreed with the verdict, but it was nothing definite. In the weeks after the verdict there had been an avalanche of speculation. Most courthouse regulars had settled on the theory that three, maybe four, of the jurors had refused to vote for the death penalty. Miss Callie was generally considered not to be in that group.

"Did the Padgitts get to them?" he asked. We were easing into the long shaded front drive of Clanton High School.

"That's the prevailing theory," I said. "But no one really knows. The last death penalty in this county for a white defendant was forty years ago."

He stopped his car and we looked at the stately oak doors of the school. "So it's finally integrated," he said.

"It is."

"Never thought I'd see it." He smiled with great satisfaction. "I used to dream of going to this school. My father worked as a janitor here when I was a little boy, and I would come over on Saturdays and walk those long hallways and see how nice everything was. I understood why I wasn't welcome here, but I never accepted it."

There was not much I could add to this, so I just listened. He seemed more sad than bitter.

We finally drove away and crossed the tracks. Back in Lowtown, I was amazed at the number of fine automobiles with out-of-state tags that were parked tightly in the streets. Large families sat on porches in the frigid air; children played in the yards and the streets. Other cars arrived, all with brightly wrapped packages in the rear windows.

"Home is where Momma is," Leon said. "And everybody comes home for Christmas."

As we stopped near Miss Callie's, Leon thanked me for befriending his mother. "She talks about you all the time," he said.

"It's all about lunch," I said, and we both laughed. At the front gate, a new aroma wafted from the house. Leon froze, took a long whiff, said, "Pumpkin pie." The voice of experience.

At various times, each of the seven professors thanked me for my friendship with Miss Callie. She had shared her life with many, had lots of close friends, but for more than eight months had especially cherished her time with me.

I left them late in the afternoon on Christmas Eve as they were preparing for church. Afterward, there would be gifts and singing. There were more than twenty Ruffins staying in the house; I couldn't imagine where everyone slept, and I was certain no one really cared.

As accepted as I was, I did feel the need to leave them at some point. Later, there would be hugs and tears, and songs and stories, and, though I was certainly welcome to experience all of it, I knew there were times when families needed to be alone.

What did I know about families?

I drove to Memphis, where my childhood home had not seen a Christmas decoration in ten years. My father and I had dinner at a Chinese joint not far from the house. As I choked down bad wonton soup I couldn't help but think of the chaos of Miss Callie's kitchen and all those wonderful dishes being pulled from the oven.

My father worked hard to seem interested in my newspaper. I obligingly sent him a copy each week, but after a few minutes of chitchat I could tell he had never read a word. He was concerned with some ominous connection between the war in Southeast Asia and the bond market.

We ate quickly and went in different directions. Sadly, neither of us had given any thought to exchanging gifts.

Christmas lunch was with BeeBee, who, unlike my father, was delighted to see me. She invited three of her little blue-haired widow friends over for sherry and ham, and the five of us proceeded to get tipsy. I regaled them with stories from Ford County, some accurate, some highly embellished. Hanging around Baggy and Harry Rex, I was learning the art of storytelling.

By 3 P.M., we were all napping. Early the next morning, I raced back to Clanton.

CHAPTER 25

One frigid day late in January, shots rang out somewhere around the square. I was sitting at my desk,
peacefully typing a story about Mr. Lamar Farlowe and
his recent reunion in Chicago with his battalion of
Army paratroopers, when a bullet shattered a window-
pane less than twenty feet from my head. A slow news
week thus came to a sudden end.

My bullet was either the second or the third in a
fairly rapid sequence. I hit the floor with all sorts of
thoughts—Where was my pistol? Were the Padgitts as-
saulting the town? Were Trooper Durant and his boys
after me? On my hands and knees I scrambled to my
briefcase as shots continued to crack through the air;
they sounded like they were coming from across the
street, but in the horror of the moment I really couldn't
tell. They sounded much louder after one hit my office.

I emptied the briefcase and then remembered the

pistol was either in my car or my apartment. I was unarmed and felt like such a weakling for not being able to defend myself. Harry Rex and Rafe had trained me better.

I was scared to the point of not being able to move. Then I remembered Bigmouth Bass was in his office downstairs, and like most real men in Clanton he had an arsenal close by. There were handguns in his desk and he kept two hunting rifles on the wall, just in case he got the urge to run out and kill a deer during lunch. Anyone trying to get me would encounter stiff resistance by my staff. I hoped so anyway.

There was a pause in the assault, then shouts of panic and chaos on the streets. It was almost 2 P.M., normally a busy time downtown. I crawled under my desk like I'd been taught in tornado warning drills. From somewhere below I heard Bigmouth yell, "Stay in your offices!" I could almost see him down there, grabbing a 30.06 and a box of shells, ducking into a doorway in great anticipation. I couldn't imagine a worse place for some nut to start shooting. There were thousands of guns within arm's reach around the Clanton square. Every pickup had two rifles in the window rack and a shotgun under the seat. These people couldn't wait to use their guns!

It wouldn't be long before the locals returned fire. That's when the war would really get ugly.

Then the shots resumed. They weren't getting any closer, I decided as I tried to breathe normally under the desk and analyze things. As the seconds slowly ticked by I realized that the assault was not aimed at me. I just happened to own a nearby window. Sirens approached, then more shots, more shouting. What in the world!

A phone rang downstairs and someone grabbed it quickly.

"Willie! You okay!" Bigmouth yelled from the bottom of the steps.

"Yeah!"

"There's a sniper on top of the courthouse!"

"Great!"

"Stay low!"

"Don't worry!"

I relaxed a little and emerged just enough to grab my phone. I called Wiley Meek at home, but he was already headed our way. Then I crawled across the floor to one of the French doors and opened it. Evidently this caught the attention of our sniper. He shattered a pane four feet above me and the glass fell like heavy rain. I dropped to my stomach and stopped breathing for what seemed like an hour. The gunfire was relentless. Whoever he was he was certainly perturbed about something.

Eight shots, each sounding much louder now that I was outside. A fifteen-second pause as he reloaded, then eight more. I heard glass shatter, bullets ricochet off bricks, bullets split through wooden posts. Somewhere in the midst of the barrage, the voices became silent.

When I could move again, I gently pulled one of the rocking chairs over on its side, then crawled behind it.

The porch had a wrought-iron railing around it, and with that and the chair in front of me, I was concealed and protected. I'm not sure why I felt compelled to move closer to the sniper, but I was twenty-four years old and owned the newspaper and knew that I would write a lengthy story about this dramatic episode. I needed details.

When I finally peeked through the chair and the railing, I saw the sniper. The courthouse had an oddly flattened dome, on top of which was a small cupola with four open windows. He'd made his nest there, and when I first saw him he was peeking just above the sill of one of the windows. He appeared to have a black face with white hair, and this sent more chills through my body. We were dealing with a world-class psycho.

He was reloading, and when he was ready he rose slightly and began shooting completely at random. He appeared to be shirtless, which, given the situation, seemed even stranger since it was around thirty degrees with a chance of light snow later in the afternoon. I was freezing and I was wearing a rather handsome wool suit from Mitlo's.

His chest was white with black stripes, sort of like a zebra. It was a white man who'd painted himself partially black.

All traffic was gone. The city police had blocked the streets and cops were darting about, squatting low and hiding behind their cars. In the store windows an occasional face popped out for a quick scan, then disappeared. The shooting stopped and the sniper ducked low and disappeared for a while. Three county deputies dashed along a sidewalk and into the courthouse. Long minutes passed.

Wiley Meek bounded up the steps of my office and was soon beside me. He was breathing so hard I thought he'd sprinted from his house out in the country. "He hit us!" he whispered, as if the sniper could hear. He was examining the broken glass.

"Twice," I said, nodding up at the broken panes.

"Where is he?" he asked as he moved a camera with a long-range lens into position.

"The cupola," I said, pointing. "Be careful. He hit that door when I opened it."

"Have you seen him?"

"Male, white, with black highlights."

"Oh, one of those."

"Keep your head down."

We stayed huddled and crouched for several minutes. More cops scurried about, going nowhere in particular and giving the distinct impression that they were thrilled to be there but had little idea what to do.

"Anybody hurt?" Wiley asked, suddenly anxious that maybe he'd missed some blood.

"How am I supposed to know?"

Then more shots, very quick and startling. We peeked and saw him from the shoulders up, blazing away. Wiley focused and began taking pictures through the long-range lens.

Baggy and the boys were in the Bar Room on the third floor, not directly under the cupola, but not far from it. In fact, they were probably the closest humans to the sniper when he began his target practice. After the shooting resumed for the ninth or tenth time, they evidently became even more frightened and, convinced they were about to be slaughtered, decided they had to take matters into their own hands. Somehow they managed to pry open the intractable window of their little hideaway. We watched as an electrical cord was thrown out and fell almost to the ground, forty feet below. Baggy's right leg appeared next as he flung it over the brick sill and wiggled his portly body through the opening. Not surprisingly, Baggy had insisted on going first.

"Oh my God," Wiley said, somewhat gleefully, and raised his camera. "They're drunk as skunks."

Clutching the electrical cord with all the grit he could muster, Baggy sprung free from the window and began his descent to safety. His strategy was not apparent. He appeared to give no slack on the cord, his hands frozen to it just above his head. Evidently there was plenty of cord left in the Bar Room, and his cohorts were supposed to ease him down.

As his hands rose higher above his head, his pants became shorter. Soon they were just below his knees, leaving a long gap of pale white skin before his black socks bunched around his ankles. Baggy wasn't concerned about appearances—before, during, or after the sniper incident.

The shooting stopped, and for a while Baggy just hung there, slowly twisting against the building, about three feet below the window. Major could be seen inside, clinging fiercely to the cord. He had only one leg though, and I worried that it would quickly give out. Behind him I could see two figures, probably Wobble Tackett and Chick Elliot, the usual poker gang.

Wiley began laughing, a low suppressed laugh that shook his entire body.

With each lull in the shooting, the town took a breath, peeked around, and hoped it was over. And each new round scared us more than the last.

Two shots rang out. Baggy lurched as if he'd been hit—though in reality there was no possible way the sniper could even see him, and the suddenness evidently put too much pressure on Major's leg. It collapsed, the cord sprang free, and Baggy screamed as he dropped like a cinder block into a row of thick boxwoods that had been planted by the Daughters of the Confederacy. The boxwoods absorbed the load, and, much like a trampoline, recoiled and sent Baggy to the sidewalk, where he landed like a melon and became the only casualty of the entire episode.

I heard laughter in the distance.

Without a trace of mercy, Wiley recorded the entire spectacle. The photos would be furtively passed around Clanton for years to come.

For a long time Baggy didn't move. "Leave the sumbitch out there," I heard a cop yell below us.

"You can't hurt a drunk," Wiley said as he caught his breath.

Eventually, Baggy rose to all fours. Slowly and painfully, he crawled, like a dog hit by a truck, into the boxwoods that had saved his life, and there he rode out the storm.

A police car had been parked three doors down from the Tea Shoppe. The sniper fired a burst at it, and when the gas tank exploded we forgot about Baggy. The crisis stepped up to the next level as thick smoke poured out from under the car, then we saw flames. The sniper found this sporting, and for a few minutes he hit nothing but cars. I was certain my Spitfire would be irresistible, but perhaps it was too small.

He lost his nerve, though, when fire was eventually returned. Two of Sheriff Coley's men stationed themselves on roofs, and when they unloaded on the cupola the sniper ducked low and was out of business.

"I got him!" one of the deputies shouted down to Sheriff Coley.

We waited for twenty minutes; all was quiet. Baggy's old wing tips and black socks could be seen from under the boxwoods, but the rest was hidden. Occasionally, Major, glass in hand, would look down and yell something at Baggy, who could have been dying for all we knew.

More cops sprinted into the courthouse. We relaxed and sat in the rockers, but we did not take our eyes off the cupola. Bigmouth, Margaret, and Hardy joined us on the balcony. They had watched Baggy's descent from the front window downstairs. Only Margaret was concerned about his injuries.

The police car burned until the fire department eventually showed up and doused it. The doors of the courthouse opened and some of the county employees came out and began smoking furiously. Two deputies managed to retrieve Baggy from the boxwoods. He was barely able to walk, and was obviously in great pain. They placed him in a patrol car and took him away.

Then we saw a deputy in the cupola, and the town was safe again. The five of us hurried over to the courthouse, along with the rest of downtown Clanton.

The third floor was sealed off. Court was not in session, so Sheriff Coley directed us to the courtroom, where he promised a quick briefing. As we were walking into the courtroom, I saw Major, Chick Elliot, and Wobble Tackett being escorted down the hall by a deputy. They were obviously drunk and laughing so hard they had trouble staying on their feet.

Wiley went downstairs to sniff around. A body was about to be removed from the courthouse, and he wanted a shot of the sniper. The white hair, black face, painted stripes—there were a lot of questions.

The deputy sharpshooters had evidently missed. The sniper was identified as Hank Hooten, the local lawyer who had assisted Ernie Gaddis in the prosecution of Danny Padgitt. He was in custody and unharmed.

When Sheriff Coley announced this in the courtroom, we were shocked and bewildered. Our nerves were pretty raw anyway, but this was too much to believe. "Mr. Hooten was found in the small stairwell that leads up to the cupola," Coley was saying, but I was too stunned to take notes. "He did not resist arrest and is now in custody."

"What was he wearing?" someone asked.

"Nothing."

"Nothing?"

"Absolutely nothing. He had what appeared to be black shoe polish on his face and chest, but other than that he was as naked as a newborn."

"What type of weapons?" I asked.

"We found two high-powered rifles, that's all I can say right now."

"Did he say anything?"

"Not a word."

Wiley said they wrapped Hank in some sheets and shoved him in the backseat of a patrol car. He shot some photos but was not optimistic. "There were a dozen cops around him," he said.

We drove to the hospital to check on Baggy. His wife worked the night shift in the emergency room. Someone had called her, woke her up, summoned her to the hospital, and when we met her she was in a foul mood. "Just a broken arm," she said, obviously disappointed that it was not more serious. "Some scrapes and bruises. What'd the fool do?"

I looked at Wiley and Wiley looked at me.

"Was he drunk?" she asked. Baggy was always drunk.

"Don't know," I said. "He fell out of a window at the courthouse."

"Oh, brother. He was drunk."

I gave a quick version of Baggy's escape and tried to make it sound as if he'd done something heroic in the midst of all that gunfire.

"The third floor?" she asked.

"Yes."

"So he was playing poker, drinking whiskey, and he jumped out of a third-floor window."

"Basically, yes," Wiley said, unable to stop himself.

"Not exactly," I said, but she was already walking away.

Baggy was snoring when we finally got back to his room. The medications had mixed with the whiskey and he appeared comatose. "He will wish he could sleep forever," Wiley whispered.

And he was right. The legend of Bouncin' Baggy was told countless times in the years that followed. Wobble Tackett would swear that Chick Elliot let go of the cord first, and Chick would argue that Major's good leg buckled first and caused a chain reaction. The town quickly believed that, whoever let go first, the three idiots Baggy left behind in the Bar Room had intentionally dropped him into the boxwoods.

———

Two days later, Hank Hooten was sent to the state mental hospital at Whitfield, where he would remain for several years. He was initially indicted for trying to kill half of Clanton, but with time the charges were dropped. He allegedly told Ernie Gaddis that he was not shooting at anyone in particular, didn't want to harm anyone, but was just upset because the town had failed to send Danny Padgitt to his death.

Word eventually drifted back to Clanton that he had been diagnosed as severely schizophrenic. "Slap-ass crazy," was the conclusion on the streets.

Never in the history of Ford County had a person lost his mind in such a spectacular fashion.

CHAPTER 26

One year after I bought the newspaper, I sent BeeBee a check for $55,000—her loan plus interest at the rate of 10 percent. She had not discussed the matter of interest when she gave me the money, nor had we signed a promissory note. Ten percent was a bit high, and I hoped it would prompt her to send the check back. I sent it, held my breath, watched the mail, and sure enough, about a week later there was a letter from Memphis.

Dear William: I enclose your check, which I was not expecting and have no use for at this time. If, for some unlikely reason, I need the money in the future, then we shall at that time discuss this matter. Your offer of payment makes me extremely proud of you and your integrity. What you have accomplished in one year down there is a source of great pride for me, and I delight in

*telling my friends about your success as a newspaper
publisher and editor.*

*I must confess that I was worried about you when you
came home from Syracuse. You appeared to lack direction
and motivation, and your hair was too long. You have
proven me wrong, and cut your hair (a little) to boot. You
have also become quite the gentleman in your dress and
manners.*

*You're all I have, William, and I love you dearly.
Please write me more often.*

Love, BeeBee

*P.S. Did that poor man really take off his clothes and
shoot up the town? What characters you have down there!*

BeeBee's first husband had died of some colorful illness in 1924. She then married a divorced cotton merchant and they had one child, my poor mother. The
second husband, my grandfather, died in 1938, leaving
BeeBee with a nice bundle. She stopped marrying and
had spent the last thirty-odd years counting her money,
playing bridge, and traveling. As the only grandchild, I
was set to inherit all she had, though I had no clue as to
the extent of her fortune.

If BeeBee wanted more letters from me, then she
could certainly have them.

I happily tore up the check, walked down to the
bank, and borrowed another $50,000 from Stan Atcav-
age. Hardy had found a slightly used offset press in Atlanta, and I bought it for $108,000. We ditched our

ancient letterpress and moved into the twentieth century. The *Times* took on a new look—much cleaner print, sharper photos, smarter designs. Our circulation was at six thousand and I could see steady, profitable growth. The elections of 1971 certainly helped.

——————

I was astounded at the number of people who ran for public office in Mississippi. Each county was divided into five districts, and each district had an elected constable, who wore a badge and a gun and whatever uniform he could put together, and if he could afford it, which he always managed, he put lights on his car and had the authority to pull over anyone at any time for any conceivable offense. No training was required. No education. No supervision from the county Sheriff or the city police chief, no one but the voters every four years. In theory he was a summons server, but once elected most constables couldn't resist the powerful urge to strap on a gun and look for folks to arrest.

The more traffic tickets a constable wrote, the more money he earned. It was a part-time job with a nominal salary, but at least one of the five in each county tried to live off the position. This was the guy who caused the most trouble.

Each district had an elected Justice of the Peace, a judicial officer with absolutely no legal training, in 1971 anyway. No education was required for the job. No experience. Just votes. The J.P. judged all the people the constable hauled in, and their relationship was cozy and suspicious. Out-of-state drivers who got nailed by a constable in Ford County were usually in for some abuse at the hands of the J.P.

Each county had five supervisors, five little kings who held the real power. For their supporters they paved roads, fixed culverts, gave away gravel. For their enemies they did little. All county ordinances were enacted by the Board of Supervisors.

Each county also had an elected sheriff, tax collector, tax assessor, chancery court clerk, and coroner. The rural counties shared a state senator and state representative. Other available jobs in 1971 were highway commissioner, public service commissioner, commissioner of agriculture, state treasurer, state auditor, attorney general, lieutenant governor, and governor.

I thought this was a ridiculous and cumbersome system until the candidates for these positions began buying ads in the *Times*. A particularly bad constable over in the Fourth District (also known as "Beat Four") had eleven opponents by the end of January. Most of these poor boys eased into our offices with an "announcement" that their wives had handwritten on notebook paper. I would patiently read them, editing, decoding, translating along the way. Then I would take their money and run their little ads, almost all of which began with either "After months of prayer . . ." or "Many people have asked me to run . . ."

By late February, the county was consumed with the August election. Sheriff Coley had two opponents with two more threatening. The deadline to file for office was

June, and he had yet to do so. This fueled speculation that he might not run.

It took little to fuel speculation about anything when it came to local elections.

———

Miss Callie clung to the old-fashioned belief that eating in restaurants was a waste of money, and therefore sinful. Her list of potential sins was longer than most folks', especially mine. It took almost six months to convince her to go to Claude's for a Thursday lunch. I argued that if I paid, then we wouldn't be wasting her money. She wouldn't be guilty of any transgression, and if I got hit with another one I really didn't care. Dining out was certainly the most benign in my inventory.

I wasn't worried about being seen in downtown Clanton with a black woman. I didn't care what people said. I wasn't worried about having the only white face in Claude's. What really concerned me, and what almost kept me from suggesting the idea in the first place, was the challenge of getting Miss Callie in and out of my Triumph Spitfire. It wasn't built for hefty folks like her.

She and Esau owned an old Buick that had once held all eight children. Add another hundred pounds and Miss Callie could still slide in and out of the front seat with ease.

She was not getting smaller. Her high blood pressure and high cholesterol were of great concern to her children. She was sixty years old and healthy, but trouble was looming.

We walked to the street and she peered down at my car. It was March and windy with a chance of rain, so the convertible top was up. In its closed state, the two-seater looked even smaller.

"I'm not sure this is going to work," she announced. It had taken six months to get her that far; we were not turning back. I opened the passenger door and she approached with great caution.

"Any suggestions?" she said.

"Yes, try the rear-end-first method."

It worked, eventually, and when I started the engine we were shoulder to shoulder. "White folks sure drive some funny cars," she said, as frightened as if she were flying in a small plane for the first time. I popped the clutch, spun the tires, and we were off, slinging gravel and laughing.

I parked in front of the office and helped her out. Getting in was far easier. Inside, I introduced her to Margaret Wright and Davey Bigmouth Bass, and I gave her a tour. She was curious about the offset press because the paper now looked so much better. "Who does the proofreading around here?" she whispered.

"You do," I said. We were averaging three mistakes per week, according to her. I still got the list every Thursday over lunch.

We took a stroll around the square and eventually made it to Claude's, the black café next to City Cleaners. Claude had been in business for many years and served the best food in town. He didn't need menus because you ate whatever he happened to be cooking that day. Wednesday was catfish and Friday was barbecue, but for the other four days you didn't know what you would eat until Claude told you. He greeted us in a dirty apron and pointed to a table at the front window. The café was half-full and we got some curious stares.

Oddly enough, Miss Callie had never met Claude. I had assumed that every black person in Clanton had at one time bumped into every other one, but Miss Callie explained that was not the case. Claude lived out in the country, and there was an awful rumor over in Lowtown that he did not go to church. She had never been anxious to meet him. They had attended a funeral together years earlier, but had not met.

I introduced them, and when Claude put her name with her face he said, "The Ruffin family. All them doctors."

"PhD's," Miss Callie said, correcting him.

Claude was loud and gruff and charged for his food and did not go to church, so Miss Callie immediately disliked him. He took the hint, didn't really care, and went off to yell at someone in the back. A waitress brought us iced tea and corn bread, and Miss Callie didn't like either. The tea was weak and almost sugarless, according to her, and the corn bread lacked enough salt and was served at room temperature, an unforgivable offense.

"It's a restaurant, Miss Callie," I said in a low voice. "Would you relax?"

"I'm trying."

"No you're not. How can we enjoy a meal if you're frowning at everything?"

"That's a pretty bow tie."

"Thank you."

My upgraded wardrobe had pleased no one more than Miss Callie. Negroes liked to dress up and were very fashion conscious, she explained to me. She still referred to herself as a Negro.

In the wake of the civil rights movement and the complicated issues it had spun, it was difficult to know exactly what to call blacks. The older, more dignified ones like Miss Callie preferred to be called "Negroes." A notch below them on the social ladder were "coloreds."

Though I had never heard Miss Callie use the word, it was not uncommon for upper blacks to refer to the lowest of their kind as "niggers."

I could not begin to understand the labels and classes, so I adhered strictly to the safety of "blacks." Those on my side of the tracks had an entire dictionary to describe blacks, little of which was endearing.

At that moment, I was the only non-Negro in Claude's, and this bothered no one.

"What y'all eatin'?" Claude yelled from the counter. A blackboard advertised Texas chili, fried chicken, and pork chops. Miss Callie knew the chicken and pork would be sub-par, so we both ordered chili.

I got a gardening report. The winter greens were especially nice. She and Esau were preparing to plant the summer crop. The *Farmer's Almanac* predicted a mild

summer with average rain—same prediction every
year—and she was excited about warmer weather and
lunch back on the porch, where it belonged. I began
with Alberto, the oldest, and half an hour later she
ended with Sam, the youngest. He was back in Milwaukee, staying with Roberto, working and taking classes at
night. All children and grandchildren were doing well.

She wanted to talk about "poor Mr. Hank Hooten."
She remembered him well from the trial, though he had
never spoken to the jury. I passed along the latest news.
He was now living in a room with padded walls, where
he would remain for some time.

The restaurant filled up quickly. Claude walked by
with an armload of plates and said, "Y'all finished, time
to go." She pretended to be insulted by this, but Claude
was famous for telling people to leave as soon as they
were finished. On Fridays, when a few whites ventured
in for barbeque and the place was packed, he put a
clock on his customers and said, loudly, "You got twenty
minutes."

She pretended to dislike the experience—the idea itself, the restaurant, the cheap tablecloth, the food,
Claude, the prices, the crowd, everything. But it was an
act. She was secretly delighted to be taken to lunch by a
well-dressed young white man. It had not happened to
any of her friends.

As I gently pulled her out of the car back in Lowtown, she reached into her purse and took out a small
scrap of paper. Only two typos that week; oddly, both
were in classifieds, an area that Margaret handled.

I walked her to the house. "That wasn't so bad now, was it?" I said.

"I enjoyed it. Thank you. Are you coming next Thursday?" She asked the same question each week. The answer was the same too.

CHAPTER 27

At noon on the Fourth of July the temperature was 101 degrees and the humidity felt even higher. The parade was led by the Mayor, even though he was not yet running for anything. State and local elections were in 1971. The presidential race was in 1972. Judicial elections were in 1973. Municipal elections were in 1974. Mississippians loved voting almost as much as football.

The Mayor sat on the rear seat of a 1962 Corvette and threw candy to the children packed along the sidewalks around the square. Behind him were two high school bands, Clanton's and Karaway's, the Boy Scouts, Shriners on mini-bikes, a new fire truck, a dozen floats, a posse on horseback, veterans from every war that century, a collection of shiny new cars from the Ford dealer, and three restored John Deere tractors. Juror number eight, Mr. Mo Teale, drove one. The rear was protected by a string of city and county police cars, all polished to perfection.

I watched the parade from the third-floor balcony of the Security Bank. Stan Atcavage threw an annual party up there. Since I now owed the bank a sizable sum, I was invited to sip lemonade and watch the festivities.

For a reason no one could remember, the Rotarians were in charge of the speeches. They had parked a long flatbed trailer next to the Confederate sentry and decorated it with bales of hay and red, white, and blue bunting. When the parade was over, the throng moved tightly around the trailer and waited anxiously. An old-fashioned courthouse hanging couldn't have drawn a more expectant audience.

Mr. Mervin Beets, president of the Rotary club, stepped to the microphone and welcomed everyone. Prayer was required for any public event in Clanton, and in the new spirit of desegregation he had invited the Reverand Thurston Small, Miss Callie's minister, to properly get things going. According to Stan, there were noticeably more blacks downtown that year.

With such a crowd, Reverend Small could not be brief. He asked the Lord to bless everyone and everything at least twice. Loudspeakers were hanging from poles all around the courthouse, and his voice echoed throughout downtown.

The first candidate was Timmy Joe Bullock, a terrified young man from Beat Four who wanted to serve as a constable. He walked across the flatbed trailer as if it were a gangplank, and when he stood behind the mike and looked at the crowd he almost fainted. He managed to utter his name, then reached into a pocket where he found his speech. He was not much of a reader, but in ten very long minutes managed to comment on the rise in crime, the recent murder trial, and the sniper. He didn't like murderers and he was especially opposed to snipers. He would work to protect us from both.

Applause was light when he finished. But at least he showed up. There were twenty-two candidates for constable in the five districts, but only seven had the courage to face the crowd. When we finally finished with the constables and the Justices of the Peace, Woody Gates and the Country Boys played a few bluegrass tunes and the crowd appreciated the break.

At various places on the courthouse lawn, food and refreshments were being served. The Lions Club was giving away slices of cold watermelon. The ladies of the garden club were selling homemade ice cream. The Jaycees were barbecuing ribs. The crowd huddled under the ancient oak trees and hid from the sun.

Mackey Don Coley had entered the race for Sheriff in late May. He had three opponents, the most popular of whom was a Clanton city policeman named T. R. Meredith. When Mr. Beets announced that it was time for the Sheriff candidates, the voters left the shade and swarmed around the trailer.

Freck Oswald was running for the fourth time. In the prior three he had finished dead last; he appeared headed for the bottom again but seemed to enjoy the fun of it. He didn't like President Nixon and said harsh things about his foreign policy, especially relations with China. The crowd listened but appeared to be a bit confused.

Tryce McNatt was running for the second time. He began his remarks by saying, "I really don't give a damn about China." This was humorous but also stupid. Swearing in public, in the presence of ladies, would cost him many votes. Tryce was upset at the way criminals were being coddled by the system. He was opposed to any effort to build a new jail in Ford County—a waste of taxpayer money! He wanted harsh sentences and more prisons, even chain gangs and forced labor.

I had heard nothing about a new jail.

Because of the Kassellaw murder and the Hank Hooten rampage, violent crime was now out of control in Ford County, according to Tryce. We needed a new Sheriff, one who chased criminals, not befriended them. "Let's clean up the county!" was his refrain. The crowd was with him.

T. R. Meredith was a thirty-year veteran of law enforcement. He was an awful speaker but he was related to half the county, according to Stan. Stan knew about such things; he was related to the other half. "Meredith'll win by a thousand votes in the runoff," he predicted. This caused quite an argument among the other guests.

Mackey Don went last. He had been the Sheriff since 1943, and wanted just one more term. "He's been saying that for twenty years," Stan said. Coley rambled on about his experience, his knowledge of the county and its people. When he finished, the applause was polite but certainly not encouraging.

Two gentlemen were running for the office of tax collector, no doubt the least popular position in the county. As they spoke, the crowd drifted away again and headed for the ice cream and watermelons. I walked down to Harry Rex's office, where another party was in progress on the sidewalk.

The speeches continued throughout the afternoon. It was the summer of 1971, and by then at least fifty thousand young Americans had been killed in Vietnam. A similar gathering of people in any other part of the country would have turned into a virulent antiwar rally. The politicians would have been heckled off the stage. Flags and draft cards would've been burned.

But Vietnam was never mentioned that Fourth of July.

I'd had great fun at Syracuse demonstrating on campus and marching in the streets, but such activity was unheard of in the Deep South. It was a war; therefore real patriots were supportive. We were stopping Communism; the hippies and radicals and peaceniks up North and in California were simply afraid to fight.

I bought a dish of strawberry ice cream from the garden ladies, and as I strolled around the courthouse I heard a commotion. From the third-floor window of the Bar Room, a prankster had dropped down an effigy of Baggy. The stuffed figure was hanging with its hands above its head—just like the real Baggy—and across its chest was a sign that said "SUGGS." And to make sure everyone recognized the butt of the joke, an empty bottle of Jack Daniel's protruded from each pants pocket.

I had not seen Baggy that day, nor would I. Later, he claimed to know nothing about the incident. Not surprisingly, Wiley managed to take numerous photos of the effigy.

"Theo's here!" someone yelled, and this excited the crowd. Theo Morton was our longtime state senator. His district covered parts of four counties, and though he lived in Baldwin his wife was from Clanton. He owned two nursing homes and a cemetery, and he had the distinction of having survived three airplane crashes. He was no longer a pilot. Theo was colorful—blunt, sarcastic, hilarious, completely unpredictable on the stump. His opponent was a young man who'd just finished law school and was rumored to be grooming himself for Governor. Warren was his name, and Warren made the mistake of attacking Theo over some suspicious legislation that had been "sneaked through" the last session and increased the state's support for nursing home patients.

It was a bristling assault. I was standing in the crowd, watching Warren blast away, and just over his left shoulder I could see "SUGGS" hanging from the window.

Theo began by introducing his wife, Rex Ella, a Mabry from right here in Clanton. He talked about her parents and her grandparents, and her aunts and uncles, and before long Theo had mentioned half the crowd. Clanton was his second home, his district, his people, the constituents he worked so hard to serve down in Jackson.

It was smooth, fluid, off-the-cuff. I was listening to a master on the stump.

He was chairman of the Highways Committee in the state senate, and for a few minutes he bragged about all the new roads he'd built in north Mississippi. His committee handled four hundred separate pieces of legislation each session. Four hundred! Four hundred bills, or laws. As chairman, he was responsible for writing laws. That's what state senators did. They wrote good laws and killed bad laws.

His young opponent had just finished law school, a notable accomplishment. He, Theo, didn't get the chance to go to college because he was off fighting the Japs in World War II. But anyway, his young opponent had evidently neglected his study of the law. Otherwise, he would've passed the bar exam on the first try.

Instead, "He flunked the bar exam, ladies and gentlemen!"

With perfect timing, someone standing just behind young Warren yelled out, "That's a damned lie!" The crowd looked at Warren as if he'd lost his mind. Theo turned to the voice and said incredulously, "A lie?"

He reached into his pocket and whipped out a folded sheet of paper. "I've got the proof right here!" He pinched a corner of the paper and began waving it about. Without reading a single word of whatever was printed on it, he said, "How can we trust a man to write our laws when he can't even pass the bar exam? Mr. Warren and I stand on equal footing—neither of us has ever passed the bar exam. Problem is, he had three years of law school to help him flunk it."

Theo's supporters were yelping with laughter. Young Warren held his ground but wanted to bolt.

Theo hammered away. "Maybe if he'd gone to law school in Mississippi instead of Tennessee then he'd understand our laws!"

He was famous for such public butcherings. He'd once humiliated an opponent who'd left the pulpit under a cloud. Pulling an "affidavit" from his pocket, Theo claimed he had proof that the "ex-reverend" had an affair with a deacon's wife. The affidavit was never read.

The ten-minute limit meant nothing to Theo. He blew through it with a series of promises to cut taxes and waste and do something to make sure murderers got the death penalty more often. When he finally wound down, he thanked the crowd for twenty years of faithful support. He reminded us that in the last two elections the good folks of Ford County had given him, and Rex Ella, almost 80 percent of their votes.

The applause was loud and long, and at some point Warren disappeared. So did I. I was tired of speeches and politics.

———

Four weeks later, around dusk on the first Tuesday in August, much of the same crowd gathered around the courthouse for the vote counting. It had cooled off considerably; the temperature was only ninety-two with 98 percent humidity.

The final days of the election had been a reporter's dream. There was a fistfight between two Justice of the Peace candidates outside a black church. There were two lawsuits, both of which accused the other side of libel and slander and distributing phony sample ballots. One man was arrested when he was caught in the act of spray painting obscenities on one of Theo's billboards. (As it turned out, after the election, the man had been hired by one of Theo's henchmen to defile the senator's signs. Young Warren still got the blame. "A common trick," according to Baggy.) The state's Attorney General was asked to investigate the high number of absentee ballots. "Typical election," was Baggy's summary. Things came to a peak on that Tuesday, and the entire county stopped to vote and enjoy the sport of a rural election.

The polls closed at six, and an hour later the square was alive and wired with anticipation. People piled in from the county. They formed little groups around their candidate and even used campaign signs to stake off their territory. Many brought food and drink and most had folding lawn chairs as if they were there to watch a baseball game. Two enormous black chalkboards were placed side by side near the front door of the courthouse, and there the returns were tallied.

"We have the results from North Karaway," the clerk announced into a microphone so loud it could've been heard five miles away. The festive mood was immediately serious.

"North Karaway's always first," Baggy said. It was almost eight- thirty, almost dark. We were sitting on the porch outside my office, waiting for the news. We planned to delay press time for twenty-four hours and publish our "Election Special" on Thursday. It took some time for the clerk to read the vote totals for every candidate for every office. Halfway through she said, "And in the Sheriff's race." Several thousand people held their breath.

"Mackey Don Coley, eighty-four. Tryce McNatt, twenty-one. T. R. Meredith, sixty-two, and Freck Oswald, eleven." A loud cheer went up on the far side of the lawn where Coley's supporters were camped.

"Coley's always tough in Karaway," Baggy said. "But he's beat."

"He's beat?" I asked. The first of twenty-eight precincts were in, and Baggy was already predicting winners.

"Yep. For T.R. to run strong in a place where he has no base shows folks are fed up with Mackey Don. Wait'll you see the Clanton boxes."

Slowly, the returns dribbled in, from places I'd never heard of: Pleasant Hill, Shady Grove, Klebie, Three Corners, Clover Hill, Green Alley, Possum Ridge, Massey Mill, Calico Ridge. Woody Gates and the Country Boys, who seemed to always be available, filled in the gaps with some bluegrass.

The Padgitts voted at a tiny precinct called Dancing

Creek. When the clerk announced the votes from there, and Coley got 31 votes and the other three got 8 combined, there was a refreshing round of boos from the crowd. Clanton East followed, the largest precinct and the one I voted in. Coley got 285 votes, Tryce 47, and when T.R.'s total of 644 was announced, the place went wild.

Baggy grabbed me and we celebrated with the rest of the town. Coley was going down without a runoff.

As the losers slowly learned their fate, they and their supporters packed up and went home. Around eleven, the crowd was noticeably thinner. After midnight, I left the office and strolled around the square, taking in the sounds and images of this wonderful tradition.

I was quite proud of the town. In the aftermath of a brutal murder and its baffling verdict, we had rallied, fought back, and spoken clearly that we would not tolerate corruption. The strong vote against Coley was our way of hitting at the Padgitts. For the second time in a hundred years, they would not own the Sheriff.

T. R. Meredith got 61 percent of the vote, a stunning landslide. Theo got 82 percent, an old-fashioned shellacking. We printed eight thousand copies of our "Election Edition" and sold every one of them. I became a staunch believer in voting every year. Democracy at its finest.

CHAPTER 28

A week before Thanksgiving in 1971, Clanton was rocked by the news that one of its sons had been killed in Vietnam. Pete Mooney, a nineteen- year-old staff sergeant, was captured in an ambush near Hue, in central Vietnam. A few hours later his body was found.

I didn't know the Mooneys, but Margaret certainly did. She called me with the news and said she needed a few days off. Her family had lived down the street from the Mooneys for many years. Her son and Pete had been close friends since childhood.

I spent some time in the archives and found the 1966 story of Marvin Lee Walker, a black kid who'd been the county's first death in Vietnam. That had been before Mr. Caudle cared about such things, and the *Times* coverage of the event was shamefully sparse. Nothing on the front page. A hundred-word story on page three with no photo. At the time, Clanton had no idea where Vietnam was.

So a young man who couldn't go to the better schools, probably couldn't vote, and more than likely was too afraid to drink from the public water fountain at the courthouse, had been killed in a country few people in his hometown could find on a map. And his death was the right and proper thing. Communists had to be fought wherever they might be found.

Margaret quietly passed along the details I needed for a story. Pete had graduated from Clanton High School in 1970. He had played varsity football and baseball, lettering in both for three years. He was an honor student who had planned to work for two years, save his money, then go to college. He was unlucky enough to have a high draft number, and in December 1970 he got his notice.

According to Margaret, and this was something I could not print, Pete had been very reluctant to report for basic training. He and his father had fought for weeks over the war. The son wanted to go to Canada and avoid the whole mess. The father was horrified that his son would be labeled a draft dodger. The family name would be ruined, etc. He called the kid a coward. Mr. Mooney had served in Korea and had zero patience for the antiwar movement. Mrs. Mooney tried the role of peacemaker, but in her heart, she too was reluctant to send her son off to such an unpopular war. Pete finally relented, and now he was coming home in a box.

The funeral was at the First Baptist Church, where the Mooneys had been active for many years. Pete had been baptized there at the age of eleven, and this was of great comfort to his family and friends. He was now with the Lord, though still much too young to be called home.

I sat with Margaret and her husband. It was my first and last funeral for a nineteen-year-old soldier. By concentrating on the casket, I could almost avoid the sobbing and, at times, wailing around me. His high school football coach gave a eulogy that drained every eye in the church, mine included.

I could barely see the back of Mr. Mooney, in the front row. What unspeakable grief that poor man was suffering.

After an hour, we escaped and made our way to the Clanton cemetery, where Pete was laid to rest with full military pomp and ceremony. When the lone bugler played "Taps," the gut-wrenching cry of Pete's mother made me shudder. She clung to the casket until they began to lower it. His father finally collapsed and was tended to by several deacons.

What a waste, I said over and over as I walked the streets alone, headed generally back to the office. That night, still alone, I cursed myself for being so silent, so cowardly. I was the editor of the newspaper, dammit! Whether I felt entitled to the position or not, I was the only one in town. If I felt strongly about an issue, then I certainly had the power and position to editorialize.

———

Pete Mooney was preceded in death by more than fifty thousand of his fellow countrymen, although the military did a rotten job of reporting an accurate count.

In 1969, President Nixon and his National Security Adviser, Henry Kissinger, made the decision that the war in Vietnam could not be won, or, rather, that the United States would no longer try and win it. They kept this to themselves. They did not stop the draft. Instead, they pursued the cynical strategy of appearing to be confident of a successful outcome.

From the time this decision was made until the end of the war in 1973, approximately eighteen thousand more men were killed, including Pete Mooney.

I ran my editorial on the front page, bottom half, under a large photo of Pete in his Army uniform. It read:

> *The death of Pete Mooney should make us ask the glaring question—What the hell are we doing in Vietnam? A gifted student, talented athlete, school leader, future community leader, one of our best and brightest, gunned down at the edge of a river we've never heard of in a country we care little about.*
>
> *The official reason, one that goes back twenty years, is that we are there fighting Communism. If we see it spreading, then, in the words of ex-President Lyndon Johnson, we are to take ". . . all necessary measures to prevent further aggression."*
>
> *Korea, Vietnam. We now have troops in Laos and Cambodia, though President Nixon denies it. Where to next? Are we expected to send our sons anywhere and everywhere in the world to meddle in the civil wars of others?*
>
> *Vietnam was divided into two countries when the*

French were defeated there in 1954. North Vietnam is a poor country run by a Communist named Ho Chi Minh. South Vietnam is a poor country that was run by a brutal dictator named Ngo Dinh Diem until he was murdered in a coup in 1963. Since then the country has been run by the military.

Vietnam has been in a state of war since 1946 when the French began their fateful attempt to keep out the Communists. Their failure was spectacular, so we rushed in to show how wars are supposed to be run. Our failure has been even grander than that of the French, and we're not finished yet.

How many more Pete Mooneys will die before our government decides to leave Vietnam to its own course?

And how many other places around the world will we send our troops to fight Communism?

What the hell are we doing in Vietnam? Right now we're burying young soldiers while the politicians who are running the war contemplate getting out.

Using bad language would be good for a few slaps on the wrist, but what did I care? Strong language was needed to give light to the blind patriots of Ford County. Before the flood of calls and letters, though, I made a friend.

When I returned from Thursday lunch with Miss Callie (lamb stew indoors by the fire), Bubba Crockett was waiting in my office. He wore jeans, boots, a flannel shirt, long hair, and after he introduced himself he thanked me for the editorial. He had some things he wanted to get off his chest, and since I was as stuffed as a Christmas turkey, I placed my feet on my desk and listened for a long time.

He'd grown up in Clanton, finished school here in 1966. His father owned the nursery two miles south of town; they were landscapers. He got his draft notice in 1967 and gave no thought to doing anything other than racing off to fight Communists. His unit landed in the south, just in time for the Tet Offensive. Two days on the ground, and he had lost three of his closest friends.

The horror of fighting could not accurately be described, though Bubba was descriptive enough for me. Men burning, screaming for help, tripping over body parts, dragging bodies off the battlefield, hours with no sleep, no food, running out of ammo, seeing the enemy crawl toward you at night. His battalion lost a hundred men in the first five days. "After a week I knew I was going to die," he said with wet eyes. "At that point, I became a pretty good soldier. You gotta reach that point to survive."

He was wounded twice, slight wounds that were treatable in field hospitals. Nothing that would get him home. He talked of the frustration of fighting a war that the government would not allow them to win. "We were better soldiers," he said. "And our equipment was vastly superior. Our commanders were superb, but the fools in Washington wouldn't let them fight a war."

Bubba knew the Mooney family and had begged Pete not to go. He had watched the burial service from a distance, and he cursed everybody he could see and many he could not.

"These idiots around here still support the war, can you believe that?" he said. "More than fifty thousand dead and now we're pulling out, and these people will argue with you on the streets of Clanton that it was a great cause."

"They don't argue with you," I said.

"They do not. I've punched a couple of them. You play poker?"

I did not, but I'd heard many colorful stories about various poker games around town. Quickly, I thought this might be interesting. "A little," I said, figuring I could either find a rule book or get Baggy to teach me.

"We play on Thursday nights, in a shed at the nursery. Several guys who fought over there. You might enjoy it."

"Tonight?"

"Yeah, around eight. It's a small game, some beer, some pot, some war stories. My buddies want to meet you."

"I'll be there," I said, wondering where I could find Baggy.

Four letters were slid under the door that afternoon, all four scathing in their criticism of me and my criticism of the war. Mr. E. L. Green, a veteran of two wars, and a longtime subscriber to the *Times*, though that might soon change, said, among other things:

> *If we don't stop Communism it will spread to every corner of the world. One day it will be at our doorstep,*

*and our children and grandchildren will ask us why we
didn't have the courage to stop it before it spread.*

Mr. Herbert Gillenwater's brother was killed in the
Korean conflict. He wrote:

*His death was a tragedy I still struggle with each day.
But he was a soldier, a hero, a proud American, and his
death helped stop the North Koreans and their allies, the
Red Chinese and the Russians. When we are too afraid to
fight, then we will ourselves be conquered.*

Mr. Felix Toliver from down in Shady Grove suggested that perhaps I'd spent too much time up North
where folks were notoriously gun-shy. He said the military had always been dominated by brave young men
from the South, and if I didn't believe it then I should
do some more research. There were a disproportionate
number of Southern casualties in Korea and Vietnam.
He concluded, rather eloquently:

*Our freedom was bought at the terrible price of the lives
of countless brave soldiers. But what if we had been too
afraid to fight? Hitler and the Japanese would still be in
power. Much of the civilized world would be in ruins. We
would be isolated and eventually destroyed.*

I planned to run every single letter to the editor, but
I hoped there might be one or two in support of my editorial. The criticism didn't bother me at all. I felt

strongly that I was right. And I was developing a rather thick skin, a fine asset for an editor.

————

After Baggy's quick tutelage, I lost $100 playing poker with Bubba and the boys. They invited me back.

There were five of us around the table, all in our mid-twenties. Three had served in Vietnam—Bubba, Darrell Radke, whose family owned the propane company, and Cedric Young, a black guy with a severe leg injury. The fifth player was Bubba's older brother David, who had been rejected by the draft because of his eyesight, and who, I think, was there just for the marijuana.

We talked a lot about drugs. None of the three veterans had seen or heard of pot or anything else prior to joining the Army. They laughed at the idea of drugs on the streets of Clanton in the 1960s. In Vietnam, drug use was rampant. Pot was smoked when they were bored and homesick, and it was smoked to calm their nerves in battle. The field hospitals loaded up the injured with the strongest painkillers available, and Cedric got hooked on morphine two weeks after being wounded.

At their urging, I told a few drug stories from college, but I was an amateur among professionals. I don't think they were exaggerating. No wonder we lost the war—everybody was stoned.

They expressed great admiration for my editorial and great bitterness for having been sent over there.

Each of the three had been scarred in some way; Cedric's was obvious. Bubba's and Darrel's was more of a smoldering anger, a barely contained rage and desire to lash out, but at whom?

Late in the game, they began swapping stories of gruesome battlefield scenes. I had heard that many soldiers refused to talk about their war experiences. Those three didn't mind at all. It was therapeutic.

They played poker almost every Thursday night, and I was always welcome. When I left them at midnight, they were still drinking, still smoking pot, still talking about Vietnam. I'd had enough of the war for one day.

CHAPTER 29

The following week I devoted an entire page to the war controversy I had created. It was covered with letters to the editor, seventeen in all, only two of which were even somewhat supportive of my antiwar feelings. I was called a Communist, a liberal, a traitor, a carpet-bagger, and, the worst, a coward because I had not worn the uniform. Every letter was proudly signed, no anonymous mail that week; these folks were fired-up patriots who disliked me and wanted the county to know it.

I didn't care. I had stirred up a hornet's nest and the town was at least debating the war. Most of the debates were one-sided, but I had aroused strong feelings.

The response to those seventeen letters was astounding. A group of high school students came to my rescue with a hand-delivered batch of their own. They were passionately against the war, had no plans to go fight in it, and, furthermore, found it odd that most of the letters the prior week were from folks too old for the armed forces. "It's our blood, not yours," was my favorite line.

Many of the the students singled out particular letters I'd printed and went after them with a hatchet. Becky Jenkins was offended by Mr. Robert Earl Huff's statement that ". . . our nation was built by the blood of our soldiers. Wars will always be with us."

She responded: "Wars will be with us as long as ignorant and greedy men try to impose their will on others."

Kirk Wallace took exception to Mrs. Mattie Louise Ferguson's rather exhaustive description of me. In his final paragraph he wrote, "Sadly, Mrs. Ferguson would not know a Communist, a liberal, a traitor, or a carpetbagger if she met one. Life out in Possum Ridge protects her from such people."

The following week, I devoted yet another full page to the thirty-one letters from the students. There were also three late arrivals from the warmongering crowd, and I printed them too. The response was another flood of letters, all of which I printed.

Through the pages of the *Times*, we fought the war until Christmas when everyone suddenly called a truce and settled in for the holidays.

———

Mr. Max Hocutt died on New Year's Day 1972. Gilma knocked on my apartment window early that morning and eventually got me to the door. I'd been asleep for less than five hours, and I needed a full day of hard sleep. Maybe two.

I followed her into the old mansion, my first visit inside in many months, and I was shocked at how badly it was deteriorating. But there were more urgent matters. We walked to the main stairway in the front foyer where Wilma joined us. She pointed a crooked and wrinkled finger upward and said, "He's up there. First door on the right. We've already been up once this morning."

Once a day up the stairs was their limit. They now were in their late seventies, and not far behind Mr. Max.

He was lying in a large bed with a dirty white sheet pulled up to his neck. His skin was the color of the sheet. I stood beside him for a moment to make sure he wasn't breathing. I had never been called upon to pronounce someone dead, but this was not a close call—Mr. Max looked as though he'd been dead for a month.

I walked back down the stairs where Wilma and Gilma were waiting right where I'd left them. They looked at me as if I might have a different diagnosis.

"I'm afraid he's dead," I said.

"We know that," Gilma said.

"Tell us what to do," Wilma said.

This was the first corpse I'd been called upon to process, but the next step seemed pretty obvious. "Well, perhaps we should call Mr. Magargel down at the funeral home."

"I told you so," Wilma said to Gilma.

They didn't move, so I went to the phone and called Mr. Magargel. "It's New Year's Day," he said. It was apparent my call had awakened him.

"He's still dead," I said.

"Are you sure?"

"Yes, I'm sure. I just saw him."

"Where is he?"

"In bed. He went peacefully."

"Sometimes these old geezers are just sleeping soundly, you know."

I turned away from the twins so they wouldn't hear me argue about whether their brother was really dead. "He's not sleeping, Mr. Magargel. He's dead."

"I'll be there in an hour."

"Is there anything else we should do?" I asked.

"Like what?"

"I don't know. Notify the police, something like that?"

"Was he murdered?"

"No."

"Why would you want to call the police?"

"Sorry I asked."

They invited me into the kitchen for a cup of instant coffee. On the counter was a box of Cream of Wheat, and beside it a large bowl of the cereal, mixed and ready to eat. Evidently, Wilma or Gilma had prepared breakfast for their brother, and when he didn't come down they went after him.

The coffee was undrinkable until I poured in sugar. They sat across the narrow prep table, watching me curiously. Their eyes were red, but they were not crying.

"We can't live here," Wilma said, with the finality that came from years of discussion.

"We want you to buy the place," Gilma added. One barely finished a sentence before the other started another one.

"We sell it to you . . ."

"For a hundred thousand . . ."

"We take the money . . ."

"And move to Florida . . ."

"Florida?" I asked.

"We have a cousin there . . ."

"She lives in a retirement village . . ."

"It's very lovely . . ."

"And they take such good care of you . . ."

"And Melberta is nearby."

Melberta? I thought she was still around the house somewhere, sneaking through the shadows. They explained that they had placed her in a "home" a few months back. The "home" was somewhere north of Tampa. That's where they wanted to go and spend the rest of their days. Their beloved mansion was simply too much for them to maintain. They had bad hips, bad knees, bad eyes. They climbed the stairs once a day—"twenty-four steps" Gilma informed me—and were terrified of falling down and killing themselves. There wasn't enough money to make it safe, and what money they had they didn't want to waste on housekeepers, grass-cutters, and, now, a driver.

"We want you to buy the Mercedes too . . ."

"We don't drive, you know . . ."

"Max always took us . . ."

Once in a while, just for fun, I would sneak a glance at the odometer of Max's Mercedes. He was averaging less than a thousand miles per year. Unlike the house, the car was in mint condition.

The house had six bedrooms, four floors and a basement, four or five bathrooms, living and dining rooms, library, kitchen, wide sweeping porches that were falling in, and an attic that I felt certain was crammed with family treasures buried there centuries ago. It would take months just to clean it before the remodelers moved in. A hundred thousand dollars was a low price for such a mansion, but there were not enough newspapers sold in the entire state to renovate the place.

And what about all those animals? Cats, birds, rabbits, squirrels, goldfish, the place was a regular zoo.

I had been looking at real estate, but, frankly, I'd been so spoiled by paying them $50 a month that I found it hard to leave. I was twenty-four years old, very single, and I was having a grand time watching the money accumulate in the bank. Why would I risk financial ruin by buying that money pit?

I bought it two days after the funeral.

On a cold, wet Thursday in February, I pulled to a stop in front of the Ruffin residence in Lowtown. Esau was waiting on the porch. "You trade cars?" he asked, looking at the street.

"No, I still have the little one," I said. "That was Mr. Hocutt's."

"Thought it was black." There were very few Mercedes in Ford County and it was not difficult keeping track of them.

"It needed painting," I said. It was now a dark maroon. I had to cover the knives Mr. Hocutt had painted on both front doors, and so while it was in the shop I decided to go with a different color altogether.

Word was out that I had somehow swindled the Hocutts out of their Mercedes. In fact, I had paid blue-book value for it—$9,500. The purchase was approved by Judge Reuben V. Atlee, the longtime chancellor in Ford County. He also approved my purchase of the house for $100,000, an apparently low figure that looked much better after two court-appointed appraisers gave their estimates at $75,000 and $85,000. One reported that any renovation of the Hocutt House would ". . . involve extensive and unforeseen expenditures."

Harry Rex, my lawyer, made sure I saw this language.

Esau was subdued, and things did not improve inside. The house, as always, simmered in the sauce of some delicious beast she was roasting in the oven. To-day it would be rabbit.

I hugged Miss Callie and knew something was terribly wrong. Esau picked up an envelope and said, "This is a draft notice. For Sam." He tossed it on the table for me to see, then left the kitchen.

Talk was slow over lunch. They were subdued, preoccupied, and very confused. Esau at times felt the proper thing to do was for Sam to honor whatever commitment his country required. Miss Callie felt like she had already lost Sam once. The thought of losing him again was unbearable.

That night I called Sam and gave him the bad news. He was in Toledo spending a few days with Max. We talked for over an hour, and I was relentless in my conviction that he had no business going to Vietnam. Fortunately, Max felt the same way.

Over the course of the next week, I spent hours on the phone with Sam, Bobby, Al, Leon, Max, and Mario, as we shared our views about what Sam should do. Neither he nor any of his brothers believed the war was just, but Mario and Al felt strongly that it was wrong to break the law. I was by far the biggest dove in the bunch, with Bobby and Leon somewhere in the middle. Sam seemed to twist in the wind and change daily. It was a gut-wrenching decision, but as the days dragged on he appeared to spend more time talking to me. The fact that he had been on the run for two years helped immensely.

After two weeks of soul-searching, Sam slipped into

the underground and surfaced in Ontario. He called collect one night and asked me to tell his parents he was okay. Early the next morning, I drove to Lowtown and delivered the news to Esau and Miss Callie that their youngest son had just made the smartest decision of his life.

To them, Canada seemed like a million miles away. Not nearly as far as Vietnam, I told them.

CHAPTER 30

The second contractor I hired to transform the Hocutt House was Mr. Lester Klump from out in Shady Grove. He had been highly recommended by Baggy, who, of course, knew exactly how to restore a mansion. Stan Atcavage at the bank also recommended Mr. Klump, and since Stan held the mortgage for $100,000 I listened to him.

The first contractor had failed to show, and when I called after waiting for three days his phone had been disconnected. An ominous sign.

Mr. Klump and his son, Lester Junior, spent days going over the house. They were terrified of the project, and knew it would be a regular nightmare if anybody got in a hurry, especially me. They were slow and methodical, even talked slower than most folks in Ford County, and I soon realized that everything they did was in second gear. I probably didn't help matters by explaining that I was already living in very comfortable quarters on the premises; thus I wasn't going to be homeless if they didn't hurry up.

Their reputation was that they were sober and generally finished on time. This put them at the top of the heap in the world of remodeling.

After a few days of scratching our heads and kicking at the gravel, we agreed on a plan whereby they would bill me weekly for their labor and supplies, and I would add 10 percent for their "overhead," which I hoped meant profit. It took a week of cursing to get Harry Rex to draft a contract reflecting this. At first he refused and called me all sorts of colorful names.

The Klumps would begin with the cleanup and demolition, then do the roof and porches. When that was over, we'd sit down and plan the next phase. In April 1972 the project began.

At least one of the Klumps appeared every day with a crew. They spent the first month scattering all the varmints and wildlife that had made the property home for decades.

A carload of high school seniors was stopped by a state trooper a few hours after their graduation. The car was full of beer, and the trooper, a rookie fresh from school where they had alerted them to such things, smelled something odd. Drugs had finally made it to Ford County.

There was marijuana in the car. All six students were

charged with felony possession and every other crime the cops could possibly throw at them. The town was shocked—how could our innocent little community get infiltrated with drugs? How could we stop it? I low-keyed the story in the paper; no sense beating up on six good kids who'd made a mistake. Sheriff Meredith was quoted as saying that his office would act decisively to "remove this scourge" from our community. "This ain't California," he said.

Typically, everybody in Clanton was suddenly on the lookout for drug dealers, though no one was quite sure what they looked like.

Because the cops were on high alert, and would love nothing more than another drug bust, poker the next Thursday was moved to a different location, one deep in the country. Bubba Crockett and Darrell Radke lived in a dilapidated old cabin with a nonpoker-playing veteran named Ollie Hinds. They called their place the Foxhole. It was hidden in a heavily wooded ravine at the end of a dirt road that you couldn't find in broad daylight.

Ollie Hinds was suffering from every manner of postwar trauma and probably several prewar ones as well. He was from Minnesota and had served with Bubba and survived their horrible nightmares. He had been shot, burned, captured briefly, escaped, and finally sent home when an Army shrink said he was in need of serious help. Apparently he never got it. When I met him he was shirtless, revealing scars and tattoos, and glassy-eyed, which, I would soon learn, was his usual condition.

I was grateful he was not playing poker. A couple of bad hands, and you got the impression he might pull an M-16 and even the score.

The drug bust, and the town's reaction to it, was the source of much humor and ridicule. Folks were acting as though the six teenagers were the very first drug users, and since they'd been caught then the county was on top of the crisis. With some vigilance and tough talk, the plague of illegal drugs could be diverted to another part of the country.

Nixon had mined the harbor at Haiphong and was bombing Hanoi with a fury. I brought this up to get a reaction, but there was little interest in the war that night.

Darrell had heard a rumor that some black kid from Clanton had been drafted and fled to Canada. I said nothing.

"Smart boy," Bubba said. "Smart boy."

The conversation soon returned to drugs. At one point Bubba admired his marijuana cigarette and said, "Man, this is really smooth. Didn't come from the Padgitts."

"Came from Memphis," Darrell said. "Mexican."

Since I knew zero about the local drug supply routes, I listened intently for a few seconds then, when it was evident no one would pursue the conversation, said, "I thought the Padgitts produced pretty good stuff."

"They should stick to moonshine," Bubba said.

"It's okay," Darrell said, "if you can't get anything

else. They struck it rich a few years back. They started growin' long before anybody else around here. Now they got competition."

"I hear they're cuttin' back, goin' back to whiskey and stealin' cars," Bubba said.

"Why?" I asked.

"A lot more narcs now. State, federal, local. They got helicopters and surveillance stuff. Ain't like Mexico where nobody gives a shit what you grow."

Gunfire erupted outside, not too far away. The others were not fazed by it. "What might that be?" I asked.

"It's Ollie," Darrell said. "After a possum. He puts on night-vision goggles, takes his M-16, goes lookin' for varmints and such. Calls it gook huntin'."

I luckily lost three hands in a row and found the perfect moment to say good night.

———————

After much delay, the Supreme Court of Mississippi finally affirmed the conviction of Danny Padgitt. Four months earlier it had ruled, by a majority of six to three, that the conviction would stand. Lucien Wilbanks filed a petition for rehearing, which was granted. Harry Rex thought that might signal trouble.

The appeal was reheard, and almost two years after his trial the court finally settled the matter. The vote to affirm the conviction was five to four.

The dissent bought into Lucien's rather vociferous argument that Ernie Gaddis had been given too much freedom in abusing Danny Padgitt on cross-examination.

With his leading questions about the presence of Rhoda's children in the bedroom, watching the rape, Ernie had effectively been allowed to place before the jury highly prejudicial facts that simply were not in evidence.

Harry Rex had read all the briefs and monitored the appeal for me, and he was concerned that Wilbanks had a legitimate argument. If five justices believed it, then the case would be sent back to Clanton for another trial. On the one hand another trial would be good for the newspaper. On the other, I didn't want the Padgitts off their island and running around Clanton causing trouble.

In the end, though, only four justices dissented, and the case was over. I plastered the good news across the front of the *Times* and hoped I would never again hear the name of Danny Padgitt.

PART
THREE

CHAPTER 31

Five years and two months after Lester Klump, Sr., and Lester Klump, Jr., first set foot in the Hocutt House, they finished the renovation. The ordeal was over, and the results were splendid.

Once I accepted their languid pace, I settled in for the long haul and worked hard selling ad copy. Twice, during the last year of the project, I had unwisely attempted to live in the house and somehow exist in the midst of the debris. In doing so I had little trouble with the dust, the paint fumes, the blocked hallways, the erratic electricity and hot water, and the absence of heating and air conditioning, but I could never adapt to the early morning hammers and handsaws. They were not early birds, which, as I learned, was unusual for contractors, but they did start in earnest each morning by eight-thirty. I really enjoyed sleeping until ten. The arrangement didn't work, and after each attempt to live in the big house I sneaked back across the gravel drive and returned to the apartment, where things were somewhat quieter.

Only once in five years was I unable to pay the Klumps on time. I refused to borrow money for the project, though Stan Atcavage was always ready to loan it. After work each Friday I would sit down with Lester Senior, usually on a makeshift plywood table in a hallway, and over a cold beer we would tally up the labor and materials for the week, add 10 percent, and I would write him a check. I filed his records away, and for the first two years kept a running total of the cost of the renovation. After two years, though, I stopped adding the weekly to the cumulative. I didn't want to know what it was costing.

I was broke but I didn't care. The money pit had been sealed off; I had teetered on the brink of insolvency, dodged it, and now I could begin stashing it away again.

And I had something magnificent to show for the time, effort, and investment. The house had been built around 1900 by Dr. Miles Hocutt. It had a distinctive Victorian style, with two high gabled roofs in the front, a turret that ran up four levels, and wide covered porches that swept around the house on both sides. Over the years the Hocutts had painted the house blue and yellow, and Mr. Klump, Sr., had even found an area of bright red under three coats of newer paint. I played it safe and stayed with white and beige and light brown trim. The roof was copper. Outside it was a rather plain

THE LAST JUROR 343

Victorian, but I would have years to jazz it up.

Inside, the heart-pine floors on all three levels had been restored to their original beauty. Walls had been removed, rooms and hallways opened up. The Klumps had finally been forced to remove the entire kitchen and build another from the basement up. The fireplace in the living room had actually collapsed under the pressure of relentless jackhammering. I turned the library into a den and knocked out more walls so that upon entering the front foyer you could see through the den to the kitchen in the distance. I added windows everywhere; the house had originally been built like a cave.

Mr. Klump admitted he had never tasted champagne, but he happily chugged it down as we completed our little ceremony on a side porch. I handed him what I hoped would be his last check, we shook hands, posed for a photograph by Wiley Meek, then popped the cork.

Many of the rooms were bare; it would take years to properly decorate the place, and it would require the assistance of someone with far more knowledge and taste than I possessed. Half-empty, though, the house was still spectacular. It needed a party!

I borrowed $2,000 from Stan and ordered wine and champagne from Memphis. I found a suitable caterer from Tupelo. (The only one in Clanton specialized in ribs and catfish and I wanted something a bit classier.)

The official invitation list of three hundred included everybody I knew in town, and a few I did not. The unofficial list was comprised of those who'd heard me say, "We'll have a huge party when it's finished." I invited

BeeBee and three of her friends from Memphis. I invited my father but he was too worried about inflation and the bond market. I invited Miss Callie and Esau, Reverend Thurston Small, Claude, three clerks from the courthouse, two schoolteachers, an assistant basketball coach, a teller at the bank, and the newest lawyer in town. That made a total of twelve blacks, and I would've invited more if I had known more. I was determined to have the first integrated party in Clanton.

Harry Rex brought moonshine and a large platter of chitlins that almost broke up the festivities. Bubba Crockett and the Foxhole gang arrived stoned and ready to party. Mr. Mitlo wore the only tuxedo. Piston made an appearance, and was seen leaving through the back door with a carry-out bag filled with rather expensive finger food. Woody Gates and the Country Boys played for hours on a side porch. The Klumps were there with all their laborers; it was a fine moment for them and I made sure they got all the credit. Lucien Wilbanks arrived late and was soon in a heated argument about politics with Senator Theo Morton, whose wife, Rex Ella, told me it was the grandest party she'd seen in Clanton in twenty years. Our new Sheriff, Tryce McNatt, dropped by with several of his uniformed deputies. (T. R. Meredith had died of colon cancer the year before.) One of my favorites, Judge Reuben V. Atlee, held court in the den with colorful stories about Dr. Miles Hocutt. Reverend Millard Stark of the First Baptist Church stayed only ten minutes and left quietly when he realized alcohol was being served. Reverend

Cargrove of the First Presbyterian Church was seen drinking champagne, and appeared to have a taste for it. Baggy passed out in a second-floor bedroom, where I found him the next afternoon. The Stukes twins, who owned the hardware store, showed up in brand-new, matching overalls. They were seventy years old, lived together, never married, and wore matching overalls every day. There was no dress requirement; the invitation said, "Open Attire."

The front lawn was covered with two large white tents, and at times the crowd spilled from under them. The party began at 1 P.M., Saturday afternoon, and would've gone past midnight if the wine and food had lasted. By ten, Woody Gates and his band were exhausted, there was nothing left to drink but a few warm beers, nothing to eat but a few tortilla chips, and nothing left to see. The house had been thoroughly seen and enjoyed.

Late the next morning, I scrambled eggs for BeeBee and her friends. We sat on the front porch and drank coffee and admired the mess made just hours before. It took me a week to clean up.

———

Through the years in Clanton I'd heard plenty of horror stories of imprisonment at the state penitentiary at Parchman. It was in sprawling farmland in the Delta, the richest farming region in the state, two hours west of Clanton. Living conditions were wretched—cramped barracks that were suffocating in the summer and frigid in the winter, ghastly food, scant medical care, a slave system, brutal sex. Forced labor, sadistic guards, the list was endless and pathetic.

When I thought of Danny Padgitt, which I did often, I was always comforted by the belief that he was at Parchman getting what he deserved. He was lucky he hadn't been strapped to a chair in a gas chamber.

My assumption was wrong.

In the late sixties, in an effort to ease the overcrowding at Parchman, the state had built two satellite prisons, or "camps" as they were known. The plan had been to place a thousand nonviolent offenders in more civilized confinement. They would obtain job training, even qualify for work release. One such satellite was near the small town of Broomfield, three hours south of Clanton.

Judge Loopus died in 1972. During the Padgitt trial, his stenographer had been a homely young woman named Darla Clabo. She worked for Loopus for a few years, and after his death left the area. When she walked into my office late one afternoon in the summer of 1977, I knew I had seen her somewhere in the distant past.

Darla introduced herself and I quickly remembered where I'd seen her. For five straight days during the Padgitt trial she had sat below the bench, next to the exhibit table, taking down every word. She was now living in Alabama, and had driven five hours to tell me something. First, she swore me to absolute secrecy.

Her hometown was Broomfield. Two weeks earlier

she had been visiting her mother when she saw a familiar face walking down the sidewalk around lunchtime. It was Danny Padgitt, strolling along with a buddy. She was so startled she tripped on the edge of a curb and almost fell into the street.

They walked into a local diner and sat down for lunch. Darla saw them through a window, and decided not to go in. There was a chance Padgitt might recognize her, though she wasn't sure why that frightened her.

The man with him wore the uniform that was common in Broomfield—navy slacks, a short-sleeved white shirt with the words "Broomfield Correctional Facility" in very small letters over the pocket. He also wore black cowboy boots and no gun whatsoever. She explained that some of the guards who handled the prisoners on work release had the option of carrying a weapon. It was hard to imagine a white man in Mississippi voluntarily declining to carry a gun if given the option, but she suspected that perhaps Danny didn't want his own personal guard to be armed.

Danny was wearing white dungarees and a white shirt, possibly issued by the camp. The two enjoyed a long lunch and appeared to be good friends. From her car, Darla watched them leave the diner. She followed from a distance as they took a leisurely stroll for a few blocks until Danny entered a building that housed the regional office of the Mississippi Highway Department. The guard got into a camp vehicle and drove away.

The following morning, Darla's mother entered the

building under the pretext of filing a complaint about a road in need of repair. She was rudely informed that no such procedure existed, and in the ensuing brouhaha managed to catch a glimpse of the young man Darla had carefully described. He was holding a clipboard and appeared to be just another useless pencil pusher.

Darla's mother had a friend whose son worked as a clerk at the Broomfield camp. He confirmed that Danny Padgitt had been moved there in the summer of 1974.

When she finished with the story, she said, "Are you going to expose him?"

I was reeling, but I could already see the story. "I will investigate," I said. "Depends on what I find."

"Please do. This ain't right."

"It's unbelievable."

"That little punk should be on death row."

"I agree."

"I did eight murder trials for Judge Loopus, and that one really sticks with me."

"Me too."

She swore me to secrecy again, and left her address. She wanted a copy of the paper if we did the story.

At six the next morning I had no trouble jumping out of bed. Wiley and I drove to Broomfield. Since both the Spitfire and the Mercedes were likely to draw attention in any small town in Mississippi, we took his Ford pickup. We easily found the camp, three miles out of

town. We found the highway department office building. At noon we took our positions along Main Street.
Since Padgitt would certainly recognize either one of
us, we faced the challenge of trying to hide on a busy
street in a strange town without acting suspicious. Wiley
sat low in his truck, camera loaded and ready. I hid behind a newspaper on a bench.

There was no sign of him the first day. We drove back
to Clanton, then early the next morning left again for
Broomfield. At eleven-thirty, a prison vehicle stopped in
front of the office building. The guard went inside, collected his prisoner, and they walked to lunch.

———

On July 17, 1977, our front page had four large photos—one of Danny walking along the sidewalk sharing
a laugh with the guard, one of them as they entered the
City Grill, one of the office building, one of the gate to
the Broomfield camp. My headline howled: NO PRISON
FOR PADGITT—HE'S OFF AT CAMP.

My report began:

Four years after being convicted of the brutal rape and
murder of Rhoda Kassellaw, and being sentenced to life
in the state penitentiary at Parchman, Danny Padgitt was
moved to the state's new satellite camp at Broomfield.
After three years there, he enjoys all the perks of a
well-connected inmate—an office job with the state
highway department, his own personal guard, and long
lunches (cheeseburgers and milk shakes) in local cafés

*where the other patrons have never heard of him
or his crimes.*

The story was as venomous and slanted as I could
possibly make it. I bullied the waitress at the City Grill
into telling me that he had just eaten a cheeseburger
with french fries, that he ate there three times a week,
and that he always picked up the check. I made a dozen
phone calls to the highway department until I found
a supervisor who knew something about Padgitt. The
supervisor refused to answer questions, and I made
him sound like a criminal himself. Penetrating Broomfield camp was just as frustrating. I detailed my efforts
and tilted the story so it sounded as though all the bu-
reaucrats were covering up for Padgitt. No one at
Parchman knew a damned thing, or if they did they
were unwilling to talk about it. I called the highway
commissioner (an elected official), the warden at Parchman (thankfully an appointed position), the Attorney
General, the Lieutenant Governor, and finally the Governor himself. They were all too busy, of course, so I
chatted with their bootlickers and made them sound
like morons.

Senator Theo Morton appeared to be shocked. He
promised to get right to the bottom of it and call me
back. At press time, I was still waiting.

The reaction in Clanton was mixed. Many of those
who called or stopped me on the street were angry and
wanted something done. They truly believed that when
Padgitt had been sentenced to life and led away in

handcuffs, that he would spend the rest of his days in hell at Parchman. A few seemed indifferent and wanted to forget Padgitt altogether. He was old news.

And among some there was the frustrating, almost cynical lack of surprise. They figured the Padgitts had worked their magic once more, found the right pockets, pulled the right strings. Harry Rex was in this camp. "What's the big fuss, boy? They've bought Governors before."

The photo of Danny walking down the street, free as a bird, frightened Miss Callie considerably. "She didn't sleep last night," Esau mumbled to me when I arrived for lunch that Thursday. "I wish you hadn't found him."

———

Fortunately, the Memphis and Jackson newspapers picked up the story, and it took on a life of its own. They turned up the heat to a point where the politicians had to get involved. The Governor and the Attorney General, along with Senator Morton, were soon jockeying to lead the parade to get the boy sent back to Parchman.

Two weeks after I broke the story, Danny Padgitt was "reassigned" to the state penitentiary.

The next day, I received two phone calls, one at the office, one at home while I was asleep. Different voices, but with the same message. I was a dead man.

I notified the FBI in Oxford, and two agents visited me in Clanton. I leaked this to a reporter in Memphis, and soon the town knew that I had been threatened, and that the FBI was investigating. For a month, Sheriff McNatt kept a patrol car in front of my office around the clock. Another one sat in my driveway during the night.

After a seven-year hiatus, I was carrying a gun again.

CHAPTER 32

There was no immediate bloodshed. The threats were not forgotten, but as time passed they became less ominous. I never stopped carrying a gun—it was always within reach—but I lost interest in it. I found it hard to believe that the Padgitts would risk the severe backlash that would come if they knocked off the editor of the local paper. Even if the town was not entirely enamored of me, as opposed to someone as beloved as Mr. Caudle, the uproar would create more pressure than the Padgitts were willing to risk.

They kept to themselves like never before. After the defeat of Mackey Don Coley in 1971, they once again proved quite adept at changing tactics. Danny had given them enough unwanted attention; they were determined to avoid anymore. They retrenched even deeper into Padgitt Island. They increased security in the wasted belief that the next sheriff, T. R. Meredith, or his successor, Tryce McNatt, might come after them. They grew their crops and smuggled them off the island in planes, boats, pickups, and flatbed trucks ostensibly loaded with timber.

With typical Padgitt shrewdness, and sensing that the marijuana business might become too risky, they began pumping money into legitimate enterprises. They bought a highway contracting company and quickly turned it into a reliable bidder for government projects. They bought an asphalt plant, a Redi-Mix concrete plant, and gravel pits around the northern part of the state. Highway construction was a notably corrupt business in Mississippi, and the Padgitts knew how to play the game.

I watched these activities as closely as possible. This was before the Freedom of Information Act and open-meetings laws. I knew the names of some of the companies the Padgitts had bought, but it was virtually impossible to keep up with them. There was nothing I could print, no story, because on the surface it was all legitimate.

I waited, but for what I wasn't certain. Danny Padgitt would return one day, and when he did he might simply disappear into the island and never be seen again. Or he might do otherwise.

———

Few people in Clanton did not attend church. Those who did seemed to know exactly which ones did not, and there was a common invitation to "come worship with us." The farewell, "See you on Sunday," was almost as common as "Y'all come see us."

I got hammered with these invitations during my first years in town. Once it was known that the owner and editor of the *Times* did not go to church, I became the most famous derelict in town. I decided to do something about it.

Each week Margaret put together our Religion page, which included a rather extensive menu of churches arranged by denominations. There were also a few ads by the more affluent congregations. And notices for revivals, reunions, potluck suppers, and countless other activities.

Working from this page, and from the phonebook, I made a list of all the churches in Ford County. The total was eighty-eight, but it was a moving target since congregations were always splitting, folding here and popping up over there. My goal was to visit each one of them, something I was sure had never been done, and a feat that would put me in a class by myself among churchgoers.

The denominations were varied and baffling—how could Protestants, all of whom claimed to follow the same basic tenets, get themselves so divided? They agreed basically that (1) Jesus was the only son of God; (2) he was born of a virgin; (3) lived a perfect life; (4) was persecuted by the Jews, arrested and crucified by the Romans; (5) that he arose on the third day and later ascended into heaven; (6) and some believed—though there were many variations—that one must follow Jesus in baptism and faith to make it to heaven.

The doctrine was fairly straightforward, but the devil was in the details.

There were no Catholics, Episcopalians, or Mormons. The county was heavily Baptist, but they were a fractured bunch. The Pentecostals were in second place, and evidently they had fought with themselves as much as the Baptists.

In 1974, I'd begun my epic adventure to visit every church in Ford County. The first had been the Calvary Full Gospel, a rowdy Pentecostal assemblage on a gravel road two miles out of town. As advertised, the service began at ten-thirty, and I found a spot on the back pew, as far away from the action as I could get. I was greeted warmly and word spread that a bona-fide visitor was present. I did not recognize anyone there. Preacher Bob wore a white suit, navy shirt, white tie, and his thick black hair was wound around and plastered tightly at the base of his skull. People started hollering when he was giving the announcements. They waved their hands and shouted during a solo. When the sermon finally began an hour later, I was ready to leave. It lasted for fifty-five minutes, and left me confused and exhausted. At times the building shook with folks stomping the floor. Windows rattled as they were overcome with the spirit and yelled upward. Preacher Bob "laid hands" on three sick folks suffering vague diseases, and they claimed to be healed. At one point a deacon stood and in an astounding display began uttering something in a tongue I had never heard. He clenched his fists, closed his eyes tightly, and let loose with a steady, fluent flow of words. It was not an act; he wasn't faking. After a few minutes, a young girl in the choir stood and began translating into English. It was a vision God was sending through the deacon. There were those present with unforgiven sins.

"Repent!" Preacher Bob shouted, and heads ducked.

What if the deacon was talking about me? I glanced around and noticed that the door was locked and guarded by two more deacons.

Things finally ran out of gas, and two hours after I sat down I bolted from the building. I needed a drink.

I wrote a pleasant little report about my visit to Calvary Full Gospel and ran it on the Religion page. I commented on the warm atmosphere of the church, the lovely solo by Miss Helen Hatcher, the powerful sermon by Preacher Bob, and so on.

Needless to say, this proved to be very popular.

At least twice a month, I went to church. I sat with Miss Callie and Esau and listened to the Reverend Thurston Small preach for two hours and twelve minutes (I timed every sermon). The briefest was delivered by Pastor Phil Bish at the United Methodist Church of Karaway—seventeen minutes. That church also got the award for being the coldest. The furnace was broken, it was January, and that may have helped shorten the sermon. I sat with Margaret at the First Baptist Church in Clanton and listened to Reverend Millard Stark give his annual sermon on the sins of alcohol. With bad timing, I had a hangover that morning and Stark kept looking at me.

I found the Harvest Tabernacle in the back room of an abandoned service station in Beech Hill, and I sat with six others as a wild-eyed doomsayer named Peter the Prophet yelled at us for almost an hour. My column that week was quite brief.

The Clanton Church of Christ had no musical instruments. The ban was based on Scripture, it was later explained to me. There was a beautiful solo, which I wrote about at length. There was also no emotion whatsoever in the service. For a contrast, I went to the Mount Pisgah Chapel in Lowtown, where the pulpit was surrounded by drums, guitars, horns, and amplifiers. As a warmup for the sermon, a full-blown concert was given with the congregation singing and dancing. Miss Callie referred to Mount Pisgah as a "lower church."

On my list, number sixty-four was the Calico Ridge Independent Church, located deep in the hills in the northeastern part of the county. According to the *Times* archives, at this church in 1965 a Mr. Randy Bovee was bitten twice by a rattlesnake during a late Sunday night worship service. Mr. Bovee survived, and for a while the snakes were put away. The legend, however, flourished, and as my Church Notes column gained popularity, I was asked several times if I intended to visit Calico Ridge.

"I plan to visit every church," was my standard reply.

"They don't like visitors," Baggy warned me.

I had been greeted so warmly in each church—black or white, large or small, town or country—that I could not imagine Christian folks being rude to a guest.

And they weren't rude at Calico Ridge, but they weren't too happy to see me either. I wanted to see the snakes, but from the safety of the back row. I went on a Sunday night, primarily because legend held that they did not "take up the serpents" during daylight hours. I searched the Bible in vain for this restriction.

There was no sign of any serpents. There were a few fits and convulsions below the pulpit as the preacher exhorted us to "come forth and moan and groan in sin!" The choir chanted and hummed to the beat of an electric guitar and a drum, and the meeting took on the spookiness of an ancient tribal dance. I wanted to leave, especially since there were no snakes.

Late in the service, I caught a glimpse of a face I'd seen before. It was a very different face—thin, pale, gaunt, topped with grayish hair. I couldn't place it, but I knew it was familiar. The man was seated in the second row from the front, on the other side of the small sanctuary, and he seemed out of touch with the chaos of the worship service. At times he appeared to be praying, then he would sit while everyone else was standing. Those around him seemed to accept him and ignore him at the same time.

He turned once and looked directly at me. It was Hank Hooten, the ex-lawyer who'd shot up the town in 1971! He'd been taken in a straitjacket to the state mental hospital, and a few years later there'd been a rumor that he had been released. No one had seen him, though.

For two days after that, I tried to track down Hank Hooten. My calls to the state mental hospital went nowhere. Hank had a brother in Shady Grove, but he refused to talk. I snooped around Calico Ridge, but, typically, no one there would utter a word to a stranger like me.

CHAPTER 33

Many of those who worshiped diligently on Sunday mornings became less faithful on Sunday nights. During my tour of churches, I heard many preachers chide their followers to return in a few hours to properly complete the observance of the Sabbath. I never counted heads, but as a general rule about half of them did so. I tried a few Sunday night services, usually in an effort to catch some colorful ritual such as snake handling or disease healing or, on one occasion, a "church conclave" in which a wayward brother was to be put on trial and certainly convicted for fancying another brother's wife. My presence rattled them that night and the wayward brother got a reprieve.

For the most part, I limited my study of comparative religions to the daylight hours.

Others had different Sunday-night rituals. Harry Rex helped a Mexican named Pepe lease a building and open a restaurant one block off the square. Pepe's became moderately successful during the 1970s with decent food that was always on the spicy side. Pepe couldn't resist the peppers, regardless of how they scalded the throats of his gringo customers.

On Sundays all alcohol was banned in Ford County. It could not be sold at retail or in restaurants. Pepe had a back room with a long table and a door that would lock. He allowed Harry Rex and his guests to use the room and eat and drink all we wanted. His margaritas were especially tasty. We enjoyed many colorful meals with spicy dishes, all washed down with strong margaritas. There were usually a dozen of us, all male, all young, about half currently married. Harry Rex threatened our lives if we told anyone about Pepe's back room.

The Clanton city police raided us once, but Pepe suddenly couldn't speak a word of English. The door to the back room was locked, and partially hidden too. Pepe turned off the lights, and for twenty minutes we waited in the dark, still drinking, and listened to the cops try to communicate with Pepe. I don't know why we were worried. The city Judge was a lawyer named Harold Finkley, who was at the end of the table slogging down his fourth or fifth margarita.

Those Sunday nights at Pepe's were often long and rowdy, and afterward we were in no condition to drive. I would walk to my office and sleep on the sofa. I was there snoring off the tequila when the phone rang after midnight. It was a reporter I knew from the big daily in Memphis.

"Are you covering the parole hearing tomorrow?" he asked. Tomorrow? In my toxic fog I had no idea what day it was.

"Tomorrow?" I mumbled.

"Monday, September the eighteenth," he said slowly.

I was reasonably certain the year was 1978.

"What parole hearing?" I asked, trying desperately to wake myself up and put two thoughts together.

"Danny Padgitt's. You don't know about it?"

"Hell no!"

"It's scheduled for ten A.M. at Parchman."

"You gotta be kidding!"

"Nope. I just found out. Evidently, they don't advertise these."

I sat in the darkness for a long time, cursing once again the backwardness of a state that conducted such important matters in such ridiculous ways. How could parole even be considered for Danny Padgitt? Eight years had passed since the murder and his conviction. He had received two life sentences of at least ten years each. We assumed that meant a minimum of twenty years.

I drove home around 3 A.M., slept fitfully for two hours, then woke up Harry Rex, who was in no condition to be dealt with. I picked up sausage biscuits and strong coffee and we met at his office around seven. We were both ill-tempered, and as we plowed through his law books there were sharp words and foul language, not aimed at each other, but at the blurry and toothless parole system passed by the legislature thirty years earlier. Guidelines were only vaguely defined, leaving ample wiggle room for the politicians and their appointees to do as they wished.

Since most law-abiding citizens had no contact with the parole system, it was not a priority with the state legislature. And since most of the state's prisoners were either poor or black, and unable to use the system to their advantage, it was easy to hit them with harsh sentences and keep them locked up. But for an inmate with a few connections and some cash, the parole system was a marvelous labyrinth of contradictory laws that allowed the Parole Board to pass out favors.

Somewhere between the judicial system, the penal system, and the parole system, Danny Padgitt's two "consecutive" life terms had been changed to two "concurrent" sentences. They ran side by side, Harry Rex tried to explain.

"What good is that?" I asked.

"It's used in cases where a defendant has multiple charges. Consecutive might give him eighty years in jail, but a fair sentence is ten. So they run 'em side by side."

I shook my head in disapproval again, and this irritated him.

I finally got Sheriff Tryce McNatt to answer the phone. He sounded as hung over as we were, though he was a strict teetotaler. McNatt knew nothing about the parole hearing. I asked him if he planned to attend, but his day was already filled with important meetings.

I would have called Judge Loopus, but he'd been dead for six years. Ernie Gaddis had retired and was fishing in the Smoky Mountains. His successor, Rufus Buckley, lived in Tyler County and his phone number was unlisted.

At eight o'clock, I jumped in my car with a biscuit and a cup of cold coffee.

———

An hour west of Ford County the land flattened dramatically and the Delta began. It was a region rich in farming and poor in living conditions, but I was in no mood to take in the sights and offer social commentary. I was too nervous about crashing a clandestine parole hearing.

I was also nervous about setting foot inside Parchman, a legendary hellhole.

After two hours, I saw fences next to fields, then razor wire. Soon there was a sign, and I turned into the main gate. I informed a guard in the booth that I was a reporter, there for a parole hearing. "Straight ahead, left at the second building," he said helpfully as he wrote down my name.

There was a cluster of buildings close to the highway, and a row of white-frame houses that would fit on any Maple Street in Mississippi. I chose the Admin A building and sprinted inside, looking for the first secretary. I found her, and she sent me to the next building, second floor. It was just about ten.

There were people at the end of the hallway, loitering

outside a room. One was a prison guard, one was a state trooper, one wore a wrinkled suit.

"I'm here for a parole hearing," I announced.

"In there," the guard said, pointing. Without knocking, I yanked open the door, as any intrepid reporter would, and stepped inside. Things had just been called to order, and my presence there was certainly not anticipated.

There were five members of the Parole Board, and they were seated behind a slightly elevated table with their name plates in front of them. Along one wall another table held the Padgitt crowd—Danny, his father, his mother, an uncle, and Lucien Wilbanks. Opposite them, behind another table, were various clerks and functionaries of the Board and the prison.

Everyone stared at me as I stormed in. My eyes locked onto Danny Padgitt's, and for a second both of us managed to convey the contempt we felt for the other.

"Can I help you?" a large, badly dressed ole boy growled from the center of the Board. His name was Barrett Ray Jeter, the chairman. Like the other four, he'd been appointed by the Governor as a reward for vote-gathering.

"I'm here for the Padgitt hearing," I said.

"He's a reporter!" Lucien practically yelled as he was standing. For a second I thought I might get arrested on the spot and be carried deeper into the prison for a life sentence.

"For who?" Jeter demanded.

"*The Ford County Times*," I said.

"Your name?"

"Willie Traynor." I was glaring at Lucien and he was scowling at me.

"This is a closed hearing, Mr. Traynor," Jeter said. The statute wasn't clear as to whether it was open or closed, so it had traditionally been kept quiet.

"Who has the right to attend?" I asked.

"The Parole Board, the parolee, his family, his witnesses, his lawyer, and any witnesses for the other side." The "other side" meant the victim's family, which in this setting sounded like the bad guys.

"What about the Sheriff from our county?" I asked.

"He's invited too," Jeter said.

"Our Sheriff wasn't notified. I talked to him three hours ago. In fact, nobody in Ford County knew of this hearing until after twelve last night." This caused considerable head-scratching up and down the Parole Board. The Padgitts huddled with Lucien.

By process of elimination, I quickly deduced that I had to become a witness if I wanted to watch the show. I said, as loudly and clearly as possible, "Well, since there's no one else here from Ford County in opposition, I'm a witness."

"You can't be a reporter and a witness," Jeter said.

"Where is that written in the Mississippi Code?" I asked, waving my copies from Harry Rex's law books.

Jeter nodded at a young man in a dark suit. "I'm the attorney for the Parole Board," he said politely. "You can testify in this hearing, Mr. Traynor, but you cannot report it."

I planned to fully report every detail of the hearing, then hide behind the First Amendment. "So be it," I said. "You guys make the rules." In less than one minute the lines had been drawn; I was on one side, everybody else was on the other.

"Let's proceed," Jeter said, and I took a seat with a handful of other spectators.

The attorney for the Parole Board passed out a report. He recited the basics of the Padgitt sentence, and was careful not to use the words "consecutive" or "concurrent." Based on the inmate's "exemplary" record during his incarceration, he had qualified for "good time," a vague concept created by the parole system and not by the state legislature. Subtracting the time the inmate spent in the county jail awaiting trial, he was now eligible for parole.

Danny's caseworker plowed through a lengthy narrative of her relationship with the inmate. She concluded with the gratuitous opinion that he was "fully remorseful," "fully rehabilitated," "no threat whatsoever to society," even ready to become a "most productive citizen."

How much did all this cost? I couldn't help but ponder that question. How much? And how long had it taken for the Padgitts to find the right pockets?

Lucien went next. With no one—Gaddis, Sheriff McNatt—not even poor Hank Hooten—to contradict or possibly throttle him, he launched into a fictional recounting of the facts of the crimes, and in particular the testimony of an "airtight" alibi witness, Lydia Vince. His reconstructed version of the trial had the jury waivering on a verdict of not guilty. I was tempted to throw something at him and start screaming. Maybe that would at least keep him somewhat honest.

I wanted to shout, "How can he be remorseful if he's so innocent?"

Lucien carped on about the trial and how unfair it had been. He nobly took the blame for not pushing hard for a change of venue, to another part of the state where folks were unbiased and more enlightened. When he finally shut up two of the board members appeared to be asleep.

Mrs. Padgitt testified next and talked about the letters she and her son had exchanged these past eight, very long years. Through his letters, she had seen him mature, seen his faith strengthen, seen him long for his freedom so he could serve his fellow man.

Serve them a stronger blend of pot? Or perhaps a cleaner corn whiskey?

Since tears were expected she gave us some tears. It was part of the show and appeared to have little sway over the Board. In fact, as I watched their faces I got the impression that their decision had been made a long time ago.

Danny went last and did a good job of walking the fine line between denying his crimes and showing remorse for them. "I have learned from my mistakes," he said, as if rape and murder were simple indiscretions where no one really got hurt. "I have grown from them."

In prison he had been a veritable whirlwind of positive energy—volunteering in the library, singing in the choral group, helping with the Parchman rodeo, organizing teams to go into schools and scare kids away from crime.

Two Board members were listening. One was still asleep. The other two sat in trancelike meditation, apparently brain dead.

Danny shed no tears, but closed with an impassioned plea for his release.

"How many witnesses in opposition?" Jeter announced. I stood, looked around me, saw no one else from Ford County, then said, "I guess it's just me."

"Proceed, Mr. Traynor."

I had no idea what to say, nor did I know what was permissible or objectionable in such a forum. But based on what I had just sat through, I figured I could say anything I damned well pleased. Fat Jeter would no doubt call me down if I ventured into forbidden territory.

I looked up at the Board members, tried my best to ignore the daggers from the Padgitts, and jumped into an extremely graphic description of the rape and the murder. I unloaded everything I could possibly remember, and I put special emphasis on the fact that the two children witnessed some or all of the attack.

I kept waiting for Lucien to object, but there was nothing but silence in their camp. The formerly comatose Board members were suddenly alive, all watching me closely, absorbing the gruesome details of the murder. I described the wounds. I painted the heartbreaking scene of Rhoda dying in the arms of Mr. Deece, and saying, "It was Danny Padgitt. It was Danny Padgitt."

I called Lucien a liar and mocked his memory of the trial. It took the jury less than an hour to find the defendant guilty, I explained.

And with a recollection that surprised even me, I recounted Danny's pathetic performance on the witness stand: his lying to cover up his lies; his total lack of truthfulness. "He should've been indicted for perjury," I told the Board.

"And when he had finished testifying, instead of returning to his seat, he walked to the jury box, shook his finger in the faces of the jurors, and said, 'You convict me, and I'll get every damned one of you.' "

A Board member named Mr. Horace Adler jerked upright in his seat and blurted toward the Padgitts, "Is that true?"

"It's in the record," I said quickly before Lucien had the chance to lie again. He was slowly getting to his feet.

"Is that true, Mr. Wilbanks?" Adler insisted.

"He threatened the jury?" asked another board member.

"I have the transcript," I said. "I'll be happy to send it to you."

"Is that true?" Adler asked for the third time.

"There were three hundred people in the courtroom,"

I said, staring at Lucien and saying with my eyes, Don't do it. Don't lie about it.

"Shut up, Mr. Traynor," a Board member said.

"It's in the record," I said again.

"That's enough!" Jeter shouted.

Lucien was standing and trying to think of a response. Everyone was waiting. Finally, "I don't remember everything that was said," he began, and I snorted as loudly as possible. "Perhaps my client did say something to that effect, but it was an emotional moment, and in the heat of the battle, something like that might have been said. But taken in context—"

"Context my ass!" I yelled at Lucien and took a step toward him as if I might throw a punch. A guard stepped toward me and I stopped. "It's in black-and-white in the trial transcript!" I said angrily. Then I turned to the Board and said, "How can you folks sit there and let them lie like this? Don't you want to hear the truth?"

"Anything else, Mr. Traynor?" Jeter asked.

"Yes! I hope this Board will not make a mockery out of our system and let this man go free after eight years. He's lucky to be sitting here instead of on death row, where he belongs. And I hope that the next time you have a hearing on his parole, if there is a next time, you will invite some of the good folks from Ford County. Perhaps the Sheriff, perhaps the prosecutor. And could you notify members of the victim's family? They have the right to be here so you can see their faces when you turn this murderer loose."

I sat down and fumed. I glared at Lucien Wilbanks and decided that I would work diligently to hate him for the rest of either his life or mine, whichever ended first. Jeter announced a brief recess, and I assumed they needed time to regroup in a back room and count their money. Perhaps Mr. Padgitt could be summoned to provide some extra cash for a Board member or two. To irritate the Board attorney, I scribbled pages of notes for the report he'd prohibited me from writing.

We waited thirty minutes before they filed back in, everyone looking guilty of something. Jeter called for a vote. Two voted in favor of parole, two against, one abstained. "Parole is denied at this time," Jeter announced, and Mrs. Padgitt burst into tears. She hugged Danny before they took him away.

Lucien and the Padgitts walked by, very close to me as they left the room. I ignored them and just stared at the floor, exhausted, hungover, shocked at the denial.

"Next we have Charles D. Bowie," Jeter announced, and there was movement around the tables as the next hopeful was brought in. I caught something about a sex offender, but I was too drained to care. I eventually left the room and walked down the hallway, half-expecting to be confronted by the Padgitts, and that was fine too because I preferred to get it over with.

But they had scattered; there was no sign of them as I left the building and drove through the main gate and back to Clanton.

CHAPTER 34

The parole hearing was front page news in *The Ford County Times*. I loaded the report with every detail I could remember, and on page five let loose with a blistering editorial about the process. I sent a copy to each member of the Parole Board and to its attorney, and, because I was so worked up, every member of the state legislature, the Attorney General, the Lieutenant Governor, and the Governor received a complimentary copy. Most ignored it, but the attorney for the Parole Board did not.

He wrote me a lengthy letter in which he said he was deeply concerned about my "willful violation of Parole Board procedures." He was pondering a session with the Attorney General in which they would "evaluate the gravity of my actions" and possibly pursue action that would lead to "far-reaching consequences."

My lawyer, Harry Rex, had assured me the Parole

Board's policy of secret meetings was patently unconsti-tutional, in clear violation of the First Amendment, and he would happily defend me in federal court. For a re-duced hourly rate, of course.

I swapped heated letters with the Board's lawyer for a month before he seemed to lose interest in pursuing me.

Rafe, Harry Rex's chief ambulance chaser, had a sidekick named Buster, a large thick-chested cowboy with a gun in every pocket. I hired Buster for $100 a week to pretend he was my own personal legbreaker. For a few hours a day he would hang around the front of the office, or sit in my driveway or on one of my porches, any place where he might be seen so folks would know that Willie Traynor was important enough to have a bodyguard. If the Padgitts got close enough to take a shot, they would at least get something in return.

———

After years of steadily gaining weight and ignoring the warnings of her doctors, Miss Callie finally relented. After a particularly bad visit to her clinic, she an-nounced to Esau that she was going on a diet—1,500 calories a day, except, mercifully, Thursday. A month passed and I couldn't discern any loss of weight. But the day after the *Times* story on the parole hearing, she sud-denly looked as though she'd lost fifty pounds.

Instead of frying a chicken, she baked one. Instead of whipping mashed potatoes with butter and thick cream and covering them with gravy, she boiled them.

It was still delicious, but my system had become accustomed to its weekly dose of heavy grease.

After the prayer, I handed her two letters from Sam. As always, she read them immediately while I jumped into the lunch. And as always, she smiled and laughed and then finally wiped a tear. "He's doing fine," she said, and he was.

With typical Ruffin tenacity, Sam had completed his first college degree, in economics, and was saving his money for law school. He was terribly homesick, and weary of the weather. To boil it all down, he missed his momma. And her cooking.

President Carter had pardoned the draft dodgers, and Sam was wrestling with the decision to stay in Canada, or come home. Many of his expatriate friends up there were vowing to stay and pursue Canadian citizenship, and he was heavily influenced by them. There was also a woman involved, though he had not told his parents.

Sometimes we began with the news, but often it was the obituaries or even the classifieds. Since she read every word, Miss Callie knew who was selling a new litter of beagles and who wanted to buy a good used riding mower. And since she read every word every week, she knew how long a certain small farm or a mobile home had been on the market. She knew prices and values. A car would pass on the street during lunch. She would ask, "Now, what model is that?"

"A '71 Plymouth Duster," I would answer.

She would hesitate for a second, then say, "If it's real

clean, it's in the twenty-five-hundred-dollar range."

Stan Atcavage once needed to sell a twenty-four-foot fishing boat he'd repossessed. I called Miss Callie. She said, "Yes, a gentleman from Karaway was looking for one three weeks ago." I checked an old section of the classifieds and found the ad. Stan sold him the boat the next day.

She loved the legal notices, one of the most lucrative sections of the paper. Deeds, foreclosures, divorce filings, probate matters, bankruptcy announcements, annexation hearings, dozens of legal notices were required by law to be published in the county paper. We got them all, and we charged a healthy rate.

"I see where Mr. Everett Wainwright's estate is being probated," she said.

"I vaguely remember his obituary," I said with a mouthful. "When did he die?"

"Five, maybe six months ago. Wasn't much of an obituary."

"I have to work with whatever the family gives me. Did you know him?"

"He owned a grocery store near the tracks for many years." I could tell by the inflection in her voice that she did not care for Mr. Everett Wainwright.

"Good guy or bad buy?"

"He had two sets of prices, one for the whites, a higher one for Negroes. His goods were never marked in any way, and he was the only cashier. A white customer would call out, 'Say, Mr. Wainwright, how much is this can of condensed milk?' and he'd holler back,

'Thirty-eight cents.' A minute later I would say, 'Pardon me, Mr. Wainwright, but how much is this can of condensed milk?' And he'd snap, 'Fifty-four cents.' He was very open about it. He didn't care. He didn't care."

For almost nine years I'd heard stories of the old days. At times I thought I'd heard them all, but Miss Callie's collection was endless.

"Why did you shop there?"

"It was the only store where we could shop. Mr. Monty Griffin ran a nicer store behind the old moviehouse, but we couldn't shop there until twenty years ago."

"Who stopped you?"

"Mr. Monty Griffin. He didn't care if you had money, he didn't want any Negroes in his store."

"And Mr. Wainwright didn't care?"

"He cared all right. He didn't want us, but he would take our money."

She told the story of a Negro boy who loitered around the store until Mr. Wainwright struck him with a broom and sent him away. For revenge, the boy broke into the store once or twice a year for a long time and was never caught. He stole cigarettes and candy, and he also splintered all the broom handles.

"Is it true he left all his money to the Methodist church?" she asked.

"That's the rumor."

"How much?"

"Around a hundred thousand dollars."

"Folks say he was trying to buy his way into heaven,"

she said. I had long since ceased to be amazed at the gossip Miss Callie heard from the other side of the tracks. Many of her friends worked as housekeepers over there. The maids knew everything.

She had once again nudged the conversation to the topic of the afterlife. Miss Callie was deeply concerned about my soul. She was worried that I had not properly become a Christian; that I had not been "born again" or "saved." My infant baptism, which I could not remember, was thoroughly insufficient in her view. Once a person reaches a certain age, the "age of accountability," then, in order to be "saved" from everlasting damnation in hell, that person must walk down the aisle of a church (the right church was the subject of eternal debate) and make a public profession of faith in Jesus Christ.

Miss Callie carried a heavy burden because I had not done this.

And, after having visited seventy-seven different churches, I had to admit that the vast majority of the people in Ford County shared her beliefs. There were some variations. A powerful sect was the Church of Christ. They clung to the odd notion that they, and only they, were destined for heaven. Every other church was preaching "sectarian doctrine." They also believed, as did many congregations, that once a person obtained salvation then it could be lost by bad behavior. The Baptists, the most popular denomination, held firm in "once saved always saved."

This was apparently very comforting for several backslidden Baptists I knew in town.

However, there was hope for me. Miss Callie was thrilled that I was attending church and absorbing the gospel. She was convinced, and she prayed about me continually, that one day soon the Lord would reach down and touch my heart. I would decide to follow him, and she and I would spend eternity together.

Miss Callie was truly living for the day when she "went Home to glory."

"Reverend Small will preside over the Lord's supper this Sunday," she said. It was her weekly invitation to sit with her in church. Reverend Small and his long sermons were more than I could bear.

"Thank you, but I'm doing research again this Sunday," I said.

"God bless you. Where?"

"The Maranatha Primitive Baptist Church."

"Never heard of it."

"It's in the phone book."

"Where is it?"

"Somewhere down in Dumas, I think."

"Black or white?"

"I'm not sure."

Number seventy-eight on my list, the Maranatha Primitive Baptist Church, was a little jewel at the foot of a hill, next to a creek, under a cluster of pin oaks that were at least two hundred years old. It was a small white-frame building, narrow and long, with a high-pitched tin roof and a red steeple that was so tall it got lost in the oaks. The front doors were open wide, beckoning any and all to come worship. A cornerstone gave the date as 1813.

I eased into the back pew, my usual place, and sat next to a well-dressed gentleman who'd been around for as long as the church. I counted fifty-six other worshipers that morning. The windows were wide open, and outside a gentle breeze rushed through the trees and soothed the rough edges of a hectic morning. For a century and a half people had gathered there, sat on the same pews, looked through the same windows at the same trees, and worshiped the same God. The choir— all eight—sang a gentle hymn and I drifted back to another century.

The pastor was a jovial man named J. B. Cooper. I'd met him twice over the years while scrambling around trying to put together obituaries. One side benefit to my tour of county churches was the introduction to all the ministers. This really helped spice up my obits.

Pastor Cooper gazed upon his flock and realized I was the only visitor. He called my name, welcomed me, and made some harmless crack about getting favorable coverage in the *Times*. After four years of touring, and seventy-seven rather generous and colorful Church Notes, it was impossible for me to sneak into a service without getting noticed.

I never knew what to expect in these rural churches. More often than not the sermons were loud and long, and many times I wondered how such good people could drag themselves in week after week for a tongue-lashing. Some preachers were almost sadistic in their condemnation of whatever their followers might have done that week. Everything was a sin in rural Mississippi, and not just the basics as set forth in the Ten Commandments. I heard scathing rebukes of television, movies, cardplaying, popular magazines, sports events, cheerleader uniforms, desegregation, mixed-race churches, Disney—because it came on Sunday nights—dancing, social drinking, postmarital sex, everything.

But Pastor Cooper was at peace. His sermon—twenty-eight minutes—was about tolerance and love. Love was Christ's principal message. The one thing Christ wanted us to do was to love one another. For the altar call we sang three verses of "Just As I Am," but no one moved. These folks had been down the aisle many times.

As always, I hung around afterward for a few minutes to speak with Pastor Cooper. I told him how much I enjoyed the service, something I did whether I meant it or not, and I collected the names of the choir members for my column. Church folk were naturally warm and friendly, but at this stage of my tour they wanted to chat forever and pass along little gems that might end up in print. "My grandfather put the roof on this building in 1902." "The tornado of '38 skipped right over us during the summer revival."

As I was leaving the building, I saw a man in a

wheelchair being pushed down the handicap ramp. It was a face I'd seen before, and I walked over to say hello. Lenny Fargarson, the crippled boy, juror number seven or eight, had evidently taken a turn for the worse. During the trial in 1970 he had been able to walk, though it was not a pretty thing to behold. Now he was in a chair. His father introduced himself. His mother was in a cluster of ladies finishing up one last round of goodbyes.

"Got a minute?" Fargarson asked. In Mississippi, that question really meant "We need to talk and it might take a while." I sat on a bench under one of the oaks. His father rolled him over, then left us to talk.

"I see your paper every week," he said. "You think Padgitt will get out?"

"Sure. It's just a question of when. He can apply for parole once a year, every year."

"Will he come back here, to Ford County?"

I shrugged because I had no idea. "Probably. The Padgitts stick close to their land."

He considered this for some time. He was gaunt and hunched over like an old man. If my memory was correct, he was about twenty-five at the time of the trial. We were roughly about the same age, though he looked twice as old. I had heard the story of his affliction—some injury in a sawmill.

"Does that frighten you?" I asked.

He smiled and said, "Nothing frightens me, Mr. Traynor. The Lord is my shepherd."

"Yes he is," I said, still warm from the sermon. Because

of his physical condition and his wheelchair, Lenny was a difficult person to read. He had endured so much. His faith was strong, but I thought for a second that I caught a hint of apprehension.

Mrs. Fargarson was walking toward us.

"Will you be there when he's released?" Lenny asked.

"I'd like to be, but I'm not sure how it's done."

"Will you call me when you know he's out?"

"Of course."

Mrs. Fargarson had a pot roast in the oven for Sunday lunch, and she wouldn't take no for an answer. I was suddenly hungry, and there was, as usual, nothing remotely tasty in the Hocutt House. Sunday lunch was typically a cold sandwich and a glass of wine on a side porch, followed by a long siesta.

Lenny lived with his parents on a gravel road two miles from the church. His father was a rural mail carrier, his mother a schoolteacher. An older sister was in Tupelo. Over roast and potatoes and tea almost as sweet as Miss Callie's, we relived the Kassellaw trial and Padgitt's first parole hearing. Lenny may have been unconcerned about Danny's possible release, but his parents were deeply worried.

CHAPTER 35

Big news hit Clanton in the spring of 1978. Bargain City was coming! Along with McDonald's and the fast-food joints that followed it around the country, Bargain City was a national chain rapidly marching through the small towns of the South. Most of the town rejoiced. Some of us, though, felt it was the beginning of the end.

The company was taking over the world with its "big box" discount warehouses that offered everything at very low prices. The stores were spacious and clean and included cafés, pharmacies, banks, even optometrists and travel agents. A small town without a Bargain City store was irrelevant and insignificant.

They optioned fifty acres on Market Street, about a mile from the Clanton square. Some of the neighbors protested, and the city council held a public hearing on whether to allow the store to be built. Bargain City had met opposition before, and it had a well-oiled and highly effective strategy.

The council room was packed with people holding red-and-white Bargain City signs—BARGAIN CITY—A GOOD NEIGHBOR and WE WANT JOBS. Engineers, architects, lawyers, and contractors were there, with their secretaries and wives and children. Their mouthpiece painted a rosy picture of economic growth, sales tax revenues, 150 jobs for the locals, and the best products at the lowest prices.

Mrs. Dorothy Hockett spoke in opposition. Her property was adjacent to the site and she did not want the invasion of noise and lights. The city council seemed sympathetic, but the vote had long since been decided. When no one else would speak against Bargain City, I stood and walked to the podium.

I was driven by a belief that to preserve the downtown area of Clanton we had to protect the stores and shops, cafés and offices around the square. Once we began sprawling, there would be no end to it. The town would spread in a dozen directions, each one siphoning off its own little slice of old Clanton.

Most of the jobs they were promising would be at minimum wage. The increase in sales tax revenues to the city would be at the expense of the merchants Bargain City would quickly drive out of business. The people of Ford County were not going to wake up one day and suddenly start buying more bicycles and refrigerators simply because Bargain City had such dazzling displays.

I mentioned the town of Titus, about an hour south of Clanton. Two years earlier, Bargain City opened there. Since then, fourteen retail stores and one café had closed. Main Street was almost deserted.

I mentioned the town of Marshall, over in the Delta. In the three years since Bargain City opened, the mom-and-pop merchants of Marshall had closed two pharmacies, two small department stores, the feed store, the hardware store, a ladies' boutique, a gift shop, a small bookstore, and two cafés. I'd had lunch in the remaining café and the waitress, who'd worked there for thirty years, told me their business was less than half of what it used to be. The square in Marshall was similar to Clanton's, except that most of the parking spaces were empty. There were very few folks walking the sidewalks.

I mentioned the town of Tackerville, with the same population as Clanton. One year after Bargain City opened there, the town was forced to spend $1.2 million on road improvements to handle the traffic around the development.

I handed the Mayor and councilmen copies of a study by an economics professor at the University of Georgia. He had tracked Bargain City across the South for the previous six years and evaluated the financial and social impact the company had on towns of less than ten thousand. Sales tax revenues remained roughly the same; the sales were simply shifted from the old merchants to Bargain City. Employment was roughly the same; the clerks in the old stores downtown were replaced by the new ones at Bargain City. The company made no substantial investment in the community, other than its land and building. In fact, it would not even allow its money to sit in local banks. At midnight, every night, the day's receipts were wired to the home office in Gainesville, Florida.

The study concluded that expansion was obviously wise for the shareholders of Bargain City, but it was economically devastating for most small towns. And the real damage was cultural. With boarded-up stores and empty sidewalks, the rich town life of main streets and courthouse squares was quickly dying.

A petition in support of Bargain City had 480 names. Our petition in opposition had 12. The council voted unanimously, 5–0, to approve it.

I wrote a harsh editorial and for a month read nasty letters addressed to me. For the first time, I was called a "tree-hugger."

Within a month, the bulldozers had completely razed fifty acres. The curbs and gutters were in, and a grand opening was announced for December 1, just in time for Christmas. With money committed, Bargain City wasted no time in building its warehouse. The company had a reputation for shrewd and decisive management.

The store and its parking lot covered about twenty acres. The outparcels were quickly sold to other chains, and before long the city had approved a sixteen-pump self-serve gas station, a convenience store, three fast-food restaurants, a discount shoe store, a discount furniture store, and a large grocery store.

I could not deny advertising to Bargain City. I didn't need their money, but since the *Times* was the only countywide paper, they had to advertise in it. (In response to a zoning flap I stirred up in 1977, a small right-wing rag called the *Clanton Chronicle* was up and running but struggling mightily.)

In mid-November, I met with a representative of the company and we laid out a series of rather expensive ads for the opening. I charged them as much as possible; they never complained.

On December 1, the Mayor, Senator Morton, and other dignitaries cut the ribbon. A rowdy mob burst through the doors and began shopping as if the hungry had found food. Traffic backed up on the highways leading into town.

I refused to give it front page coverage. I buried a rather small story on page seven, and this angered the Mayor and Senator Morton and the other dignitaries. They expected their ribbon cutting to be front and center.

The Christmas season was brutal for the downtown merchants. Three days after Christmas, the first casualty was reported when the old Western Auto store announced it was closing. It had occupied the same building for forty years, selling bicycles and appliances and televisions. Mr. Hollis Barr, the owner, told me that a certain Zenith color TV cost him $438, and he, after several price cuts, was trying to sell it for $510. The identical model was for sale at Bargain City for $399.

The closing of Western Auto was, of course, front page news.

It was followed in January by the closing of Swain's pharmacy next to the Tea Shoppe, and then Maggie's Gifts, next door to Mr. Mitlo's haberdashery. I treated each closing as if it were a death, and my stories had the air of obituaries.

I spent one afternoon with the Stukes twins in their hardware store. It was a wonderful old building, with dusty wooden floors, saggy shelves that held a million items, a wood-burning stove in the back where serious things got debated when business was slow. You couldn't find anything in the store, and you weren't supposed to. The routine was to ask one of the twins about "the little flat gizmo that screws into the washer at the tip of that rod thing that fits into the gadget that makes the toilet flush." One of the Stukes would disappear into the slightly organized piles of debris and emerge in a few minutes with whatever it took to make the toilet flush. Such a question could not be asked at Bargain City.

We sat by the stove on a cold winter day and listened to the rantings of one Cecil Clyde Poole, a retired Army major, who, if put in charge of national policy, would nuke everyone but the Canadians. He would also nuke Bargain City, and in some of the roughest, most colorful language I'd ever heard he ripped and blasted the company with great gusto. We had plenty of time to talk because there were almost no customers. One of the Stukes told me their business was down 70 percent.

The following month they closed the doors to the store their father had opened in 1922. On the front page, I ran a photo of the founder sitting behind a counter in 1938. I also fired off another editorial, sort of a wise-ass "I-told-you-so" reminder to whoever was out there still reading my little tirades.

"You're preachin' too much," Harry Rex warned me over and over. "And nobody's listenin'."

———

The front office of the *Times* was seldom attended. There were some tables with copies of the current edition strewn about. There was a counter that Margaret sometimes used to lay out ads. The bell on the front door rang all day long as people came and went. About once a week a stranger would venture upstairs where my office door was usually open. More often than not it was some grieving relative there to discuss an upcoming obituary.

I looked up one afternoon in March 1979 and there was a gentleman in a nice suit standing at my office door. Unlike Harry Rex, whose entrance began on the street and was heard by everyone in the building, this guy had climbed the stairs without making a sound.

His name was Gary McGrew, a consultant from Nashville, whose area of expertise was small-town newspapers. As I fixed a pot of coffee, he explained that a rather well-financed client of his was planning to buy several newspapers in Mississippi during 1979. Because I had seven thousand subscribers, no debt, an offset press, and because we now ran the printing for six smaller weeklies, plus our own shoppers' guides, his client was very interested in buying *The Ford County Times*.

"How interested?" I asked.

"Extremely. If we could look at the books, we could value your company."

He left and I made a few phone calls to verify his credibility. He checked out fine, and I collected my current financials. Three days later we met again, this time at night. I did not want Wiley or Baggy or anyone else hanging around. News that the *Times* was changing hands would be such hot gossip that they'd open the coffee shops at 3 A.M. instead of 5.

McGrew crunched the numbers like a seasoned analyst. I waited, oddly nervous, as if the verdict might drastically change my life.

"You're clearing a hundred grand after taxes, plus you're taking a salary of fifty grand. Depreciation is another twenty, no interest because you have no debt. That's one-seventy in cash flow, times the standard multiple of six, comes to one million twenty thousand."

"And the building?" I asked.

He glanced around as if the ceiling might collapse any moment. "These places typically don't sell for much."

"A hundred thousand," I said.

"Okay. And a hundred thousand for the offset press and other equipment. The total value is somewhere in the neighborhood of one-point-two million."

"Is that an offer?" I asked, even more anxious.

"It might be. I'll have to discuss it with my client."

I had no intention of selling the *Times*. I had stumbled into the business, gotten a few lucky breaks, worked hard writing stories and obituaries and selling pages of ads, and now, nine years later, my little company was worth over a million dollars.

I was young, still single though I was tired of being lonely and living alone in a mansion with three leftover Hocutt cats that refused to die. I had accepted the reality that I would not find a bride in Ford County. All the good ones were snatched up by their twentieth birthday, and I was too old to compete at that level. I dated all the young divorcées, most of whom were quick to hop in the sack and wake up in my fine home, and dream about spending all the money I was rumored to be making. The only one I really liked, and dated off and on for a year, was saddled with three small children.

But it's funny what a million bucks will do to you. Once it was in play, it was never far from my thoughts. The job became more tedious. I grew to resent the ridiculous obituaries and the endless pressure of the deadlines. I told myself at least once a day that I no longer had to hustle the street selling ads. I could quit the editorials. No more nasty letters to the editor.

A week later, I told Gary McGrew that the *Times* was not for sale. He said his client had decided to buy three papers by the end of the year, so I had time to think about it.

Remarkably, word of our discussions never leaked.

CHAPTER 36

On a Thursday afternoon in early May, I received a phone call from the attorney for the Parole Board. The next Padgitt hearing would take place the following Monday.

"Convenient timing," I said.

"Why's that?" he asked.

"We publish every Wednesday, so I don't have time to run a story before the hearing."

"We don't monitor your paper, Mr. Traynor," he said.

"I don't believe that," I snapped.

"What you believe is irrelevant. The Board has decided that you will not be permitted to attend the hearing. You violated our rules last time by reporting on what happened."

"I'm banned?"

"That's correct."

"I'll be there anyway."

I hung up and called Sheriff McNatt. He, too, had been notified of the hearing, but wasn't sure if he could attend. He was hot on the trail of a missing child (from Wisconsin), and it was obvious he had little interest in getting mixed up with the Padgitts.

Our District Attorney, Rufus Buckley, had an armed robbery trial scheduled for Monday in Van Buren County. He promised to send a letter opposing the parole, but the letter never made it. Circuit Judge Omar Noose was presiding over the same trial, so he was off the hook. I began to think that no one would be there to speak in opposition to Padgitt's release.

For fun I asked Baggy to go. He gasped, then quickly let loose with an impressive list of excuses.

I walked over to Harry Rex's with the news. He had an ugly divorce trial starting Monday in Tupelo; otherwise he might have gone with me to Parchman. "The boy's gonna be released, Willie," he said.

"We stopped it last year," I said.

"Once the parole hearings start, it's just a matter of time."

"But somebody has to fight it."

"Why bother? He's gettin' out eventually. Why piss off the Padgitts? You won't get any volunteers."

Volunteers were indeed hard to find as the entire town ducked for cover. I had envisioned an angry mob packing into the parole board hearing and disrupting the meeting.

My angry mob consisted of three people.

Wiley Meek agreed to ride over with me, though he had no interest in speaking. If they were serious about banning me from the room, Wiley would sit through it and give me the details. Sheriff McNatt surprised us with his presence.

Security was tight in the hall outside the hearing room. When the Board attorney saw me he became angry and we exchanged words. Guards in uniforms surrounded me. I was outnumbered and unarmed. I was escorted from the building and placed in my car, then watched by two thick-necked ruffians with low IQs.

According to Wiley, the hearing went like clockwork. Lucien was there with various Padgitts. The Board attorney read a staff report that made Danny sound like an Eagle Scout. His caseworker seconded the nomination. Lucien spoke for ten minutes, the usual lawyerly bullshit. Danny's father spoke last and pleaded emotionally for his son's release. He was desperately needed back home, where the family had interests in timber, gravel, asphalt, trucking, contracting, and freight. He would have so many jobs and work so many hours each week that he couldn't possibly get into more trouble.

Sheriff McNatt gamely stood up for the people of Ford County. He was nervous and not a good speaker, but did a credible job of replaying the crime. Remarkably, he neglected to remind the Board members that a jury drawn from the same pool of people who elected him had been threatened by Danny Padgitt.

By a vote of 4–1, Danny Padgitt was paroled from prison.

———————

Clanton was quietly disappointed. During the trial, the town had a real thirst for blood and was bitter when the jury didn't deliver the death penalty. But nine years had passed, and since the parole hearing it had been accepted that Danny Padgitt would eventually get out. No one expected it so soon, but after the hearing we were over the shock.

His release was influenced by two unusual factors. The first was that Rhoda Kassellaw had no family in the area. There were no grieving parents to arouse sympathy and demand justice. There were no angry siblings to keep the case alive. Her children were gone and forgotten. She had lived a lonely life and left no close friends who were willing to press a grudge against her murderer.

The second was that the Padgitts lived in another world. They were so rarely seen in public, it was not difficult to convince ourselves that Danny would simply go to the island and never be seen again. What difference did it make to the people of Ford County? Prison or Padgitt Island? If we never saw him, we wouldn't be reminded of his crimes. In the nine years since his trial, I had not seen a single Padgitt in Clanton. In my rather harsh editorial about his release, I said "a cold-blooded killer is once more among us." But that wasn't really true.

The front page story and the editorial drew not a single letter from the public. Folks talked about the release, but not for long and not very loudly.

Baggy eased into my office late one morning a week after Padgitt's release, and closed the door, always a good sign. He'd picked up some gossip so juicy that it had to be delivered with the door shut.

On a typical day I arrived for work around 11 A.M. And on a typical day he began hitting the sauce around noon, so we usually had about an hour to discuss stories and monitor rumors.

He glanced around as if the walls were bugged, then said, "It cost the Padgitts a hundred grand to spring the boy."

The amount did not shock me, nor did the bribe itself, but I was surprised that Baggy had dug up this information.

"No," I said. This always spurred him to tell more.

"That's what I'm tellin' you," he said smugly, his usual response when he had the scoop.

"Who got the money?"

"That's the good part. You won't believe it."

"Who?"

"You'll be shocked."

"Who?"

Slowly, he went through his extended ritual of lighting a cigarette. In the early years, I would hang in the air as he delayed whatever dramatic news he had picked up, but with experience I had learned that this only slowed down the story. So I resumed my scribbling.

"It shouldn't come as a surprise, I guess," he said, puffing and pondering. "Didn't surprise me at all."

"Are you gonna tell me or not?"

"Theo."

"Senator Morton?"

"That's what I'm tellin' you."

I was sufficiently shocked, and I had to give the impression of being so or the story would lose steam. "Theo?" I asked.

"He's vice chairman of the Corrections Committee in the Senate. Been there forever, knows how to pull the strings. He wanted a hundred grand, the Padgitts wanted to pay it, they cut a deal, the boy walks. Just like that."

"I thought Theo was above taking bribes," I said, and I was serious. This drew an exaggerated snort.

"Don't be so naive," he said. Again, he knew everything.

"Where did you hear it?"

"Can't say." There was a chance that his poker gang had cooked up the rumor to see how fast it would race around the square before it got back to them. But there was an equally good chance Baggy was on to something. It really didn't matter, though. Cash couldn't be traced.

———

Just when I had stopped dreaming of an early retirement, of cashing in, walking away, jetting off to Europe, and backpacking across Australia, just when I had resettled into my routine of covering stories and writing obits and hawking ads to every merchant in town, Mr. Gary McGrew reentered my life. And he brought his client with him.

Ray Noble was one of three principals in a company that already owned thirty weekly newspapers in the Deep South and wanted to add more. Like my college friend Nick Diener, he had been raised in the family newspaper business and could talk the talk. He swore me to secrecy, then laid out his plan. His company wanted to buy the *Times*, along with the papers in Tyler and Van Buren Counties. They would sell off the equipment in the other two and do all the printing in Clanton because we had a better press. They would consolidate the accounting and much of the ad sales. Their offer of $1.2 million had been at the high end of the appraisal.

Now they were offering $1.3 million. Cash.

"After capital gains, you'll walk away with a cool million," Noble said.

"I can do the math," I said, as if I closed such deals on a weekly basis. The words "cool million" were rumbling through my entire body.

They pressed a little. Offers were on the table for the other two papers, and I got the impression that the deal wasn't exactly coming together as they wished. The key element was the *Times*. We had better equipment and a slightly larger circulation.

I declined again and they left; all three of us knew it was not our last conversation.

Eleven years after he fled Ford County, Sam Ruffin returned in much the same manner as he left—on a bus in the middle of the night. He'd been home for two days before I knew it. I arrived for my Thursday lunch and there sat Sam, rocking on the porch, with a smile as wide as his mother's. Miss Callie looked and acted ten years younger now that he was safely back home. She fried a chicken and cooked every vegetable in her garden. Esau joined us and we feasted for three hours.

Sam now had one college degree under his belt and was planning on law school. He had almost married a Canadian woman but things blew up over her family's heated opposition to the union. Miss Callie was quite relieved to hear of the breakup. Sam had not mentioned the romance in letters to his mother.

He planned to stay in Clanton for a few days, very close to home, venturing out of Lowtown only at night. I promised to talk to Harry Rex, to fish around and see what I could learn about Trooper Durant and his sons. From the legal notices we printed, I knew that Durant had remarried, then divorced for the second time.

He wanted to see the town, so late that afternoon I picked him up in my Spitfire. Hiding under a Detroit Tigers baseball cap, he took in the sights of the small town he still called home. I showed him my office, my house, Bargain City, and the sprawl west of town. We circled the courthouse and I told him the story of the sniper and Baggy's dramatic escape. Much of this he'd heard in letters from Miss Callie.

As I dropped him off in front of the Ruffin home, he said, "Is Padgitt really out of prison?"

"No one's seen him," I said. "But I'm sure he's back home."

"Do you expect trouble?"

"No, not really."

"Neither do I. But I can't convince Momma."

"Nothing will happen, Sam."

CHAPTER 37

The single shot that killed Lenny Fargarson was fired from a 30.06 hunting rifle. The killer could have been as far as two hundred yards away from the front porch where Lenny died. Thick woods began just beyond the wide lawn around the house, and there was a good chance whoever pulled the trigger had climbed a tree and had a perfectly concealed view of poor Lenny.

No one heard the shot. Lenny was sitting on the porch, in his wheelchair, reading one of the many books he borrowed each week from the Clanton library. His father was delivering mail. His mother was shopping at Bargain City. In all likelihood, Lenny felt no pain and died instantly. The bullet entered the right side of his head, just over the jaw, and created a massive exit wound above his left ear.

When his mother found him, he'd been dead for some time. She somehow managed to control herself and refrain from touching his body or the scene. Blood was all over the porch, even dripping onto the front steps.

Wiley heard the report on his police scanner. He called me with the chilling announcement, "It has begun. Fargarson, the crippled boy, is dead."

Wiley swung by the office, I jumped in his pickup, and we were off to the crime scene. Neither of us said a word, but we were thinking the same thing.

Lenny was still on the porch. The shot had knocked him out of his wheelchair and he lay on his side, with his face toward the house. Sheriff McNatt asked us not to take photos, and we readily complied. The paper would not have used them anyway.

Friends and relatives were flocking over, and they were directed by the deputies to a side door. McNatt used his men to shield the body on the front porch. I backed away and tried to take in that horrible scene— cops hovering over Lenny while those who loved him tried to get a glimpse of him as they hurried inside to console his parents.

When the body was finally loaded onto a gurney and placed in an ambulance, Sheriff McNatt came over and leaned on the pickup next to me.

"Are you thinkin' what I'm thinkin'?" he said.

"Yep."

"Can you find me a list of the jurors?"

Though we had never printed the names of the jurors, I had the information in an old file. "Sure," I said.

"How long will it take you?" he asked.

"Give me an hour. What's your plan?"

"We gotta notify those folks."

As we were leaving, the deputies were beginning to comb the thick woods around the Fargarson home.

———————

I took the list to the Sheriff's office, and we looked over it together. In 1977, I had written the obituary for juror number five, Mr. Fred Bilroy, a retired forest ranger who died suddenly of pneumonia. As far as I knew, the other ten were still alive.

McNatt gave the list to three of his deputies. They dispersed to deliver news that no one wanted to hear. I volunteered to tell Callie Ruffin.

She was on the porch watching Esau and Sam wage war over a game of checkers. They were delighted to see me, but the mood quickly changed. "I have some disturbing news, Miss Callie," I said somberly. They waited.

"Lenny Fargarson, that crippled boy on the jury with you, was murdered this afternoon."

She covered her mouth and fell into her rocker. Sam steadied her, then patted her shoulder. I gave a brief description of what happened.

"He was such a good Christian boy," Miss Callie said. "We prayed together before we began deliberating." She wasn't crying, but she was on the verge. Esau went to fetch her a blood pressure pill. He and Sam sat beside her rocker while I sat in the swing. We were all bunched together on the small porch, and for a long time little was said. Miss Callie lapsed into a long, brooding spell.

It was a warm spring night, under a half-moon, and Lowtown was busy with kids on bikes, neighbors talking across fences, a rowdy basketball game under way down the street. A gang of ten-year-olds became infatuated with my Spitfire, and Sam finally ran them off. It was only the second time I had been there after dark. "Is it like this every night?" I finally asked.

"Yes, when the weather's nice," Sam said, anxious to talk. "It was a wonderful place to grow up. Everybody knows everybody. When I was nine years old I broke a car windshield with a baseball. I turned tail and ran, ran straight home, and when I got here Momma was waiting on the front porch. She knew all about it. I had to walk back to the scene of the crime, confess, and promise to make full restitution."

"And you did," Esau said.

"Took me six months to work and save a hundred and twenty bucks."

Miss Callie almost smiled at the memory, but she was too preoccupied with Lenny Fargarson. Though she hadn't seen him in nine years, she had fond memories of him. His death truly saddened her, but it was also terrifying.

Esau fixed sweet tea with lemon, and when he returned from the inside of the house he quietly slid a double-barrel shotgun behind the rocker, within his reach but out of her sight.

As the hours passed, the foot traffic thinned and the

neighbors withdrew. I decided that if Miss Callie stayed at home she would be a very difficult target. There were houses next door and across the street. There were no hills or towers or vacant lots within sight.

I didn't mention this, but I'm sure Sam and Esau were having the same thoughts. When she was ready for bed, I said my good nights and drove back to the jail. It was crawling with deputies, and had the carnival-like atmosphere that only a good murder could bring. I couldn't help but flash back nine years to the night Danny Padgitt was arrested and hauled in with blood on his shirt.

Only two of the jurors had not been found. Both had moved, and Sheriff McNatt was trying to track them down. He asked about Miss Callie and I said she was safe. I did not tell him Sam was home.

He closed the door to his office and said he had a favor to ask. "Tomorrow, can you go talk to Lucien Wilbanks?"

"Why me?"

"Well, I could, but, personally, I can't stand the bastard, and he feels the same way about me."

"Everybody hates Lucien," I said.

"Except . . ."

"Except . . . Harry Rex?"

"Harry Rex. What if you and Harry Rex go talk to Lucien? See if he will act as go-between to the Padgitts. I mean, at some point I gotta talk to Danny, right?"

"I guess. You're the Sheriff."

"Just have a chat with Lucien Wilbanks, that's all.

Feel him out. If it goes well, then maybe I'll talk to him. It's different if the Sheriff goes bargin' in at first."

"I'd rather be lashed with a bullwhip," I said, and I wasn't joking.

"But you'll do it?"

"I'll sleep on it."

———

Harry Rex wasn't too thrilled with the idea either. Why should both of us get involved? We kicked it around over an early breakfast at the coffee shop, an unusual meal for us but then we didn't want to miss the first tidal wave of downtown gossip. Not surprisingly, the place was packed with anxious experts who were repeating all sorts of details and theories about the Fargarson murder. We listened more than we talked, and left around eight-thirty.

Two doors down from the coffee shop was the Wilbanks Building. As we walked by, I said, "Let's do it."

Pre-Lucien, the Wilbanks family had been a cornerstone of Clanton society, commerce, and law. In the golden years of the last century, they owned land and banks, and all of the men in the family had studied law, some at real Ivy League schools. But they had been in decline for many years. Lucien was the last male Wilbanks of any consequence, and there was an excellent chance he was about to be disbarred.

Ethel Twitty, the longtime secretary, greeted us rudely, almost sneering at Harry Rex, who mumbled to me under his breath, "Meanest bitch in town." I think she heard him. It was obvious they had been catfighting for many years. Her boss was in. What did we want?

"We want to see Lucien," Harry Rex said. "Why else would we be here?" She rang him up as we waited. "I don't have all day!" Harry Rex snapped at her at one point.

"Go ahead," she said, more to get rid of us than anything else. We climbed the steps. Lucien's office was huge, at least thirty feet wide and long with ten-foot ceilings and a row of French doors overlooking the square. It was on the north side, directly across from the *Times*, with the courthouse in between. Thankfully, I couldn't see Lucien's balcony from my porch.

He greeted us indifferently, as if we had interrupted a long serious meditation. Though it was early, his cluttered desk gave the impression of a man who'd worked all night. He had long grayish hair that ran down his neck, and an unfashionable goatee, and the tired red eyes of a serious drinker. "What's the occasion?" he asked, very slowly. We glared at each other, both conveying as much contempt as possible.

"Had a murder yesterday, Lucien," Harry Rex said. "Lenny Fargarson, that crippled boy on the jury."

"I'm assuming this is off the record," he said in my direction.

"It is," I said. "Completely. Sheriff McNatt asked me to stop by and say hello. I invited Harry Rex."

"So we're just socializing?"

"Maybe. Just having a little gossip about the murder," I said.

"I got the details," he said.

"Have you talked to Danny Padgitt lately?" Harry Rex asked.

"Not since he was paroled."

"Is he in the county?"

"He's in the state, I'm not sure exactly where. If he crosses the state line without permission he violates the conditions of his parole."

Why couldn't they parole him to, say, Wyoming? It seemed odd that he would be required to stay close to where he committed his crimes. Get rid of him!

"Sheriff McNatt would like to talk to him," I said.

"Oh does he? Why should that concern you and me? Tell the Sheriff to go talk to him."

"It's not that simple, Lucien, and you know it," Harry Rex said.

"Does the Sheriff have any proof against my client? Any evidence? Ever hear of probable cause, Harry Rex? You can't just round up the usual suspects, you know? Takes a little more than that."

"There was a direct threat against the jurors," I said.

"Nine years ago."

"It was still a threat, and we all remember it. Now, two weeks after he's paroled, one of his jurors is dead."

"That's not enough, fellas. Show me more and I might consult with my client. Right now there's nothing but naked speculation. Plenty of it, but this town's always good for a flood of gossip."

"You don't know where he is, do you, Lucien?" Harry Rex said.

"I assume he's on the island, with the rest of them." He used the word "them" as if they were a bunch of rats.

"What happens if another juror gets shot?" Harry Rex pressed on.

Lucien dropped a legal pad on his desk and rested there on his elbows. "What am I supposed to do, Harry Rex? Call the boy up, say 'Hey, Danny, I'm sure you're not killin' your jurors, but, if by chance you are, then, hey, be a good boy and stop it.' You think he'll listen to me? This wouldn't have happened if the idiot had followed my advice. I insisted that he not take the stand in his own defense. He's an idiot, okay, Harry Rex! You're a lawyer, God knows you've had idiot clients. You can't do a damned thing to control them."

"What happens if another juror gets shot?" Harry Rex repeated.

"Then I guess another juror will die."

I jumped to my feet and headed for the door. "You're a sick bastard," I said.

"Not a word of this in print," he snarled behind me.

"Go to hell," I yelled as I slammed his door.

——————

Late in the afternoon Mr. Magargel called from the funeral home and asked if I could hustle over. Mr. and Mrs. Fargarson were there, picking out a casket and making the final arrangements. As I had done many times, I met them in Parlor C, the smallest viewing room. It was seldom used.

Pastor J. B. Cooper of the Maranatha Primitive Baptist Church was with them, and he was a saint. They leaned on him for every decision.

At least twice a year, I met with a family after the tragic death of a loved one. It was almost always a car wreck or some gruesome farm injury, something unexpected. The surviving members were too shocked to think clearly, too wounded to make decisions. The strong ones simply sleepwalked through the ordeal. The weak ones were often too numb to do anything but cry. Mrs. Fargarson was the stronger of the two, but the horror of finding her son with half his head blown off had reduced her to a shuddering ghost. Mr. Fargarson just stared at the floor.

Pastor Cooper gently extracted the basics, many of which he already knew. Since his spinal injury fifteen years earlier, Lenny had dreamed of going to heaven, of having his body restored, of walking every day hand in hand with his Savior. We worked on some language to this effect, and Mrs. Fargarson was deeply appreciative. She handed me a photo, one of Lenny sitting by a pond with a fishing pole. I promised to put it on the front page.

As always with grieving parents, they thanked me profusely and insisted on hugging me tightly as I tried to leave. Mourners cling to people like that, especially at the funeral home.

I stopped by Pepe's and bought an array of Mexican carryout, then drove to Lowtown, where I found Sam playing basketball, Miss Callie asleep inside, and Esau guarding the house with his shotgun. Eventually, we ate on the porch, though she only nibbled at the foreign food. She wasn't hungry. Esau said she'd eaten little during the day.

I brought my backgammon board and taught Sam the game. Esau preferred checkers. Miss Callie was certain any activity that involved the rolling of dice was patently sinful, but she wasn't up to a lecture. We sat for hours, deep into the night, and watched the rituals of Lowtown. School had just turned out for the summer, the days were longer and hotter.

Buster, my part-time pit bull, drove by every half hour. He would slow in front of the Ruffins, I'd wave as if things were fine, he'd ease away and return to the driveway of the Hocutt House. A patrol car parked two doors down from the Ruffin house and sat for a long time. Sheriff McNatt had hired three black deputies, and two of them had been assigned to keep an eye on the home.

Others were watching as well. After Miss Callie went to bed, Esau pointed across to the street to the darkened screened porch where the Braxtons lived. "Tully's over there," he said. "Watchin' everythin'."

"He told me he'd stay up all night," Sam said. Lowtown would be a dangerous place to start a gunfight.

I left after eleven, crossed the tracks, and drove the empty streets of Clanton. The town pulsed with tension, with anticipation, because whatever had been started was far from over.

CHAPTER 38

Miss Callie insisted on attending the funeral of Lenny Fargarson. Sam and Esau objected strenuously, but, as always, once she made up her mind, then all conversations were over. I discussed this with Sheriff McNatt, who summed things up by saying, "She's a grown lady." He knew of no other jurors who planned to attend, but then it was difficult to monitor such things.

I also called Pastor Cooper to forewarn him. His response was, "She will be very welcome in our little church. But get here early."

With rare exceptions blacks and whites did not worship together in Ford County. They fervently believed in the same Lord, but chose very different styles of worshiping him. The majority of whites expected to be outside the church building at five past noon on Sunday, and seated for lunch by twelve-thirty. Blacks really didn't care what time the service broke up, or what time it began for that matter. On my church tour I visited twenty-seven black congregations and never saw a benediction before 1:30—3 P.M. was the norm. Several simply went all day, with a short break for lunch in the fellowship hall, then back to the sanctuary for another round.

Such zealotry would have killed a white Christian.

But funerals were very different. When Miss Callie, along with Sam and Esau, walked into the Maranatha Primitive Baptist Church, there were a few quick stares but nothing more. Had they walked in on a Sunday morning for regular worship, there would have been resentment.

We arrived forty-five minutes early, and the lovely little sanctuary was almost filled. I watched through the tall open windows as the cars kept coming. A loudspeaker had been hung from one of the ancient oaks, and a large crowd gathered around it after the building was full. The choir started with "The Old Rugged Cross," and the tears began flowing. Pastor Cooper's soothing message was a gentle warning for us not to question why bad things happen to good people. God is always in control, and though we are too small to understand His infinite wisdom and majesty, He will one day reveal Himself to us. Lenny was with Him now, and that was where Lenny longed to be.

They buried him behind the church, in an immaculate little cemetery inside a wrought-iron fence. Miss Callie clutched my hand and prayed fervently when the casket was lowered into the ground. A soloist sang

"Amazing Grace," then Pastor Cooper thanked us for coming. There was punch and cookies in the fellowship hall behind the sanctuary, and most of the crowd hung around for a few minutes to visit, or to have one last word with Mr. and Mrs. Fargarson.

Sheriff McNatt caught my attention and nodded as if he wanted to talk. We walked to the front of the church where no one could hear us. He was in uniform with his standard toothpick in his mouth. "Any luck with Wilbanks?" he asked.

"No, just the one meeting," I said. "Harry Rex went back yesterday and got nowhere."

"I guess I'll talk to him," he said.

"You can, but you won't get anywhere."

The toothpick shifted from one side of his mouth to the other, in much the same way Harry Rex could slide his cigar over without missing a word. "We got nothin' else. We've combed the woods around the house, not a track or a trace of anything. You're not printin' this, are you?"

"No."

"There are a bunch of ol' loggin' trails deep in the woods around the Fargarson place. We've tiptoed everyone of 'em, found absolutely nothin'."

"So your only evidence is a single bullet."

"That and a dead body."

"Has anybody seen Danny Padgitt?"

"Not yet. I keep two cars up on 401, where it turns to go into the island. They can't see everything, but at least the Padgitts know we're there. There are a hundred ways off and on the island, but only the Padgitts know them all."

The Ruffins were slowly moving toward us, talking to one of the black deputies.

"She's probably the safest one," McNatt said.

"Is anybody safe?"

"We'll find out. He'll try again, Willie, you mark my word. I'm convinced of it."

"Me too."

———

Ned Ray Zook owned four thousand acres in the eastern part of the county. He farmed cotton and soybeans, and his operations were large enough to maintain sufficient profits. He was rumored to be one of the few remaining farmers who made good money from the soil. It was on his property, deep in a wooded area, in a converted cattle barn, that Harry Rex had taken me nine years earlier to watch my first and last cockfight.

Sometime during the early hours of June 14, a vandal entered Zook's vast equipment shed and partially drained the oil from the engines of two of his big tractors. The oil was collected in cans and hidden among the supplies, so when the operators arrived around 6 A.M. for the day's work there was no sign of foul play. One operator checked the oil as he was supposed to do, saw the shortage, thought it odd, said nothing, and added four quarts. The other operator had checked his the afternoon before, as was his habit. The second tractor ground to a sudden halt an hour later, as its engine locked up. Its operator hiked half a mile back to the shed and reported the breakdown to the farm manager.

Two hours later, a green-and-yellow service truck bounced along the field road and maneuvered itself close to the disabled tractor. Two servicemen slowly got out, inspected the hot sun and cloudless sky, then walked around the tractor for an initial look. They reluctantly opened up the panels of the service truck and began removing tools and wrenches. The sun baked them and they were soon sweating.

To make their day somewhat more pleasant, they turned on the radio in their truck and cranked up the volume. Merle Haggard could be heard wafting across the soybean field.

The music muffled the crack of a distant rifle shot. It hit Mo Teale directly in the upper back, ripped through his lungs, and tore a hole in his chest as it exited. Teale's partner, Red, said over and over that the only thing he heard was a fierce grunt just a second or two before Mo fell under the front axle. He thought at first that something from the tractor had snapped loose in a violent way and injured Mo. Red dragged him to the truck and raced away, much more concerned about his buddy than what might have injured him. At the equipment shed, the farm manager called an ambulance, but it was too late. Mo Teale died there, on the concrete floor of a small, dusty office. "Mr. John Deere" we'd called him during the trial. Middle of the front row, bad body language.

At the time of his death he was wearing the same

type of bright yellow uniform shirt he'd worn every day of the trial. It made for an easy target.

I saw him at a distance, through the open door. Sheriff McNatt allowed us inside the shed with the now standard prohibition against taking photos. Wiley had left his cameras in his pickup.

Once again Wiley had been monitoring the police scanner when the report came across—"Got a shooting at Ned Ray Zook's farm!" Wiley was always near his scanner, and in those days he wasn't alone. Given the high state of anxiety in the county, every scanner was being listened to and every possible shooting was reason to hop in the pickup and go for a look.

McNatt soon asked us to leave. His men found the cans of oil that had been drained by the vandal, and they found a window that had been pried open for entry into the shed. They would dust for fingerprints and find none. They would look for footprints on the gravel flooring, and find none. They would scour the woods around the soybean field and find no sign of the killer. In the dirt beside the tractor they did find the 30.06 shell, and it was quickly matched with the one that killed Lenny Fargarson.

———

I hung around the Sheriff's office until well after dark. As expected it was a busy place, with deputies and constables loitering about, comparing stories, creating new details. The phones rang nonstop. And there was a new wrinkle. Random townsfolk, unable to control their curiosity, began stopping by and asking anyone who would listen if there was anything new.

There was not. McNatt barricaded himself in his office with his top boys and tried to decide what to do next. His priority was the protection of the surviving eight jurors. Three were already dead—Mr. Fred Bilroy (of pneumonia), and now Lenny Fargarson and Mo Teale. One juror had moved to Florida two years after the trial. At that moment, each of the eight had a patrol car parked very near their front doors.

I left and went to the office to work on the story about the murder of Mo Teale, but I was sidetracked by the lights at Harry Rex's. He was in his conference room, knee-deep in depositions and files and all sorts of lawyerly debris, the sight of which always gave me an instant headache. We grabbed two beers out of his small office refrigerator and went for a drive.

In a working-class section of town known as Coventry we drove along a narrow street and passed a house with cars parked like fallen dominoes in the front yard. "That's where Maxine Root lives," he said. "She was on the jury."

I vaguely remembered Mrs. Root. Her small red-brick house had no front porch to speak of, so her neighbors were scattered around the carport in folding lawn chairs. Rifles were visible. Every light in the house was on. A patrol car was parked by the mailbox, two deputies leaning on its hood, smoking cigarettes and watching us very closely as we drove by. Harry Rex stopped and said, "Evenin', Troy," to one of the deputies.

"Hey, Harry Rex," Troy said, taking a step toward us.

"Quite a party they got goin', huh?"

"It'd take a fool to start trouble around here."

"We're just passin' by," Harry Rex said.

"Better keep movin'," Troy said. "They got itchy fingers."

"Take care." We eased away and swung around behind the livestock barn north of town where a long shady lane dead-ended near the water tower. Halfway down, the street was lined on both sides with cars. "Who lives here?" I asked.

"Mr. Earl Youry. He sat on the back row, farthest from the spectators."

A crowd was huddled on the front porch. Some sat on the steps. Others were in lawn chairs out on the grass. Somewhere in that pack Mr. Earl Youry was hidden and very well protected by his friends and neighbors.

Miss Callie was no less defended. The street in front of her house was packed with cars and barely passable. Groups of men sat on the cars, some smoking, some holding rifles. Next door and across the street the porches and yards were filled with people. Half of Lowtown had gathered there to make sure she felt secure. There was a festival atmosphere, the feeling of a unique event.

With white faces, Harry Rex and I received closer

scrutiny. We didn't stop until he could speak with the deputies, and once they approved our presence the pack relaxed. We parked and I walked to the house where Sam met me at the front steps. Harry Rex stayed behind, chatting with the deputies.

She was inside, in her bedroom, reading her Bible with a friend from church. Several deacons were on the porch with Sam and Esau, and they were anxious for details of the Teale murder. I filled them in with as much as I could tell, which wasn't much at all.

Around midnight, the crowd began to slowly break up. Sam and the deputies had organized a rotation of all-night sentries, armed guards on both the front and back porches. There was no shortage of volunteers. Miss Callie never dreamed her pleasant and God-fearing little home would become such an armed fortress, but under the circumstances she could not be disappointed.

We drove the anxious streets to the Hocutt House, where we found Buster asleep in his car in the driveway. We found some bourbon and sat on a front porch, swatting an occasional mosquito and trying to appreciate the situation.

"He's very patient," Harry Rex said. "Wait a few days when all these neighbors get tired of porch sittin', when everybody relaxes a little. The jurors can't live long locked inside their homes. He'll wait."

One chilling little fact that had not been released was a service call received by the tractor dealership a week earlier. At the Anderson farm south of town a tractor had been disabled under similar circumstances. Mo Teale, who was one of four chief mechanics, had not been sent to repair it. Someone else's yellow shirt had been watched through the scope of a hunting rifle.

"He's patient and meticulous," I agreed. Eleven days had passed between the two murders, and no clues had been left behind. If it was indeed Danny Padgitt, there was a stark contrast between his first murder—Rhoda Kassellaw—and his last two. He'd advanced from a brutal crime of passion to cold-blooded executions. Perhaps that's what nine years in prison had taught him. He'd had plenty of time to remember the faces of the twelve people who'd sent him away, and to plan his revenge.

"He's not finished," Harry Rex said.

One murder might be considered a random act. Two meant there was a pattern. The third would send a small army of cops and vigilantes onto Padgitt Island for an all-out war.

"He'll wait," Harry Rex said. "Probably for a long time."

"I'm thinking about selling the paper, Harry Rex," I said.

He took a long drink of bourbon, then said, "Why would you do that?"

"Money. This company in Georgia is making a serious offer."

"How much?"

"A lot. More than I ever dreamed of. I wouldn't work for a long time. Maybe never."

The idea of not working hit him hard. His daily routine was ten hours of nonstop chaos with some very emotional and high-strung divorce clients. He often worked nights, when the office was quiet and he could think. He made a comfortable living, but he certainly scraped for every penny. "How long have you had the paper?" he asked.

"Nine years."

"Kinda hard to imagine the paper without you."

"Maybe that's a reason to sell it. I don't want to be another Wilson Caudle."

"What will you do?"

"Take a break, travel, see the world, find a nice lady, marry her, get her pregnant, have some kids. This is a big house."

"So you wouldn't move away?"

"To where? This is home."

Another long sip, then, "I don't know. Let me sleep on it." With that, he walked off the porch and drove away.

CHAPTER 39

With the bodies piling up, it was inevitable the story would attract more attention than the *Times* could give it. The next morning, a reporter I knew from the Memphis paper arrived in my office, and about twenty minutes later one from the Jackson paper joined us. Both covered northern Mississippi, where the hottest news was usually a factory explosion or another indicted county official.

I gave them the background on both murders, the Padgitt parole, and the fear that had gripped the county. We were not competitors—they wrote for large dailies that barely overlapped. Most of my subscribers also took either the Memphis or Jackson papers. The Tupelo daily was also popular.

And, frankly, I was losing interest; not in the current crisis, but in journalism as a vocation. The world was calling me. As I sat there drinking coffee and trading stories with those two veterans, both of whom were older than me, each of whom earned about $40,000 a year, I found it hard to believe that I could walk away right then with a million bucks. It was difficult to stay focused.

They eventually left to pursue their own angles. A few minutes later Sam called with a rather urgent, "You need to come over."

A ragtag little unit was still guarding the Ruffin porch. All four were bleary-eyed and in need of sleep. Sam cleared me through the bivouac and we went to the kitchen table where Miss Callie was shelling butter beans, a task she always performed on the rear porch. She gave me a warm smile and the standard bear hug, but she was a troubled woman. "In here," she said. Sam nodded and we followed her into her small bedroom. She closed the door behind us as if intruders were lurking, then she disappeared into a narrow closet. We waited awkwardly while she rattled around in there.

She finally emerged with an old spiral notebook, one that had obviously been well hidden. "Something doesn't make sense," she said as she sat on the edge of the bed. Sam sat beside her and I backed into an old rocker. She was flipping through the pages of her handwritten notes. "Here it is," she said.

"We gave our solemn promises that we would never talk about what happened in the jury room," she said, "but this is too important not to tell. When we found Mr. Padgitt guilty, the vote was quick and unanimous. But when we came to the issue of the death penalty, there was some opposition to it. I certainly didn't want to send anyone to die, but I had promised to follow the law. Things got very heated, there were sharp words, even some accusations and threats. Not a pleasant thing to sit through. When the battle lines became clear, there were three people opposed to the death penalty, and they were not about to change their minds."

She showed me a page in her notebook. In her clear and distinctive handwriting there were two columns—one had nine names, the other had only three—L. Fargarson, Mo Teale, and Maxine Root. I gawked at the names, thinking that maybe I was looking at the killer's list.

"When did you write this?" I asked.

"I kept notes during the trial," she said.

Why would Danny Padgitt be killing the jurors who refused to give him the death penalty? The ones who had effectively saved his life?

"He's killing the wrong ones, isn't he?" Sam asked. "I mean, it's all wrong, but if you're out for revenge why go after the folks who tried to save you?"

"As I said, it doesn't make sense," Miss Callie said.

"You're assuming too much," I said. "You're assuming he knows how each juror voted. As far as I know, and I snooped around for a long time, the jurors never told anyone how the vote went. The trial was overshadowed rather quickly by the desegregation order. Padgitt was shipped off to Parchman the same day he was found guilty. There's a good chance he's picking off the easy ones first, and Mr. Fargarson and Mr. Teale just happened to be more accessible."

"That's very coincidental," Sam said.

We pondered that for a long time. I wasn't sure if it was plausible; I wasn't sure of anything. Then I had another thought: "Keep in mind, all twelve jurors voted guilty, and that was just after he made his threat."

"I suppose," Miss Callie said, unconvinced. We were trying to make sense of something that was completely incomprehensible.

"Anyway, I need to give this information to the Sheriff," I said.

"We promised we'd never tell."

"That was nine years ago, Mother," Sam said. "And no one could have predicted what's happening now."

"It's especially important for Maxine Root," I said.

"Don't you think some of the other jurors have come forward with this same information?" Sam said.

"Maybe, but it was a long time ago. And I doubt if they kept notes."

There was a commotion at the front door. Bobby, Leon, and Al had arrived. They had met in St. Louis, then driven all night to Clanton. We had coffee around the kitchen table, and I filled them in on the most recent developments. Miss Callie suddenly sprang to life and was pondering meals and making a list of vegetables for Esau to pick.

———

Sheriff McNatt was out making the rounds, visiting each juror. I had to unload on someone, so I barged into Harry Rex's office and waited impatiently while he finished a deposition. When we were alone, I told him about Miss Callie's list and the division of the jurors. He'd been haggling with a room full of lawyers for the past two hours, so he was in a feisty mood.

As usual, he had a different, far more cynical theory.

"Those three were supposed to hang the jury on guilt," he said after a quick analysis. "They caved for some reason, probably thought they were doin' the right thing by keepin' him out of the gas chamber, but of course Padgitt ain't thinkin' that way. For nine years he's been pissed because his three stooges didn't hang the jury. He figures he'll get them first, then go after the rest."

"There's no way Lenny Fargarson was a stooge for Danny Padgitt," I argued.

"Just because he's crippled?"

"Just because he was a very devout Christian."

"He was unemployed, Willie. He was once able to work, but he knew his condition would only deteriorate over the years. Maybe he needed money. Hell, everybody needs money. The Padgitts have trucks full of cash."

"I don't buy it."

"It makes more sense than any of your screwball theories. What are you sayin'—somebody else is pickin' off the jurors?"

"I didn't say that."

"Good, because I was about to call you a flamin' dumb-ass."

"You've called me worse."

"Not this morning."

"And under your theory, Mo Teale and Maxine Root also took cash from the Padgitts, then double-crossed Danny on the issue of guilt, then reversed themselves on the issue of death, and will now pay the ultimate price because they didn't hang the jury to begin with? Is that what you're saying, Harry Rex?"

"Damned right!"

"You're a flaming dumb-ass, you know that? Why would an honest, hardworking, crime-hating, church-going man like Mo Teale agree to take money from the Padgitts?"

"Maybe they threatened him."

"Maybe! Maybe they didn't!"

"So what's your best theory?"

"It's Padgitt, and it just so happens that the first two he picked off happened to be two of the three who voted no to the death penalty. He doesn't know how the vote went. He was in Parchman twelve hours after the verdict. He's made his list. Fargarson was first because he was such an easy target. Teale was second because Padgitt could choose the setting."

"Who's third?"

"I don't know, but these folks won't stay locked in their homes forever. He'll bide his time, let things die down, then secretly start making plans again."

"He could have some help, you know."

"Exactly."

Harry Rex's phone had never stopped ringing. He glared at it during a pause, then said, "I got work to do."

"I guess I'll go see the Sheriff. See you later." I was out of his office when he yelled, "Say, Willie. One other thing."

I turned to face him.

"Sell it, take the money, go play for a while. You've earned it."

"Thanks."

"But don't leave Clanton, you hear?"

"I won't."

————

Mr. Earl Youry ran a road grader for the county. He graded the rural roads that ran into very remote places, out from Possum Ridge and far beyond Shady Grove. Since he worked alone, it was decided that he should hang around the county barn for a few days where he had many friends, all of whom had rifles in their trucks and were on high alert. Sheriff McNatt huddled with Mr. Youry and his supervisor and worked out a plan to keep him safe.

Mr. Youry called the Sheriff and said he had important information. He admitted his recollection was less than thorough, but he was certain that the crippled boy and Mo Teale had been adamant in their refusal to impose the death penalty. He remembered that they had a third vote, maybe it was one of the women, maybe the colored lady. He just couldn't recall exactly, and, after all, it had been nine years. He posed the same question to McNatt—"Why would Danny Padgitt be killing the jurors who refused to give him the death penalty?"

When I walked into the Sheriff's office, he had just finished his conversation with Mr. Youry, and he was as bewildered as he should have been. I closed the door and relayed my conversation with Miss Callie. "I saw her notes, Sheriff," I said. "The third vote was Maxine Root."

For an hour we rehashed the same arguments I'd had with Sam and Harry Rex, and again it made no sense. He did not believe that the Padgitts had bought or intimidated either Lenny or Mo Teale; he wasn't so sure about Maxine Root since she came from a rougher family. He more or less agreed with me that the first two killings had been coincidental, and that Padgitt, in all likelihood, did not know how the jurors had voted. Interestingly, he claimed that he found out about a year after the verdict that it had been a 9–3 split on the issue of death, and that Mo Teale had become almost violently opposed to such a sentence.

But, both of us conceded, with Lucien Wilbanks involved it was entirely possible Padgitt knew more about the deliberations than we did. Anything was possible.

And nothing made sense.

While I was sitting in his office, he called Maxine Root. She worked as a bookkeeper at the shoe factory north of town, and had insisted on going to work. McNatt had been in her office that morning, inspecting the place, talking with her boss and coworkers, making sure everyone felt safe. Two of his deputies were outside the building, watching for trouble and waiting to haul Maxine back home at quitting time.

They chatted on the phone like old friends for a few minutes, then McNatt said, "Say, Maxine, I know that you and Mo Teale and the Fargarson boy were the only three who voted against the death penalty for Danny Padgitt . . ." He paused as she interrupted.

"Well, it's not important how I found out. What's important here is that makes me real nervous about your safety. Extra nervous."

He listened to her for a few minutes. As she rambled on he interrupted occasionally with such things as: "Well, Maxine, I can't just charge out there and arrest the boy."

And, "You tell your brothers to keep those guns in their trucks."

And, "I'm workin' on the case, Maxine, and when I get enough evidence I'll get a warrant for his arrest."

And, "It's too late to give him the death penalty, Maxine. You did what you thought was right at the time."

She was crying when the conversation ended. "Poor thing," McNatt said, "her nerves are shot to hell."

"Can't really blame her," I said. "I'm ducking under windows myself."

CHAPTER 40

The funeral for Mo Teale was held at the Willow Road Methodist Church, number thirty-six on my list and one of my favorites. It was barely in the city limits of Clanton, south of the square. Because I had never met Mr. Teale, I did not go to his funeral. However, there were many in attendance who had never met him.

Had he died of a heart attack at the age of fifty-one, it would have been sudden and tragic and his final service would have drawn an impressive crowd. But being gunned down in a revenge killing by a freshly paroled murderer was simply too much for the curious to resist. The mob included long-forgotten high school acquaintances of Mr. Teale's four adult children, and meddling old widows who seldom missed a good funeral, and out-of-town reporters, and several gentlemen whose only contact with Mo was the fact that they owned John Deere tractors.

I stayed away and worked on his obituary. His oldest son had been kind enough to stop by the office and give me the details. He was thirty-three—Mo and his wife jump-started their family—and he sold new Fords over in Tupelo. He stayed for almost two hours and desperately wanted me to assure him that Danny Padgitt was about to be hauled in and stoned.

Interment was at the Clanton cemetery. The funeral procession stretched for blocks and, for good measure, swung by the square and proceeded down Jackson Avenue, just outside the *Times*. It did not disrupt traffic at all—everyone was at the funeral.

Using Harry Rex as an intermediary, Lucien Wilbanks arranged a meeting with Sheriff McNatt. I was specifically mentioned by Lucien, and specifically not invited. Didn't matter; Harry Rex took notes and told me everything, with the understanding that nothing would get printed.

Also present in Lucien's office was Rufus Buckley, the District Attorney who had succeeded Ernie Gaddis in 1975. Buckley was a publicity hog who, though reluctant to meddle in Padgitt's parole, was now anxious to lead the mob to lynch him. Harry Rex despised Buckley, and the feelings were mutual. Lucien despised him too, but then Lucien disliked virtually everyone because everyone certainly disliked him. Sheriff McNatt hated Lucien, tolerated Harry Rex, and was forced to work the same side of the street with Buckley, though he loathed him in private.

Given those conflicting sentiments, I was quite pleased not be invited to the meeting.

Lucien began by saying that he had talked with both Danny Padgitt and his father, Gill. They had met somewhere outside of Clanton and away from the island. Danny was doing fine, working each day in the office of the family's highway contracting firm, that office being conveniently located within the safe harbor of Padgitt Island.

Not surprisingly, Danny denied any involvement in the murders of Lenny Fargarson and Mo Teale. He was shocked by what was happening and angry that he was widely considered to be the chief suspect. Lucien emphasized that he grilled Danny at length, even to the point of irritating him, and he never showed the slightest hint of dishonesty.

Lenny Fargarson was shot on the afternoon of May 23. At that time, Danny was in his office, and there were four people who could vouch for his presence there. The Fargarson home was at least a thirty- minute drive from Padgitt Island, and the four witnesses were certain that Danny was either in his office or very close to it throughout the afternoon.

"How many of these witnesses are named Padgitt?" McNatt asked.

"We're not giving names, yet," Lucien said, stonewalling as any good lawyer should.

Eleven days later, on June 3, Mo Teale was shot at approximately nine-fifteen in the morning. At that precise moment, Danny was standing beside a newly paved highway in Tippah County, getting documents signed by one of the Padgitt construction foremen. The foreman, along with two laborers, was willing to testify as to exactly where Danny was at that moment. The highway job was at least two hours away from Ned Ray Zook's farm in eastern Ford County.

Lucien presented airtight alibis for both murders, though his small audience was very skeptical. Of course the Padgitts would deny everything. And given their capacity to lie, break legs, and bribe with serious cash, they could find witnesses for anything.

Sheriff McNatt voiced his skepticism. He explained to Lucien that his investigation was continuing, and if and when he had probable cause, he would get his arrest warrant and descend upon the island. He had spoken several times with the state police, and if a hundred troopers were necessary to flush out Danny, then so be it.

Lucien said that would not be necessary. If a valid arrest warrant was obtained, he would do his best to bring the boy in himself.

"And if there's another killing," McNatt said, "this place will erupt. You'll have a thousand rednecks crossin' the bridge and shootin' every Padgitt they can find."

Buckley said that he and Judge Omar Noose had spoken twice about the killings, and he was reasonably confident that Noose was "almost ready" to issue a warrant for Danny's arrest. Lucien attacked him with a barrage of questions about probable cause and sufficient

evidence. Buckley argued that the threat by Padgitt during his trial was ample reason to suspect him of the
murders.

The meeting deteriorated as the two argued heat-
edly over nitpicking legalities. The Sheriff finally broke
it up by announcing he'd heard enough and walked out
of Lucien's office. Buckley followed. Harry Rex hung
around and chatted with Lucien in a much more relaxed setting.

"You got liars protectin' liars," Harry Rex growled as
he paced around my office an hour later. "Lucien tells
the truth only when it sounds good, which, for him and
his clientele, is not very often. The Padgitts have no
concept of what the truth really is."

"Remember Lydia Vince?" I asked.

"Who?"

"The slut at the trial, the one Wilbanks put on the
stand, under oath. She told the jury Danny was in her
bed when Rhoda was murdered. The Padgitts found
her, bought her testimony, and handed her to Lucien.
They're all a bunch of lying thieves."

"Then her ex got shot, right?"

"Just after the trial. Probably got hit by one of the
Padgitt goons. No evidence other than the bullets. No
suspects. Nothing. Sounds familiar."

"McNatt didn't buy anything Lucien said. Neither
did Buckley."

"And you?"

"Naw. I've seen Lucien cry before in front of juries. He can be very persuasive at times, not often, but occasionally. I got the impression he was working way too hard to convince us. It's Danny, and he's got some help."

"Does McNatt believe that?"

"Yep, but he has no proof. An arrest is a waste of time."

"It'll keep him off the streets."

"It's temporary. With no proof you can't keep him in jail forever. He's patient. He's been waiting for nine years."

———

Though the pranksters were never identified, and they had enough sense to take their secret to their graves, there was considerable speculation in the months that followed that they were the two teenaged sons of our Mayor. Two youngsters were seen sprinting away from the scene, much too fast to be caught. The Mayor's boys had a long and colorful track record as creative and brazen jokesters.

Under the cover of darkness, they boldly sneaked through a thick hedgerow and came to a stop less than fifty feet from the corner of the front porch of Mr. Earl Youry's house. There they watched and listened to the crowd of friends and neighbors camped out on the front lawn, protecting Mr. Youry. They waited patiently for just the right moment to launch their attack.

A few minutes after eleven, a long strand of eighty-four

Black Cat firecrackers was tossed in the general direction of the porch, and when they began popping Clanton almost erupted into an all-out war. Men yelled, ladies screamed, Mr. Youry hit the planks and scurried into his house on all-fours. His sentries out front rolled over in their lawn chairs, clawed around for their guns, and hid low in the grass as the Blacks Cats bounced and popped in a smoky frenzy. It took thirty seconds for all eighty-four to finish exploding, and during that time a dozen heavily armed men were darting behind trees, pointing their guns in every direction, ready to shoot anything that moved.

A part-time deputy named Travis was jolted from his sleep on the hood of his patrol car. He yanked out his .44 Magnum and dashed low and hard in the general direction of the Black Cats. Armed neighbors were scampering everywhere in Mr. Youry's front yard. For some reason, and neither Travis nor his supervisor ever revealed the official explanation, if in fact there was one, he fired a shot into the air. A very loud shot. A shot heard well above the firecrackers. It caused another itchy finger, someone who never admitted to pulling the trigger, to unload a .12-gauge shotgun shell into the trees. No doubt many others would have commenced firing and who knows how many might have been slaughtered had not the other part-time deputy, Jimmy, screamed loudly, "Hold your fire, you idiots!"

At which point the gunfire ceased immediately, but the Black Cats had a few rounds left. When the last one popped the entire gang of vigilantes walked over to the smoldering patch of grass and inspected things. Word spread that it was just fireworks. Mr. Earl Youry peeked through the front door and eventually eased outside.

Down the street, Mrs. Alice Wood heard the assault and was running to the rear of her house to lock the door when the two youngsters blew by her back entrance, sprinting and laughing furiously. She would report that they were about fifteen and white.

A mile away, in Lowtown, I had just walked down the steps of Miss Callie's front porch when I heard the distant explosions. The late shift—Sam, Leon, and two deacons—jumped to their feet and gazed into the distance. The forty-four sounded like a howitzer. We waited and waited, and when all was still again Leon said, "Sounds like firecrackers."

Sam had sneaked inside to check on his mother. He came back and said, "She's asleep."

"I'll go check it out," I said. "And I'll call if it's anything important."

Mr. Youry's street was alive with the red and blue lights of a dozen police cars. Traffic was heavy as the other curious fought to get near the scene. I saw Buster's car parked in a shallow ditch, and when I found him a few minutes later he told me the story. "Coupla kids," he said.

I found it funny, but I was in the distinct minority.

CHAPTER 41

In the nine years since I'd bought the *Times*, I had never left it for more than four days. It went to press every Tuesday, was published every Wednesday, and by every Thursday of my life I was facing a formidable deadline.

One reason for its success was the fact that I wrote so much about so many in a town where so little happened. Each edition had thirty-six pages. Subtracting five for classifieds, three for legals, and about six for advertisements, I was faced each week with the task of filling approximately twenty-two pages with local news.

The obits consumed at least one page, with me in charge of every word. Davey Bigmouth Bass took two pages for sports, though I often had to help with a summary of a junior high football game or an urgent story about a trophy buck shot by some twelve-year-old. Margaret put together one page for Religion and one page for Weddings and another for classifieds. Baggy, whose production nine years earlier had been feeble at best, had succumbed almost completely to booze and was now good for only one story each week, which, of course, he always wanted on the front page. Staff reporters came and went with frustrating regularity. We usually had one on board, sometimes two, and they were often more trouble than they were worth. I had to proofread and edit their work to the point of wishing I had simply done it myself.

And so I wrote. Though I'd studied journalism, I had not noticed a propensity to produce vast amounts of words in short periods of time. But once I suddenly owned the paper, and it was time to sink or swim, I discovered an amazing ability to crank out windy and colorful stories about almost everything, and nothing. A moderately severe car wreck with no fatalities was front page news with breathless quotes from eyewitnesses and ambulance drivers. A small factory expansion sounded like a boon to the nation's Gross National Product. A bake sale at the Baptist Ladies' WMU could run for eight hundred words. A drug arrest sounded as if the Colombians were advancing unchecked upon the innocent children of Clanton. A blood drive by the Civitan Club carried the urgency of a wartime shortage. Three stolen pickups in one week had the feel of organized crime.

I wrote about the people of Ford County. Miss Callie's was my first human interest story, and over the years I tried to run at least one a month. There was a survivor of the Bataan death march, the last local veteran of

World War I, a sailor who had been at Pearl Harbor, a retiring minister who'd served one small country congregation for forty-five years, an old missionary who'd lived for thirty-one years in the Congo, a recent graduate who was dancing in a musical on Broadway, a lady who'd lived in twenty-two states, a man who'd been married seven times and was anxious to share his advice with future newlyweds, Mr. Mitlo—our token immigrant, a retiring basketball coach, the short-order cook at the Tea Shoppe who'd been frying eggs forever. And on and on. These stories were immensely popular.

However, after nine years the list of interesting people in Ford County had very few names on it.

I was tired of writing. Twenty pages a week, fifty-two weeks a year.

I woke up each morning thinking of either a new story or a new angle for an old one. Any bit of news or any unusual event was inspiration to puff up a piece and stick it somewhere in the paper. I wrote about dogs, antique trucks, a legendary tornado, a haunted house, a missing pony, Civil War treasure, the legend of a headless slave, a rabid skunk. And all the usual stuff—court proceedings, elections, crime, new businesses, bankrupt businesses, new characters in town. I was tired of writing.

And I was tired of Clanton. With some reluctance the town had come to accept me, especially when it became obvious I wasn't leaving. But it was a very small place, and at times I felt suffocated. I spent so many weekends at home, with little to do but read and write, that I became accustomed to it. And that frustrated me greatly. I tried the poker nights with Bubba Crocket and the Foxhole gang, and the redneck cookouts with Harry Rex and company. But I never felt as though I belonged.

Clanton was changing, and I was not happy with its direction. Like most small towns in the South, it was sprawling in all directions with no plan for its growth. Bargain City was booming, and the area around it was attracting every fast-food franchise imaginable. Downtown was declining, though the courthouse and the county government would always draw people. Strong political leaders were needed, folks with vision, and they were in short supply.

On the other hand, I suspected the town was weary of me. Because of my preachy opposition to the war in Vietnam, I would always be considered a radical liberal. And I did little to diminish this reputation. As the paper grew and the profits increased, and as a direct result my skin got thicker, I editorialized more and more. I railed against closed meetings held by the city council and the county Board of Supervisors. I sued to get access to public records. I spent one year bitching about the almost complete lack of zoning and land-use management in the county, and when Bargain City came to town I said way too much. I ridiculed the state's campaign finance laws, which were designed to allow rich people to elect their favorites. And when Danny Padgitt was set free, I unloaded on the parole system.

Throughout the seventies, I was always on a soapbox.

And while this made for interesting reading and sold papers, it also transformed me into something of an oddity. I was viewed as a malcontent, one with a pulpit. I don't think I was ever a bully; I tried hard not to be. But looking back, there were fights I started not only out of conviction but also out of boredom.

As I grew older, I wanted to be a regular citizen. I would always be an outsider, but that didn't bother me anymore. I wanted to come and go, to live in Clanton as I saw fit, then leave for long periods of time when I got bored. Amazing how the prospect of money can change your future.

I became consumed with the dream of walking away, of taking a sabbatical to some place I'd never been, of seeing the world.

The next meeting with Gary McGrew was at a restaurant in Tupelo. He'd been to my office several times. One more visit and the staff would start whispering. Over lunch we again looked at my books, talked about his client's plans, negotiated this point and that one. If I sold, I wanted the owner to honor the new five-year contracts I'd given to Davey Bigmouth Bass, Hardy, and Margaret. Baggy would either retire soon or die of liver poisoning. Wiley had always been a part-timer, and his interest in chasing subjects for photos was waning. He was the only employee I'd told about the negotiations, and he had encouraged me to take the money and run.

McGrew's client wanted me to stay on for at least a year, at a very high salary, and train the new editor. I would not agree to this. If I walked away, then I walked away. I didn't want a boss, and I didn't want the local heat that would come for selling the county's paper to a large firm from outside the state.

Their offer was at $1.3 million. A consultant I'd hired in Knoxville had valued the *Times* at $1.35 million.

"Confidentially, we've bought the papers in Tyler and Van Buren Counties," McGrew said, late in a very long lunch. "Things are falling into place."

He was being almost completely honest. The owner of the paper in Tyler County had agreed in principle, but the documents had not been signed.

"But there's a new wrinkle," he said. "The paper in Polk County might be for sale. Frankly, we're taking a look at it if you pass. It's quite a bit cheaper."

"Ah, more pressure," I said.

The *Polk County Herald* had four thousand readers and lousy management. I saw it every week.

"I'm not trying to pressure you. I'm just putting everything on the table."

"I really want a million and a half bucks," I said.

"That's over the top, Willie."

"It's high, but you'll earn it back. Might take a little longer, but look ten years down the road."

"I'm not sure we can go that high."

"You'll have to if you want the paper."

A sense of urgency had arisen. McGrew hinted at a deadline, then finally said, "We've been talking for months now, and my client is anxious to reach a conclusion. He wants to close the deal by the first of next month, or he'll go elsewhere."

The tactic didn't bother me. I was tired of talking too. Either I sold, or I didn't. It was time to make a decision.

"That's twenty-three days from now," I said.

"It is."

"Fair enough."

———————

The long days of summer arrived, and the insufferable heat and humidity settled in for their annual three-month stay. I made my usual rounds—to the churches on my list, to the softball fields, to the local golf tournament, to the watermelon cuttings. But Clanton was waiting, and the wait was all we talked about.

Inevitably, the noose around the neck of each remaining juror was loosened somewhat. They quite naturally got tired of being prisoners in their homes, of altering their lifelong routines, of having packs of neighbors guard their homes at night. They began to venture out, to try and resume normal lives.

The patience of the killer was unnerving. He had the advantage of time, and he knew his victims would grow weary of all that protection. He knew they would drop their guard, make a mistake. We knew it too.

After missing three consecutive Sundays, for the first time in her life, Miss Callie insisted on going to church. Escorted by Sam, Esau, and Leon, she marched into the sanctuary on Sunday morning and worshiped the

Lord as if she'd been gone a year. Her brothers and sisters embraced her, and prayed for her fervently. Reverend Small revised his sermon on the spot and preached on God's protection of his followers. Sam said he went on for almost three hours.

Two days later, Miss Callie slid into the backseat of my Mercedes. With Esau beside her and Sam riding shotgun, we hurried out of Clanton with a deputy behind us. He stopped at the county line, and an hour later we were in Memphis. There was a new shopping mall east of town that was all the rage, and Miss Callie dreamed of seeing it. Over a hundred stores under one roof! For the first time in her life, she ate a pizza; she saw an ice rink, two men holding hands, and a mixed-race family. She approved only of the ice rink.

After a full hour of Sam's atrocious navigating, we finally found the cemetery in south Memphis. Using a map from the guardhouse, we eventually located the grave of Nicola Rossetti DeJarnette. Miss Callie placed a bouquet of flowers she'd brought from home on the grave, and when it became apparent she planned to spend some time there, we walked away and left her in peace.

In memory of Nicola, Miss Callie wanted Italian food. I had reserved a table at Grisanti's, a Memphis landmark, and we had a long, delightful dinner of lasagna and ravioli stuffed with goat cheese. She managed to overcome her bias against bought food, and, to protect her from sin, I insisted on paying for it.

We didn't want to leave Memphis. For a few hours

we had escaped the fear of the unknown and the anxiety of the waiting. Clanton seemed a thousand miles away, and that was too close. Going back late that night, I found myself driving slower and slower.

Though we didn't discuss it, and the conversation grew quieter the closer we got to home, there was a killer loose in Ford County. Miss Callie's name was on his list. If not for the two dead bodies, that would have been impossible to believe.

According to Baggy, and verified by research in the *Times* archives, there had been no unsolved murders that century. Almost every killing had been some impulsive act where the smoking gun had been seen by witnesses. Arrests, trials, and convictions had been prompt. Now, there was a very smart and very deliberate killer out there, and every one knew his intended victims. For such a law-abiding, God-fearing community, it was inconceivable.

Bobby, Al, Max, and Leon had, at various times, argued strenuously for Miss Callie to go stay with any of them for a month or so. Sam and I, and even Esau, had joined in these rather vigorous requests, but she would not budge. She was in close contact with God, and he would protect her.

In nine years, the only time I lost my temper with Miss Callie, and the only time she rebuked me, was during an argument about spending a month in Milwaukee with Bobby. "Those big cities are dangerous," she had said.

"No place is as dangerous as Clanton right now," I had replied.

Later, when I raised my voice, she told me she did not appreciate my lack of respect, and I quickly shut up.

As we crossed into Ford County late that night, I began watching my rearview mirror. It was silly, but then it wasn't. In Lowtown, the Ruffin home was guarded by a deputy parked in the street, and a friend of Esau's on the porch.

"It's been a quiet night," the friend said. In other words, no one had been shot or shot at.

Sam and I played checkers for an hour on the porch while she went to sleep.

The waiting continued.

CHAPTER 42

Nineteen seventy-nine was a year for local elections in Mississippi, my third as a registered voter. It was much quieter than the first two. The Sheriff's race was uncontested, something that was unheard of. There had been a rumor that the Padgitts had bought a new candidate, but after the parole debacle they backed off. Senator Theo Morton drew an opponent who brought me an ad that screamed the question— WHY DID SENATOR MORTON GET DANNY PADGITT PAROLED? CASH! THAT'S WHY! As much as I wanted to run the ad, I had neither the time nor the energy for a libel suit.

There was a constable's race out in Beat Four with thirteen candidates, but other than that the races were fairly lethargic. The county was fixated on the murders of Fargarson and Teale, and, more important, on who might be next. Sheriff McNatt and the investigators from the state police and state crime lab had exhausted every possible clue and lead. All we could do was wait.

As July Fourth approached, there was a noticeable lack of excitement about the annual celebration. Though almost everyone felt safe, there was a dark cloud hanging over the county. Oddly, rumors persisted that something bad would happen when we all gathered around the courthouse on the Fourth. Rumors, though, had never been born with such creativity, nor spread as rapidly, as in the month of June.

———

On June 25, in a fancy law office in Tupelo, I signed a pile of documents that transferred ownership of the *Times* to a media company owned in part by Mr. Ray Noble of Atlanta. Mr. Noble handed me a check for $1.5 million, and I quickly, and somewhat anxiously, walked it down the street, where my newest friend, Stu Holland, was waiting in his rather spacious office in the Merchants Bank. News of such a deposit in Clanton would leak overnight, so I buried the money with Stu, then drove home.

It was the longest one-hour drive of my life. It was exhilarating because I had cashed in at the market's peak. I had squeezed top dollar out of a well-heeled and honorable buyer who planned to make few changes to my newspaper. Adventure was calling me, and I now had the means to answer.

And it was a sad drive because I was giving up such a large and rewarding part of my life. The paper and I had grown and matured together; me as an adult, it as a prosperous entity. It had become what any small-town paper should be—a lively observer of current events, a recorder of history, an occasional commentator on politics and social issues. As for me, I was a young man who had blindly and doggedly built something from scratch. I suppose I should've felt my age, but all I wanted to do was find a beach. Then a girl.

When I returned to Clanton, I walked into Margaret's office, closed the door, and told her about the sale. She burst into tears, and before long my eyes were moist as well. Her fierce loyalty had always amazed me, and though she, like Miss Callie, worried way too much about my soul, she had grown to love me nonetheless. I explained that the new owners were wonderful people, planned no drastic changes, and had approved her new five-year contract at an increased salary. This made her cry even more.

Hardy did not cry. By then he had been printing the *Times* for almost thirty years. He was moody, cantankerous, drank too much like most pressmen, and if the new owners didn't like him then he'd simply quit and go fishing. He did appreciate the new contract though.

As did Davey Bigmouth Bass. He was shocked at the news, but rallied nicely at the idea of earning more money.

Baggy was on vacation somewhere out West, with his brother, not his wife. Mr. Ray Noble had been reluctant to agree to another five years' of Baggy's sluggish reporting, and I could not, in good conscience, make him a part of the deal. Baggy was on his own.

We had five other employees, and I personally broke the news to each of them. It took all of one afternoon, and when if it was finally over I was drained. I met Harry Rex in the back room at Pepe's and we celebrated with margaritas.

I was anxious to leave town and go somewhere, but it would be impossible until the killings stopped.

———————

For most of June, the Ruffin professors scrambled back and forth to Clanton. They juggled assignments and vacations, trying their best to make sure at least two or three of them were always with Miss Callie. Sam seldom left the house. He stayed in Lowtown to protect his mother, but also to keep his own profile low. Trooper Durant was still around, though he was married again and his two renegade sons had left the area.

Sam spent hours on the porch, reading voraciously, playing checkers with Esau or whoever stopped by to help guard things for a while. He played backgammon with me until he figured out the strategy, then he insisted that we bet a dollar per game. Before long I owed him $50. Such blatant gambling was a deadly secret on Miss Callie's porch.

A hasty reunion was put together for the week before July Fourth. Because my house had five empty bedrooms and a woeful lack of human activity, I insisted that it be filled with Ruffins. The family had grown considerably since I first met them in 1970. All but Sam were married, and there were twenty-one grandchildren. The total came to thirty-five Ruffins, not counting Sam, Callie, and Esau, and thirty-four made it to Clanton. Leon's wife had a sick father in Chicago.

Of the thirty-four, twenty-three moved into the Hocutt House for a few days. They drifted in from different parts of the country, mostly up North, coming in shifts at all hours of the day, with each new arrival greeted with great ceremony. When Carlota and her husband and two small children arrived at 3 A.M. from Los Angeles, every light in the house came on and Bobby's wife, Bonnie, began cooking pancakes.

Bonnie took over my kitchen, and three times a day I was sent to the grocery store with a list of things she urgently needed. I bought ice cream by the ton and the kids soon learned I would fetch it for them at any hour of the day.

Since my porches were long and wide and seldom used, the Ruffins gravitated toward them. Sam brought Miss Callie and Esau over late in the afternoons for serious visiting. She was desperate to get out of Lowtown. Her warm little house had become a prison.

At various times, I heard her children talk with great concern about their mother. The obvious threat of somehow getting shot was discussed less than her health. Over the years she had managed to lose somewhere around eighty pounds, depending on whose version you heard. Now it was back, and her blood pressure had the doctors concerned. The stress was taking its toll. Esau said she slept fitfully, something she blamed on medications. She was not as spry, didn't smile as much, and had noticeably less energy.

It was all blamed on the "Padgitt mess." As soon as he got caught and the killings stopped, then Miss Callie would bounce back.

That was the optimistic view, the one generally shared by most of her children.

On July 2, a Monday, Bonnie and company prepared a light lunch of salads and pizzas. All available Ruffins were there, and we ate on a side porch under slow-moving and practically useless wicker fans. There was a slight breeze, however, and with the temperature in the nineties we were able to enjoy a long lazy meal.

I had yet to find the right moment to tell Miss Callie that I was leaving the paper. I knew she would be shocked, and very disappointed. But I could think of no reason why we couldn't continue our Thursday lunches. It might even be more fun counting the typos and mistakes made by someone else.

In nine years we had missed only seven, all due to illness or dental work.

The lazy postmeal chatter suddenly came to a halt. There were sirens in the distance, somewhere across town.

The box was twelve inches square, five inches deep, white in color with red and blue stars and stripes. It was gift package from the Bolan Pecan Farm in Hazelhurst,

Mississippi, sent to Mrs. Maxine Root by her sister in Concord, California. An Independence Day gift of real American pecans. It came by mail, delivered by the postman around noon, placed in the mailbox of Maxine Root, then hauled inside, past the lone sentry sitting under a tree in the front yard, and into the kitchen where Maxine first saw it.

It had been almost a month since Sheriff McNatt had quizzed her about her vote on the jury. She had reluctantly admitted that she had not been in favor of the death penalty for Danny Padgitt, and she recalled that the two men who stuck with her were Lenny Fargarson and Mo Teale. Since they were now dead, McNatt had delivered the grave news that she might be the next victim.

For years after the trial, Maxine had wrestled with the verdict. The town was bitter over it and she felt the hostility. Thankfully, the jurors kept their vows of silence, and she and Lenny and Mo avoided any additional abuse. With the soothing passage of time, she had been able to distance herself from the aftermath.

Now the world knew how she'd voted. Now a crazy man was stalking her. She was on leave from her job as a bookkeeper. Her nerves were shot; she couldn't sleep; she was sick of hiding in her own home; sick of a yard full of neighbors gathering every night as if it was time for a social event; sick of ducking under every window. She was taking so many different pills that they were all counteracting each other to the point that nothing worked.

She saw the box of pecans and started crying. Someone out there loved her. Her precious sister Jane was thinking about her. Oh how she'd love to be in California with Jane at that very moment.

Maxine started to open the package, then had a thought. She went to the phone and dialed Jane's number. They had not talked in a week.

Jane was at work, thrilled to hear from her. They chatted about this and that, then about the horrible situation in Clanton. "You're a dear to send the pecans," Maxine said.

"What pecans?" Jane asked.

A pause. "The gift box from Bolan Pecans down in Hazelhurst. A big one, three pounds."

Another pause. "Not me, sis. Must've been someone else."

Maxine hung up moments later and examined the box. A sticker on the front said—A Gift from Jane Parham. Of course she knew of no other Jane Parhams.

Very gently, she picked it up. It seemed a bit heavy for a three- pound tin of pecans.

Travis, the part-time deputy, happened by the house. He was accompanied by one Teddy Ray, a pimple-faced boy with an oversized uniform and a service revolver that he had never fired. Maxine hustled them into the kitchen where the red, white, and blue box sat benignly on the counter. The lone sentry was also tagging along, and for a long minute or so the four of them just stared at the package. Maxine recounted verbatim her conversation with Jane.

With great hesitation, Travis picked up the box and shook it slightly. "Seems a might heavy for pecans," he observed. He looked at Teddy Ray, who'd already gone pale, and at the neighbor with a rifle, who seemed ready to duck at anything.

"You think it's a bomb?" the neighbor asked.

"Oh my God," Maxine mumbled and appeared ready to collapse.

"Could be," Travis said, then gawked down in horror at what he was holding.

"Get it outside," Maxine said.

"Shouldn't we call the Sheriff?" Teddy Ray managed to ask.

"I guess so," Travis said.

"What if it's got a timer or something?" asked the neighbor.

Travis hesitated for a moment, then with the voice of absolutely no experience, said, "I know what to do."

They stepped through the kitchen door onto a narrow porch that ran the length of the rear of the house. Travis carefully placed the box at the very edge, three feet or so above the ground. When he removed his .44 Magnum, Maxine said, "What are you doing?"

"We're gonna see if it's a bomb," Travis said. Teddy Ray and the neighbor scurried off the porch and took up a safe position in the grass about fifty feet away.

"You're gonna shoot my pecans?" Maxine asked.

"You got a better idea?" Travis snapped back.

"I guess not."

With most of his body inside the kitchen, Travis

leaned out through the screen door with his thick right arm, and his rather large head, and took aim. Maxine was right behind him, crouching low and peeking around his waist.

The first shot missed the porch entirely, though it took the breath out of Maxine. Teddy Ray shouted, "Nice shot," and he and the neighbor had a quick laugh.

Travis aimed and fired again.

The explosion ripped the porch completely from the house, tore a gaping hole in the back wall behind the kitchen, and sprayed shrapnel for a hundred yards. It shattered windows, peeled up planks, and it wounded the four observers. Teddy Ray and the neighbor both took bits of metal in their chests and legs. Travis's right arm and his firing hand were mangled. Maxine was hit twice in the head—one piece of glass ripped off the lobe of her right ear, and a small nail penetrated her right jaw.

For a moment, they were all unconscious, knocked silly by three pounds of plastic explosives packed with nails, glass, and ball bearings.

As the sirens continued to wail across town, I went to the phone and called Wiley Meek. He was just about to call me. "They tried to blow up Maxine Root," he said.

I told the Ruffins there'd been an accident and left them on the porch. When I got near the subdivision where the Roots lived, the main roads were blocked and traffic was being turned away. I hustled over to the hospital and found a young doctor I knew. He said that there were four injured, none of whom appeared to be in grave danger.

———

Judge Omar Noose was holding court in Clanton that afternoon. In fact, he later said that he heard the explosion. Rufus Buckley and Sheriff McNatt met with him for over an hour in chambers, and what they discussed was never revealed. As we waited in the courtroom, Harry Rex and most of the other lawyers loitering there were certain that they were debating how to handle an arrest warrant for Danny Padgitt when there was so little proof that he'd done anything wrong.

But something had to be done. Someone had to be arrested. The Sheriff had a population to protect; he had to take action, even if it wasn't entirely proper.

We got a report that Travis and Teddy Ray had been transported to one of the hospitals in Memphis for surgery. Maxine and her neighbor were under the knife at that very moment. Again, it was the opinion of the doctors that no life was in jeopardy. Travis might lose his right arm, though.

How many people in Ford County knew how to make package bombs? Who had access to explosives? Who had motive? As we argued these questions in the courtroom, they were evidently being argued back in chambers as well. Noose, Buckley, and McNatt were all elected officials. The good people of Ford County needed their protection. Since Danny Padgitt was the only conceivable suspect, Judge Noose finally issued a warrant for his arrest.

Lucien was notified, and he took the news without objection. At that moment, not even Padgitt's lawyer could argue with the strategy of bringing him in for processing. He could always be released later.

A few minutes after 5 P.M., a convoy of police cars blew out of Clanton and headed for Padgitt Island. Harry Rex now owned a police scanner (there were quite a few new ones in town) and we sat in his office, sipping beer, listening to it squawk with unchecked fury. It had to be the most exciting arrest in the history of our county, and many of us wanted to be there. Would the Padgitts block the road and thwart the arrest? Would there be gunfire? A small war?

From the chatter, we were able to follow most of what was happening. At Highway 42, McNatt and his men were met by ten "units" of the state highway patrol. We assumed a "unit" meant nothing more than a car, but it sounded far more serious. They proceeded to Highway 401, turned onto the county road that led to the island, and at the bridge where everyone expected some dramatic showdown, there sat Danny Padgitt in the car with his lawyer.

The voices on the scanner were quick and anxious:

"He's with his lawyer!"

"Wilbanks?"

"Yep."

"Let's shoot both of them."

"They're gettin' out of the car."

"Wilbanks is holdin' up his hands. Smart-ass!"

"It's Danny Padgitt, all right. Hands held high."

"I'd like to knock that smile off his face."

"They got the cuffs on him."

"Dammit!" Harry Rex yelled across his desk. "I wanted some gunfire. Just like in the old days."

We were at the jail an hour later when the parade of red and blue lights came swarming in. Sheriff McNatt had wisely placed Padgitt in the patrol car of a state trooper; otherwise his deputies might have roughed him up during the ride. Two of their colleagues were in surgery in Memphis, and feelings were pretty raw.

A mob had gathered outside the jail. Padgitt was jeered and cursed as he was rushed inside, then the Sheriff angrily told the hotheads to go home.

Seeing him in handcuffs brought a great sense of relief. And the news that he was in custody was like a balm for the entire county. The heavy cloud had been lifted. Clanton came to life that night.

When I returned to the Hocutt House after dark, the Ruffin clan was in a festive mood. Miss Callie was as relaxed as I'd seen her in a long time. We sat on the porch for a long time, telling stories, laughing, listening to Aretha Franklin and the Temptations, even listening to an occasional burst of fireworks.

CHAPTER 43

Unknown to anyone, Lucien Wilbanks and Judge Noose struck a deal in the hectic hours before the arrest. The Judge was worried about what might happen if Danny Padgitt chose to retreat into the safety of the island, or, worse, resist the arrest with force. The county was a powder keg waiting for a match. The cops were ready for blood because of Teddy Ray and Travis, whose gunslinging stupidity was being temporarily ignored while they recovered from their wounds. And Maxine Root came from a notoriously rough family of loggers, a large fierce clan known to hunt year round, live off their land, and leave no grudge unchallenged.

Lucien appreciated the situation. He agreed to deliver his client on one condition—he wanted an immediate bail hearing. He had at least a dozen witnesses who were willing to provide "airtight" alibis for Danny, and Lucien wanted the folks in Clanton to hear their testimony. He truly believed that someone else was behind the killings, and it was important to convince the town.

Lucien was also one month away from being disbarred in an unrelated mess. He knew the end was coming, and the bail hearing would be his last performance.

Noose agreed to a hearing and set it for 10 A.M. the next day, July 3. In a scene eerily reminiscent of one nine years earlier, Danny Padgitt once again packed the Ford County Courthouse. It was a hostile crowd, anxious to get a look at him, hopeful that he might be strung up on the spot. Maxine Root's family arrived early and sat near the front. They were angry, thick-chested, bearded men in overalls. They frightened me, and we were ostensibly on the same side. Maxine was reported to be resting well and expected home in a few days.

The Ruffins had little to do that morning, so the excitement at the courthouse could not be missed. Miss Callie herself insisted on arriving early and getting a good seat. She was happy to be downtown again. She wore a Sunday dress and delighted in sitting in such a public gathering surrounded by her family.

The reports from the hospital in Memphis were mixed. Teddy Ray had been sewn together and was recuperating. Travis had had a rough night, and there was much concern about saving his arm. Their comrades were in the courtroom in full force, waiting for another chance to scowl at the bomb maker.

I saw Mr. and Mrs. Fargarson sitting in the rear, two rows from the back, and I couldn't begin to comprehend what they were thinking.

There were no Padgitts present; they had enough sense to stay clear of the courtroom. The sight of one of them would've touched off a riot. Harry Rex whispered that they were huddled together upstairs in the jury room, with the door locked. We never saw them.

Rufus Buckley arrived with his entourage to represent the State of Mississippi. One advantage in selling the *Times* was that I would never be forced to spend time with him. He was arrogant and pompous, and everything he did was designed to get him to the Governor's office.

As I waited and watched the courtroom fill up, I realized it was the last time I would cover such a proceeding for the *Times*. I found no sadness in that. I had mentally checked out, mentally spent some of the money. And now that Danny was in custody, I was even more anxious to escape Clanton and go see the world.

There would be a trial in a few months. Another Danny Padgitt circus, but I doubted seriously if it would be held in Ford County. I didn't care. It would be a story for someone else.

At 10 A.M., all seats were filled and a thick row of spectators lined the walls. Fifteen minutes later, there was a shuffle behind the bench, a door opened, and Lucien Wilbanks emerged. It had the feel of a sporting event; he was a player; we all wanted to boo. Two bailiffs quickly followed him, and one announced, "All rise for the Court!"

Judge Noose ambled forth in his black robe and sat on his throne. "Please be seated," he said into the microphone. He surveyed the crowd and seemed astonished at the number of us out there.

He nodded, a side door opened, and Danny Padgitt, handcuffed, shackled at the ankles, and sporting the orange jail jumpsuit he'd worn before, was led in by three deputies. It took a few minutes to unlock him from his various restraints, and when he was finally free he leaned over and whispered something to Lucien.

"This is a bail hearing," Noose announced, and the courtroom was still and quiet. "There's no reason why it cannot be handled judiciously and briefly."

It would be much briefer than anyone anticipated.

———

A cannon exploded somewhere above us, and for a split second I thought we'd all been shot. Something cracked sharply through the heavy air of the courtroom, and for a town so jittery to begin with we all froze in one horrible snapshot of disbelief. Then Danny Padgitt grunted in a delayed reaction, and all hell broke loose. Women screamed. Men screamed. Someone yelled, "Get down!" as half the spectators ducked low, some hitting the floor. Someone shouted, "He's been shot!"

I lowered my head a few inches, but I didn't want to miss anything. Every deputy yanked out a service revolver and looked in a different direction for someone to shoot. They pointed up and down, front and back, here and there.

Though we argued about it for years, the second shot was no more than three seconds behind the first. It hit Danny in the ribs, but it had not been necessary. The first had gone through his head. The second shot drew the attention of a deputy in the front of the courtroom. I was ducking even lower, but I saw him pointing to the balcony.

The double doors to the courtroom flew open, and the stampede was on. In the hysteria that followed, I stayed in my seat and tried to take in everything. I remember seeing Lucien Wilbanks hovering over his client. And Rufus Buckley on his hands and knees, scurrying in front of the jury box in an effort to escape. And I'll never forget Judge Noose, sitting calmly at the bench, reading glasses perched on the tip of his nose, watching the chaos as if he saw it every week.

Each second seemed to last a minute.

The shots that hit Danny were fired from the ceiling above the balcony. And, though the balcony was filled with people, no one saw the rifle drop down a few inches ten feet above their heads. Like the rest of us, they were preoccupied with getting a first glance at Danny Padgitt.

The county had patched and renovated the courtroom at various times over the decades, whenever a few spare bucks could be squeezed from the coffers. Back in the late sixties, in an effort to improve the lighting, a dropped ceiling had been installed. The sniper found the perfect spot on a heating duct just above a panel in the ceiling. There, in the dark crawl space, he waited patiently, watching the courtroom below through a five-inch slit he'd created by lifting one of the water-stained panels.

When I thought the shooting was over, I crept closer to the bar. The cops were yelling for everybody to get out of the courtroom. They were shoving people and barking all sorts of contradictory instructions. Danny was under the table, attended to by Lucien and several deputies. I could see his feet, and they were not moving. A minute or two passed, and the confusion was subsiding. Suddenly, there was more gunfire; thankfully, now it was outside. I looked out a courtroom window and saw people scampering into the stores around the square. I saw an old man point upward, sort of above my head, to something on the top of the courthouse.

Sheriff McNatt had just found the crawl space when he heard shots above him. He and two deputies climbed the stairs to the third floor, then slowly took the cramped circular stairway through the dome. The door to the cupola was jammed shut, but just above it they could hear the anxious footsteps of the sniper. And they could hear shell casings hit the floor.

His only target was the law offices of Lucien Wilbanks, specifically the upstairs windows. With great deliberation he was blowing them out, one by one. Downstairs, Ethel Twitty was under her desk, bawling and screaming at the same time.

I finally left the courtroom and hustled downstairs to

the main floor, where the crowd was waiting, uncertain what to do. The police chief was telling everyone to stay inside. Between bursts of gunfire, the chatter was fast and nervous. When the shooting started, we gawked at one another. Each one of us was thinking, "How long will this go on?"

I huddled with the Ruffin family. Miss Callie had fainted when the first shot jolted the courtroom. Max and Bobby were clutching her, anxious to get her home.

————

After holding the town hostage for an hour, the sniper ran out of ammunition. He saved the last bullet for himself, and when he pulled the trigger he fell hard on the small passage door in the floor of the cupola. Sheriff McNatt waited a few minutes, then managed to shove the door up and open. The body of Hank Hooten was naked again. And as dead as fresh roadkill.

A deputy ran down the stairs and yelled, "It's over! He's dead! It's Hank Hooten!"

The bewildered expressions were almost amusing. Hank Hooten? Everyone said the name but no words came out. Hank Hooten?

"That lawyer who went crazy."

"I thought he got sent away."

"Isn't he in Whitfield?"

"Thought he was dead."

"Who's Hank Hooten?" Carlota asked me, but I was too confused to give an answer. We spilled outside under the shade trees and lingered for a while, not certain whether we should stay in case there was another incredible event, or go home and try to comprehend the one we'd just lived through. The Ruffin clan left quickly; Miss Callie was not feeling well.

Eventually, an ambulance carrying Danny Padgitt pulled away from the courthouse and left in no hurry whatsoever. The removal of Hank Hooten was a bit more demanding, but with time they wrestled down his corpse, then rolled it out of the courthouse on a gurney, covered from head to toe with a white sheet.

I walked to my office, where Margaret and Wiley were sipping fresh coffee and waiting for me. We were too stunned to engage in intelligent conversation. The entire town was muted.

I eventually made some phone calls, found who I wanted, and around noon left the office. As I drove around the square, I saw Mr. Dex Pratt, who owned the local glass company and ran an ad in the *Times* every week, on the balcony at Lucien's, already removing the French doors and replacing panes. I was sure Lucien was home by then, already hitting the sauce on his porch, from where he could see the dome and the cupola of the courthouse.

Whitfield was three hours to the south. I wasn't sure if I would make it that far, because at any moment I was likely to turn right, head west, cross the river at Greenville or Vicksburg, and be somewhere deep in Texas by dusk. Or take a left, head east, and find a very late dinner somewhere close to Atlanta.

What madness. How did such a pleasant little town end up in such a nightmare? I just wanted out.

I was near Jackson before I came out of my trance.

————

The state mental hospital was twenty miles east of Jackson on an interstate highway. I bluffed my way through the guardhouse, using the name of a doctor I'd located fishing around with the phone.

Dr. Vero was very busy, and I read magazines for an hour outside his office. When I informed the girl at the desk that I was not leaving, and that I would follow him home if necessary, he somehow found the time to squeeze me in.

Vero had long hair and a grayish beard. His accent was clearly upper midwest. Two diplomas on his wall tracked him through Northwestern and Johns Hopkins, though in the dingy light of his debris-strewn office I couldn't read the details.

I told him what had happened that morning in Clanton. After my narrative he said, "I can't talk about Mr. Hooten. As I explained on the phone, we have a doctor-patient privilege."

"Had. Not have."

"It survives, Mr. Traynor. It's still alive, and I'm afraid I can't discuss this patient."

I'd been around Harry Rex long enough to know that you never took no for an answer. I launched into a long and detailed account of the Padgitt case, from the trial to the parole to the last month and the tension in

Clanton. I told the story of seeing Hank Hooten late one Sunday night in the Calico Ridge Independent Church, and how no one seemed to know anything about him during the last years of his life.

My angle was that the town needed to know what made him snap. How sick was he? Why was he released? There were many questions, and before "we" could put the tragic episode behind "us," then "we" needed the truth. I caught myself pleading for information.

"How much will you print?" he asked, breaking the ice.

"I'll print what you tell me to print. And if something's off-limits, just say so."

"Let's take a walk."

On a concrete bench, in a small shaded courtyard, we sipped coffee from paper cups. "This is what you can print," Vero began. "Mr. Hooten was admitted here in January 1971. He was diagnosed as schizophrenic, confined here, treated here, and released in October 1976."

"Who diagnosed him?" I asked.

"We now go off the record. Agreed?"

"Agreed."

"This must be confidential, Mr. Traynor. I must have your word on this."

I put away my pen and notepad and said, "I swear on the Bible that this will not be printed."

He hesitated for a long time, took several sips of his coffee, and for a moment I thought he might clam up and ask me to leave. Then he relaxed a little, and said, "I treated Mr. Hooten initially. His family had a history of schizophrenia. His mother and possibly his grandmother suffered from it. Quite often genetics play a role in the disease. He was institutionalized while he was in college, and remarkably, managed to finish law school. After his second divorce, he moved to Clanton in the mid-sixties, looking for a place to start over. Another divorce followed. He adored women, but could not survive in a relationship. He was quite enamored with Rhoda Kassellaw and claimed he asked her to marry him repeatedly. I'm sure the young lady was somewhat wary of him. Her murder was very traumatic. And when the jury refused to send her killer to death, he, shall I say, slipped over the edge."

"Thank you for using layman's terms," I said. I remembered the diagnosis around town—"slap-ass crazy."

"He heard voices, the principal one being that of Miss Kassellaw. Her two small children also talked to him. They begged him to protect her, to save her. They described the horror of watching their mother get raped and murdered in her own bed, and they blamed Mr. Hooten for not saving her. Her killer, Mr. Padgitt, also tormented him with taunts from prison. On many occasions I watched by closed circuit as Mr. Hooten screamed at Danny Padgitt from his room here."

"Did he mention the jurors?"

"Oh yes, all the time. He knew that three of them—Mr. Fargarson, Mr. Teale, and Mrs. Root—had refused to bring back a death penalty. He would scream their names in the middle of the night."

"That's amazing. The jurors vowed to never discuss their deliberations. We didn't know how they voted until a month ago."

"Well, he was the assistant prosecutor."

"Yes, he was." I vividly remembered Hank Hooten sitting beside Ernie Gaddis at the trial, never saying a word, looking bored and detached from the proceedings. "Did he express a desire to seek revenge?"

A sip of coffee, another pause as he debated whether to answer. "Yes. He hated them. He wanted them dead, along with Mr. Padgitt."

"Then why was he released?"

"I can't talk about his release, Mr. Traynor. I wasn't here at the time, and there might be some liability on the part of this institution."

"You weren't here?"

"I left for two years to teach in Chicago. When I returned eighteen months ago, Mr. Hooten was gone."

"But you've reviewed his file."

"Yes, and his condition improved dramatically while I was away. The doctors found the right mix of antipsychotic drugs and his symptoms diminished substantially. He was released to a community treatment program in Tupelo, and from there he sort of fell off our radar. Needless to say, Mr. Traynor, the treatment of the mentally ill is not a priority in this state, nor in many others. We are grossly understaffed and underfunded."

"Would you have released him?"

"I cannot answer that. At this point, Mr. Traynor, I think I've said enough."

I thanked him for his time, for his candor, and once again promised to protect his confidence. He asked for a copy of whatever I printed.

I stopped at a fast-food place in Jackson for a cheeseburger. At a pay phone I called the office, half-wondering if I'd missed more shootings. Margaret was relieved to hear my voice.

"You must come home, Willie, and quickly," she said.

"Why?"

"Callie Ruffin has had a stroke. She's in the hospital."

"Is it serious?"

"I'm afraid so."

CHAPTER 44

A county bond issue in 1977 had paid for a handsome renovation to our hospital. At one end of the main floor there was a modern, though quite dark, chapel where I'd once sat with Margaret and her family as her mother passed away. It was there that I found the Ruffins, all eight children, all twenty-one grandchildren, and every spouse but Leon's wife. Reverend Thurston Small was there, along with a sizable contingent from the church. Esau was upstairs in the intensive care unit, waiting outside Miss Callie's room.

Sam told me that she had awakened from a nap with a sharp pain in her left arm, then numbness in her leg, and before long she was mumbling incoherently. An ambulance rushed her to the hospital. The doctor was certain it was initially a stroke, one that precipitated a mild heart attack. She was being heavily medicated and monitored. The last report from the doctor had been around 8 P.M.; her condition was described as "serious but stable."

Visitors were not allowed, so there was little to do but wait and pray and greet friends as they came and went. After an hour in the chapel, I was ready for bed. Max, third in the birth order but the undeniable leader, organized a schedule for the night. At least two of Miss Callie's children would be somewhere in the hospital at all times.

We checked with the doctor again around eleven, and he sounded reasonably optimistic that she was still stable. She was "asleep" as he put it, but upon further questioning admitted that they had her knocked out to prevent another stroke. "Go home and rest," he said. "Tomorrow could be a long day." We left Mario and Gloria in the chapel, and moved en masse to the Hocutt House where we ate ice cream on a side porch. Sam had taken Esau home to Lowtown. I was delighted that the rest of the family preferred staying at my place.

Of the thirteen adults there, only Leon and Carlota's husband, Sterling, would touch alcohol. I opened a bottle of wine, and the three of us passed on the ice cream.

Everyone was exhausted, especially the children. The day had begun with an adventure to the courthouse for a peek at the man who'd been terrorizing our community. That seemed like a week ago. Around midnight, Al gathered the family together in my den for one last word of prayer. A "chain prayer" as he called it, in which every adult and child gave thanks for something and asked for God's protection of Miss Callie. Sitting there on my sofa, fervently holding hands with Bonnie and with Mario's wife, I felt the presence of the Lord. I knew my beloved friend, their mother and grandmother, would be fine.

Two hours later I was lying in bed, wide awake, still hearing the sharp crack of the rifle in the courtroom, the thud of the bullet as it hit Danny, the panic that followed. I rewound and replayed every word of Dr. Vero's, and wondered in what manner of hell poor Hank Hooten had been living for the past few years. Why had he been set loose on society again?

And I worried about Miss Callie, though her condition seemed to be under control and she was in good hands.

I eventually slept for two hours, then eased downstairs where I found Mario and Leon drinking coffee at the kitchen table. Mario had left the hospital an hour earlier; there'd been no change. They were already plotting the stringent weight reduction plan the family would impose on Miss Callie when she was back home. And she would begin an exercise program that would include long walks each day around Lowtown. Regular checkups, vitamins, lean foods.

They were serious about this new health regimen, though everyone knew that Miss Callie would do exactly as she wished.

———

A few hours later, I began the chore of boxing up the things and junk I'd collected in nine years, and cleaning out my office. The new editor was a pleasant lady from Meridian, Mississippi, and she wanted to get started by the weekend. Margaret offered to help, but I wanted to go slowly and reminisce as I emptied drawers and files. It was a personal moment, and I preferred to be alone.

Mr. Caudle's books were finally removed from the dusty shelves where they had been placed long before I arrived. I planned to store them somewhere at home, in case an ancestor of his showed up and asked questions.

My emotions were mixed. Everything I touched brought back a story, a deadline, a trip deep into the county to chase a lead, interview a witness, or meet someone I hoped would be interesting enough for a profile. And the sooner I finished the packing, the closer I would be to walking out of the building and catching an airplane.

Bobby Ruffin called at nine-thirty. Miss Callie was awake, sitting up, sipping some tea, and they were allowing visitors for a few minutes. I hurried to the hospital. Sam met me in the hall and led me through the maze of rooms and cubicles in ICU. "Don't talk about anything that happened yesterday, okay?" he said as we walked.

"Sure."

"Nothing exciting. They won't even allow the grandkids in; afraid that would make her heart rate go crazy. Everything is real quiet."

She was awake, but barely. I had expected to see the bright eyes and brilliant smile, but Miss Callie was barely conscious. She recognized me, we hugged, I patted her right hand. The left one had an IV. Sam, Esau, and Gloria were in the room.

I wanted a few minutes alone so I could finally tell her I was selling the paper, but she was in no condition for such news. She'd been awake for almost two hours, and she obviously needed more sleep. Perhaps in a day or so we could have a lively chat about it.

After fifteen minutes, the doctor showed up and asked us to leave. We left, we came back, and the vigil continued throughout the Fourth of July, though we were not allowed inside the ICU again.

———

The Mayor decided there would be no fireworks for the Fourth. We'd heard enough explosions, suffered enough from gunpowder. Given the town's lingering jumpiness, there was no organized objection. The bands marched, the parade went on, the political speeches were the same as before, though with fewer candidates. Senator Theo Morton was a conspicuous no-show. There was ice cream, lemonade, barbecue, cotton candy—the usual food and snacks on the courthouse lawn.

But the town was subdued. Or maybe it was just me. Maybe I was just so tired of the place that nothing seemed right about it. I certainly had the remedy.

After the speeches, I left the square and drove back to the hospital, a little detour that was becoming monotonous. I spoke to Fuzzy, who swept the hospital parking lot, and to Ralph, who washed the windows of the lobby. I stopped by the canteen and bought another lemonade from Hazel, then spoke to Mrs. Esther Ellen Trussel, who was manning the front information desk on behalf of the Pink Ladies, the hospital's auxiliary. In the waiting room on the second floor I found Bobby with Al's wife; they were watching television like two zombies. I had just opened a magazine when Sam came running in.

"She's had another heart attack!" he said.

The three of us jumped to our feet as if we had somewhere to go.

"It just happened! They got the red team in there!"

"I'll call the house," I said, and stepped to the pay phone in the hall. Max answered the phone, and fifteen minutes later the Ruffins were streaming into the chapel.

The doctors took forever before giving us an update. It was almost eight P.M. before her treating physician entered the chapel. Doctors are notoriously hard to read, but his heavy eyes and wrinkled brow conveyed an unmistakable message. As he described a "significant cardiac arrest" the eight children of Miss Callie deflated as a group. She was on a respirator, no longer able to breathe by herself.

Within an hour, the chapel was full of her friends. Reverend Thurston Small led a nonstop prayer group near the altar, and people joined it and left it as they wished. Poor Esau sat on the back row, slumped over, thoroughly drained. His grandchildren surrounded him, all very quiet and respectful.

For hours, we waited. And though we tried to smile

and be optimistic, there was a feeling of doom. It was as if the funeral had already begun.

Margaret stopped by and we chatted in the hallway. Later, Mr. and Mrs. Fargarson found me and asked to speak to Esau. I led them into the chapel, where they were welcomed warmly by the Ruffins, all of whom expressed great sympathy for the loss of their son.

By midnight we were numb and rapidly losing track of time. Minutes dragged by, then I would look at the clock on the wall and wonder where the past hour went. I wanted to leave, if only to walk outside and breathe fresh air. The doctor, however, had warned us to stay close.

The horror of the ordeal hit when he gathered us around and gravely said it was time for a "final moment with the family." There were gasps, then tears. I'll never forget hearing Sam say out loud, "A final moment?"

"This is it?" Gloria asked in absolute terror.

Frightened and bewildered, we followed the doctor out of the chapel, down the hall, up a flight of stairs, all of us moving with the heavy feet of someone marching to his own execution. The nurses helped herd us through the maze in ICU, their faces telling us what we dreaded the most.

As the family filed into the cramped little room, the doctor touched my arm and said, "This should be just for the family."

"Right," I said, stopping.

"It's okay," Sam said. "He's with us."

We packed around Miss Callie and her machines,

most of which had been disconnected. The two smallest grandchildren were placed at the foot of her bed. Esau stood closest to her, gently patting her face. Her eyes were closed; she did not appear to be breathing.

She was very much at peace. Her husband and children touched some part of her, and the crying was heartbreaking. I was in a corner, wedged behind Gloria's husband and Al's wife, and I simply could not believe where I was or what I was doing.

When Max got his emotions under control, he touched Miss Callie's arm and said, "Let us pray." We bowed our heads and most of the crying stopped, for a moment anyway. "Dear Lord, not our will but yours. Into thine hands we commend the spirit of this faithful child of God. Prepare a place for her now in your heavenly kingdom. Amen."

———

At sunrise, I was sitting on the porch outside my office. I wanted to be alone, to have a good cry in private. The crying around my house was more than I could bear.

As I had dreamed of traveling the world, I had the recurring vision of returning to Clanton with gifts for Miss Callie. I'd bring her a silver vase from England, linens from the Italy she would never see, perfumes from Paris, chocolates from Belgium, an urn from Egypt, a small diamond from the mines of South Africa. I would present these to her on her porch, before we had lunch, then we would talk about the places they came from. I would send her postcards at every stop. We would review my photographs in great detail. Through me, she would vicariously see the world. She would always be there, waiting eagerly for my return, anxious to see what I'd brought her. She would fill her home with little pieces of the world, and own things that no one, black or white, had ever owned in Clanton.

I ached with the loss of my dear friend. Its suddenness was cruel, as it always is. Its depth was so immense that I could not, at that time, imagine a recovery.

As the town slowly came to life below me, I walked to my desk, shoved some boxes out of the way, and sat down. I took my pen, and for a long time stared at a blank notepad. Eventually, slowly, with great agony, I began the last obituary.

AUTHOR'S NOTE

Very few laws remain the same. Once enacted, they are likely to be studied, modified, amended, then often repealed altogether. This constant tinkering by judges and lawmakers is usually a good thing. Bad laws are weeded out. Weak laws are improved. Good laws are fine-tuned.

I took great liberty with a few of the laws that existed in Mississippi in the 1970s. The ones I mistreated in this book have now been amended and improved. I misused them to move my story along. I do this all the time and never feel guilty about it, since I can always disclaim things on this page.

If you spot these mistakes, please don't write me a letter. I acknowledge my mistakes. They were intentional.

Thanks to Grady Tollison and Ed Perry of Oxford, Mississippi, for their recollections of old laws and procedures. And to Don Whitten and Mr. Jessie Phillips of *The Oxford Eagle*. And to Gary Greene for technical advice.